Death in Summer

Lina Areklew was born in Stockholm 1979 and grew up at the High Coast. Today she lives part time in a house northwest of Stockholm and part time in a croft outside Örnsköldsvik. After a career as a project manager within telecommunications, she studied literature and now works as a freelance copy editor. Her debut novel is set in Stockholm and on the island Ulvön outside Örnsköldsvik.

DEATH
IN
SUMMER

LINA AREKLEW

CANELOCRIME

First published in Sweden in 2020 by Bazar Publishing

This edition published in the United Kingdom in 2022 by

Canelo
Unit 9, 5th Floor
Cargo Works, 1–2 Hatfields
London, SE1 9PG
United Kingdom

A CIP catalogue record for this book is available from the British Library.

Print ISBN 978 1 80032 982 9
Ebook ISBN 978 1 80032 981 2

This book is a work of fiction. Names, characters, businesses, organizations, places and events are either the product of the author's imagination or are used fictitiously. Any resemblance to actual persons, living or dead, events or locales is entirely coincidental.

First published as *Ur Askan – Beneath the Surface*

Translation by Tara F. Chace

Look for more great books at www.canelo.co

Printed and bound in Great Britain by Clays Ltd, Elcograf S.p.A.

Prologue

MS Estonia, *September 28, 1994*

His sweater was stuck up under his life jacket so his back was exposed. His shoes were missing, maybe still inside, but he didn't feel any cold. A woman yelled heartbreakingly, pleading for his help, but there was no time or opportunity to help. He abandoned her without a moment's hesitation, lunging for the railing. People were fighting for their lives to hold on as the ship listed. Should he try to get back inside, to his mother and father? But something told him that he was alone now. He had to make it on his own. With a new resolve, he pulled himself over the railing. The angle increased with every wave and he would be able to slide down the outside of the ferry soon. He looked down at the listing ship. He had time to think that it looked like a dying whale with the white belly visible just above the surface. So many remained in its bowels.

Fear ached in his chest, but he kept going. His feet slipped forward over the metal hull. He bumped into other people in the darkness, confused and panic-stricken people who were all waiting for the wave that would carry them away into the black void. Everywhere there were desperate cries for loved ones. He thought of his mother and father again. He hadn't seen Niklas since he pulled himself up the listing stairs in the middle of a chain of people.

He stepped on one of the windows from the outside, feeling with his foot the contrast between its thick plastic and the cold hull. The cabin within was empty. The family staying in there must have gotten out. Blankets, pillows, and luggage lay in a jumble on top of the closed door. A pink teddy bear lay wedged in the hat rack.

The lights flickered on one final time and then the signal horn blared sharply. The sky glowed red with emergency flares.

The whole world had capsized.

He looked up and watched wave after wave hit the life rafts that had made it into the water. The wind lifted them up, causing them to tumble along the surface. He had to decide now: stay put and go down with the ship, or jump into the frigid water.

There was no surviving this. He realized that. His life would end this night.

Thursday, June 20, 2019

1.

The vomit poured out of Fredrik Fröding, like an unchecked waterfall. It burned in his nose when he tried to catch his breath between heaves. He was kneeling in front of the toilet with one hand convulsively clutching the toilet paper holder as he spewed out the last of his stomach contents.

He stood up, his legs shaking, and felt frightened when he saw his own reflection. The whites of his eyes were a light pink with angry red blood vessels pointing in toward the irises.

His gray face and unshaven jawline made him look away.

He tried to take a step toward the door, but his legs wouldn't support him, and he collapsed onto the floor. He lay there on the bathmat, his eyes focused on the dusty plastic cover over the sink's drainpipe as he tried to get the room to stop spinning.

It had gotten to be too many again. He hadn't waited more than half an hour after the first two pills before taking two more. Now he had finished the whole blister pack. The alcohol in his bloodstream had sped up the effect. And the side effects. The dizziness had hit him like a sandbag and the vomiting had followed not long afterward. Do not mix anti-anxiety pills with alcohol. That was the cardinal rule which had been impressed on him ever since his very first pill. And he had been careful about it for all these years. The last time he had screwed up was in college almost fifteen years ago now. That time, he had woken up in a stairwell holding his knocked-out front teeth in his hand.

Fredrik lay there on the bathmat for a while, allowing his breathing to calm down. He had to get up soon. He would lose his appointment with Torsten Bredh if he did not stand up, walk down the stairs, and get to the subway. He tried to picture the path before him, imagining the knot inside himself gradually untying with each step he took in his visualization. With some effort, he managed to make it up onto all fours. His legs wobbled beneath him, but in the end he was finally standing on the cold plastic bathmat. Without letting go of the bathroom wall, he made it into the shower and turned on the water. Steam soon began to seep out over the shower curtain. He cautiously let go of the wall with one hand and pulled off his boxer shorts. He avoided looking at himself in the mirror over the sink as he stepped naked into the scalding water.

Forty-five minutes later, he was standing out on Karlavägen. People hurried past with bags in their hands, the same as always, looking stressed out, seemingly completely unaware of how quickly life could change. Fredrik envied them. He used to daydream about the people he saw shopping at the ICA Super-market Esplanad. Sweaty dads holding the hands of little kids, plowing their way from the taco shell aisle to the vegetables. Imagine what it would be like to be one of them, someone who planned Friday night dinner, changed diapers, and took all-inclusive family-friendly vacations.

He zipped up his leather jacket and descended the stairs stooping over forwards, focusing on the escalator on the other side of the barriers. He sat down heavily on the bottom step and rubbed his face with his hands as he caught his breath. People cleared their throats and sighed audibly at him as they pushed their way past, but he ignored them. He closed his eyes and raised his face in the cool air that wafted up from the dark tunnels. He imagined it sweeping away his dizziness and nausea.

His anxiety had been in remission for almost five years this time. Five years of calm, but it was all back now with a force that frightened him. He knew what had triggered it, but he couldn't avoid it. It was like a force that drew him in, and he found himself standing by all the newspapers, flipping through

Sunday supplements with headlines like "Life After the MS *Estonia*" or articles about mothers holding the hands of cute little kids laying flowers at the memorial on Stockholm's Djurgården Island: "Elsa never got to meet her grandmother." Even after so many years the journalists and photographers still had him in their sights. Sometimes there would be a phone call or two around the anniversary, sometimes even several in one day. The milestone anniversaries were the worst, although on the other hand people gave up much faster. It wasn't like in the beginning, when they had pretty much lived outside the hospital and then camped out on the street outside his grandmother's apartment for weeks after he got home. They hadn't hesitated to photograph him, his friends, his school. They had coaxed, wheedled, threatened, and bribed, anything to land the best possible story about the devastated thirteen-year-old who had lost his entire family in Europe's worst ferry disaster.

And now here they went again. Time to start filing stories for the commemorative inserts. Even though they hadn't been particularly aggressive in their attempts thus far, they had been intrusive enough to send him into this downward spiral, which had brought him to Thomas Bredh's office with regard to his post-traumatic stress.

Fredrik stood up unsteadily. He could see the platform. Three minutes until the next train.

–

Sofia Hjortén contemplated the available parking space next to the fully loaded motorhome. The Volkswagen Golf she kept out on Ulvön Island was rusty and had several dents on its doors. It was a beater. On the mainland, however, she was more cautious about where she parked. Her black Volvo XC60 was only a year old and she didn't want it to get scratched. She looked one more time and decided that the parking space was wide enough.

A mother was sitting on a stool in the shade outside the motorhome breastfeeding a baby. A brown dog drank lazily out of a plastic water bowl by her feet. Amused, Sofia noted several similar vehicles and drivers in the lot. Always mothers with varying assortments of children and pets that needed to be walked, but never any fathers.

She locked her car and walked into the outlet store. The hunting and fishing supply store on highway E4 was a popular stop for many tourists, and in the summer months the crowds could easily become annoying, usually in the clothing department where visiting urbanites scrambled through half-price down jackets and warm hiking boots that would never see hide nor hair of an actual mountain. Sofia was usually the only representative of her sex in the fishing gear department.

Bengt walked over and gave her a hug. She didn't actually feel like they knew each other well enough to hug. They had fished together on the same competitive pike fishing team for the last three years. That was all. In her eyes they were more like acquaintances than friends, but she knew that she didn't have the same social interaction criteria as normal people.

"Are you excited about this weekend? Norway, can you believe it? It's been years since I've fished there. Remember though, the bus is leaving at nine a.m. sharp on Saturday," Bengt warned her over his shoulder. "That means no Midsummer's Eve partying! Or is the detective perhaps working this weekend?"

He nodded toward a glass counter in the back of the store to indicate that she should follow him over there.

"No, actually this detective is taking Midsummer off," Sofia said. This would be the first Midsummer holiday that she wouldn't be working since she had started with the Örnsköldsvik Police Station's investigative unit.

Bengt ducked down behind the counter, rummaged through a bunch of cardboard boxes that hadn't been unpacked yet, pulled something out of a wad of bubble wrap, and then reverently held up a gold-colored fishing reel.

8

"Here she is, a Shimano Calcutta Conquest 400, in the flesh." Bengt bowed slightly and presented the reel to her. "You are right-handed, right?"

Sofia nodded and accepted it. She tried disengaging the clutch and casting, enjoying for a second the nearly silent Japanese precision.

"Nice, huh?"

This reel was going to cost her a small fortune, but it would be worth it. Her team had won the prize at last year's Pike Challenge, but she had lost two of her best Wolfcreek trolling spoons and her last Shimano reel in the process.

"It'll hold 110 meters of 0.35 mm line. That ought to do the trick for you. Do you need any lures or bait to go with that? A rubber, maybe?" He grinned at his own joke. Sofia couldn't resist the expectant look on his face.

"You do know that real men use jerkbait, right?"

Bengt chuckled as he took the reel back from her and packed it back up again.

"Two more days," he beamed. "And then away we go!"

2.

"Fredrik?" said Torsten Bredh, snapping his fingers and cocking his head to the side, trying to catch Fredrik's eye.

The sun was shining outside the psychiatrist's window and Fredrik was contemplating the grimy streaks on the unwashed windowpanes. He was lost in his own thoughts, hearing the sounds of the ropes rubbing against the rubber life raft, feeling Niklas's cold hand clinging convulsively to his as the waves crashed in.

At first they had laughed, weeping with joy at how absurd it was that they had both managed to get out and down into the same raft. But the longer it took before the rescuers arrived, the quieter they had grown. Fredrik had comforted his little brother, trying to convince him that everything would be all right despite the thoughts that were tearing him up inside, thoughts about all the people who were still on the ferry, in the water, on the bottom, thoughts about their mother and father. In the end they had just clung to each other, holding on tight, and whispering soothing words that didn't mean anything. Two people had died right next to them, but none of them had said anything about it. They had all just sat there as if turned to stone. Right up until that last wave came...

Fredrik looked up, gazing around at Torsten's third-floor office on Sveavägen in the heart of Stockholm with its hippie furnishings. This place was like his second home. The public healthcare sector had given up hope on him a long time ago. The only alternative Fredrik had had left was private healthcare or in his case private mental healthcare. Torsten had opened his practice, focused on grief counseling and post-traumatic stress, right when Fredrik's doctor had shrugged and started discussing long-term disability or early retirement. His medical records had been sent over to Torsten and that's where he had remained.

By this point most of Torsten's other patients had moved on, starting new lives, allowing their wounds to heal. But not him.

"Fredrik?"

"Yes?" He directed his gaze toward the psychiatrist's green plaid shirt pocket.

"I asked you what you were thinking about."

"Niklas."

Torsten did his best to hide his disappointment, but his raised eyebrows revealed that that wasn't the answer he had wanted to hear.

"I saw him again yesterday," Fredrik said.

Torsten lowered his gaze, the air audibly escaping his nostrils in a prolonged exhalation.

"Ah, I see. So where did he turn up this time?"

Fredrik shrugged, fully aware that Torsten's questions did not stem from any sort of genuine interest.

"Does it matter?"

Torsten responded with a shoulder shrug of his own. This was a well-rehearsed dance between the two of them.

"It'll be twenty-five years this year, right?" Torsten asked.

The question was rhetorical, but Fredrik nodded anyway.

"Have the newspapers contacted you?"

Yet another nod.

Torsten leaned back in his chair.

"So tell me," Torsten continued, "where did you see him?"

This was how their dance ended, an ending that was hardly in line with any of the many treatment programs and methods Torsten had tried on Fredrik in the hopes that he would move on. Instead, he would let him talk over and over again about the grief, anxiety, and suffocating guilt he lived with. The guilt he felt for having let go of his brother's hand that night. How he had let him slip away into the black water, only seconds before the rescuers had reached them.

"Where did you see him?" Torsten repeated.

Fredrik closed his eyes and rested his head in his hands.

He had been walking down Karlavägen and had been in a good mood. Two of his colleagues in the passport office in Sollentuna had asked if he wanted to grab a beer with them after work to celebrate the start of the summer holidays. They had ended up sitting outside near Stureplan and one beer had become several beers. They had discussed work and their summer plans. Fredrik had lied and said that he was going sailing with some friends. It had felt good, almost like having a real life. On his way home he had stopped in at Pressbyrån, the convenience store, to buy a soda. He had been drunk. The combination of four anxiety pills with several beers had affected him quickly. He had had a hard time focusing his eyes to enter his pin number when he bought his soda, and he staggered as he squeezed past the line on his way out of the store.

That was when it had happened.

A man in a black cap and a light hoodie passed him moving at high speed just as he came out of the store, so close that Fredrik had to slow down to avoid bumping into him. He watched the man as he walked over to the crosswalk and then crossed the street with his head down, as if he were looking at his shoes or wanted to hide his face. But one glimpse of his profile was enough for Fredrik.

It was Niklas. He knew it.

Before he had had a chance to react, the light had turned red and the cars had started moving again on the four-lane road. He had shouted. Over and over again he had shouted to Niklas, but the man hadn't reacted. Without thinking, Fredrik had darted out into traffic, running until his heart threatened to explode in his chest. He had darted in and out between people out on evening walks, trying to keep his eyes on that black cap, which was quickly making its way through the crowd. He had last spotted Niklas heading for the door of the Ceder City East hotel by the corner of Humlegården Park, shaking hands with a redheaded man standing out front and then entering the hotel. Fredrik had stood there, as if stunned, suddenly unsure if he had seen correctly.

"Fredrik."

He opened his eyes and looked up at Torsten who was reaching for his laptop, which was on his desk a little to their right, a sure sign that he was going to write a new prescription. Torsten was always careful to move his chair around to Fredrik's side, so that the desk didn't come between them. As if the psychiatrist needed to sit physically close to his patient in order to understand the internal disarray that prevailed within him and all the other poor devils who wound up in this office.

You'll never understand. No matter where you put your chair.

"Fredrik, if you're experiencing hallucinations again it's my duty to discuss placing you in a psychiatric clinic. I'm reluctant to prescribe more pills for you until we have a plan for where we go from here."

Fredrik nodded and his breath caught. Torsten wasn't usually stingy with medication. Torsten was usually available to see him at any hour of the day, to listen, and to prescribe pills, although occasionally he would demand something in return. More than once he had sent Fredrik to a specialty clinic for experimental treatment. Sometimes it helped for a while, sometimes it didn't, but the anxiety always came back and when it did, he needed his pills.

Torsten looked him in the eye.

"Fredrik? You know your little brother is dead, right?"

Fredrik looked out the window again, shuddering as he heard the door of a truck hitting the asphalt with a bang. That was the sound he remembered best. How the water seemed to be boiling around him. The cabin windows exploding from the pressure. One by one, like firecrackers.

It didn't matter what Torsten said, what anyone said. Niklas must have made it onto another life raft. There had been several nearby. Not to mention the helicopters. He had had a life jacket on. Maybe he had been too traumatized to tell them his name, or had been confused with someone else? Or maybe he… No, Niklas must have survived.

When Fredrik emerged from Torsten's office, the backs of his hands itched so that they burned. He walked quickly up Sveavägen and into the first pharmacy he found. As soon as he was out the doors again, he ripped open the package and took two pills before heading over to the hotel. He hadn't dared to go into it the day before, afraid of being wrong yet again.

But he had made up his mind now. He was going to go in.

Fredrik stopped across the street from it and watched people coming and going through the wide glass doors. He pushed his dark, uncut hair off his forehead with both hands, hesitated for a few seconds, but then he headed for the entrance, walking decisively.

A doorman in a blue blazer courteously opened the door for him. He let an elderly couple by, who were on their way out, each pulling their own carry-on bag, and then he stopped in the middle of the gold-colored lobby. An enormous crystal chandelier hung from the ceiling and a long chrome reception desk ran the length of one wall. Standing behind it were young women and men wearing the same type of blue blazers as the doorman. His field of vision grew blurry around the edges. Fredrik had to rotate his entire body to scan the room. He walked over to the reception desk, reaching out his hand and leaning against it, and a man with black hair parted on the side spoke to him.

"I'm sorry, sir. How may I help you?"

Fredrik turned away so as not to hear the desk clerk's voice. He scanned the room again, in the vain hope that Niklas would be standing there, alive, forgiving. The man with the side part came around from behind the reception desk and approached him.

"Is there anything I can help you with?" He scrutinized Fredrik's worn leather jacket.

"Has a Niklas Fröding checked in here?" Fredrik's tongue felt thick and to his horror he could hear that he was slurring his words.

The man, whose embroidered shirt pocket said his name was Theodor Hake and that he was the manager, put his hand on Fredrik's arm and pulled him aside.

"Unfortunately we can't disclose the identity of our guests. If there's nothing else, then…" He nodded meaningfully toward the main entrance.

"He was here yesterday." Fredrik's raised voice attracted attention. "I saw him come in yesterday."

The hotel manager took a firm hold of Fredrik's elbow, pushing him toward the doors. Fredrik yanked his arm.

"Let go of me!"

One of the other front desk workers came out from behind the counter and two of the guests who were waiting to check in eyed them apprehensively.

"If you don't calm down, sir, I'm afraid I'll be forced to summon security." The manager reached into his pocket for his phone.

Fredrik tried in vain to pull free. Just as the manager began explaining the situation to security over the phone, a redheaded man walked calmly over to them.

Fredrik recognized him immediately. It was the man Niklas had greeted out in front of the hotel the day before.

"What's going on here?" His voice was authoritative.

Fredrik managed to free his arm and straighten his jacket.

"I'm looking for my brother Niklas, Niklas Fröding."

The man scrutinized him.

"I'm Adam Ceder. I'm the owner of this hotel. Follow me." He walked around behind the reception desk, clicked away on a terminal's keyboard for a few seconds, and then looked up. His cold eyes gave Fredrik the shivers.

"There must be some misunderstanding. We don't have any guest by that name." Ceder smiled self-consciously at him.

A liar's smile, there was no doubt about that. Fredrik slapped his hands down on the counter and reached for Ceder.

"You're lying!"

Out of the corner of his eye, Fredrik saw the manager coming back over, but Ceder calmly shook his head and held up his hand without taking his eyes off Fredrik.

"As I said, there must be some misunderstanding." The manager didn't have a chance to say any more before two security guards approached them. They took hold of Fredrik by his upper arms, a firm grip that didn't brook any contradictions.

"You can't do this!" Fredrik yelled back over his shoulder.

Ceder didn't move, watching him thoughtfully.

"I want to see Niklas!"

Friday, June 21, Midsummer's Eve

3.

Sofia carefully freed her arm and inched a bit away from Kaj. The crook of her arm was sticky with sweat from his neck and her hand had fallen asleep. His salt and pepper hair curled at his temples from the heat.

She lay still on her back for a long time, staring at the balcony door. It was ajar, letting in a cool sea breeze. In the distance she could hear the waves striking the rocky shoreline.

Kaj was supposed to be back with his wife in Stockholm by this evening, but she didn't mind. That's what their arrangement looked like, and she had her fishing competition in Norway to look forward to tomorrow.

To her relief Kaj had turned down her offer of a boat ride to the mainland, so she only needed to drop him off down by Ulvö Harbor and he would take the ferry back across on his own. Sofia would have the whole afternoon to get her fishing gear ready. She would give her boat a little love, too, even if it wasn't suitable for fishing trips. Tord, her godfather, was storing her costly Riva Ariston for her over the winter, the Horse as her father used to call the boat, his Italian baby with the temperament of a colt, sometimes gentle, sometimes unruly, but fast like the wind when it put its back into something. Now the Horse was hers, whether she wanted it or not. She needed to try to get her own boathouse renovated by next year so she could store it over the winter herself. Tord was getting on in years. It was enough that he went out to her house every other week to shovel the snow off the deck in the winter while she sat comfortably in her warm apartment in Örnsköldsvik like some pasha. Her father would roll over in his grave if he knew. His daughter, a paper pusher on the mainland.

Sofia reached for her cellphone and pulled her finger across the screen to see what time it was. Nine fifteen. The whole morning was gone.

Kaj sighed in his sleep and rolled over so his back was to her. The covers went with him, his long body rolled up in it as if in a cocoon. Sofia was left lying naked on the warm bottom sheet. She looked down at her body. It looked unappealing in the sharp morning light.

Her stomach flat, the hipbones jutting out, and those skinny legs. She had always looked like a child. Her small breasts with their light pink nipples were the only thing that gave her away as a grown woman.

But Kaj had never complained about her lack of femininity. Quite the contrary, he found her desirable. She had never understood why. They had been seeing each other off and on for more than ten years, but their passion had never cooled. Kaj had never expressed any desire to shake things up in their sex life. He was a generation behind her when it came to sex. To him it was still something beautiful between two people who loved each other. Kaj Marklund had no interest in Brazilian waxes, one-night stands, or online dating, which made their arrangement all the more remarkable.

Sofia carefully sat up in the bed. Sometimes she had a hard time understanding what he saw in her. Despite their twenty-three-year age difference, one might think that she was the older one, the boring one. Kaj had an active social life with many friends, while Sofia barely left the house. And compared to Mette Severin Marklund, the colorful, bon vivant peacock Kaj was married to, Sofia was ordinary at best.

Sometimes she wondered what it would have been like if she hadn't gotten pregnant. Would she still have been in Stockholm then? Maybe. Even so, the pregnancy had been a positive surprise for her. She had always wanted to have children, a chance to give a little person the childhood she herself had been deprived of due to Claire. But having a baby with a superior was an indignity she wasn't prepared to bear. It was bad enough that several people around them had already started to whisper about Sofia's fast-moving career. Sleeping her way to the top was not part of her world view, but there was no quashing the rumors. It didn't matter that Kaj was the one who had pursued her from the beginning and not the other way around.

Three days after she had found out about the pregnancy, Sofia exited the relationship and her job as an investigator with the Stockholm Police working in their major crimes unit. She had known that Kaj would take it hard, and she imagined that she was doing what was best for everyone. She hadn't been prepared to give up the child and knew that she wasn't strong enough to stand up to Kaj pressuring her if he insisted on an abortion. So she had packed her bags, called her boss and said that she wanted to move back home to Örnsköldsvik on northeastern Sweden's High Coast, and had had the unbelievable luck to start almost immediately. Kaj had pursued her for months, calling and sending letters and flowers, but she had consistently refused to answer. By the time she had her second ultrasound, he had given up. Sofia had seen the pictures of the baby she bore in her belly by herself, her and Kaj's daughter.

In the beginning she had been content with her choice. She had felt strong and ready to tackle the future as a single mother, but then everything had fallen apart. The terrible miscarriage and the medical leave of absence that followed had isolated her. Her awkward attempts to re-create a social life in the town she had been away from for so long, a place that was now a blend of new and old, had failed and when she finally returned to work, she had been pigeonholed as a loner. People who didn't know about the miscarriage assumed that she had hit the wall after only a couple of weeks in her new job, so she was also labeled as a weakling. Her years in Stockholm had also branded her as a city slicker and earned her the dishonorable nickname of "Zero

Eight," Stockholm's area code, pretty much the worst thing you could call a Norrlander.

Her loneliness had become like a mantle that she wore, first out of necessity, but later with a sort of pride. She didn't know why she had picked up the phone and dialed Kaj's number that February day four months ago, but he had been thrilled. Even though three years had passed, he was ready to resume the relationship. Everything was back to normal aside from the fact that in the meantime Kaj had met Mette and gotten married and now Sofia had to settle for the role of the other woman.

She gathered her long, blond hair into a bun high on her head and secured it with the hairband she always wore around her wrist.

"Good morning."

She jumped when she heard Kaj's gruff morning voice. He reached for her and pulled her back in under the covers. She let herself be caught but arched her back to avoid his sweaty chest.

"I had a dream about you," he mumbled, his lips against her neck.

"It's already after nine." Sofia carefully pulled away. "I want to fit in a run before breakfast."

"You mean lunch?"

Ah, Midsummer's Day lunch. She suppressed the sigh that rose from her lungs. Kaj was a stickler for eating the traditional holiday lunch of pickled herring and schnapps on Midsummer. Traditions were important to her married lover.

"You know, you could get a little exercise if you stayed right here," he tried, pulling the covers down to reveal his morning wood. But Sofia was already on her way out of bed.

"You stay. I'll take the long route."

Kaj gave her a disappointed look.

"OK, I'll have lunch ready when you get back."

Sofia took a pair of running shoes out of her travel bag which she hadn't had time to unpack yet. Kaj watched her.

"How much time are you taking off work for the summer holidays?"

She pulled on a faded t-shirt with the pike fishing team's logo and then bent down to tie her shoes.

"Four weeks. As long as nothing happens at work."

Kaj smiled.

"What would happen up here?"

4.

The night had felt both short and long. Fredrik had barely made it home before his anxiety had ripped a hole in his chest. Oh, that sexless creature that danced on his chest with its sharp heels until only shreds were left. He had already taken six pills, and this was the last prescription he was going to get. Torsten had been very clear on that point. He had been given a phone number to call, a clinic outside of Sundsvall about four hours north of Stockholm. If he wanted more pills, he needed to do at least four weeks of intensive inpatient treatment there.

He sat down on the Windsor chair in his tiny kitchen. Outside the window the sun was rising, throwing a sharp light across the floor. His apartment was in shambles. At one time it had been a miniature version of a cozy and stylish place. Now the parquet flooring was worn and lacking both rugs and furniture. There were piles of cardboard boxes and bags stacked along the walls and drifts of dust bunnies in all the corners. The last time he had been out of work for an extended sick leave, he had been forced to sell his grandmother's Afghan rug and several pieces of antique furniture online. Only the bed, the Windsor chair, and the round kitchen table were left. The salary the police paid for the most monotonous and lowest ranked jobs, like the one he held in the passport office, barely paid the bills. But it was the closest he had come to a real job as a policeman.

His pay wasn't enough to build up any savings either, even though he didn't have any major expenses—food, rent, cell phone, and maybe a night out at the movies now and then. His social life for the last year had consisted entirely of those beers he had drunk after work the day before yesterday. Apart from that, January through June had passed without a single social gathering outside of work. The tragic nature of that realization left a lump in his throat.

Fredrik looked around his apartment. He could feel his grandmother's reproachful eyes watching him from the photo that sat alone on the deep window ledge, covered with dust. She had been so proud when he was admitted to the police academy. He remembered how they had gone out to eat that night at Restaurant Riche the way they always did when they were celebrating something. She had taken every opportunity to inform the waitstaff that her grandson was going to be a policeman. Fredrik smiled at the memory of his grandmother, Greta. She had become his mother, father, and breadwinner overnight, even though her youthful vigor had already been far behind her by that point. In the beginning they had argued. Fredrik was thirteen, an orphan, and longed to return to his friends in Bromma on the western side of Stockholm. His grandmother Greta had been a dedicated Rotary Club member for sixty-five years and lived a very uneventful life in a one-bedroom apartment in Östermalm, a more affluent neighborhood on the eastern side of Stockholm. He remembered with shame the times she had had to come pick him up from the principal's office. First she would scold him and then comfort him, well aware of the grief he bore. Slowly, a new existence had evolved that over time he had come to both accept and eventually thrive in. They had lived in their nontraditional family constellation for almost ten years, right up until the morning when Fredrik had found her in bed, her lips cold and gray, following a massive stroke.

It was as if a glass crusher started tumbling inside him at the thought of his grandmother. He couldn't stay here. He had to go do something, talk to someone.

Stockholm was just waking up as Fredrik stepped out the front door. It smelled pleasantly of gravel and freshly mowed grass. The subway car was almost empty, and he took a seat in the very back. The sun was already shining from a deep-blue sky and down below the Traneberg Bridge families were packing their boats full of food and drinks for the day's Midsummer celebrations. Traffic was still light. Fredrik leaned his head against the cool window and admired the view. The city sparkled in its morning pajamas and summer apparel.

He transferred onto the Tvärbanan light rail line and got off at Ålstens Gård Manor and started walking to Philip's house. The Lindén family lived on the same street Fredrik had lived on for most of his childhood. The simple charm of the white, Lego-like rowhouses and their proximity to downtown Stockholm had caused the housing prices here to skyrocket over the last couple of decades. Housing here was much more expensive now than it had been in the mid-nineties when they had been forced to sell his own childhood home.

For as long as he could remember Hans and Inga Lindén had talked about selling when they got older and moving to an apartment in the city. He suspected that they would have done it a long time ago if only their 38-year-old son had moved out.

Fredrik knocked hard on their front door. If Philip had gone to bed, he might be knocking for a good long while before he woke up, but it was Hans who opened the door instead of his childhood friend.

"Philip was up all night. He just went to bed. You go on in, but you're going to have to fight for a bit to get some life into him," Hans explained. Then he looked Fredrik over and asked, "How are you doing?"

"Great," Fredrik lied.

Fredrik walked right in and headed for the basement stairs to escape any further questioning. The rowhouses were identical on the inside and, just like his had been, Philip's bedroom was in the rec room. He pushed open the door without knocking.

Philip was lying on his stomach in bed with the covers wrapped around his legs. Several computer monitors stood strewn across his desktop. The rest of the room was taken up by a leather sofa directly in front of a big screen TV. There were drifts of cords and consoles on the floor for various video games and computers.

They had known each other for as long as Fredrik could remember, carefree best friends who had played soccer and floorball on the asphalt outside, ridden mopeds, and hung out at the youth center. Philip was just like everyone else on the outside, but on the inside he was different. He got stuck on things easily and had a hard time getting unstuck. When everyone else rode their bikes home to eat, he might sit there in the woods and carefully sort their cache of pornographic magazines by date or color or whatever occurred to him, completely uninterested in the contents that the rest of them could hardly stop thinking about. Hans and Inga had often had to go out looking for him in the evenings. Fredrik accepted Philip's idiosyncrasies, but one by one the rest of their friends had moved on. Philip became increasingly isolated, and a profound fear of the world took root in him. When Fredrik moved to his grandmother's place, Philip stopped going out, and started living through his video games. He had received his education from his rec room and later did his job as a freelance software developer there, a job that required minimal human contact and could be done from anywhere in the world.

"Philip." Fredrik gently shook his skinny shoulder.

His friend rolled over onto his back and opened one eyes.

"What the hell, Freddy... what time is it?"

"Almost nine thirty."

"Go away! I just fell asleep." Philip rolled back over onto his stomach again and gave Fredrik the finger behind his back.

Fredrik walked over to the rectangular basement window just below the ceiling and opened it to let a little air in. When he turned around he saw himself reflected in the grid of mirrors over the bed that had been there since Philip was a teenager. The sight was not appealing. His dark, unwashed hair was long enough to wear in a bun. He needed to make an appointment for a haircut.

Fredrik sat down heavily on the sofa and looked at the skinny figure in the bed.

"It was him," Fredrik said. "I'm one hundred percent sure it was Niklas this time."

Philip didn't respond at first, but Fredrik could tell from the tension in his back that he hadn't fallen back asleep.

"Freddy..." Philip reluctantly rolled over in bed and swung his legs over the edge. His voice sounded both compassionate and irritated. He rubbed his face with his palms.

"Are you taking too much benzo again?"

Fredrik looked down and started picking at his cuticles. The only sound was the muted hum from the abundant electronics in the room.

"This isn't exactly the first time you've seen him."

It had happened before, many times, but this time was different. Fredrik was sure it was Niklas he had seen outside the hotel, completely sure. He couldn't understand why Adam Ceder had had him thrown out, claiming he didn't know who Niklas was, or why his brother would want to stay hidden from him.

Fredrik pulled the box of pills out of his pocket, purposefully pushed two pills through the foil backing, and then swallowed them. His childhood friend looked on disapprovingly as Fredrik closed his eyes and leaned back on the sofa waiting for the chemicals to seep into his blood. After a while, his breathing began to calm down and the itching in his hands eased up, but his heartbeat remained irregular in his chest.

"Don't you get that it wasn't real?" Philip eyed him reproachfully. "Ugh, why are you taking that shit?"

"Adam Ceder," Fredrik said, opening his eyes. "Do you know who he is?"

"No, should I?" Philip sounded tired.

"The Ceder hotel chain?"

Philip nodded in recognition.

"OK... and?" Philip said. "What the hell does that have to do with this?"

"I saw Niklas with Ceder outside his hotel." He heard a vacuum cleaner turn on upstairs.

"Freddy, what the hell..."

"Fine!" Fredrik threw his hands up in the air. "You don't need to believe me. All I'm asking is for you to look into that Ceder guy. I'm positive that he knows something about Niklas."

"Why don't you look into him yourself? You could probably just ask somebody at work, right?"

"How would that look?"

"Right? How would that look?" Philip repeated sarcastically.

His sarcasm didn't bother Fredrik. He needed to find out more about Ceder. Why would his brother go to that man's hotel? And why would Adam Ceder lie about having met Niklas?

Philip reluctantly got up and walked over to his desk, his blanket still wrapped around him, and woke up his laptop.

"If I do this and I don't find anything on him, then you'll let this go? Once and for all?"

"I swear." Fredrik nodded, getting up from the sofa.

Philip looked into his eyes and they both knew it wasn't true. Fredrik would never let go of Niklas. Not again.

"Hey, where are you going?" Philip asked as Fredrik headed for the stairs.

"I'm going to confront Adam Ceder."

Things were hopping outside Ceder City East. Everyone definitely hadn't left the city to go spend Midsummer out in the archipelago or at their summer homes, far from it. Taxis dropped off a steady stream of tourists who all marveled at the lush greenery right in the heart of the city. Adam Ceder came out in person to greet one group who arrived in black cars with hordes of bodyguards before they vanished again just as quickly as they had appeared, into the hotel entrance.

Fredrik knew better than to follow them. He had decided to keep an eye on Ceder from a distance to start. While he waited, he pushed out two more pills and swallowed them without water. The bitter taste calmed him even before they had a chance to start working. Torsten had said no more than four a day. Fredrik looked down at the blister pack. He had already taken four, and it wasn't even lunchtime yet.

After his visit to Philip he had taken the subway home and retrieved his car, which he kept parked in a parking garage a few blocks away. This, too, had been his grandmother's, a silver-colored Skoda. It was hardly fancy or high-powered, but it was in good condition. The car was one of the few things he hadn't sold yet. It gave him a sense of freedom even though he rarely or essentially never drove it anywhere.

Ceder wouldn't be able to dodge his questions this time. Stalking someone was definitely taking things too far, but since Ceder refused to tell him the truth about Niklas, there wasn't any other option. He would wait until Ceder came back out of the hotel and then follow him and demand to know why Niklas had come to his hotel. According to Swedish search engine hitta.se, Ceder lived in a house in Djursholm, a suburb just north of Stockholm. When they got there, Fredrik would jump out of the car and pin Ceder against the wall, far away from his guards. That was the plan.

Fredrik didn't need to wait very long. Adam Ceder turned up in front of the hotel again by noon. He was casually dressed in a yellow polo shirt and khaki shorts now and carrying a sports bag. He chatted for a bit with the doorman before a black Mercedes SUV pulled up in front of the hotel. The driver stepped out and handed the keys to Ceder who hopped in and drove away once his bag had been loaded into the trunk. Fredrik turned on his engine, slowly pulled out onto the road, and followed the black SUV.

30

He quickly realized that they were not headed to Djursholm. Ceder went north on Karlavägen and nimbly worked his way toward highway E4, changing lanes frequently. Fredrik followed at a safe distance. As soon as they were on highway E4, Ceder sped up to eighty miles per hour. The Skoda protested as Fredrik tried to maintain the same speed.

The traffic jams to get out of the city for the holiday hadn't started yet, and soon they had passed both Arlanda Airport and the city of Uppsala. Fredrik cast a worried glance at his gas gauge. How far was Ceder actually going to go? Fredrik struggled to extract his phone from his jeans pocket as he drove and with one eye on the road and one on his phone, he tried to figure out if the Ceder family owned any summer houses north of Stockholm, but all he found was more Ceder hotels.

Two hours later they were still driving. They had passed Gävle now. This was the farthest north Fredrik had ever been. He felt a burning sensation in the pit of his stomach from his anxiety. Should he turn around? No, he couldn't. Ceder knew Niklas, just as surely as he was sitting here. If Fredrik wanted any chance at finding out where his brother was, he had to talk to Ceder.

5.

Kaj had lunch ready on the deck when Sofia returned from her run. The table was set with one of her grandmother's embroidered linen tablecloths from the hall cupboard with a vase of wildflowers as a centerpiece. Kaj had laid out pickled herring, deviled eggs, flatbread, and beer with a schnapps glass for himself and a Ramlösa mineral water for Sofia.

She wasn't hungry, but since Kaj insisted that they should eat Midsummer luncheon together, she sat down and put a napkin in her lap. Kaj went into the kitchen to fetch the boiled fingerling potatoes. She spread butter on a piece of flatbread and took a cautious bite.

"Ah, this view!" Kaj sat down and enjoyed a sip of his beer. "Just think if Mette could see this. She loves the water."

Sofia didn't respond. She didn't have anything against Kaj's wife, but she drew the line at inviting her out to her summer house.

"We're going to Yxland tomorrow," Kaj continued in an attempt to get a conversation going. Sofia nodded vaguely, turning her attention to the dock and the boat.

"How are things going at the station? Missing boat motors and illegal fishing?" Kaj took a big bite of herring in mustard sauce and potatoes and smiled wryly.

Even though they had never worked together on a case, work was the one topic of conversation that never failed to bring them together. Criminal profiling and major crimes went hand in hand, and more than once they had worked out theories together over the dinner table. Rarely over the years they had been together had there ever been any line between their personal lives and work.

"Honestly, Sofia, isn't it time you moved back home?"

"Um, this is home for me."

"You know what I mean," Kaj said. "Move back to Stockholm. Good grief, you've not even forty yet. What kind of career opportunities do you have to look forward to here?"

"Well, there's a rumor that Vera's going to retire."

"I'll believe that when I see it," Kaj scoffed.

He was well acquainted with Sofia's boss. They had worked together on a difficult case several years earlier. A missing mother of two had been found raped and murdered, and Kaj and his colleagues from the criminal profiling group had been brought in to help with the investigation. That had been before Sofia had moved back up to Örnsköldsvik.

"How old is Vera, actually?"

"Not old enough to retire at any rate," Sofia said with a shrug.

"You mean not as old as I am?" Kaj smiled at her over his beer glass and Sofia couldn't help but smile back.

"Something like that."

He wiped his mouth with his napkin and then set it on top of his silverware on his plate.

"Well, you could think about it anyway," he said.

"Think about what?"

"Moving back. I'd really like to see you more often."

Sofia nodded, but inside she knew it would never happen. She would never leave the place where her father was buried.

And her daughter.

—

As five thirty approached, Fredrik had been following Adam Ceder's SUV for more than five hours. An infinite amount of forest seemed to have passed by outside the windows. He had considered turning back several times but changed his mind at the last second each time. Surely Ceder would reach wherever he was going in just a few more miles and then he would stop. And yet, he hadn't stopped, aside from a quick stop at a gas station in Tönnebro, where Ceder had hopped out, filled up his tank, and run inside the gas station to buy a cup of coffee. Fredrik had barely had time to put a few liters of gas into the Skoda before Ceder continued north.

They had driven for another three hours before Ceder finally pulled off the E4 near Bjästa, just south of Örnsköldsvik, and proceeded to the Köpmanholmen ferry terminal.

Fredrik kept his distance and parked as far away from Ceder as possible. He had an alarming, sinking feeling in his stomach as he saw Ceder stroll calmly over to the wide dock where scores of tourists were standing in front of a red wooden building waiting in line to buy tickets. Visible across the bay there was dark green, old growth forest, like a blanket on top of the steep, reddish-brown cliffs: Sweden's High Coast. Fredrik understood now how the region had gotten its name.

He stayed in his car for a while. What should he do? Ceder was obviously planning to take the ferry. Should he try to confront him here, before he got on the boat? Fredrik didn't have time to think any farther than that before he saw the ferry pulling into the wide bay from the Gulf of Bothnia and Ceder vanished into the crowd. Fredrik threw his phone charger and wallet into the cloth tote bag with the Coop logo on it that his grandmother always kept in the glove compartment and opened his door.

As he stepped out of the car he was hit by the scent of the sea air. It smelled like death.

His hands started itching instantly and he scratched nervously at the back of one hand. As he ran over to the ticket window, he pushed two round pills out of the blister pack, and swallowed them. Six pills in one day, two too many.

A few teenagers were jostling each other and laughing in the line in front of him. Behind him the line filled up with travelers.

This was the last sailing of the day and everyone seemed to be in a hurry to get aboard. The horde of people started moving the instant the ferry docked. He could see Ceder's yellow polo shirt farther ahead in the line.

One step forward and then another. His scalp hurt. His heart was pounding so hard it was painful, but he couldn't stop now. A woman with a scarf around her hair sighed impatiently when he hesitated before taking that last step onto the gangway.

One more step. Panic set in and he nearly tripped. A member of the crew in a white shirt with tattooed forearms grabbed his hand at the last second.

"Here, let me take your bag." He smiled and reached for the tote bag, but Fredrik snatched it back out of his hand.

"It's OK," Fredrik mumbled and jogged over to the stairs that led to the aft deck. He sat down on a white bench as far from the bow as he could get and wiped away the cold sweat that kept beading up on his forehead. The first step was done. Now the actual ferry crossing was all that remained. He shielded his eyes with his hand and looked up at the barren, rocky cliffs. Would he be able to swim that far if the boat sank? Probably not.

6.

Ulvön Island, 1979

Adam hung out over the railing, watching the waves foaming around the bow. Little drops of saltwater splashed his face.

It was sunny and the ferry was packed. A little boy of about six jumped up and down in excitement as he spotted Ulvö Harbor come into view from behind the cape.

"I can get ice cream, right, Dad?"

The father laughed and hugged the little boy.

The others were waiting farther back on the deck. There were twelve of them on their way to the camp. Adam already thought it felt like a prison. They had spent more than seven hours on the bus yesterday. By the time they arrived the last ferry had already left so they spent the night with an acquaintance of the pastor's, a fat lady who smelled unpleasantly of cooking and sweat. He had had to share a bumpy mattress with Thomas, and they were awakened at six in the morning to get to the ferry. He felt like they were on their way to Alcatraz, the island prison he had read about in school.

Suddenly someone pinched his sides. He jumped and nearly fell headfirst over the railing.

"Cut it out!" Adam exclaimed.

"What? I thought you wanted to swim," laughed Thomas, who had snuck up on him from behind.

The Russian girls had come out, too, and were giggling with glee at Thomas's prank.

He winked at them and yelled in his not-very-good English.

"You want swim?"

They laughed and nodded.

Thomas walked up to one girl, picked her up by the waist, and pretended to chuck her over the railing. Adam turned back around to face the water again. He couldn't understand why everyone was so excited. They were going to be away from home for four weeks. Even if his mother was annoying, he would rather be home in the city than stuck on a stupid island in the middle of nowhere.

They were approaching the harbor. A long string of red boathouses lined the bay. The place looked deserted and spooky despite the nice weather. A small group of people stood waiting at the dock, the pastor in his white collar and black robes, and two girls Adam's age. One of the girls was in a wheelchair. She raised her hand and waved at them. Adam waved back discreetly. Thomas laughed.

"Look at that!" Thomas laughed. "Lamest roller derby contestant ever!"

The Russian girls laughed, too, even though they didn't understand what Thomas had said.

Thomas's loud voice echoed across the bay and the girl in the wheelchair fidgeted.

Adam took a breath and looked up at the sky.

He would be home again soon.

7

After two horrific hours, the captain announced over the loud-speakers that they would soon be arriving in Ulvö Harbor. Fredrik had sat outside on the deck for the whole ferry ride, his eyes locked on the horizon. He didn't dare go down into the lounge, not even to the bathroom. He didn't want to risk being caught in the vessel's innards if it sank or being spotted by Ceder. He didn't release his convulsive grip on the bench until the thick mooring lines were securely wrapped around the wharf bollards. He opened and closed his hands a few times to bring some life back into his stiff fingers as he looked around at the harbor. The wharf was full of people and the collective mood was upbeat. Bicycles, strollers, and coolers were schlepped ashore with everyone pitching in. Some of the passengers had people waiting for them with wheelbarrows or carts to haul their luggage. People hugged and waved. Fredrik spotted Ceder, who walked unfalteringly down the gangway and then turned off to the right along an unpaved road.

Fredrik hurried to disembark the ferry. Just to the left there was a simple little wooden shop, painted red with a colorful, clown-shaped GB ice cream sign out front. Next to that there was a gas station with a bulletin board mounted on the front. He pushed his way past a flock of young girls in too-short cropped tops, but he made sure to keep his distance from Ceder. As Fredrik passed the bulletin board, Ceder stopped to look at his phone.

Fredrik stopped, too, pretending to study the map that was posted on the bulletin board. It turned out Ulvön Island, which meant Wolf Island, was actually two different islands, North Ulvön and South Ulvön separated by Ulvö Strait. The hotel was less than a kilometer to the east on North Ulvön, which was the island he was on. Presumably that was where Ceder was headed. According to the map, there were a few other villages on the island, Fjären, Norrbyn, Norrbysbodarna, and Sörbyn a few kilometers to the north. Otherwise it seemed to be sparsely populated. An ad for a fishing village in Sandviken caught his eye, a heritage site from the middle of the seventeenth century with fishing huts available for overnight rentals. He peeked in Ceder's direction but when he saw that the hotel owner was still standing in the same spot he continued reading the bulletin board. "Ulvön Island is home to Sweden's most traditional salting house where Baltic herring are fermented to make surströmming and an iron ore mine that dates back to the seventeenth century..."

Finally Ceder started moving again.

Fredrik hesitated for a second. A hard shove on his shoulder nearly made him fall over backwards.

"Oh, I'm sorry! I..."

A blond woman smiled at him apologetically. He was just about to move on after Ceder when the woman touched his arm.

"Fredrik Fröding?" She leaned in close to him, and before Fredrik could defend himself, she gave him a clumsy hug. When she took a step back, he looked into her green eyes and tried in vain to place her familiar face. It took him far too long before he realized that it was Sofia Hjortén. She had already started to squirm and looked like she was having trouble deciding if she should remind him who she was.

"Sofia," he said.

They both exhaled.

"It's been ages," she said.

She was still beautiful. Those green eyes rimmed with thick, pale eyelashes and that long blond hair pulled back into a high ponytail.

"It sure has. How have you been?" Fredrik pulled his hand through his uncombed hair.

"Good."

"What are you doing here?" He gave her a friendly smile and Sofia returned the smile.

"I live here. At least in the summers. I have a house out by Norrbysbodarna. Maybe you saw it on your way in with the ferry? White, with triangular windows over the deck."

Fredrik nodded, impressed. He had indeed seen the big, white house that sat like a bright star in the middle of the thick woods only a hundred meters from the water.

"So you didn't stay in Stockholm?"

"No, I moved back up here several years ago," she said. "How about you?"

"I still live in the same apartment on Brahegatan."

She blushed slightly when he mentioned the apartment. She shaded her eyes with her hand and looked at him.

"Are you working for the police?"

"No, I... no, that didn't work out."

Fredrik looked up at the dirt road. Ceder was gone.

"Look, I have to go. It was great to see you again. Have a nice Midsummer," he mumbled anxiously and walked off before she had even answered.

Ceder was already way ahead of him. Fredrik spotted Ceder's yellow polo shirt every now and then as he quickly walked eastward. This was a beautiful island. Little picturesque summer homes and boathouses bordered the gravel road that ran through the little harbor village parallel to the shore. Every house featured a new sun-faded color, but otherwise they looked the same. The windows were trimmed with lace curtains, and old-fashioned nautical-themed knick-knacks were visible on the windowsills. It was as if the place had been taken right out of an Astrid Lindgren story. The Midsummer holiday festivities seemed to be well underway. Tipsy teenagers staggered aimlessly along the road. In the distance, Fredrik could hear a singer performing and people clapping their hands.

Less than ten minutes later he had reached the spot where the Ulvö Hotel was supposed to be, but there was no sign of the tired, red wooden building with the ornate balcony railing that he had googled on his phone as he walked. Instead, a trendy new hotel for the yachting crowd towered before Fredrik, with a fenced-in pool below a large deck covered in wicker furniture. The hotel's pier was enormous, and every slip had a boat in it.

Ceder strode purposefully toward the glass front entrance. Fredrik waited outside while Ceder talked to the desk clerk. Keys changed hands and Ceder disappeared up a staircase. Once he was no longer in sight, then Fredrik dared to enter.

A woman in her fifties with long, blond hair worn up in a clip greeted him. "Mona" was embroidered in white on her black shirt. He needed to decide what he was going to do.

But he had come this far, so he just had to follow through on his plan now. He needed to pin Ceder up against a wall.

"I need a room for the night."

Mona eyed him skeptically for a few seconds, but then turned her eyes to a ledger on the front desk.

"Our IT system is being upgraded. Really inconvenient during the Midsummer rush."

She flipped through the ledger.

"We're usually fully booked over Midsummer weekend," she stated, as if he should have realized that on his own. "But we actually received a cancellation this afternoon. You would have to check out tomorrow, but if you want the room for tonight, it's yours."

Fredrik accepted and after she took his name and credit card information, Mona motioned with her hand for him follow her. On their way up the stairs she proudly told him about all the famous hockey players, royals, and politicians who had stayed in the newly built hotel. Fredrik occasionally had trouble following because of her heavy local dialect, but he nodded, impressed, whenever he recognized someone's name while at the same time remaining on the lookout for Ceder as they passed the hotel bar and the entrance to the restaurant. They reached his room and she courteously handed over the key.

"Well, in that case I'll wish you a pleasant Midsummer's Eve."

She had told him that this was one of their nicer rooms. The decor was bucolic, the color scheme white and gray. Fredrik opened the window which looked out at Ulvö Strait toward South Ulvö Island, nicknamed "Anersia," which meant "the other side" in the local Norrland dialect. He had learned that from Mona as well.

He sat down on the edge of the bed. The water outside sparkled in the sunlight and he could hear laughter and voices from the hotel restaurant. Images of Niklas flickered before his eyes, jerky movie sequences that seemed out of focus. The movie started playing faster and faster and he began to trouble breathing.

What have I done?

He was trapped on an island. He had followed a complete stranger more than 300 miles, and now no matter what he did, he was going to have to get back on the ferry if he ever wanted to leave again. The realization was numbing. The walls of the room felt like they were closing in on him, and his heart was beating like crazy in his chest. He leaned forward and tried to exhale calmly. He focused on each breath and counted his inhalations and exhalations as Torsten had taught him, but it didn't help. He dug around in his pocket for more pills and looked for something to wash them down with. His eyes landed on a miniature wine bottle and two wineglasses sitting on a table by the window. Do not combine the pills with alcohol under any circumstances. That warning had been deeply ingrained on him, but he had already broken that rule once this week. What would one more time matter? What did anything matter right now?

He got up off the bed and opened the bottle.

8.

The smell of moss and old growth forest embraced Sofia as she ran. This was her second run of the day. She shouldn't actually run this much, the connective tissues in her legs took such a beating. But her body suffered from the kind of restlessness that only running could deal with. It was still hot out even though it was late in the evening, almost night. She was forced to stop and pull off her t-shirt only a few kilometers down the forest path heading down to Sandviken. She was just in her sports bra and training tights now. Every once in a while a dry fir branch jutting out over the path would scratch her arms, but that didn't matter. That was part of it. The dark woods didn't scare her. She had run here for so many years that her feet knew the way over the smallest roots without her needing to even look down. Her father had worried when she decided to take up orienteering at the age of thirteen. There are bears and wolves in these woods, he used to say, looking at her with a worried wrinkle between his eyebrows. I could probably outrun a bear or a wolf, she had retorted, even though they both knew that no one had ever seen a wolf or bear on the island. Moose occasionally crossed the ice during a really cold winter, but she wasn't afraid of moose. As long as you kept your distance when they had calves with them, you had nothing to fear.

Orienteering and pike fishing, what kinds of hobbies were those for a pretty girl to pursue? She had heard that her whole life from her mother, but never from her father. Why not take up dancing or singing in the choir like Claire had done when she was little? The fact that it drove her mother crazy had been half the fun. Sometimes she still thought it was part of the fun.

Sofia veered off toward Norrby Tarn as she climbed the hill. She checked her fitness tracker and found that she was a couple of seconds under her standard time.

Her thoughts turned to Fredrik. After she had seen Kaj off at the ferry, she had literally walked right into him. He had just been standing there in the middle of the crowd like a lost child who couldn't find his mother. Seeing him again had felt like a kick in the gut.

It had been more than ten or fifteen years since she had seen him last. He was skinnier than she remembered, but still intimidatingly good-looking, wearing jeans and a light-colored shirt with the sleeves rolled up, revealing his sinewy forearms and olive skin. His dark eyes had looked right at her, right through her. For a minute she had thought he didn't recognize her.

He was the first man she had ever fallen in love with. Pathetic, sure, not to have fallen in love until the age of twenty-three, but there just hadn't been anyone before him. Sometimes she wasn't sure if there had been anyone since, either. Of course she loved Kaj, but not the way she had loved Fredrik. She had lusted after Fredrik for that whole six-week-long summer course in criminology that they had both taken. He had barely noticed her existence, until that night they rode the subway together. He was on his way home to the turn-of-the-century, one-bedroom apartment he had inherited, with the high ceilings and the deep window ledges. She was on her way back to the shabby student room she was renting in Spånga, which cost nine times more than what she would have paid back home in her far less urban hometown of Örnsköldsvik, 500 kilometers north of Stockholm. She talked so much during that subway ride that she accidentally got off at his stop by mistake, which was so unlike her that she was surprised at herself. When they got to his door, he had laughed and asked if she lived there, too, knowing full well that she didn't. She had been embarrassed, but he had just kept laughing and then invited her in for a cup of tea. They never got to the tea, but she had stayed in his apartment for the next two days anyway. The memories of those days lingered with her still. She could still recall those images in her mind at any time, her and Fredrik together in his bed with the window open to the late summer night. How he had touched her… Pull yourself together! Sofia shook herself as she ran. She didn't believe for a second that those nights had meant as much to him as they had to her, not that it mattered.

This wasn't the first time she had run into someone up here from her years in Stockholm. Ulvön Island attracted thousands of tourists every year, and she had gotten used to running into former colleagues and classmates disembarking the ferry with their families in tow to soak up the island's history and taste some surströmming. It wasn't so strange that Fredrik had also shown up here at some point. It meant absolutely nothing.

Sofia picked up her pace. She tried to think about the upcoming fishing competition.

She was looking forward to going. Her bags were packed and sat waiting in her front hall with her rods and reels. The team was gathering early on Midsummer's day to take a charter bus to Norway together. The only thing bugging her about her vacation was that her overly ambitious colleague, Mattias Wikström, wasn't taking any time off. He would still be in the office in the summer heat eyeing Vera's position like a hawk.

Chief Inspector Vera Nordlund had held the coveted position as head of the investigative division with the Örnsköldsvik Police Department for more than ten years. She was one of the few people who knew about Sofia's miscarriage, not that they shared any real personal connection. Just like everyone else, Vera maintained a certain emotional distance from Sofia, even though they had been working together for almost three years. Having worked in Stockholm was both a feather in Sofia's cap and a target on her back. Particularly up in this part of Sweden, she knew it was culturally taboo to be too full of oneself. The difference between the way Vera kept her at a distance and the way the others did was that Vera treated everyone that way. She kept to herself and never discussed her private life at work. In all the years Sofia had been back in Örnsköldsvik, she had never heard Vera say a peep about a grandchild's soccer game or a vacation to the Canary Islands. She didn't even talk about the local ice hockey team, Modo Hockey, even though that was practically a statutory requirement for anyone residing within the Örnsköldsvik municipal boundaries. Work was Vera's life. But rumor had it now that she was starting to talk about retiring, and people were baring their fangs and sharpening their claws. A lot of people wanted that coveted job, and Sofia was one of them.

She kept running, sweat pouring down her body. She grabbed her t-shirt from where she had tucked it into the back of her training tights and mopped her face, her stomach, and her back. She had already run more than five kilometers but decided to keep going the whole way to the old seventeenth-century fishing village in Sandviken. That would make the run more than ten kilometers, farther than she usually went, but that didn't matter. She had several weeks of vacation to rest her weary muscles.

Sofia held her arms out away from her body and let the cool air refresh her as she ran down toward the sand dunes. Her sneakers sank into the soft sand with every step. To avoid periostitis pain she needed to keep her strides short and keep her weight on her forward foot.

It was best if she didn't run downhill at all, but her endorphins were pumping now and it was hard to stop. She veered off to the right along the rocky waterfront, picked up her pace, and turned up toward the forest trail. She kept her eyes on her fitness tracker and sped up even more through sheer willpower.

This was going to be a record time.

9.

He peered into the dark boathouse. Despite the pale blue light from the open end, it was really hard to see. His eyes adjusted quickly, and he was able to make out a metallic boat with double motors, which had been winched up and was hanging from the rafters overhead. There were hooks, nets, and floats to his right. The surface of the water outside was smooth. A silvery fish jumped and broke the stillness. He stood there for a while watching the ring pattern of the ripples expand and then fade away before he entered the boathouse. When he stepped over the threshold, he stepped wrong and staggered even though he had only had one shot of whiskey.

Was this really the right place? He pulled out his phone and with some effort managed to reread the message. The letters were swimming together. How could he have gotten so drunk from only two fluid ounces? Yeah, the description matched. But where was she?

"Hello? I'm here now."

He was standing there waiting awkwardly in the dark boathouse when a sound made him turn around. A fast, rhythmic clicking followed by a bell that dinged. He quickly discovered where it came from.

There was a toy angel in the doorway, a delicate, white angel twirling around with her hands out in front of her body clasped together in prayer. His mother had had a similar toy when he was little, only it had been a dog with a blue collar. It sat on the bookshelf in the living room and smiled mockingly at him when she scolded him. Her most cherished possession which you weren't allowed to touch since there was a risk of breaking the delicate springs in the dog's back.

He leaned forward to pick up the angel and perceived a pale face with icy blue eyes that met his gaze from the darkness.

"Hi." The voice was childish and soft.

Then came the blow.

The sound of his skull being crushed filled his whole being. His ears were ringing. He fell backward onto the hard, wooden planks. He wanted to scream, but no sound came out. His body was paralyzed, he couldn't tell if it was out of fear or from the injury, but nothing would obey. His arms lay limp, against his body, as if he were a soldier who had fallen at his post. His head was tilted to one side, and he saw the wind-up angel spinning around on her white wooden base only a few inches from his face. As the key in her back stopped, a pair of naked, suntanned feet approached. The woman picked her toy back up. He saw her long fingers tenderly caress the doll as she whispered loving words into its deaf, porcelain ears. He realized that he was dying but felt neither pain nor fear. Out of the corner of his eye he watched the angel begin spinning again. Rosy cheeks on a chalk-white face and golden hair falling in curls down her back. The angel's slight smile felt almost comforting.

It was becoming harder to breathe and he coughed with difficulty. Red drops rained onto the angel.

A minute passed, maybe an hour. His rattling breaths were the only thing that disturbed the silence. And the angel, which was lifted up as soon as it stopped. Over and over again.

The bell dinged again.

Then silence.

Saturday, June 22, Midsummer Day

10.

Even as Sofia opened the door, she recognized the smell of fear. The feeling was so familiar, so frightening in its simplicity. She went into the kitchen. As soon as she stepped over the threshold, she saw it. A yellowish-brown dog lying on its side. Its mouth was open, and those dead eyes looked at her pleadingly. It was covered in blood. The gash where its belly had been split open gaped wide, a nasty sight. She looked over at the kitchen table. A little boy sat underneath it with his legs pulled up under his chin and his light-blue pajama top pulled down over his knees. He couldn't be more than three years old.

"Hi, I'm Sofia. I'm a police officer." She reached in under the table. "Come on, let's go to a different room." The boy didn't react as she placed her hand on his cold feet.

Suddenly there was a bang. A chair was yanked and overturned, and an arm closed in around her throat. Sofia was pulled to her feet so fast that the back of her head hit the table.

"Don't you touch him, you god damned pussy cop!" The man reeked of alcohol and cigarettes. His movements were wobbly, but his grip on her neck was firm. At first she panicked, but then her experience took over, muscle memory. She managed to loosen the drunk man's arm enough that she could turn toward him and punch the inside of his shoulder. He lost his balance and they fell over backward onto the floor together, on top of the lifeless dog.

"Let go of her!" Vera stood in the kitchen doorway with her gun drawn.

The man's knee hit Sofia full force in the gut, and she felt something rupture inside her. A blow so hard that it resonated throughout her body. The pain was so intense that for a second she thought Vera had shot her by mistake. Vera reached her quickly and twisted the man's arm behind his back. Sofia got up onto her knees, coughing. Her hand moved to her stomach, down between her legs. Her jeans were red with blood.

Sofia woke up. She was pressing both hands to her belly to stop the blood flow, but when she looked down there was no blood. The dream had felt so real that she almost couldn't make sense of it. She looked up and tried to orient herself. She was sitting on her sofa with a cardigan on, still in her workout clothes. Oh, good Lord, how long had she been asleep? Shit, the fishing competition! The bus was supposed to leave at nine.

Her cell phone rang angrily from the kitchen counter. The display said 5:10 a.m.

"Sofia Hjortén."

"Hi, it's Karim. I just talked to the captain. Are you out at your place on Ulvön?" Her colleague's voice sounded as if he had just woken up, just like her.

"Yes, why?"

"Vera is on her way over with the Coast Guard. They found a dead man down below the bathrooms near the hotel pier. You need to get over there before the tourists wake up. The body is lying out in the open. Vera and Mattias will be there within thirty minutes."

The phone made two chimes to announce that she had a call waiting from Vera Nordlund. Sofia ended her call with Karim and answered.

"We're on our way out. Head down there and cordon off the area," Vera said without any additional explanation.

"I don't keep crime scene tape here in my house."

"Just use whatever and make sure no one comes near the body. Get help from a couple of the hotel staff if you need!"

Sofia stuffed her phone into the pocket of her cardigan. She didn't bother to change even though she did keep a uniform and some of her official police polo shirts at home. On the way to her car, she grabbed her plastic clothesline, which had been rolled up in a basket. She thought about the ominous dream about the day when she had lost her baby. She hadn't had that dream for a long time. She rubbed her neck anxiously. Was it some kind of warning?

There was no one around when she pulled up by the hotel. Since there was essentially no vehicle traffic on the island, there wasn't really anywhere to park, so she parked the car on the sloping drive to the left of the hotel. Before she got out, she cast a quick glance in her rearview mirror and pulled her ponytail tighter.

Luckily the hungover Midsummer tourists weren't awake yet. Ideally they would have time to move the body without too much fuss. Sofia looked out at the water. Twenty minutes had passed since Karim's call and the Coast Guard boat should be arriving at any moment. A slender woman in her twenties stood below the hotel's front entrance, nervously fiddling with her server's apron. Sofia walked over and introduced herself.

"Sofia Hjortén. I'm with the police. Could you show me where the body is?"

The girl nodded silently and they walked in silence past the oversized hotel pier with the swimming pool, past the restrooms and the staff housing. A short way down the strip of beach along the rocky coastline, an older woman with long, blond hair worn up in a clip came into view. When she saw Sofia, she came over to her and held out her hand. She smiled, pale beneath her sunburn. Little beads of sweat gleamed on her upper lip and her eyes darted back and forth between Sofia and the hotel.

"I'm Mona Höglund. I run the hotel along with Christine Karst."

She introduced herself formally even though she and Sofia had met at least a handful of times. She was obviously in shock.

"I found the…" She pointed awkwardly toward the rocky slope that led down to the water.

"Have you walked over to the body or touched it?"

"Yes, at first I thought he had just passed out. It wasn't until I got closer that I saw the head injury." She cleared her throat to steady her voice. "I felt to see if he had a pulse. I'm a nurse by training."

"Do you know who he is?"

"He checked in yesterday. I'll have to check on his name, but I'm quite sure it's the same man," Mona replied without looking her in the eye.

Sofia nodded and then pointed to the young server.

"Could you run up to the hotel and bring a blanket or a sheet to cover him with?" Then she turned to Mona. "I want you to hold onto this so I can try to cordon off the area."

The woman obediently held the end of the short laundry line and Sofia stretched it between two lampposts to block off access to the rocky slope. She regarded her work and determined that at least it would prevent people from going down to the water where the body was. When she was done with that, the server returned with the blanket. Sofia took it and carefully climbed down the steep, rocky slope so as not to disturb any evidence. Even though she didn't have gloves, shoe coverings, or step plates available, she didn't want to wait any longer before covering the body. The boaters would start waking up soon and start making their way to the bathrooms and showers.

Sofia squatted down and took a few deep breaths looking out at the water before looking down at the body.

The man lay on his back with his arms and legs stretched straight out like a starfish.

Only his head and one shoulder were on the shore. The rest of his body was in the water. His skin gleamed white and spongy below the surface. His shirt had ridden up, exposing his chest, which was unnaturally thin, almost sunken. One eye was sealed shut by blood, the other stared up at the sky, unseeing. He had several abrasions on his forehead, but his body wasn't bloated or discolored. An open wound gaped above his right ear and something messy was stuck in his hair. The man was obviously beyond rescuing.

The island only had about thirty permanent residents, so Sofia could tell right away that he was a tourist. She respectfully spread the blanket over the man and turned around just as Vera came tromping over in her boots to Sofia's clumsy, makeshift crime scene tape with one of the forensic techs in tow. Her tall figure cast long shadows over the rocky shoreline.

She wore protective shoe covers over her size ten feet.

"What kind of infernal fucknuggetry have we got here?" Her voice echoed over the strait. Chief Inspector Vera Nordlund had her own special way with words, swear words to be specific. Sofia had never met anyone who could cram more colorful curse words into a single sentence.

"He doesn't look like he's been lying here for very long," Sofia said, scanning the beach around them. A light breeze was gently ruffling the water, but otherwise everything was calm. "Do you think this was an accident?"

Vera lifted the blanket and looked at the body without responding. She pushed her glasses up on top of her head and leaned in closer. Her nostrils flared.

"Well, he doesn't smell like booze anyway, but that looks damned brutal to have been an accident."

Sofia nodded.

"We'll see what the forensic techs say. The medical examiner is on her way out from Umeå."

A couple of hours later, the hotel was in full activity. Early risers were out on the patio eating breakfast and watching the K-9 teams crossing the pier back and forth. They had managed to get two dogs out to the island despite the holiday weekend. Sofia could just make out the other one at the end of the steep rocky beach. The German shepherd bitch waved her tail to keep her balance as they made their way over the rocks down to the water.

A white tent had been erected by the edge of the water to cover the body, which was still lying in the shallow water. A handful of police officers who had been brought over stood in a circle by the crime scene tape. Mattias stood beside Vera, talking on the phone, as Sofia approached. There were eight officers in total at the scene. Several of her colleagues had had to cut short their vacations to come in. Sofia smiled sympathetically at David, one of the cadets, who had been extra unlucky to answer his phone this morning. He had been at a family reunion and hadn't actually even gone to bed yet. She noted that there were several others besides him that were really in no shape to be working, but they needed every resource they could bring in right now.

"OK, could everyone gather here?" Vera waved them over and the circle closed in around her. "Our victim was found at 4:25 a.m. on the shore here by a hotel employee. The man has a visible head injury. The area has been cordoned off and medical examiner Caroline Fridell has just arrived. As usual, she wants us to steer clear of the body. Do as she says, people. Otherwise you'll be in an assload of trouble." Vera glanced at her watch and pointed to the west. "The first ferry has already left. We have exactly four hours before the next one goes. We are currently considering the incident to be a crime, and I want you to follow the protocol. Don't go overboard, no fucking wild-west interrogations, people."

One of the techs, who was wearing a full-body protective suit, apologized and pushed his way into the circle of officers. He whispered a few words to Vera before disappearing back down toward the tent.

"We don't have permission to halt commercial boat traffic and the questionings will cause delays, so prepare yourselves for a bunch of bellyaching. And then it's all going to go even more to hell once all the hungover tourists try to leave. We need to talk to as many people as possible before they leave the island!"

The rest of the day was a zoo. After a quick questioning, the shaken young server was transported to Örnsköldsvik Hospital along with Mona Höglund, who had discovered the body.

Nothing of interest had come from knocking on the doors of the residents who lived in the immediate vicinity of the hotel. Vera had asked Mattias to help her question the hotel guests, and the staff had set up a temporary questioning room in the hotel's conference room. Sofia couldn't help worrying about the fact that she hadn't been questioned, but she knew better than to complain. Instead, she stood with two colleagues and took the names and phone numbers of everyone waiting for the ferry. In the beginning most people were accommodating and genuinely horrified to learn of the death, but as time went by in the summer heat, people grew grumpier. It had been several hours and they still hadn't received a single promising tip. No one had heard or seen anything unusual.

11.

When Fredrik woke up, at first he didn't know where he was. He blinked with difficulty and looked around. The wall next to him was covered with white wooden paneling and there was a draft. His head throbbed and he was lying at a weird angle. He groped around and his fingertips felt cold porcelain.

A bathtub.

His watch showed that lunchtime had come and gone. With a good deal of effort, Fredrik heaved himself out of the tub and landed on the floor with a thud. He just managed to crawl to the toilet before his stomach turned inside out. He leaned back against the bathroom wall in exhaustion and closed his eyes. He reviewed his scant recollections from the previous day, but he couldn't remember how many drinks he had had after he went down to the hotel bar. He had one foggy, fleeting memory of a waitress asking if he was OK. And there was something about Adam Ceder, too.

Suddenly he pictured Ceder's face in front of him. His jaw tense and his hands trembling with rage. *What are you doing here? Are you following me? Leave me alone. Otherwise I promise you you're going to regret it!* The words rang in his head. Ceder had been standing very close to him. So close that he could feel the angry puffs of Ceder's breath on his face. Or was that a dream? Had he said anything about Niklas? Fredrik couldn't remember. The last thing he remembered was someone helping him to his room. After that, nothing.

After showering and helpfully tidying up his hotel room, Fredrik started packing his things. Since he barely had anything

58

with him, it didn't take long. He set his cloth tote bag by the door and walked back into the room to make one last sweep to make sure he hadn't knocked over or broken anything the day before.

That was when he discovered it.

The bag was tucked under the bed.

At first he thought someone must have forgotten it there and that he had simply missed it when he checked in. He sat down on the edge of the bed and pulled it out. It was a black sports bag. The logo on the outside revealed that it was an expensive brand. Fredrik carefully opened the zipper. Some shirts, a pair of pants, a razor, a toiletry bag, a plastic folder with some papers in it, and a silver-colored laptop, the same make that he had at home. He looked through it and turned things over without finding any indication of who the owner was.

Until he opened the laptop.

Shocked, he dropped the computer on the bed and wiped off his hands on his pants, as if they had been contaminated with a contagious virus. The itching returned immediately, and he scratched the backs of his hands anxiously. His eyes came to rest on a sticker.

Adam Ceder, Ceder City East. There was a phone number after the name.

How the hell had Ceder's bag ended up in his room? Had Ceder broken into his room?

All Fredrik remembered was that their conversation had been brief and loud, and then they had gone their separate ways. Or had they?

Obviously he needed to return the bag. This had all gotten completely out of control.

What was he doing? Following a stranger and stealing his stuff. And why would Ceder lie about Niklas? What possible reason could he have for doing that? None. Fredrik ran his hand over the pack of pills in his pocket, aware that there were even fewer pills in it now than there had been yesterday. This had to end. These pills were ruining his life, rattling his perception of reality. Maybe it was time to really get to the root of the problem instead of covering it up with medications that just created more problems? He had to go home. In a worst-case scenario, Ceder would report him to the police, but he would just have to deal with that if it happened. He would explain his history and tell them about the pills and the booze. He would apologize to Ceder and ask him to forget the whole ridiculous history.

And Niklas.

He should go see Torsten, too, as soon as Midsummer was over, to discuss that inpatient stay at the clinic in Sundsvall. Yes, that's what he would do.

Then a thought struck him. He could just take the bag with him and leave it at the front desk. That way he would still be doing the right thing but could avoid a police report. He could say that he found it in the hallway. Given that he couldn't remember, that could easily have been how it happened. Although he suspected that wasn't the case.

A young woman with ash-blond hair in a bun stood behind the front desk, talking to a uniformed policeman.

"I'm checking out? Fredrik Fröding."

The clerk searched for his name on a list and nodded to the police officer.

"That's the last one." The policeman watched Fredrik.

Damn it. He couldn't hand over the bag right in front of the police.

The female desk clerk ripped the list of hotel guests off her pad of paper and gave it to the policeman who took a picture of it with his cell phone, but showed no sign of leaving.

"Has something happened?" Fredrik avoided making eye contact.

"An accident," the desk clerk mumbled as she inserted Fredrik's credit card into the card reader. Nothing happened.

"Hm, it doesn't seem to be going through. Did you have a different card?"

Fredrik shook his head. His stomach was still burning.

"Let me run it again." The receipt paper immediately started humming inside the device. The nausea was coming in waves now, but Fredrik was able to keep himself from throwing up. He accepted the receipt and was preparing to walk across the lobby to the entrance, when a hand on his arm stopped him.

"You're coming with me."

"Why?" Fredrik asked, looking at the officer.

The policeman didn't respond, just motioned with one hand for Fredrik to follow him up the stairs. Fredrik didn't understand how the policeman could already know about the bag, but he made no attempt to protest. Although, how could Ceder know that he was the one who had taken it? Had he caught Fredrik stealing it? Oh God, he could only remember a couple of hours out of the whole previous evening.

But it didn't matter how they knew. It was enough that they knew. There was no getting out of this now.

The policeman stopped outside two big doors on the third floor and gestured with his hand that Fredrik should enter. Someone had set up a folding table and three chairs in what appeared to be a conference room. The rest of the furniture was still folded and stored along the walls. Fredrik caught a glimpse of the water out the window.

There was a tall, blond man about his age seated at the table. The dark blue polo with the police emblem was stretched tight around his muscular upper arms. He was ridiculously attractive and seemed to be well aware of that fact. An equally tall woman wearing a gray blazer sat beside him. She got up, came over to Fredrik, and shook his hand. Her short hair was dyed a plum red tone, shifting to gray at the temples. She radiated a calm and obviously commanding presence.

"Vera Nordlund."

The man on the other side of the table nodded his head in greeting without saying anything.

Vera placed her hand authoritatively on Fredrik's shoulder and showed him to a chair. The gesture was done kindly, but it made him feel uncomfortable anyway.

She sat back down and shuffled around some of the papers on the table in front of her, straightened her notepad, and then looked up at him.

"Well then, maybe we should get started?"

She started the recording device that sat between them on the table.

"Witness examination with Fredrik Fröding, Saturday, June 22nd. Present: Chief Inspector Vera Nordlund and Inspector Mattias Wikström." She pushed the recorder closer to Fredrik and leaned back in her chair.

"Are you aware that a dead man was found here on Ulvön Island this morning?"

Fredrik shook his head.

"You need to respond with a yes or a no," Vera said in a friendly voice, pointing to the recorder.

"No."

"We suspect this is a criminal matter."

Fredrik looked at the blond police officer and then at Vera.

"When did you arrive on the island?"

"Yesterday, on Midsummer eve. I drove up from Stockholm. I had planned to stay longer, but they only had a room available for one night."

Vera enthusiastically took notes even though everything they said was being recorded.

"Do you have any way to corroborate that?"

Fredrik dug around and pulled a bundle of receipts out of the pocket of his leather jacket and found the ticket from the ferry.

Vera pulled a pair of glasses out of her chest pocket and studied the ticket for a while before she stuffed it into a plastic pouch without asking him if she could keep it.

"Did you see anything unusual last night? Anyone who was acting strange? Anyone arguing or fighting?"

Fredrik shook his head and Vera gestured toward the recorder again.

"No."

"Are you sure?"

"Yes."

"What do you do for a living?" Mattias chimed in.

"I'm a manager in the passport office in Sollentuna."

Mattias smirked and snorted faintly.

"Do you have a background in law enforcement?" Vera eyed him with curiosity.

"I went to the police academy, but never finished my training. What does that have to do with this?"

She raised one hand reassuringly and shook her head.

"Nothing," she said. "We just find it interesting to meet one of our own. Where were you yesterday evening and last night?"

"Here at the hotel. I drove all day yesterday and I was tired. I had a glass of wine in the bar and then I went to bed."

"Not much of a Midsummer celebration then?" Vera made a knowing smacking sound with her tongue. Her tone of voice was friendly, but there was something sharp behind that.

"Is there anyone who can confirm that you were here all night?"

"There was a waitress…"

Mattias was at the ready with his pen.

"Her name?"

Fredrik shook his head.

"Wait here for a moment," Vera said, pushing her chair back and standing up. "I'll be right back."

Mattias stayed seated and eyed him arrogantly as Vera left the room. Fredrik looked down at his lap without trying to make small talk. Vera returned after only a couple of minutes.

"All right, Fredrik." She drummed her fingers on the edge of the table as she sat down.

"I talked to one of the servers and she remembers you quite well. Is there anything else you'd like to add about last night?"

Fredrik fidgeted in his seat.

"I was pretty drunk," he mumbled.

"I'm sorry? I didn't catch that."

"I was drunk. I drank too much and… I was drunk, that's all."

"According to the server you were so drunk that they had to stop serving you."

"That's probably true." He shrugged, embarrassed. "I don't know what time it was, but I don't think I left until the bar closed."

"Did you talk to anyone after that?"

"The desk clerk. She accompanied me upstairs."

"You'll have to speak louder!" Vera pushed the recorder closer to him. "Did a hotel staff member help you into your room?"

Fredrik nodded.

"Or, no, not into my room. I think. I don't really remember."

"You don't really remember," Vera repeated. "Can you perhaps remember what her name was?"

"I don't know her last name, but her first name might have been Mona."

"Her name is Mona Höglund, and she's also the hotel manager," Vera noted bitingly.

"Apparently you were in no condition to unlock your door on your own. She deposited you outside your room at two thirty in the morning. Is that correct?"

"That's possible." Fredrik sighed.

Vera sucked air in through her teeth in annoyance without saying anything more.

Mattias pulled a phone out of his pocket and brought up a picture. Then he set it in front of Fredrik with a bang. He tapped on the screen urgently.

"Do you recognize him?"

64

Fredrik felt his breath catch in his throat. He wanted to look away but couldn't take his eyes off the macabre photo. It showed a man lying on a rocky beach. The right side of his head was bloody, and his red hair lay in sticky clumps around his ear. Fredrik swallowed a wave of nausea and looked up. The chief inspector watched him calmly.

"Is he the one who…?" His hands sought each other out.

"Have you seen him before?"

Yes.

Fredrik shook his head fitfully.

"No," he answered.

"Are you sure? He was a guest here at the hotel last night."

Fredrik couldn't remember anything besides their brief argument. What had actually happened? Oh my God, did the police think that he…

The room started shrinking around him. He would never be allowed to leave. They would arrest him. He didn't have any alibi. He had Ceder's bag. He glanced up at Vera and thought he saw long wolves' teeth growing out of her mouth. His mind was reeling, and he grabbed the armrest to keep from falling forward.

Had he killed someone?

Had he killed Adam Ceder?

Fredrik opened his mouth. He should admit everything and let the police take care of the rest. But Vera beat him to it. She turned the phone away and looked him in the eye.

"Well then, Fredrik, thank you for your time. We would appreciate it if you could make sure you're reachable for the next few weeks." She pulled a business card out of her chest pocket and passed it to him.

"If you think of anything, anything at all, we want you to give us a call."

Fredrik nodded without daring to make eye contact with either of the officers.

"I'm sorry, do you mind if I use the bathroom?"

"Just out to the right." Vera pointed out at the corridor.

"Thank you." He snatched up the bag, which he had set next to the door, before squeezing past the uniformed officer who was still standing outside. His eyes burned into Fredrik's back.

A fire alarm was going off in his head. Fredrik saw the door to the restroom, but kept walking. His legs moved of their own accord, down the stairs and out into the lobby. Only a few steps left. The glass doors slid open silently before him and soon he was standing outside.

Free.

12.

Afternoon was approaching and the sun beat down mercilessly on the waiting ferry passengers, but no one wanted to give up their spot in line to find shade. A ferry had just arrived and put out its gangway. The rush resulted in a woman being knocked into the water and needing to be fished out, resulting in additional delays.

"What have you got?" Mattias panted through Sofia's cell phone. It sounded as if he were walking around outside.

"Nothing yet."

He made an exaggerated sigh, as if the entire investigation hinged on what Sofia could squeeze into a few hours of work.

"How about you?" she asked.

"Would I be calling you if I had anything?"

The fact that Mattias hadn't learned anything either was yet another small gain for her.

"Are you talking to Sofia?" Vera's voice was audible in the background and the phone changed hands.

"Keep talking to everyone who boards the ferry," Vera instructed her. "And anyone moored in Ankarviken on a private boat. We have two men at the Köpmanholmen terminal on the mainland waiting to greet the ferry when it docks."

Sofia heard Vera drink something, probably her tenth cup of coffee for the day.

"We just questioned the last hotel guest," Sofia said. "No one saw or heard anything."

"How about the hotel staff?"

"Same there. We have been able to ID the victim at any rate. Only one guest was missing, Adam Ceder. The family will obviously have to confirm it, but it is most likely him."

"Adam Ceder, as in the Ceder hotel chain?"

"Yes, according to the hotel manager, Mona Höglund," Sofia confirmed. "She checked him in yesterday afternoon but hadn't seen him since then. The forensic team went through his room, but it was more or less empty, no luggage or valuables. They've already ruled out the hotel room as the murder location."

"No luggage?"

"No," Sofia replied. "We're working on gaining access to the server room behind the front desk. The surveillance camera footage is in there. Mona Höglund is the only one with the code and she's still at the hospital."

Vera cleared her throat and spit somewhere away from the phone.

"We'll question everyone to begin with, and then we'll see what the medical examiner has to say."

"Are you going back to the station?" Sofia asked.

"Yes, there's not much more we can do out here right now. The Coast Guard is going to take us back across. Hey, I'm sorry about your trip to Norway…"

Sofia wanted to throw her phone in the water and tell Vera to go to hell.

"I'm just going to stop by my house. Then I'll come back across in my own boat first thing tomorrow."

–

Fredrik walked back toward the harbor where he had gotten off the ferry the day before. He wanted to hurry, but he couldn't. His body felt numb, aside from his hand which was convulsively clutching Ceder's bag.

The bright sunlight had the sweat pouring off him inside his shirt. He couldn't shake the feeling that that tall chief inspector was right on his heels with the blond policeman in tow.

He looked back over his should every now and then, but saw only other sweaty travelers staring blankly and hurrying toward the pier.

As he came over the hilltop, he stopped and looked around. Irritated people crowded amidst bicycles, tents, grocery bags, and strollers. The line for the ferry coiled around past the gas station and well up the gravel road. The boat was just coming in and the crowd moved together toward the ferry dock. Yesterday's Midsummer idyll was shattered now. One battered man on a beach had abruptly caused the herring and dancing around the maypole to be replaced with police interviews and expedited trips back home. Several uniformed police officers were circulating around the line of waiting passengers, asking questions and taking notes. Fredrik noticed at least four of them, who seemed to be making their way back through the line toward him.

He rubbed his eyes with his palms. Adam Ceder, whom he had chased by car for 300 miles and whose bag he was now carrying, was dead. He couldn't make sense of it. He swallowed with great effort. His mouth tasted like acid. On all sides people seemed to be staring at him. A mother holding a little girl by the hand leaned over to her husband and whispered something. Were they talking about him? The two closest police officers seemed to seek out eye contact with him. The more he stared at them, the more convinced he became that they were starting to move in his direction. He backed away a couple of steps, but promptly bumped into the person in line behind him. An elderly woman in white boat shoes and a navy blue dress opened her pursed lips to say something, but changed her mind and quickly got out of his way when she saw his wide eyes and clammy, sweaty face.

He had to get out of here. The ferry, the police, the bag. Adam Ceder was dead. The backs of his hands burned as if they were on fire and he scratched aggressively with his bitten-down nails.

He apologized and got out of the line without taking his eyes off the police officers. When he reached the shade behind the gas station, he broke into a run.

—

When Sofia finished the last of her interviews, she walked back to the hotel to retrieve her red Golf. Before she put her key into the ignition, she dialed Eva's number. Their administrative assistant and the Örnsköldsvik Police Station's Renaissance woman, not to mention the only one of her coworkers who seemed to genuinely like Sofia.

"Are they back yet?" Sofia asked.

"They arrived fifteen minutes ago."

Sofia started her car and reversed it toward the dock, careful not to run over the technicians' equipment which was all packed up and sitting by the miniature golf course just outside the front door of the hotel. Two of them were packing up the tent and gathering up the step plates and flags. The blue and white crime scene tape was still up.

She was grateful that the technical investigations had gone so quickly. Only a few hours after the body had been found, worried businessmen had started getting in touch, shop owners, vacation cabin renters, and restaurant owners, everyone who depended financially on the stream of tourists continuing. Since she had connections with both the police and the local island community, her voice mail was full of questions about how long the police presence around the hotel would last and when people could expect things to go back to normal. No one wanted to put any pressure on the investigation, but they still wondered—very deferentially of course—if it couldn't be hurried along. And even though she found it distasteful to think about money when someone had just lost his life, she understood their concerns. The summer months were short enough as it was. An interruption to the flow of paying visitors coming in could be a death sentence for Ulvön.

"Was your fishing trip canceled?" Eva asked her.

Sofia murmured her assent into her phone, which she was holding squeezed between her ear and her shoulder as she slowly drove down the dirt road. Even though there were only twenty or so cars on the island, vehicle traffic and the speed limit were contentious issues, and as a police officer, she knew it was important to set a good example.

"Do you have time to help me with something?" Sofia asked.

"Sure." Sofia could hear Eva typing away on her computer keyboard as she chatted.

"Could you look up a Christine Karst for me?"

Vera had said that Mona Höglund was the only one who had the code to the server room, but Sofia assumed that the hotel's owner would also have access to it, even if she rarely or never set foot on the island anymore. If she could get her hands on the surveillance footage before Mattias did, that would please her very much.

"Karst?" Eva scrolled her mouse quickly on the other end of the line. "They've already tried to contact her. Mattias was just in here asking me to pull up her information."

"OK." Sofia tried not to sound disappointed. Eva had a tendency to fan the flames of all sorts of rumors regarding rivalries and conflicts from her glass cage in the middle of police headquarters.

"I'm at my house now," Sofia said. "I've got to go. I'll see you tomorrow."

Eva hung up and Sofia turned off her engine, but froze with her hand on the handle of the car door.

Someone was sitting on her front porch.

13.

A crunching sound from the gravel path made Fredrik jump. He had fallen asleep leaning against the front door, and the second he opened his eyes he encountered Sofia's suspicious eyes through the windshield of a red Golf. He grabbed her front porch railing and tried to pull himself up onto his feet, but he was forced to sit back down again. The bag, which he had forgotten he had on his lap, slid off and then down the stairs onto the gravel walkway. Sofia slowly opened her car door and got out.

"Fredrik? Did you walk all the way out here?"

There was an uncomfortable buzzing in his ears and sour bile rose up his throat.

"Did something happen? I mean, you're obviously welcome to stop by, but…"

She shut her car door and squinted into the evening sun.

"…given that you haven't been in touch for fifteen years, it is a bit of a surprise," she said and then smiled. "You look like you've been through the wringer, actually."

In a few strides she reached him and helped him to his feet. Before he had a chance to greet her, she had picked up the bag and slung it over her shoulder. She jumped when the laptop hit her on the back.

"Oh my God, what do you have in this thing? Bricks, or something?"

Fredrik attempted a laugh, but it sounded more like a raspy whimper. He had no choice but to follow Sofia into the house. She set the bag down inside the door and dropped her keys into a bowl that sat on a blue folk-art cabinet. A staircase on the right led to the upstairs and straight ahead he could see the kitchen and the spectacular view of the water out the kitchen window. Sofia showed him through the house and opened the door in the living room that led out onto the deck. She gestured to the deck furniture, made of wood and painted blue, and he took a seat.

"Soda or coffee?"

"Coffee, thanks."

Sofia disappeared into the house but kept talking to him through the open door.

"Did you overdo it a little with your Midsummer celebrations?"

Fredrik didn't have a chance to respond before she returned with two cups and a silver carafe. She poured him a cup and then sat down in the rocking chair facing him.

"Are you staying at the hotel?"

He looked up at her and shook his head.

"No, I checked out. I have to go home."

"But you heard what happened?"

He nodded.

"But I didn't notice anything unusual," he hurried to add. "I had had a few too many and I went to bed."

Fredrik looked out at the water and the sun, which was slowly sinking toward the horizon. A flock of gulls was circling over some invisible meal out by one of the little islets.

The same horrible ocean, but it seemed almost peaceful when viewed from Sofia's balcony.

"How are you doing, actually?"

She drank some coffee and watched him over her cup.

"Not so good," he admitted.

"Why not?" Sofia said, raising one eyebrow.

"Well, I have pretty severe anxiety. Sometimes I need to take pills to... I've done several stints of inpatient treatment." He met Sofia's gaze shamefacedly.

They looked at each other for a while.

"You look like you could use some sleep," Sofia finally said.

Her mildly authoritarian voice made him realize how tired he was.

"Would it be OK if I lay down for a bit?"

"There are clean sheets on the bed in the guest room."

Sunday, June 23rd

14.

The scent of coffee caressed Sofia's nostrils and she rolled over tiredly in bed. She fell back into her dream for a few seconds. She was naked, and rough hands were caressing her body...

A loud clatter from the utensil drawer, like the clash of her grandfather's alarm clock that had stopped working long ago. She opened her eyes. The realization that she wasn't alone in the house cleared away the last of her drowsy thoughts. He was really here, not just a foggy shadow in an erotic dream. Fredrik Fröding was downstairs in her kitchen. Fifteen years had passed since their days together. It felt almost like a lifetime.

When Sofia came downstairs, Fredrik had set coffee cups on a tray along with soft-boiled eggs and the sourdough bread that Kaj had left. He was standing at the kitchen counter in jeans with no shirt on. He gave her an embarrassed look as she sat down.

"I hope it's OK that I stayed? I was so tired yesterday..."

Sofia nodded and tried to keep her eyes from roaming over his wiry torso. She reached for a coffee cup and an egg. She didn't actually know if this was OK. Could you just show up in someone's life after such a long time and pretend like nothing had happened? And was it her job to deal with his anxiety? No. Although she did like having him here.

"How are you doing today?"

"Better. I really needed to sleep."

They ate in silence. The coffee was strong and bracing, borderline undrinkable, but she drank it anyway, let it flow into her veins and wake up her body as she looked out at the water. Not a ripple and the sun was pouring glitter over the whole channel. It would be a quick trip to the mainland today. She turned around and looked at the kitchen clock next to the fridge.

"I have to go to work."

"On a Sunday?" Fredrik looked at her sadly with red-rimmed puppy dog eyes that seemed to look right into her soul. The words tumbled out of her mouth before she could stop them.

"You can stay here if you want, but I might not be back until late."

"That doesn't matter," he said, brightening.

Sofia finished her coffee, got up, and put her cup in the sink. She could feel Fredrik following her with his eyes as she walked out into the hall, opened a closet door, and started looking for a clean polo shirt. By the time she returned, Fredrik had also finished his breakfast and had loaded the dishes into the dishwasher. She put on her windbreaker and her backpack.

"Please try not to burn down the whole kitchen."

Fredrik turned around and smiled for the first time since she had found him out there on her doorstep the day before.

A smile that took root deep within her.

–

Fredrik stood for a long time, watching Sofia's mahogany boat disappear over the shimmering blue water. A white fold of churned-up wake followed her boat.

The boathouse and the dock way down at the bottom of Sofia's yard were surrounded a rocky shoreline. A few dry reeds stuck out of the clumps of grass at the end of her dock. It didn't look anywhere near as scary as the ferry terminal in Ulvö Harbor. Even though the whole situation was absurd, a calm settled over him. The acute anxiety of the day before was gone and his hangover had subsided. He had pills left in his blister pack but hoped he wouldn't have to take any.

By this point the tourists and the police would probably have emptied out of the harbor. Maybe he could go home now with the bag without being discovered, but home to what? The loneliness in his grandmother's apartment?

He thought about Sofia. They hadn't known each other very long, not at all actually. A few days was all they had had together. Even so, this had felt like coming home. To both of them, he thought. Two lonely searchers who had found each other. It was completely inconceivable that he could have forgotten her.

They had ended up sitting next to each other in a summer course on criminology. She was going to be a social worker, and he was almost done with the police academy. He had just started as a trainee. He was excited about policework and wanted to make his grandmother proud. He took extra academic courses and did volunteer work for Children's Rights in Society. He was passionate about making a difference and giving back.

But only a few days after that, previews had started to come out for memorial editions for the tenth anniversary of the *Estonia* disaster, and everything had fallen apart. Special inserts, church services, memorial events. The pills became his life preserver again and it wasn't long before Torsten shipped him off for inpatient treatment. He never went back to the criminology course and he hadn't even called Sofia after the days they had spent together in his bed.

Fredrik cleared the kitchen table and poured the rest of the coffee down the drain. He had made it far too strong and the coffee grounds lay like a tarry sand beach in the bottom of the cup. He didn't know how to fill a percolator-style coffee maker. After one more attempt to measure out the right amount of grounds, he gave up, left the coffee on the counter, and returned to the guest room. His shirt was hanging over a chair and Ceder's bag was underneath it. Along with his cloth tote bag, phone charger, and wallet, those were all the possessions he had in the world right now.

He realized that he should get rid of Ceder's bag, but at the same time he wanted to know. Was there anything in it that could explain what had happened to Ceder? And why?

Fredrik emptied the contents out onto the bed. Clothes, toiletry bag, razor, computer, and a plastic folder. The pockets of the shirts and pants were empty. He checked the zipper compartments on the bag and finally turned it inside out. He didn't know what he was looking for, but his hands kept fiddling with it, searching for answers. He opened the computer and booted it up. A window appeared right away asking for the password. He tried Adam, Ceder, Adam Ceder, Ceder Hotels, but none of these unimaginative attempts worked. He closed the computer again and put it back in the empty bag.

He carefully tipped the papers out of the folder and spread them out on the bed. He pulled the chair closer, pushing his shirt off onto the floor. He flipped through the documents at random. Bank statements, credit reports, copies of mortgages. They all seemed to have to do with the Ulvö Hotel. Fredrik stared off into space. Did Ceder want to buy the hotel? Had his fate been sealed because of a business deal?

There was also a white envelope addressed to Adam Ceder in the folder. When Fredrik checked the postmark he saw that it had been sent just a few weeks ago. He opened it and pulled out a folded sheet of paper, a color copy of a photograph. The date stamp in the right corner said that it had been taken June 22, 1979. The picture showed a pastor in a black robe with about ten kids around him, standing rigidly in front of a Midsummer maypole. One girl was in a wheelchair. In the background there was a gray wooden building with a bell tower in front of it. It took a second before Fredrik recognized the chapel he had walked by on his way from the ferry to the Ulvö Hotel.

A skinny boy with bright red hair and freckles stood way off to the right. Even though he was forty years younger in the photograph, you could tell it was him.

Adam Ceder.

When Fredrik inspected the picture more closely he saw that someone had poked Ceder's eyes out with a pin.

What the hell was this? He looked at the envelope again and discovered a thin, yellowed piece of paper that looked like it had been ripped out of a book. With a growing sense of discomfort, he read the section that was circled in pen:

> *Go in and out from gate to gate throughout the camp, and slay every man his brother, and every man his companion, and every man his neighbor.*

Was that a threat? Had someone been trying to scare Ceder? Slay every man... Could this be the reason Ceder was dead?

Fredrik was about to get out his phone and start looking for information about Ulvön Island in the late 1970s when a noise in the kitchen interrupted him. A broad shadow fell over him from the doorway.

"Who are you?"

15.

Ulvön Island, 1979

Adam sat in the kitchen with the others. The rain beat angrily against the windowpanes. They were supposed to be out having a soccer tournament today against some of the village kids, but it had been called off because of the weather. Instead they had all crammed into the kitchen, waiting for the rain to let up. The girls were playing Monopoly at one of the tables and the boys were playing cards at another. Ester sat in her wheelchair in the next room along with the girls from Russia. They were playing records and trying to talk to each other in a blend of English and Swedish.

But Adam didn't want to be with any of them. Instead he sat on the floor, his back resting against the kitchen bench, flipping through a women's magazine. The pastor had a bookshelf in the living room, but all the books were about God. Adam was reading about a new oven from America that used electromagnetic fields to heat the food. It sounded cool, he thought, a little like science fiction.

"Are you looking for cookie recipes, or what?" teased Thomas, who was lying on the bench with his knees up. The red cat that usually prowled around the house was sitting on his stomach. The pastor had told them not to feed it, but they did anyway, when Bodil and Ester weren't looking. The cat purred and preened as Thomas scratched its back.

Mona looked up from the game and wrinkled her nose at the cat.

"Ugh," she said, "You know cats have fleas, don't you?"

Thomas didn't pay any attention to her, just kept scratching the cat. Soon it stood up and jumped awkwardly down to Adam, landing on his magazine. He laughed and pulled the magazine out from under the cat. The page about ovens got stuck in its flexing claws.

"So, you want to be with me, huh?" he said to the cat.

Adam had always wanted a cat, but his mother said no. She didn't want a bunch of cat fur in the house. He cautiously stroked the cat's back and listened to it purr. When no one was looking he buried his nose in its red fur.

"So what should we call you?" he whispered. "Maybe Cookie?"

Marianne, who was sitting closest, heard him even though he was whispering. She always had to poke her nose into other people's business.

"Cookie is such a stupid name," she laughed, and Christine agreed. Christine never missed an opportunity to suck up to Marianne.

"You want go outside and smoke?" Mats sauntered by, waving a pack of cigarettes in front of his face, but Adam shook his head. It was pouring outside, and the pastor had said that they weren't allowed to smoke or drink at his house. Plus, his mother wouldn't be happy if she discovered he had misbehaved. Again.

"What about you, Thomas?" Mats asked.

Thomas shook his head as well. In the doorway, Mats ran into Bodil, the pastor's eldest daughter. She looked at the pack of cigarettes in his hand but didn't say anything. As long as they didn't smoke inside the house she didn't usually tattle to Aron. Instead she walked over to the stove and lifted the lid on the potatoes, which were at a rolling boil. She turned down the heat and put the lid back on. In mid-motion, she stiffened and turned around.

"You let a cat in?" Her voice was loud and strident.

"It's raining outside, you dimwit," Thomas answered for Adam. "Go out there yourself if you think it's so nice to get soaked."

"You can't be serious!" Bodil snapped, angrily wiping her hands on the apron she wore tied around her waist. "Ester is insanely allergic to cats."

Ester had rolled her wheelchair over to the threshold to the kitchen and was following Bodil's movements attentively as she stomped over to Adam and reached for the cat. He put his arms around it protectively, but Bodil grabbed it by the scruff of its neck and snatched it up. The cat squealed in pain.

Before Adam knew what was going on, she had dragged it away out into the hall, opened the front door, and tossed it over the railing, out into the storm.

"You're an idiot!" Thomas glared angrily at Bodil, who made a show of washing her hands under the tap before drying them off on her apron. Then she left the room without a word.

16.

Sofia moored in her slip in front of Saltmagasinet Italian restaurant next to the Örnsköldsvik Visitors Marina and quickly strolled through the empty town up to the police station. When she stepped inside, it felt as if the building was sealed in a silent vacuum. The receptionist wasn't in yet, but she could hear Eva messing around somewhere behind the glass-screened front desk. It was a weekend and a holiday one at that, and that was evident.

The waiting room consisted of three bland wooden sofas with burgundy seat cushions, a few well-used plastic toys, and an oak coffee table with informational flyers about the neighborhood watch program. It was hardly inviting. She nodded to the stuffed, 700-pound brown bear that stood at the end of the room. With a foolish look in its eyes and limply dangling paws, it watched over anyone sitting in the waiting room. A sign beside it explained that it had been shot in legitimate self-defense a few years earlier, but since the bear hunting quota had been filled, the animal had become the property of the government and had ended up in the Örnsköldsvik police station via Sweden's Environmental Protection Agency.

Sofia swiped her access card. The heavy, lacquered brown door buzzed and opened, and she continued up the stairs to her office on the third floor. Sofia set her backpack on the spare chair and turned on the lights. Her thoughts kept constantly turning back to Fredrik. He was at her house right now, in her home. A warm feeling spread through her belly and a smile twitched at the corners of her mouth.

She inserted her service card into the card reader on her keyboard and turned on the computer. As it struggled to start, she walked down to the lunchroom for a cup of coffee.

"Aren't you supposed to be on vacation?" a colleague from financial crimes asked, poking his head out of his office as she walked by.

"You know how it is," Sofia replied with a shrug.

"Yeah, we picked a real winner of a career, huh?" He laughed and wheeled his chair back to his desk.

Sofia had never harbored any lifelong dream of becoming a police officer. To the contrary, the profession had always scared her when she was little. An everyday life filled with so many people, abuse, drugs, and especially alcohol. She had wanted to be a social worker, to help people who had suffered from abuse and neglect, people like her. But some of the girls in her orientation team had dreamt of joining the force. They had idealistically longed for a more just world. When Claire heard about it, she had flipped out. Proper young women did not go around pursuing murderers and rapists. That in and of itself had been enough reason to convince Sofia to apply to the police academy as well. It had been a half-hearted attempt, and she didn't get any farther that first year, but the idea of becoming a police officer had grown more and more appealing to her. The role she pictured for herself had begun to change. She wasn't going to save children who had been subjected to injustice. She was going to help them before they even needed the help. She moved to Stockholm even though she hadn't gotten into the police academy. She studied sociology and criminology while she waited until she could reapply. On her second attempt, she made it as far as the physical tests, but since she wasn't quite in good enough condition, she missed the running cutoff by six seconds. On her third attempt she got in.

Thirteen years in the police and she had come to love it.

The kitchen was empty when she came down. As the freshly ground black coffee brewed, she stood by the kitchen island

and skimmed the newspapers. The local paper didn't put out a Sunday edition, but the national newspapers were all reporting on the man who had been found dead on Ulvön Island. People were speculating as to whether he had gotten drunk, fell in the water, and drowned, or was murdered.

"Good morning."

Vera walked into the lunchroom. She opened a bag clip and dumped out a plastic bag on the kitchen island while she grunted something that could have been "help yourself." Homemade cinnamon rolls bounced out of the bag. Sofia held her hands out as a barrier to stop them from tumbling onto the floor. Vera wadded up the bag and stuffed it into the trash without a word.

Mattias Wikström and Karim Jansson came in right behind her. Despite it being early on a Sunday morning, their loud, energetic conversation was audible as they approached in the hallway. They formed a stark contrast to Vera's sullenness.

Mattias had attended the police academy in Umeå immediately after completing his mandatory military service and had started working for the Örnsköldsvik police almost immediately after graduation. He still lived in the same little village north of Örnsköldsvik, where he had been born and grown up, but now with his wife and children. He rarely left the county and avoided traveling whether for work or vacation. Mattias's entire existence seemed to revolve around his job and his daughters' soccer and hockey teams, which he coached. And his summer cabin of course.

"I didn't know you baked." Karim smiled at Vera.

"I don't," she muttered grumpily, snatching two roles for herself. "Library, now!" She tossed that last bit out over her shoulder as she headed for the stairs.

Karim didn't let their boss's grumpy mood bother him, just contentedly selected a couple cinnamon rolls and nodded to Sofia.

"The dragon woke up early today," he whispered as they followed Vera up the stairs.

Sofia smiled. Karim's voice was like a warm blanket. She had never met anyone whose intonation made her feel so safe. His Finland-Swedish/Arabic accent was striking and he had acquired his unusual combination of first and last names in part through his Finland-Swedish wife, Irja Jansson. They had met in Iran when she was interning as a midwife there and then they had moved to Sweden together. They had four daughters and just like Mattias, Karim was dedicated to the girls' various athletic pursuits.

"As you can see there's some interest in our victim. Adam Ceder was a well-known figure, not just in his own social circle but throughout the Swedish business community," Vera began once everyone had taken a seat. "We're going to be under a tremendous amount of media pressure with this case."

Mattias smoothed his blond hair with a habitual motion and leaned forward on the table on his elbows. Dealing with the media was his strong suit. Sofia readily admitted that Mattias was an attractive man, at least on the outside. He was always tan and well dressed, like a sailor, and had more of the look of a Nautica or Gant advertising model than a policeman.

"What do we know?"

"All of Ceder's possessions are missing. We haven't found his wallet, cell phone, or clothes. According to the forensics team, it's extremely unlikely that he died on the beach where he was found. There was virtually no blood around the body and no sign of a struggle. The rocks on the slope appeared untouched."

"What about the dogs?" Karim asked.

"The dogs didn't pick up any scent trails to or from the body aside from the ones left by Mona Höglund and Sofia." Vera took two big bites of the cinnamon roll she was holding.

"Upon initial examination, the medical examiner noted diffuse, scattered areas of livor mortis discoloration on the body that indicate that he may have floated around for a while. The appearance of his hands and feet show that he was in the water for at least a few hours. She estimated a maximum of 24 hours, but she couldn't be any more specific until she did an autopsy. Other than that the head injury suggests that this wasn't an accident."

"So, murder?" Sofia said.

"Yes, exactly. So, murder." Vera gave her a grim look.

"And when do you think the autopsy will happen?" Karim asked.

"You know how it goes, right? They have to establish the victim's identity before they can start. I've asked for help getting some pressure from above, but we need to wait until someone from Ceder's family has made it up here to take a look at him."

"When is Marie coming?"

Sofia's question caused Vera to look even gloomier and she immediately regretted having asked it. Marie Fransson was going to lead the preliminary investigation. She was from the Criminal Investigations Unit in Sundsvall, was the gentlest person in all of Västernorrland county, and to top it all off a devout Christian. Basically everything that Vera wasn't. As so many times before, Marie would join the regional team and take charge of the detective work.

"Tomorrow. We can review the situation again after she arrives and decide how to proceed from there. For the time being we'll keep calling our way through the witness lists from Midsummer's Day and reading the transcripts from the questioning sessions we've completed. There were a lot of people for whom all we had time to do was take down their names and phone numbers."

"No one else was checked into the room Ceder was staying in at the hotel. It seems like he was alone on the island," Sofia said.

"Surely it's too early to say that for sure?" Mattias, who seemed upset, trained his eyes on Vera. "Ceder's family hasn't even been questioned yet! Just because no one reported him missing, that doesn't mean that he was there by himself."

His meaning was clear. Sofia was not well liked, she knew that. Some of her colleagues tolerated her, some even chatted with her, but no one asked her to join them for lunch or to go out after work or to watch a hockey match. Least of all Mattias. He absolutely wasn't the sexist type. To the contrary. With two daughters of his own, he was passionate about women's rights, both in sports and in the professional world. Even so, she seemed to infuriate him. Without anyone either reprimanding him or agreeing with him, Mattias had taken to calling her "Your Highness," every time she arrived late or made a suggestion based on her experiences from working as a detective in Stockholm. Sofia had wondered many times if that wasn't the very definition of harassment, but had let it slide. Complaining to your boss about the boys on the team picking on you felt like a sure-fire way to get demoted. If you wanted to play the game, you had to put up with the game... or something like that.

"Sure, he could have met someone we haven't interviewed yet." Sofia nodded to Mattias.

"Our colleagues in Stockholm have talked to Ceder's family. His father is dead, but his mother, Maj Ceder, is still around along with a sister, Nina Ceder, both living at the same address in Älvsjö."

"They live together?" Sofia asked.

"It seems like some sort of two-story place with separate entrances. I can ask Stockholm to clarify that in their memo if you think that would be of value for the investigation." Mattias smirked.

She shook her head without looking him in the eye.

"I don't know if it's of interest, but the sister did time in Ystad Women's Prison. Sometime in the early 80s, but still."

"Whoops!" Karim said.

"Assault. She hit her ex-boyfriend in the head with a glass bottle. We'll take a closer look at that. She had no idea Ceder was coming to Ulvön for Midsummer. The mother was shocked to hear about it."

"What about the owner of the hotel?" Karim flipped through his papers looking for the name. "Christine Karst?"

"She was here for a brief visit," Mattias said shaking his head, "but apparently she left the island late on Midsummer's Eve to travel back to her mother's place in Alicante, Spain. It sounds like she has been living down there since her divorce. We haven't gotten ahold of her or her mother yet."

"What the hell is wrong with people?" Vera snorted in exasperation. "What kind of person doesn't answer their phone after someone goes and get murdered in your hotel?"

17.

A gray-haired man in boots, loose-fitting jeans, and a plaid shirt was leaning in the doorway, digging into a container of snus as he calmly eyed Fredrik.

"Did Sofia start one of those bed and breakfasts or whatever you call them?" The man had kind of a severe smile and his thick Norrland Swedish dialect sang in Fredrik's ears.

Fredrik scrambled to his feet and reached out his hand in greeting, but had to wait until the man had stuffed the snus tobacco in under his lip and wiped his hand off on his jeans.

"I'm Fredrik Fröding. Sofia and I took a class together ages ago." His crisp Stockholm dialect sounded impertinent compared to the older man's softer way of speaking.

"Tord Grändberg." Without further introduction, Tord turned around and strode purposefully into the kitchen and the percolator, which he immediately began to fill with water.

Fredrik followed him, pulling the door to the guest room closed behind him. His whole body was yearning for some proper coffee and Tord did not disappoint. When he came and sat down after a couple of moments of silence, it was with two steaming cups of black coffee.

"Is this your first trip to Ulvön Island?"

Fredrik sipped the hot drink before he replied.

"Yes, how about yourself?"

Tord chuckled and shook his head.

"Good Lord, boy. I was born and raised here. I've never lived anywhere else."

Fredrik nodded, impressed.

"It's beautiful place," he said.

Tord drank his coffee without saying anything more. Fredrik did the same but couldn't really relax. Small talk had never been his strong suit, but Tord seemed perfectly satisfied to sit in someone else's kitchen and savor someone else's coffee with a stranger in total silence.

Once the silence grew so ponderous that they could both clearly hear the pendulum of the traditional Mora clock in the next room, Fredrik couldn't take it anymore.

"So how do you know Sofia?"

"Godfather." Tord made no attempt to say anything more, just sat contentedly with one leg resting on the chair next to him and the coffee cup still in his hand. Fredrik thought about the picture he had found. Tord had lived on the island his whole life... It couldn't hurt to ask, could it?

"Do you happen to know if the church held any youth gatherings here on Ulvön back in the late 70s?"

"Why?" A deep wrinkle appeared between Tord's gray eyebrows.

Fredrik opened his mouth, but realized too late that he had no answer. He couldn't tell Tord about the picture. Or that he had Ceder's bag. Or about the hotel.

"I'm writing," he replied evasively.

"About Ulvön?"

Fredrik nodded even though he had no idea what he would say if there were any follow-up questions, but Tord seemed lost in his own thoughts.

"You know, Fredrik, I know every stretch of woods, every lake, and every rock on this here island. Those of us who live out here stick together and work together like one big organism, one communal body. It's always been like that. I can feel the pulses and the breaths in that body as if they were my own. But when I look back, I see the Dirk family as a tumor. It was as if their years here on the island somehow tarnished us."

It was clear that Tord's previous silence shouldn't be interpreted as a lack of anything to say or an inability to express

93

himself. The poetic image he painted captivated Fredrik, even though he didn't understand a word of what it meant.

"Aron Dirk. He had kids here on the island for the summer back in the late 70s. The church organized it. Summer camps, that kind of thing." His voice faded away and his eyes seemed to lock onto something far back in time. He scratched absent-mindedly at the gray hair at his temple. "Poor unfortunate devil."

"Why?"

Tord pulled the old snus pouch out from under his lip and immediately replaced it with a fresh one. He wiped his index finger off on the edge of his snus tin.

"His wife, Elisabeth, died in a car accident when the girls were little. Ester, the younger one, ended up in a wheelchair. The sister, Bodil, had to take care of her after that."

Fredrik thought of the picture. So Ester was the girl in the wheelchair with her hands clasped on her lap and the long, blond hair down over her shoulders. That must be her sister standing next to her. Their hair was the same color, but Bodil wore hers in a braid that was draped over one shoulder. Her face looked stern and her left hand rested on the wheelchair's hand grip, like a protective claw.

"They came to the island because Aron's mother lived here, but they had scarcely set foot on the dock before she died of a stroke. So there he was, Aron, with no wife and his two little girls with no mother. That's how the summer camps came about. Kids who had tough situations at home would come here from all over the country to get a taste of the outdoors and island life. All officially run by the church, of course."

"That still sounds like a good ending to a sad story?"

"It could have been."

"But?"

"But there was something about that family… something that wasn't right."

Fredrik laughed, but quickly realized that Tord wasn't joking.

"Something was always going wrong out there at the parsonage. That first year the house almost burned down after a fire escaped from the woodstove in the kitchen. The next year one of the women who helped Aron look after the girls fell down the stairs and broke a vertebra so badly that she had to spend six months in bed." Tord leaned in over the table and lowered his voice. "And then, a couple of years after the campers started coming, there was a boy who hung himself over there." He shuddered and shook his head. "They moved back to Stockholm after that. You'd think that that would have been enough, but then the year after they moved, Ester died in an apartment fire. Aron nearly died himself."

Tord leaned back in his chair and drank some coffee.

"Like I said. He was a poor unfortunate devil, that Aron."

Fredrik didn't know what to say. And what did all this have to do with a dead hotel owner?

"If you're interested in the summer camp and the Dirk family, I think you ought to talk to Marianne Nordin, she used to hang out with the Dirks in the summers. Born on the island, she was. Or with Gösta. He was the sacristan at the church. If anyone knew Aron and the girls, it was him."

Was he interested in that? Fredrik didn't know. He wanted to know why he had woken up with Ceder's bag in his room. He wanted to not be accused of murder and not get caught up in a police investigation. The question was if that would even be possible now?

He took out his phone.

"What's Gösta's last name?"

"Björnberg." Fredrik typed in both names and looked back up at Tord. "Do you know where they live?"

Tord laughed.

"Marianne lives next door to me and Gösta lives in Sandviken. I can drive you over there if you want, but unfortunately not today. I'm actually going over to Marianne's place tomorrow to smoke whitefish. Why don't you come along?"

18.

In an Upstairs Bedroom

Sins thrive. Fat pigs wallowing in their own feces. Rooting around in the muck their own misdeeds created. I smell the stench of them. Unclean, dishonest evildoers.

Remember Romans 13:4!

"But if thou do that which is evil, be afraid; for he beareth not the sword in vain: for he is the minister of God, a revenger to execute wrath upon him that doeth evil."

You are the minister, the revenger, my child. Yours is the sword.

19.

As Sofia approached the cove where her boathouse and dock awaited, even from far away she could see that her deck door was open. She hadn't dared to think anything other than that Fredrik had given up, and it bothered her that yet again little threads were tugging the corners of her mouth upward. Not to mention that her lawn was now freshly mowed and the branches that had blown down over the winter lay neatly stacked in a pile by the woodshed. The two-foot-tall pink and purple lupins were still there around the house, but the gravel path had been weeded and raked.

Fredrik sat on the steps that led up to the deck, brushing off his bare feet as she walked up the bank. The soles of his feet were a greenish black. Apparently he had not located her father's old rain boots in the shed.

"Impressive," she said. "I didn't think you Stockholm people knew how to use a lawnmower."

"Well, we have to give you country bunnies a helping hand every now and then. But it was the least I could do. For letting me stay here, I mean."

She sat down next to him. He poured water from a carafe and handed her a glass.

Sofia drank in big gulps.

"Good day at work?"

She nodded, but then changed her mind and shook her head instead.

"It's really beautiful here," Fredrik said looking out at the water.

"It's not so bad, but there is a lot to look after. My godfather helps out in the winter. He actually owns the land." Sofia laughed. "Well actually he owns about half of the island and sees it as a bit of his duty to help those of us who are financially less well endowed."

"Tord?"

Sofia turned to him.

"Yeah. How did you know that?"

"He stopped by today."

Of course. You couldn't find a more curious man. And since Tord didn't think all that highly of Kaj, he would probably be thrilled to spread the rumor across half the island that she had a new male guest in the house. She would have to talk to him before the rumor mill really got going.

"If this were my house, I would sit here nonstop." Fredrik didn't take his eyes off the horizon.

Sofia smiled.

"That's pretty much what I do," Sofia said.

He lifted the corner of his shirt to mop off his forehead. And she caught a glimpse of his flat stomach underneath. Then he pulled his cell phone out of his pocket and rolled it around nervously between his fingers.

"No reception."

"It's a little spotty out here," Sofia confirmed. "It's better down in the village."

They ran out of meaningless things to say and both grew quiet. But the fact that much remained unsaid was palpable in the air. Their brief but intense connection had come to an unfortunate end. She had called him several times, but he hadn't answered or gotten in touch with her. Sofia had felt so shaken and humiliated that she hadn't tried again. Much later she had heard through the grapevine that Fredrik had dropped out of the police academy when all he had left to do was his trainee service. She wanted to ask him why, but didn't dare.

She looked up at the sky. Thin wavelike clouds moved across it, but the evening sun bravely forced its way through them.

It was going to be a beautiful evening even though it wasn't exactly warm out.

"There's clothes in the wardrobe in the guest room, my dad's old ones, so I'm sure you can find something to wear. If you want to stay here tonight, I mean, but obviously you don't have to if..."

Fredrik's hand on top of her own stopped her.

"I'd like to stay."

She left that alone and felt the warmth between their hands moving up through her arm and then into her chest and then continuing farther down.

"Are you hungry?"

He nodded gratefully.

"The fridge is awfully empty as you may have already noticed, but with a little imagination I might be able to scrounge up a sandwich and a cup of tea at any rate."

She held out her hand to him and pulled him up onto his feet.

Sofia had to dig well into the clumps of ice to find last year's smoked trout. There was some doubt as to whether it would still be edible, but it was all she had. They had finished off the last of her eggs and bread for their breakfast that morning, but there was crisp bread in the pantry and boiled potatoes from the Midsummer's Day lunch the other day.

Fredrik was taciturn as they each prepared and ate their own poor version of a sandwich. Afterward, they took their teacups and went out onto the deck.

Fredrik sat down on one of the sofas and she took the rocking chair. A cold wind was blowing in off the water and Sofia pulled her feet up underneath her. Her father had dreamed of putting in a beautiful, glass-enclosed veranda, where they could sit out until late in the fall. And even though Sofia had thought about calling a handyman many times to implement that dream, it had never happened. And soon the summer holidays would make it impossible to get ahold of anyone.

"Tell me about the house." Fredrik looked at her.

"My dad's grandfather built it in 1909. He gave it to my grandparents when they had kids. My dad and his sister were both born in the bedroom in there." She pointed to the nearest window. "My dad loved this house."

He really had. She remembered his last summer so well. When her father had gotten sick, Claire had wanted to sell this place and move to the mainland for good, but he had refused. Their compromise had been a two-bedroom condo in downtown Örnsköldsvik. That had been sold a long time ago, but Sofia refused to get rid of this house. Her father had struggled his way out here every weekend. They had sat on the deck in the evenings, tied flies, and planned fishing trips that at that point they knew would never happen.

"And your mom?"

Claire. Sofia couldn't even think of her as her mother. The stranger with the wineglass permanently in her hand. Claire had gotten pregnant almost immediately after she and Sten had met. They had tried in the beginning, moving to his childhood home and playing house, but Claire was young and restless and thirsted for the kind of social life that you couldn't find on a small island. Once the headiness of their first love had faded, the chasm between them was already cemented. Sure, her father had tried to make Claire happy, but when it came to choosing between Sofia and Claire, Sten had chosen Sofia. Claire had chosen bitterness and the bottle.

"Mom was an addict, an alcoholic," she answered briefly. "We don't have any contact now."

–

After another cup of tea, the sun had begun to set. They stayed out on the deck, without saying much. Fredrik's muscles ached from dealing with the lawnmower all day, but he still felt energized in some way, proud at having accomplished something. His anxiety and worries about Adam Ceder and the bag remained in the background. For long periods of the evening he hadn't noticed it at all. As if the island were an antidote to agony.

Sofia sat in the rocking chair, leaning back with her eyes closed, her hand moving absentmindedly over her abdomen.

"Do you only live here in the summer?" he asked.

"Yes, although sometimes I think about moving out here permanently. But at the same time, I'm afraid to do it. I spent a whole winter here by myself a few years ago when I separated from my boyfriend. He was one of the instructors when you were at the police academy. Kaj Marklund?"

"Kaj?" Fredrik remembered him well. He had taught several of the courses for the program. Marklund had been hot stuff back then, even though he was twice as old as most of the students. A legend, like crime writer Leif G.W. Persson, but with a well-honed physique and thick, salt and pepper hair that he wore brushed back. Fredrik had never liked him, but there was no discounting the legendary status he had achieved in the police world. He routinely appeared on TV and in the papers. It was impressive that Sofia had been the one to snag him.

"What, didn't you think a—what was that you called me, a country bunny?—could get a man, or what?" she laughed with feigned indignation, leaning forward toward him. Her smile faded and she looked earnestly into his eyes. It was time for the question they had been avoiding all night.

"Why didn't you call?" She didn't sound accusatory in the least. Fredrik looked down at his hands and rubbed the backs of them. The months of inpatient care had been like lying on his back and floating downstream. Day after day, with the same routines, the same staff, the same conversations. When he did finally emerge, everyone else had swum on past him, and it was impossible for him to catch up. School was over, his traineeship had gone to someone else, and without having completed the academy there were very few job opportunities open to him. And the ferry with his family inside was still lying on the bottom of the Baltic.

He had the urge to tell her. About everything. About the accident, about his parents, about Niklas. Why he was on the island and about Adam Ceder. But how do you explain a disaster to someone who wasn't there? People screaming and sobbing, desperate mothers convulsively trying to hold onto their children with their arms as the whole world capsized. The terrible cold that cut through the skin and the flesh right to the very bone. The sounds of ropes rubbing against rubber rafts. Every time a wave washed over them, they had to count. Sometimes someone was missing.

Fredrik fiddled nervously with the handle of his teacup and cleared his throat.

"I was admitted that summer. My doctor said I was suffering from PTSD. That's why I have anxiety and panic attacks. I get flare-ups and I relapse. Usually I'm healthy for several years in between."

"What's it from?"

"My mother, Gunnel, had just turned 50. We were going to celebrate, my dad, me, and my brother. Niklas and I didn't actually want to go. We had a soccer competition in Västerås. I was mad at my mom because she didn't want to stay home and take us to the competition. And because they forced us to go. The last time I talked to my parents we argued…"

He realized that he was rambling, and he could tell that Sofia didn't understand what he was trying to say.

"What happened?"

"They died in an accident. In the fall of '94."

For some reason, he laughed. He had never voluntarily told anyone even this much before, and it felt almost pleasurable. He rubbed his hand over his mouth, embarrassed at his own reaction. Sofia got up from the rocking chair and came over to sit next to him on the outdoor sofa. She patted him tentatively on the back. Her hand burned through his shirt, right into his soul. He realized for the first time how desperately lonely he had been. Sure, there had been women at times, but he had never really allowed anyone to get close to him.

It was as if something was starting to come undone inside of him. A dam that had been under pressure for far too long. His breathing became fitful and he wiped his cheeks with his palms in astonishment. He was crying.

Somewhere in the distance he heard seagulls squawking.

His tears kept flowing and he let them. He leaned his head on Sofia's shoulder, exhausted. She was sitting so close that he could smell the scent of her. Her tan hand rested on his knee as she stroked his back with her other one. He looked up and their eyes met.

Everything was still there between them.

Sofia seemed to sense it, too, because her hand on his back became still. They just sat there for several seconds, close to each other. The water lay smooth, waiting for the sunset. The gulls had moved on and not a sound could be heard around them. Sofia tentatively caressed his knee and against his will he felt his excitement rising. He leaned closer to her and she did the same. The taste of her lips blended with his tears and made his head spin. He moved slightly, afraid of ruining something, but she didn't seem to waver. Instead she took his hand and led him into the house.

Once they were inside the deck door, Sofia pulled him to her and kissed him. She barely came up to his chin and had to stand on her tiptoes to pull his shirt over his head. He tried to take his time, but she urged him on, as if there was no time to lose.

Monday, June 24

20.

Sofia lay still on her side and watched Fredrik, who was sleeping with his mouth closed and the blanket pulled up high over one shoulder. She smiled to herself. He was beautiful—dark, sharp features and a strong, slightly crooked nose. She thought it made him look Roman even though she didn't really know what that meant.

He twitched in his sleep and she ran her fingers over his cheek. She felt like something heavy inside her chest had dissolved. What did she care if she didn't get to succeed Vera? What did it matter if Mattias despised her? Suddenly the job and the career she had fought so hard for felt less important than they had yesterday.

As carefully as she could, Sofia snuck out of bed from her side and reached for her thin robe, which was draped over the white rattan armchair in the corner. Both her and Fredrik's clothes were still downstairs, lying on the living room floor. At some point overnight they had moved upstairs to the bed, but she couldn't remember which time that was out of all the times they had made love. Or fucked. *At least I had time to change the sheets after Kaj*, she thought embarrassed.

On her way down the stairs, cool drafts blew up her legs. The door to the deck had been wide open all night and the cold had now crept in off the water and settled like an invisible carpet over the wooden floor. She closed the door and put the coffee on. While the percolator bubbled, she turned on her cell phone. It wasn't even seven yet and she shouldn't have any trouble making it to her morning meeting at eight thirty.

Sofia wondered if she should wake Fredrik up, but decided not to. She didn't want to have to discuss the future. Today she just wanted to remain in her endorphin bubble.

With her coffee cup in her hand, she went into the laundry room to get some clean clothes. A dark shadow moved suddenly outside the frosted-over windows of the front door. She jumped and spilled hot coffee on her foot.

"Damn it!"

A key was inserted into the door and a second later, Tord stood before her.

"What are you swearing about, girl?"

Sofia wiped off the top of her foot with her hand.

"You scared me half to death. What are you doing here so early?"

"Forgot my hat." Tord reached for the red hat hanging next to Fredrik's leather jacket on the hooks under the hat shelf. She squeezed past him and continued into the laundry room to get dressed.

"So, you still have a visitor, I see?" Tord remarked.

"Yes." She smiled again. It was like some kind of a spasm. What, was this going to become a habit now?

"Nice boy."

When she returned, Tord had poured himself a cup of coffee and taken a seat at the kitchen table.

"Don't you have your own coffee at your place?"

He didn't respond, just eased his snus tin out of his chest pocket and tapped it against the palm of his hand the way he usually did.

"So is your old beast of burden out of the picture now?"

"Kaj?" she said. "I didn't say that."

Tord snorted and then took off the hat that was apparently so important to him and hung it on the back of his chair.

"Are you going to work?"

Sofia nodded and walked back over to the front door and put on her jacket and running shoes.

"Fredrik's sleeping. Please don't scare the hell out of him when he comes down."

"I guess we'll see."

—

It took Fredrik a few seconds to figure out where he was when he woke up. A gentle breeze blew in the open window, but despite the sunshine there no warmth in the air.

He lay there for a while, breathing in the scent of Sofia from the blanket and pillows. He listened for his anxiety. It was still there, but it was resting calmly deep inside him. For a second he permitted himself to mull over the thought that Niklas might actually not be alive anymore, but he refused to go any farther than that. He didn't want to awaken the beast. But it was as if the terrible emptiness and the feelings of guilt were starting to be replaced by something new. Was it hope? Would he maybe be able to get his anxiety under control this time? Be able to cope without the pills, return to life?

There was scarcely time to air that thought before it burst as he remembered the bag lying downstairs. He didn't have time to start over again or try to look for love. A man was dead and he had to learn more. He had to equip himself with something he could strike back with if the police found out that he and Ceder had argued the night before and that now he had Ceder's bag. It was unthinkable for him to stop now.

Before Sofia had come home from work yesterday, he had packed up all of Ceder's things, apart from the picture, and stuffed his bag under the bed in the guestroom. He had agreed with Tord that they would get together during the day today to meet the church sacristan, Gösta Björnberg, and Marianne Nordin, who were both familiar with the history of the Dirk family. Fredrik had been contemplating what to do, and he had decided to take the risk of showing Ceder's picture. He had no choice. It was the only clue he had.

The sound of a faucet running got him out of bed. All his clothes were downstairs and with no other option, he wrapped the blanket around himself and went downstairs.

"Young master Fredrik Fröding."

Tord looked pleased, rolling his snus tin back and forth across the kitchen table. He seemed like he had been waiting for a while, because there was an empty coffee cup in front of him and a completed crossword puzzle next to him.

"Sleeping until the middle of the day out here, I see." He grinned and tapped his watch with a dirty black fingernail. Fredrik glanced at the wall clock by the fridge to see what Tord considered the middle of the day. It was nine fifteen.

"Did Sofia already leave for work?"

Tord nodded.

"Well, hop to it," Tord said. "You'd better put some clothes on now! Björnberg is waiting for us out in Sandviken."

Fredrik tried to recollect the map he had seen on the bulletin board down by the harbor. If he was remembering right, Sandviken was at least a couple miles away.

"Do you have a car?"

"A moped with a cargo bed," Tord replied, straightening his red cap.

Thirty minutes later, a pummeled Fredrik extracted himself the wooden cargo rack attached to Tord's moped. The trip over the island's unpaved roads reminded him of the time he and his parents had ridden camels in Tunisia the year before the accident. His testicles had been bruised for a week after that.

Tord parked by Gösta Björnberg's gate and walked right into the house without knocking. Fredrik limped after him. The former church sacristan was waiting in his kitchen doorway. The log cabin had a low ceiling and high thresholds. The decor was cozy with red geraniums at the windows and paintings with maritime motifs on the walls.

Gösta Björnberg was tall, with a wiry build not unlike Fredrik's own. He was wearing jeans and trendy neon-purple running shoes. He must be at least 80, older than Tord, but he still had a full head of hair and lively eyes. He gave Fredrik a very strong, firm handshake.

"Fredrik Fröding."

"Gösta Björnberg." Gösta stepped aside so they could come into the kitchen. There was a pot of coffee simmering Turkish style on a woodstove in one corner. "Come in. The place is a bit of a mess. My missus was the one who used to keep things tidy. She passed away last year." He brushed a few crumbs off the kitchen table and got out three coffee cups. After checking to make sure they were acceptably clean, he set them on the table.

"Things are mostly going all right, but it's a little iffy with the cleaning."

Gösta sat down directly across from Fredrik and Tord and immediately started rocking back in his chair.

"Women'll drive you crazy, but you sure miss them when they're gone. We had fifty years together, Maud and I." He proudly twisted his wedding ring around and Tord nodded approvingly.

"Maud was a lovely woman. Not like my crazy old broad."

"No, you really didn't have her under control, did you?" Gösta laughed. "Although as I seem to recall she didn't feel like she had you under control either, eh?"

Tord grunted something in response. The two men seemed to have a warm relationship with each other.

"Have you lived here long?" Fredrik asked in a cautious attempt to guide the conversation to what he had come here to talk about. Although he himself wasn't exactly sure what that was.

"Yes." Gösta stretched. "Maud and I built this cabin right after we got married. We never did have any children." He looked up at Fredrik as if he had realized that he'd said too much. "Which is to say that the cabin was enough space for the two of us."

"It's beautiful. Are you a carpenter?"

Gösta lit up.

"No, goodness gracious! I worked at the herring saltery up until 1974, and then after that I was the sacristan at the Ulvö Chapel. I've been retired for a long time now, of course, but you've got to stay in shape." He laughed and flexed his biceps.

"Well, I have a few questions about a summer camp," Fredrik said. "Tord says you knew the family that ran it."

"That's right. I started working as the sacristan in 1975, the same year Aron Dirk and his family moved here. Taking care of the chapel was part of that."

"So, you knew the family well?"

"Yes, I suppose you could say that," Gösta said, stroking his chin. "As well as anyone could know them. He did a lot of good, Aron did. But he was very religious, almost a fanatic. His daughters, too. I don't know about his wife, Elisabeth. She had already passed by the time they moved here."

The sacristan balanced on his chair for a bit without saying anything. They heard an ATV race by outside at high speed. Gösta followed the sound with his eyes even though you couldn't see the road from the window.

"Terrible story, that one. There were only pieces left of the car. Part of the windshield came off in the crash and Elisabeth… well, she lost her head so to speak."

"Lost her head?"

"It was severed. They had to cut Ester free. She was trapped in the front seat next to her mother. She was only nine at the time."

"Ew…" Fredrik shuddered. "What year did Aron Dirk stop running the camps?"

"Seventy-nine." The answer came like the crack of whip.

The same year as on the date in the photo Ceder had a copy of in his bag. Fredrik reached for the folded printout of the picture from the inside pocket of his leather jacket.

"Can you identify the people shown here?"

Gösta took the printout, set it down on the table and pointed to the youngsters one by one.

"That's Ester, and then Bodil of course. Then that one is Gisela Karst's daughter, Christine, she was friends with the girls and she played over there a lot for several years. That must be Marianne Nordin, Siw-Inger Hörnberg, and her sister Annika, and then two girls from the Soviet Union, or Russia as I suppose it's called now. There was some kind of exchange program through the Church of Sweden. Mona Höglund—the woman who runs the hotel for the Karsts—may have been involved, too, but she's not in this picture."

"What about the boys?"

Gösta peered at the picture and thought about it. He didn't seem to reflect on the fact that the eyes had been poked out. Or maybe he didn't notice that, Fredrik thought. He was almost eighty.

"Oh, I'm not as sure about them. Most of them were from far away. You know, messed up boys who needed to come out to the countryside for a bit of fresh air. I think this one was named Mats." Gösta pointed to a moody-looking boy with dark hair. "And then that's Jan Dagegård. He was a good kid. The one to his left is Thomas Nilsson. I seem to recall that that redheaded boy's name was Adam."

Fredrik nodded and made a note of the names on his cell phone. He tried not to seem more interested in Adam Ceder than any of the others. If word got out that he was running around asking questions about him, that would put a quick end to things.

"Thomas." Gösta handed the printout back and lowered his voice. "He hung himself. And then Ester up and died as well…"

He drank a sip of his coffee which had grown cold as they talked.

Fredrik wondered what he should ask in order to learn more.

"Are you in touch with any of them now? The kids that came here, or with Aron and Bodil?"

Gösta shook his head and leaned forward, as if the bushes outside might be full of listening ears.

"After that boy hung himself, no one ever heard from Bodil again. It was as if she went up in smoke. There was a rumor that Aron sent her to that Bible school in Uppsala, but I don't know."

"What do you mean?"

Tord and Gösta exchanged glances across the table and Gösta squirmed in his seat. He smiled awkwardly.

"I'm sorry, but I'm afraid I need to get going. They're hosting a lunch bingo event down by the harbor. If you get there late, they run out of chips."

Fredrik shook Gösta's hand across the crumb-strewn table.

"Thank you for taking the time to talk to me."

21.

Ulvön Island, 1979

Mona and Christine were sitting on the bench below the stoop. Bodil was hanging the laundry on the line strung between the alder trees in front of the house. There was no sign of Ester, but Christine knew that she usually kept an eye on them from her bedroom window.

Adam, Mats, Thomas, and Marianne were sitting on a blanket on the lawn a little farther away. Christine wanted to go over and join them but didn't dare. The wooden shoes with the buckles that she had borrowed were too high, and she was afraid she would fall but also that they would say she couldn't join them.

There was a deck of cards between them, but no one was dealing the cards. Thomas was leaning against Marianne's knees and sunbathing. Thomas didn't have a shirt on and his belly was bulging out over his waistband.

"How long are we going to sit here?" Marianne complained. "I'm dying of boredom!"

When no one responded, she got up abruptly so that Thomas's head fell back onto the blanket. He cursed and got up on all fours. His belly crumpled like dough as he wriggled back up and out of the corner of her eye Christine could see how Mona pursed her lips in disgust.

"Look at him," she whispered, leaning against Christine. "Fat as a pig. Surely God made a mistake when He created someone like Thomas?" She scoffed and nudged Christine in the side with her elbow. Christine didn't respond. She had no idea how God had created them. She also had no interest in Thomas. She just wanted to sit there and look at Adam, wishing that he was hers.

"I think I'll call him piggy from now on," Mona continued.

Thomas had gotten to his feet now and was standing next to his friends on the blanket and drinking big gulps out of a soda bottle.

"Did you hear that, Bodil? We're bored." He concluded with a loud burp and the others laughed. Bodil focused on the laundry without turning around.

"There's a dance at the hotel tonight," he continued. "A band and everything on the open-air dance floor. We had been planning to bike over there, but that plan was not to the liking of our rolling saint." When Bodil still didn't respond, Thomas raised his voice.

"Tattling, your sister's good at that, you know? So now the pastor says we can't go." Bodil turned around and looked deliberately at Thomas. He took a few steps toward her.

"Maybe someone ought to teach her a lesson for ratting out her friends?"

Bodil walked up to him with the laundry basket under her arm.

"If you touch Ester, I'll strangle you. Do you hear me?"

Thomas held up his hands, laughing.

"Hey, come on, take it easy. A little lesson couldn't hurt, right? Snitching on people is just as much a sin as going to a dance, isn't it?"

Mats chimed in from over on the blanket.

"Yeah, maybe our saint needs a little spanking?"

Thomas laughed crudely, but Bodil didn't respond. To Christine's dismay, Mona raised her voice next to her and called out across the lawn, "Gluttony is also a sin. Didn't you know that, you pig?"

Thomas froze for a hundredth of a second, but then headed right for them. Christine froze and couldn't move. Out of the corner of her eye, she saw Adam watching them. Her cheeks burned with shame.

Mona kept yelling.

"Look at how he wobbles, that pig! Oink, oink!"

Thomas would reach them soon.

"You take that back!"

But Mona just looked at him stubbornly. He aimed a kick at her leg, but missed. His next kick hit Mona's thigh and she screamed. Everyone was on their feet in a flash. Adam came running over and tried to pull Thomas away. He kept kicking but missing. Instead he threw his soda bottle which sprayed all over Christine and Mona.

Thomas put up quite a fuss as Adam and Mats dragged him into the house. They could hear him swearing all the way into the boys' bedroom.

Bodil stood there with the laundry basket under her arm and watched. Her voice was barely a whisper.

"Someone ought to teach him a lesson."

22.

The investigative team had gathered in the library once again. Marie Fransson from the Criminal Investigations Unit in Sundsvall had just arrived. As Sofia sat down, Mattias and Karim were involved in a heated discussion about the previous day's soccer practice as usual.

Their daughters, who were the same age, were on the same team and they never seemed to run out of things to say on the topic. Vera called for their attention in her usual, down-to-earth way.

"Pipe the fuck down, would you!"

Marie combed her old-lady bangs with her fingers and smiled uncomfortably. It was clear that the strictly religious investigator was not thrilled with Vera's choice of words, but at least she had enough sense not to say so. Even though Marie had been brought in to lead the preliminary investigation, Sofia knew that Vera would still be holding the reins. The two women had established their interpersonal hierarchy many years ago with Marie reluctantly accepting the subordinate role.

"Well then, maybe we should get started." Vera rubbed her index finger against her thumb as if she were holding an invisible rosary, an unmistakable sign that she was irritated.

"As you know, Adam Ceder was found dead below the Ulvö Hotel at 5:25 a.m. yesterday morning. He had a room at the hotel and had checked in on Midsummer's Eve."

"Witnesses?" Marie asked.

Vera shook her head.

"We've knocked on doors, questioned people on-site and over the phone, but without results. So far we haven't found anything that suggests that Ceder had company or had arranged to meet anyone. Until the autopsy, we can't do more than we've already done. His sister is on her way up to Umeå to ID him and should be there sometime this afternoon. Fridell was extremely reluctant to cut into him before that."

Marie wrinkled her nose at this choice of words.

"But at any rate, she did agree to share a highly informal guess," Vera continued. "She thinks the victim died from the head injury and not from drowning. In other words, we're dealing with a murder. His head was really badly battered. But he was completely spared from animal attacks, so he can't have been lying in the water for very long. We'll find out more once the report comes back."

"Was she able to say anything about the murder weapon?" Marie asked.

"No."

"How about how long he's been dead?"

"No."

"Has she found any other potential clues on the body?"

"No."

Marie was tossing out questions and with each no, Sofia noticed the look in Vera's eyes growing grimmer.

"The question is, how did Ceder end up at that specific location?" Karim asked, holding up a picture of the body from the beach. "We haven't found any tracks leading to or from the body's location."

Vera opened her notepad. A quick toss of her head and her reading glasses slid down from where she had had them on top of her head to land neatly on her nose. She pushed them into place with the back of her hand.

"Fridell mentioned that he had abrasions on his forehead and on his hands. Given the diffuse suggillation pattern, the most likely conclusion seems to be that he was thrown into the water and then carried to the beach below the hotel by the currents. Otherwise the suggillations would only be on his back, since he was lying in a supine position when he was found."

"That sounds likely," Sofia said. "The guest pier starts only a few meters from where he was found, and it was packed with boats on Midsummer's Eve. You don't pass a whole marina full of people and then dump a dead body unnoticed. Not even if you're drunk."

Karim rubbed his forehead between his eyebrows.

"Could he have floated ashore from Rensviken on South Ulvön Island, maybe?" he asked.

"We've had a southerly wind for at least two days," Sofia said, "so that's not impossible. And that is a local hangout for teenagers. I'll talk to the Coast Guard and see what they think."

"Well, he's hardly a teenager, but, yes, check on that," Vera muttered.

"Christine Karst, the owner of the hotel, have you gotten ahold of her?" Marie asked.

"No."

"Mona Höglund, then? Has she been in touch about the surveillance footage?"

"No, but we're still trying to access the footage." Vera shut her notepad and shoved it across the table. A heavy silence settled over the room.

"Do we have a point person for the media?" Marie asked.

"Mattias?" Vera passed the question on.

A crime of this type was rare in Västernorrland county. Vera was responsible for media communications, but she usually delegated it to Mattias. Sofia reluctantly had to concede that the role suited him. Not just because he looked good in the photos, but also because he had a way of making the journalists settle for whatever he doled out to them. If he hadn't gone into policework, he would have made an excellent politician.

"I can put together a press release." Mattias pulled his hand through his hair, unable to conceal that he relished being asked to do so.

"Sofia, you make sure we get ahold of Karst," Vera said. "The rest of us will keep working on what we have until Ceder has been IDed and autopsied."

"What we have?" There was no overlooking the annoyance in Marie's voice, despite her affable smile.

"I'm aware that we don't have very much to go on right now, but we should keep digging. Somewhere out there there's someone who saw something. The poor guy can't just have fallen out of the sky!"

Marie pursed her lips and was about to say something, but Vera interrupted her.

"Well, let's get started then." Vera looked at her watch. "I want us to have something by our afternoon meeting, OK?"

–

Fredrik's already battered backside was, if possible, even sorer when he yet again extracted himself from the moped's cargo bed with as much dignity as he could muster. They had left the northern part of the island's winding woodland track and come down to the village once again. On the last steep downhill section, which Tord called Malabacken, Fredrik had nearly toppled right off the cargo bed. His heart was still racing from the surge of adrenalin. And yet it wasn't an unpleasant feeling. He felt alive for the first time in a long time. So much so that he had almost forgotten the reason for their outing. Gösta's awful story had made him even more convinced that Adam Ceder's death had something to do with that summer camp.

"Well, that was fun!" Tord laughed as he parked the moped below the fire station on the hill, not far from the old chapel. They were at the heart of the island, right where the road to Sandviken and Norrbysbodarna, where Sofia lived, took off from the unpaved pedestrian street that ran along the waterfront at Ulvö Harbor to the hotel. On the other side of the pedestrian street, down by the water, there was a long row of colorful houses built right in against each other and tucked neatly behind colorful picket fences. Between the houses, Fredrik caught glimpses of red painted boathouses with docks.

Tord left the keys dangling from the moped's handlebars in the event that someone needed to borrow it and pointed proudly to the gray building about 30 feet away.

"And here you have Ulvö's old chapel."

The seventeenth-century chapel sat on an unstable-looking foundation of smooth, loosely stacked old stones and its minimal churchyard was surrounded by a rickety-looking wooden fence. Fredrik looked up at the tall bell tower before them. This was where the row of teenagers had been standing in the photo. It looked exactly the same now as it had forty years ago.

They walked around the chapel and stopped by the fence. Tord pointed to the two buildings on the neighboring property uphill from the chapel.

"There on the right you have my humble abode," Tord said.

Fredrik looked up the grassy slope. There was a red cabin with a green door. Not much bigger than Gösta Björnberg's, but in far better condition. The decorative trim—the barge-boards and window frames—gleamed with a coat of fresh white paint and the lawn around the house had been neatly mowed and trimmed.

"The other one there is Nordin's house. I own the land, but we share it." About twenty yards up to the left of the cabin, Fredrik saw a large house, painted white with a glassed-in porch and windows with white mullions. An overgrown stone wall ran down the middle between the two houses, and a little farther up there was a gap in the wall that was almost completely filled by an enormous lilac. Tord seemed unaware of the almost laughable difference between the two houses. He really was a man of contrasts, Fredrik thought. Gruff and poetic, wealthy and down to earth.

Tord looked at his watch.

"Marianne's in the chapel now. You go on in. I'm just going to visit the little boy's room." Then without further ado he disappeared though a gate and up toward his cabin which he appeared to have left unlocked during their travels around the island.

Fredrik took off his leather jacket and tried to stretch out his muscles which still felt knocked out of commission by the bumpy ride. He rolled up the sleeves of the shirt he had borrowed from the wardrobe full of Sofia's dad's clothes. He hadn't found any underwear, and even if he had, he wasn't particularly thrilled with the idea of borrowing another man's underwear.

He walked back around to the chapel's entrance and had to lift his feet high to step over the old building's lopsided threshold. There was a wooden bench with brochures about the chapel and a stack of worn hymnals. A woman with brown hair in a pageboy cut stood at the far end of the aisle wearing a dress that came down to her ankles. She waved for him to come closer, without pausing the presentation she was giving in error-free, British English that was holding the rapt attention of a group of Asian tourists. It was warm inside and smelled of dry wood and dust.

"The chapel was built in 1622, and the paintings you see here were done by Roland Johansson Öberg in 1719. He was the son of one of the farmers here on Ulvön Island."

Fredrik took a seat in the back row of pews, tilting his head so far back that he could easily look at the chapel's ceiling. Every inch of the rough log construction, walls and ceiling alike, were covered with paintings. Swirly floral patterns, strict, biblical motifs, and what appeared to be some completely ordinary, everyday situations—people cooking, riding horseback, or tending their animals. At the front of the chapel there was a green pulpit with carved details that were painted red and brown. To the left of the altar, a beautiful votive ship with white sails and blue railings hung from the ceiling.

"Ulvön Island was historically a fishing community. The fishermen who attended services in this chapel in the eighteenth century often couldn't read or write, so the paintings were intended to help them understand the pastor's sermons. As you can see many of the motifs are related to fishing."

Fredrik nodded in agreement even though no one was looking at him where he sat way in the back. There were men in neatly buttoned seventeenth-century coats putting out their nets or fishing with rods.

Fredrik had always had a soft spot for religion. Maybe his life would have looked different if he had found God? But he had put his faith in pills instead.

"Thank you for your attention. I hope you've enjoyed your tour. Now, please go and enjoy some herring."

The Asian tourists crowded into the central aisle to make their way out of the warm chapel. Fredrik stood up and followed them out into the sunshine. Marianne Nordin was standing in the little anteroom chatting with the tourists who flocked past her on their way out.

He held out his hand to greet her and she shook it. Her hand was cool and dry in his.

"Fredrik Fröding. I'm a friend of Tord's. He invited me to come meet you and ask a couple of questions about the history of Ulvön Island if that's all right. You're clearly an expert."

Marianne smiled, revealing a perfect set of white teeth.

"I suppose you could say that."

They quickly walked around the clock tower and out onto the road before turning to walk through the gate to Tord's property. After they pushed their way past the lilac bush in the gap in the old stone wall, she invited him to sit on the stairs leading up to the glassed-in veranda while she filled a watering can from a faucet on the side of the house. She wasn't at all what he had expected. At least fifteen years older than he was, maybe more, but her face was smooth and tan. She looked like a movie star, but Fredrik couldn't place which one. Which movie had he seen her in? Maybe Ingmar Bergen's "Fanny and Alexander"? At any rate, the likeness was striking. The fullness of her lips and the unnatural firmness of her body given her age told him that Marianne was a woman of means, eager to hold onto what the years had tried to take from her. She was tall and slim and wore a sundress with thin shoulder straps that extended all the way to her ankles. He was just about to say something courteous about the house or the yard when Tord's loud voice cut him off.

"For crying out loud, Marianne! When are you going to cut down this darned tree?"

He squeezed his way around the lilac bush that separated their yards and swore softly as his sweater caught on a branch.

"That is a bush not a tree, if you please. And my answer is never. It's beautiful."

Marianne smiled teasingly at Tord. He snorted something inaudible in response and dropped a crate of shiny silver fish at their feet. He deftly pulled his snus tin out of his chest pocket and gathered himself a liberal pinch as he nodded at Fredrik.

"I see that you two have met."

Marianne nodded.

"Well, let's get smoking, boy. If you want to eat, you need to do your share."

23

Sofia heard Karim's and Mattias's voices in the hallway outside her office at eleven twenty-five. They were on their way to their usual lunch place at their usual lunchtime. She didn't expect to be invited to join them and she wasn't, even though her door was open when they went by.

Vera rarely ate lunch and Marie had gone to her hotel to check in. Sofia tried to decide if she was hungry, but the endorphin rush from her night of lovemaking had shut down any need for food. The thought of Fredrik's hands on her body made her lose her focus for a second, and she jumped when the hold music started playing on the other end of the line, grating and far too loud. One of the guards in Christine Karst's gated community in Alicante answered promptly in English with a Spanish accent.

"Hi, my name is Sofia Hjortén and I'm with the Swedish police. I'm trying to get ahold of a Swedish citizen who lives there, in…" Sofia clicked through to the email she had received from the Ulvö Hotel's human resources manager, "…apartment 4D, on Carrer de Tabarca."

"Ah, you mean Gisela!" the guard laughed. "Unfortunately she's not home." The man rattled off a long place name in Spanish that Sofia didn't catch. "She's playing piano. You know, concert."

Sofia knew. Gisela Karst, Christine's mother, was Ulvön Island's local pride and joy, the world-renowned pianist.

"Do you know if her daughter Christine is there, staying in her apartment?"

"No." The man suddenly sounded depressed. "She comes sometimes but can't stay long. Always on the go. Anxiety… you know?" he added to make sure that his somewhat poor English had conveyed what he had intended.

"According to her coworkers, she planned to travel to her mother's place the day before yesterday. Apparently, she's staying with her mother during her divorce?"

"Unfortunately, the apartment is empty. I went by there yesterday morning."

After having asked the man to email her the name of the place where Gisela had gone, and to keep an eye out for Christine and ask her to contact them if she returned, Sofia thanked him and hung up.

Her next call was to Mona Höglund. Sofia had tried to reach her several times the previous day, but without luck. Mona had left the hospital on Midsummer night along with the server who had helped Sofia cover Ceder's body. According to the hotel staff, Mona hadn't arrived at work yet even though the morning was pretty much over. Sofia had asked them to tell both Mona and Christine to call her as soon as possible if either of them got in touch.

After another hour of making calls, she reached Christine's ex-husband, who lived in Nacka just outside Stockholm. He hadn't seen or spoken with his former wife in several months, since she had been spending almost all her time at her mother's apartment in Alicante following the divorce. He gave Sofia a tip to call one of Christine's female friends, who in turn was able to confirm that Christine was planning to have a layover in Stockholm on Midsummer's Day after catching the morning flight from Örnsköldsvik. Then she was going to continue on to Alicante. Yet again, Sofia hung up having left the message to have Christine to contact them as soon as possible.

She was not looking forward to facing Vera empty-handed.

—

There was a hint of a storm in the air despite the scorching sunshine. The clouds lay densely packed on the horizon and Fredrik thought he felt a thunderstorm coming on. He sat leaning against the wall of the house, waiting for the whitefish to finish smoking while Marianne told him about the island, the chapel, the fishermen who came here in the eighteenth century and the construction of the new Ulvö Hotel. She was interested in history and gave the tours of the chapel in her free time.

Tord carried the crates of fish between the boathouse below the pedestrian street and the smokehouse in the corner of Marianne's yard. Fredrik had proven to be supremely useless when it came to either cleaning the fish or lighting the juniper in the fish smoker and had therefore been invited to stay out of the way with a thermos of coffee and a plate of almond biscotti, an assignment that he undertook with relish. Despite his inauspicious night at the hotel and Ceder's death, he couldn't help but enjoy himself. This was almost like living in a parallel reality. The house, the sun, the view of Ulvö Harbor, and the two friendly strangers who didn't know a thing about his life or what he had been through.

Marianne sat in a chair with a pail between her knees, cleaning fish. Her hands sparkled with iridescent fish scales and she had to use the back of her hand to brush a lock of her dark brown pageboy out of her face. When she raised her arm, Fredrik saw several long scars that ran from the inside of her elbow down to her wrist. Marianne followed his gaze, embarrassed.

"Come, give us a hand, young'un!" Tord called from the smoker. "You ought to be able to empty out a smoker even if you are from the city."

"Well, let's hope so," Fredrik said. He set down his coffee cup and got up.

"Be careful not to burn yourself," Marianne warned. The lock of hair fell down again and she tried in vain to blow it off her face. She gave up after several attempts, and Fredrik leaned forward and tucked it behind her ear. She nodded in gratitude and smiled up at him.

Once all the fish had been taken out, Tord and Fredrik sat down on the lawn furniture outside the house. Tord handed him a beer and Marianne disappeared inside. Fredrik took a tentative sip. He probably shouldn't drink, but then it hit him that he hadn't taken any pills since Midsummer's Eve. That was the longest he'd gone without for this whole bout. Was the tide turning now?

He leaned back and looked out at the boathouses and farther out across the strait. His eyes followed the mast of a big sailboat as it squeezed through the Ulvö Strait and was now chugging toward the hotel. New potatoes with dill were cooking on the stove and the aroma made Fredrik's stomach rumble.

"What a strange story that is about the Dirks," Fredrik said.

Tord nodded and pinched some snus. He brushed his hands emphatically so black grains rained down over the white cotton tablecloth.

"They were all strange, the whole family. Nowadays you'd probably call them fanatics, like members of a sect. God and Jesus and the devil and his great aunt." He shook his head. "Aron used to preach that his youngest daughter Ester had been spared, that God had sent an angel to protect her in the car crash. He probably wanted to believe that everything had a meaning, which is understandable, but it got a little out of hand. Several of the kids believed what Aron said and many of them were afraid of Ester, that poor girl."

"Time to eat now," Marianne said, appearing in the window above them, "before the potatoes get cold."

24

Everyone was there in the library for the last check-in of the day. The room had originally acquired its name because for many years people had had to come here to look up information in the law books. Now that everything was digitized, the room was used as a conference room, although the bookshelves were still there. Sofia sat down next to Marie, who good-heartedly pulled out a chair for her and smiled broadly.

"You look so fresh, Sofia. Did you do something to your hair?"

Sofia shook her head.

"Maybe it's something about your eyes." Marie leaned in so close that their shoulders touched. "Did you meet a man?"

Sofia's cheeks flushed and she couldn't help but be amazed at Marie's astuteness. Was it that obvious?

"If you two are done whispering, maybe we could start the meeting?" Vera stood at the short end of the table, drumming on the tabletop in irritation with a whiteboard marker. Marie winked at Sofia and turned to Vera with a smile.

"Absolutely," Marie said cheerfully. "Go right ahead."

"Thank you," Vera replied sourly. She secured a picture of Christine Karst to the whiteboard with some adhesive putty. The picture had come from the local newspaper's photo archives and showed a tan, smiling Christine at the opening of the new Ulvö Hotel. The mayor at that time, Elvy Söderström, had been cut out of the picture, but you could still see her arm around Christine's narrow shoulders.

"Any luck getting ahold of her?"

"No. Her ex-husband hasn't talked to her in several months and Gisela Karst is apparently away performing and unreachable. It's been almost three days now since we found Adam Ceder murdered outside the hotel and Christine still hasn't gotten in touch with us, despite repeated attempts to reach her."

"That is strange," Karim agreed.

Vera pursed her lips and wrote a question mark next to the photo.

"But just because Christine said she was going to Alicante, that doesn't mean she actually did," Sofia continued. "I talked to the ferry crew. They are positive that she didn't take the first ferry across on Midsummer's Day. She's well known on the island and apparently that crossing wasn't so crowded that they could have missed her. I'll request the passenger lists from the flight to Spain and see what that tells us."

Vera nodded.

"What did the Coast Guard say?" Marie turned to Sofia, who shrugged.

"They couldn't say anything about where he had floated in from. He could certainly have drifted in from the strait."

"Could his death have something to do with the hotel?"

"There have been rumors for a while that it's for sale, but I don't know if that's true. Ceder was also in the hotel business. So maybe there's a motive there? Maybe he was planning to buy it?" Sofia looked at Vera.

"Maybe, but why should that have led to his death?" Mattias sounded doubtful.

"We'll have to look into that." Vera pointed to the picture of Adam Ceder from the homepage for Ceder Hotels, which was also up on the whiteboard. He was smiling cheerfully at the camera.

"Sofia, I want you to go down to Stockholm and talk to Ceder's mother and sister. And to the employees at the corporate headquarters for the hotel chain, too. And call Marklund! We need to get someone from Profiling up here. I can't think of anyone who would be a better fit."

Sofia had never worked on a case that required criminal profiling before, but it was bound to happen at some point. So now she and Kaj were going to work side by side? The idea was not at all pleasant. Especially not now that she had met Fredrik again. But this was a workplace, not a stage for some corny love triangle.

"Should I look into the rumors that the hotel was for sale then?" Karim asked.

"Do it." Vera turned back to the whiteboard.

"I talked to the press officer…," Mattias began, but was interrupted by Sofia's cell phone vibrating on the table. It was the receptionist's number.

"There's a woman from Ulvön Island down here looking for you. It's in regard to someone named Fredrik Fröding."

"I'm in a meeting," Sofia said, a blush spreading up her neck. "Take her number and tell her I'll call her back in an hour."

"It's Mona Höglund. She says it has to do with the investigation. I'll put her through."

The other end of the line went quiet and then a faint voice could be heard.

"Hi, this is Mona Höglund. I run the Ulvö Hotel. We saw each other…"

"We've been trying to reach you." Sofia's tone was harsher than it needed to be.

"I haven't been sleeping well since we found that man, and…"

"We need to talk to you, but at the moment I'm busy in a meeting. Can I call you back in a little while?"

Mona pulled herself together and cleared the tiredness out of her voice.

"The night before Midsummer we had a guest by the name of Fredrik Fröding. He was quite drunk and I saw him standing down by the pool that night yelling at a man."

Sofia spun her chair around discreetly so as not to disrupt the meeting.

"And what does this have to do with the investigation?"

"I'm not positive, but the man he was yelling at looked like the guy who was found down by the water. Adam Ceder, I mean. I'm quite sure it was him. I should have thought of that before. After all, I was the one who found him, but I think I was in shock and…"

"Thank you. I'll get back to you once we've confirmed that."

When Sofia looked up, she discovered that the meeting had ground to a halt. Vera was looking questioningly at her blushing face.

"We'll hold off on the media."

"Why?" Mattias eyed Vera angrily.

"Because we have a witness who saw the victim arguing with one of the hotel guests the night before," Sofia said.

Vera leaned back in her chair and crossed her arms.

"I see, and who the hell would that be?"

—

"Oh my God, I'm stuffed!" Marianne set her utensils down on her plate and leaned back in her wicker chair with a bottle of beer in her hand. "Good thing I'm not wearing pants or I'd have to undo the button." She patted her flat stomach contentedly.

It had been a lovely afternoon. Tord had regaled them with crazy fish stories and Marianne had sat in the shade under the lilac, mending nets and cleaning fish while they waited for the smoker. In addition to the whitefish, a tin of fermented surströmming had also found its way out. The white and blue tin was still on the table and the stench was really out of this world. Fredrik pushed it a little farther away from himself, but he had to admit that it didn't taste anything like it smelled. When Marianne had opened the tin, he had thought he might be sick. He was never going to stuff something that smelled like that in his mouth, not in this lifetime! But on a piece of flatbread with some potato and red onion, the fermented herring was actually really good.

"So, Fredrik, now you've been initiated into Ulvön Island's ancient tradition and are now officially a member of our community," Tord stated solemnly and then bowed over the table with his hat in his hand.

"Very kind of you," Fredrik said with a laugh. "I could have done without the smell, though."

"Ah, you get used to it. Next time you'll have it without the flatbread, just with a little schnapps to go with it." Tord pushed his plate of whitefish and fermented herring aside and gathered another pinch of snus. He rarely seemed to be without a big, black wad of it under his lip.

"That really was delicious," Fredrik acknowledged. "Thank you for letting me stay for dinner."

"Not at all." Marianne opened another beer and dropped the cap on the tablecloth. "Is there any particular reason you're interested in the island's history?"

"I'm actually most curious about the summer camps."

Marianne's hand stopped halfway to her mouth and then she slowly set her beer bottle back down on the table again.

"Why do you want to know more about those?"

"He's writing about the island." Tord laughed, as if he'd never heard anything so ridiculous.

"Tord tells me that you knew the Dirk family?" Fredrik pulled the printout of the photograph out of his leather jacket, which was draped over the chair next to him. Marianne pulled one leg up underneath herself in her wide wicker chair. She avoided looking at the picture.

"Well, it depends on what you mean by knowing. My parents belonged to the same congregation as Aron. They worked for the Church of Sweden in Ireland. I lived with the Dirks whenever they were away, before we moved abroad permanently."

"Were you friends with the sisters?"

Marianne looked down the hill, out over the long row of houses and boathouses across the pedestrian street.

"No, not really."

"The boy who hung himself at the end of the 70s, did you know him?"

"No, I can't say that I did. I was only at the Dirks' place now and then, and when the actual... incident occurred, on Midsummer night that year, I had left Sweden."

"Are you still in touch with anyone from the summer camp?"

She shook her head.

"There were so many children who stayed with the Dirks over the years, even when there wasn't a camp going on. People came and went, so you didn't really have time to get attached to anyone. We were all kids from the island who obviously already knew each other, but not so much so that we've kept in touch. I've lived abroad for so long. I didn't move back until early this spring."

"The Karsts' girl, then? Christine?" Tord interjected.

"Yes, she was there a lot, but like I said there were a lot who hung out there in the summers. Half the island seemed to have something to do with the Dirks at some point."

"She was just here for Midsummer." Tord nodded toward the hotel.

"I heard that. I had planned to visit her, but she seems to have left again already. I don't understand why the Karsts insist on holding onto that hotel. They're never here to look after the place."

Tord nodded in agreement.

"What was it like at that camp?" Fredrik asked, trying to steer the conversation away from village gossip.

Marianne shook her head, without making eye contact.

"It was like any other summer camp, I would imagine. I've mostly suppressed all that... It was actually a pretty unpleasant time." She looked up and her eyes locked onto Fredrik's as if seeking support. "We were young, all of us. We didn't want to sit around thinking about life and death and Jesus's suffering.

We wanted to have fun. You know, run down to the village, sneak out to smoke, go to dances."

There was silence and Fredrik watched Marianne's fingers methodically tearing at the edges of the label on her beer bottle until it came off in one piece. The heat lingered like a steaming lid over them, but the dark clouds had begun to creep closer. A cool wind swept in over the grassy slope.

"Your house is really amazing." Fredrik changed the topic to lighten the mood. Marianne lit up.

"It is, isn't it? When my husband and I got divorced, I knew right away that I wanted to come home to Sweden, to my parents' home. I've moved enough for a whole lifetime. Before I'd even set down my bags in Dublin, my parents had started looking around for a new project somewhere out in the world." She laughed. "I've lived in everything from fancy dormitories to huts in the jungle. Aside from with my husband in London, this house is probably the only place I've ever spent more than six months. It was in really sorry shape when I came back, but my handy neighbor here helped me get it into shape again." She winked at Tord, who appeared pleased with the compliment.

She set her now label-free beer bottle on the table.

"My son still lives in London. They just had a little boy. He's five months old. I had already decided to move home to Sweden when they told me they were expecting him, but I was able to be there when he came home from the hospital anyway. I'm going back in September to see them." She smiled genuinely and pulled her cell phone out of her dress pocket. She swiped her finger across the screen a few times and then proudly showed him a picture of the baby. Fredrik nodded in approval the way one is expected to when a proud grandparent shows you a picture of a grandchild.

"You'd have to look hard to find a more beautiful grand-mother, right, Fredrik?" Tord smiled.

Marianne blushed and kept looking at her picture of her grandchild with a smile. No one said anything for a while.

"Well, you kids. It's getting to be time for me to hit the hay!" Tord slapped his knee and got up. Fredrik patted him on the shoulder as he wriggled his way past him around the table. Marianne got up and gave Tord a kiss on the cheek.

"Thanks for a nice day."

"Will you drive the youngster home?" Tord asked.

Marianne nodded.

"Adios, then!" Tord tipped his hat and strolled off toward the lilac bush. They watched him as he pushed his way through the foliage muttering curse words. Soon they heard the green door bang shut.

"Would you like to have a cup of coffee down by the boathouse?" Marianne stood up and started gathering the dishes. Fredrik nodded and made an effort to help, but she put her hand on his shoulder and pushed him benevolently back into his seat.

"You sit and enjoy the warmth while it lasts. The storm will be upon us soon."

He opened another beer and leaned back.

Marianne returned promptly with a basket in her hand.

"All right, let's go."

25

"Can you believe this heat?!" Vera's grumpy voice echoed through the investigative unit, which had mostly emptied out for the night. "Karim! Come in here and help me open this window!"

Karim's rapid footsteps could soon be heard in the hallway. The office air conditioning system had fought the good fight during the day, but in the end it hadn't been a match for the humid heat. Now there was a thunderstorm brewing and it was stifling and stuffy inside. The company that maintained their HVAC system was on summer vacation and the few poor souls left in the police station simply had to cope with the heat.

Sofia shifted her position to keep from sticking to the seat of her chair. Her hand rested listlessly on her mouse, but she couldn't really make her brain process the information on the screen in front of her. Her thoughts were continually turning to the surreal situation she found herself in.

Fredrik Fröding was back in her life.

And at the same time also a part of her investigation.

Why would this all happen right now? Why the hell did Fredrik have to come into her life and start mucking things up? And what did he have to do with Ceder? Mona Höglund had said the two of them had argued. About what? Fredrik had claimed that he hadn't noticed anything unusual. But arguing with someone who was then found dead the next day could hardly be considered a common occurrence, could it?

Sofia ran her hand over her neck, feeling irritated. She had been so taken aback by Mona's phone call that she had forgotten to ask her for the surveillance footage. Could Fredrik really have been involved somehow? What else hadn't he told her? It struck her that she knew almost nothing about him. She hadn't asked him a single question about what he was doing now or why he was on Ulvön Island. She had just welcomed him with open arms, lies and all. She was so profoundly ashamed that she wanted to crawl out of her own skin.

Sofia drank a sip of water and forcibly redirected her thoughts to her work. She clicked mechanically through the photos of Adam Ceder's hotel, Ceder City East, the home of the hotel chain's headquarters. Located at a pretentious address in the heart of Östermalm with white marble columns outside its front entrance. It looked American, excessive. Ceder Sky at the Stockholm airport, Ceder Sea in Vaxholm, and a long list of other hotels with similar names. The chain even owned hotels outside of Sweden. Sofia had stayed at a Ceder hotel in Rome many years ago. She and Kaj had dolefully agreed that it had been a poor choice and the word tasteless had come up more than once on that vacation. If she wasn't remembering wrong, the taps in the bathtub had been gold-plated dolphins.

She clicked back and forth between the few tabs in the investigation file. Her own memo about finding the body came first along with several notes from the policemen who had notified the family in Stockholm of the death.

Vera stepped in without knocking and sat down on the visitor's chair.

"Nina Ceder has just officially IDed him as Adam Erik Johannes Ceder. A resident of Djursholm, on the finer side of life."

Sofia nodded absentmindedly, her eyes still on her screen.

"No children, divorced," Vera continued. "We haven't found any obvious commonalities between this Fröding and Ceder yet. By the way, did you know that he went to the police academy? Fröding, I mean."

Vera leaned across Sofia's desk and snuck a peek at the screen.

"Sofia?"

They heard a patrol car exit the garage and speed away down Viktoriaesplanaden with its sirens wailing.

This isn't happening.

"Sofia?"

She looked up.

"I thought we'd start with his Facebook page." Vera snorted. "In my day…"

Sofia wasn't listening, just staring intently at her screen trying to think of something to say.

"The Flashback message board about the murder is full of comments."

Vera got right down to business.

"Damn it, it's weird how those fools always know more than we do, and faster to boot!" When Sofia didn't respond, she continued. "Mattias is calling his way through the last of the witness lists and Karim is working on finding out more about the hotel's potentially being for sale. Have you booked your tickets to Stockholm yet?"

Sofia rubbed the bridge of her nose. How should she handle this? What was she going to say to Kaj? What would happen when her colleagues found out that she and Fredrik… Oh God, she had to get ahold of him, get him to stay at her house so they could get to the bottom of this. Before someone else beat her to it.

"Not yet. I'll do that before I go home."

"Good. Marie contacted Ceder's wireless carrier and bank to obtain a list of his calls and withdrawals so we can plot out the final few days of his life. We'll also request tower dumps to see where his cell phone went after he got to Örnsköldsvik. Ideally we'll be able to determine which ferry he took to the island and where he last connected."

Vera crossed her arms in front of her broad chest and leaned back.

"And this Fröding…" She shook her head. "We'll get in touch with him for further questioning. Mattias will look up anything we have on him from before. If there is anything."

Sofia looked down at her desk.

"Can you handle the questioning or should I put Mattias on that?"

"Mattias," Sofia replied far too quickly.

"All right, that's settled then." Vera got up but stopped in the doorway.

"Are you OK? You look pale."

–

Fredrik stood up. The beer left his legs feeling wobbly. Marianne started walking down the grassy slope and grabbed two terrycloth towels off the clothesline below her house on the way.

"In case we feel like a swim. I usually borrow the Bohmans' dock. They're in Mallorca," she said as they passed the chapel. "That's Tord's boathouse." Marianne pointed to one of the little red buildings along the shore.

They crossed the pedestrian street and she lifted the latch on the gate before they stepped onto the Bohmans' property. The walkway between their boathouse and the neighbor's wasn't more than a few feet across. The door was open and Fredrik could see the water through the opening. It smelled like saltwater and a little musty. Marianne led the way with a firm grip on the basket and sat down at the far end of the dock. She patted the spot next to her and poured coffee into the cups.

"I missed this view so much when I was living abroad."

"I can see that." Fredrik sat down with his legs dangling over the side of the dock. The water sparkled as if the strait were covered with bits of broken mirror despite the heavy storm clouds in the east. They could see South Ulvön Island across the strait. There were still boats and jet skis out even though it was getting late.

Marianne looked at him.

"Hey, that thing about the Dirks?"

"Yeah?"

"There's more to that story about Thomas than Tord knows about. I didn't want to say anything with him there. It's very embarrassing."

Fredrik set down his cup and looked at Marianne. It was obvious that this was hard for her to talk about. Her lower lashes already glistened with tears and she wiped them carefully with her little fingers to keep her mascara from running.

"I'm so embarrassed. It feels like it was all our fault. Thomas was the instigator, but we were always ready to go along with everything he said. Although he did pay for it later…"

Fredrik handed her a napkin from the basket. She took it and loudly blew her nose.

"Who was we?" he asked.

"Me, Siw-Inger, Annika, everybody, a ragtag bunch of kids thrown together at that camp because our parents couldn't cope or didn't have time for us. But that's no excuse for how we treated Ester. I've felt so terrible about it all these years."

Marianne crumpled up the used napkin and stuffed it down into the basket.

"She was never included when we did things. We used to leave her upstairs when we went swimming, and she didn't have any way to come down on her own. I remember one time when Thomas locked her in the chapel and put a viper in there. Children can be so cruel…"

Fredrik knew all about that. And not just children. Grown-ups could also take pleasure at pressing on other people's sore spots. He had met all sorts over the years. The ones who silently respected his preference not to talk about what had happened and the ones who could barely refrain from blurting out morbid questions. *What was it like in there? Did you see anyone die? Do you have survivor's guilt?*

"Why didn't Aron do anything?"

"Aron didn't need to do anything."

Marianne changed position. They heard thunder rumbling out over the water even though above them the sun was still shining from a clear blue sky. The storm would be upon them soon.

"What do you mean?" Fredrik asked.

"He didn't need to take care of Ester. Bodil did that. She never left her sister's side. Bodil would have walked through fire for her."

"But what did you mean that Thomas paid for it later? He took his own life, didn't he?"

Marianne gazed out at the water. A canoe slid past in front of the dock. The young paddlers raised their paddles and said hello.

"Those are the neighbor girls," Marianne explained before she continued in a quiet voice. She leaned over so close that her forehead almost grazed Fredrik's.

"I'm quite certain that it wasn't suicide at all. Thomas was pushed."

26.

In an Upstairs Bedroom

You innocent, chaste as the new fallen snow.

No one can keep you from your revenge. You are entitled to it, granted by God in his mercy.

Let them know the cleansing flames and the sting of the whip. Let the knotted strands whistle over their backs until flesh is torn from bone.

God is with us. And together we will carry out his work.

27.

After Marianne dropped Fredrik off outside Sofia's house and waved goodbye, he went inside and turned on the lights in the kitchen and the living room. It had started raining and the thunder was booming over the water. It was late, but Sofia wasn't home yet. He could still feel the effects of the beer, but he sat down anyway and made one last attempt to get into Ceder's computer without success. He still didn't know what he was looking for.

A thought had struck him on his way back to Sofia's place. What if the hotel had security cameras? Had he been caught on film taking the bag or leaving the hotel with it? If so, it would just be a matter of time before the police closed in on him. He needed to find out what Ceder had been involved in and why someone had threatened him. Then he could contact the police and tell them everything.

He pulled out the printout of the photo from the summer camp that was in his jacket pocket. There were twelve teenagers in total. After having talked about them all day, he was starting to feel like he knew them. Twelve apostles. Two dead and one missing. One hanged and one burned to death in a fire, and now Adam Ceder was dead, too. But what did all this have to do with Ceder's murder? Did it have anything to do with it at all? He hadn't dared to ask Marianne any more questions. But the threat to Ceder had something to do with that summer camp, Fredrik could sense it. And he was going to find out what.

He was tired and he longed to go to bed, to let his body to rest after smoking all the fish and touring the island by moped, to take a break from thinking about forgotten tragedies and suspicious deaths for a while.

The problem was that he couldn't decide which bed to get into. It felt presumptuous to assume that he had now earned a place in Sofia's bed upstairs, but would she feel hurt if he went to bed in the guest room? Fredrik decided to wait until she came home so that he didn't need to make this decision on his own. He longed for the chance to be close to her again so much it was like a fire inside him, and yet at the same time he wished he could get out of seeing her. The conversation about the future couldn't be far off. But he couldn't stay here forever and play house. The bubble of happiness would pop soon, and he wanted to be far away from Sofia when that happened.

The landline out in the hall started ringing with an urgent ring that Fredrik hadn't heard for years. No one had a landline anymore. He let it ring and walked over to switch on the TV, but only a couple of seconds after the last ring faded away, it started ringing again. It occurred to him that it might be Tord, so he answered it.

"Sofia Hjortén's house. This is Fredrik speaking."

"Oh, I'm so glad you picked up." Sofia sounded stressed.

Fredrik drew his finger over the textured wallpaper.

"I miss you," he said, but regretted the ridiculous words the instant he said them.

Luckily Sofia pretended she hadn't heard him.

"Are you still at the house? Of course you are since you answered the phone. I tried your cell phone, but reception is pretty... Anyway, I'm so glad you answered."

Fredrik walked around the front hall with the phone receiver wedged between his ear and his shoulder. He encountered his reflection in the mirror with its orangey-brown pine frame. Without thinking about what he was doing, he opened the drawer of the low table that stood under the mirror, also made

146

of pine. A few hairclips, an old phone book. He closed the drawer and waited for Sofia to say something more.

"Look, here's the thing…"

The spiral phone cord rubbed against his shoulder as Fredrik opened the closet door next to the hall table.

"We need to talk."

He looked at the clothes hanging there. It smelled stuffy, like mothballs. A red raincoat, a jacket with suede patches on the elbows, and a bunch of very familiar dark blue polo shirts. The creeping sensation in his body and the itching on the backs of his hands returned immediately. He carefully pushed the hangers apart and stared at the black and yellow emblem near the shoulder of the shirts.

"I don't understand?" His question was directed just as much to Sofia as to himself.

"I want you to stay in the house until I get back. We need to talk." Sofia's voice was steadier now, with a sharpness that hadn't been there before, and it didn't take any more than that for the realization to hit Fredrik like a slap on the face.

The bag.

She had tricked him. She had never cared about him. She was a police officer. And she knew.

"Yeah, of course I'll stay." He sounded cheerful and relaxed, a relaxation that could be cut with a knife. "I'll see you in a bit."

Fredrik hung the phone up and stared numbly into the closet.

Then he ran to the bedroom.

28.

An old man with wrinkly hands sat in front of him in the chapel's pews. He flipped back and forth through the hymnal. Two elderly women in floral sundresses sat beside him. They spoke softly to each other, laughing occasionally. Adam turned around to look for the others. None of them were them were there yet, aside from Jan and Siw-Inger. They were already standing by the entrance to help Aron hand out the hymnals.

He wanted to go home, wanted to get out of sitting here and talking about God and Jesus day in and day out in that dilapidated old parsonage. Just because his mother couldn't cope.

The parsonage. It was so creepy that he shivered just thinking about it. There was always something creaking or squeaking there, rats running around in the walls. And then Thomas. Not that he thought Ester was so much fun either, but it was starting to get out of hand. He was staying in the room underneath hers and he could hear her crying sometimes. She couldn't be feeling good at all. Why didn't Aron do something?

The door to the chapel opened. Thomas came in and sat down beside him in the pew. Mats, Christine, Mona, and the Russian girls came in after him and sat down behind them. Soon Aron came in as well. He wobbled along down the aisle in his long, white cassock. Then came Ester. Bodil guided her solemnly along in front of her as if she were sacred.

Thomas turned and not so quietly whispered, "Here comes the rolling saint. Praise the Lord!"

Christine hushed him curtly.

"Don't you know that Ester was chosen by God? She's protected by a holy angel."

Thomas burst out laughing and Mats promptly joined him.

Adam looked down at his watch, wishing he could magically make the time pass.

29.

He looked down at his feet, panic-stricken. The icy cold water was rushing in under the door. He kicked at the door with all his might, but the weight of the tremendous volume of water made it impossible to budge. The water level rose second by second and he backed away in terror toward to rear wall of the cabin. His back hit the window and when he turned around he saw that greenish black water filled the entire outside of the windowpane. He saw naked, white bodies outside. They were being pushed down into the darkness by the weight of the ferry. Terrified eyes. The door was bulging alarmingly inward, seconds from breaking. Despite the roaring mass of water outside, he heard Niklas clearly, screaming in terror from the hallway.

The door was ripped from the frame, and water gushed into the cabin.

He screamed.

Fredrik looked around in confusion. The ferry. The steady hum of the fully functioning engines below him. His clothes were plastered to his body. He discreetly stuck his hand between his legs to make sure he hadn't wet himself. The woman across the aisle looked at him and he forced a placating smile.

"Nightmare."

When the ferry reached the Köpmanholmen ferry terminal, Fredrik was the first person to get off. There had only been a handful of passengers on the boat. The backs of his hands were itching like crazy, but he felt a certain amount of pride at having handled the crossing. With his eyes riveted on the horizon, he had convulsively clutched the handrailing outside under the roof on the aft deck. He had just barely succeeded in parrying the rough seas. The rain ran in swift streams down the red paint on the vehicle deck, but he didn't dare enter the lounge. A more experienced traveler probably wouldn't have even blinked at the gentle summer swells, but to him every rocking motion felt like the ferry was capsizing. He shivered. His leather jacket was still at Sofia's place and all he had was the thin, soaking shirt on his back. In the end he had been forced to relent and, very much against his will, he had gone down into the lounge where at least it was warm and dry. The condensation on the windows had helped him ignore the fact that he was sitting on a boat. Ultimately he had fallen asleep from sheer exhaustion.

The Skoda was still there waiting for him in the almost empty parking lot. Ceder's SUV was also still there with police tape wrapped around it. So the police had found it. Yet again, Fredrik was struck by how unreal the situation was. It had only been a couple of days since he had been here, but everything that had happened since then had made a mess of time. When he thought back to himself, just a few steps behind Adam Ceder right here on this dock on Midsummer Eve, it felt like he was watching a movie, an unrealistic movie. He walked over to use the restroom in the restaurant at the ferry terminal. It was late already and he was going to need to drive all night to get home.

The restaurant, creatively named Kajen, meaning The Dock, was in a red wooden building. The place was empty aside from a few construction workers with suntanned arms and reflective vests eating schnitzel. Fredrik slipped past them and into the bathroom.

He pulled his phone out of his pocket and dialed Philip's number.

"Freddy." He sounded distracted, and Fredrik could hear muffled battle sounds and cries from a video game in the background.

"I need your help. I'm in one hell of a predicament."

The video game noises stopped abruptly, and Philip's voice took on a new edginess.

"What happened?"

"You're not going to like it. I have a computer that I can't get into. It's not mine, but…"

"Forget it!" Fredrik just had time to hear the video game resume before Philip hung up on him.

He didn't bother calling back. It was better to go there in person. He rinsed his face thoroughly with cold water and dried himself with a paper towel. His anxiety had returned with the force of a wrecking ball. This was serious. The police must have found out about his argument with Ceder and knew that he had the bag. Did they think he had killed him? Why hadn't Sofia arrested him right away? Fredrik reached for the blister pack of pills in his pocket. He had taken two pills at Sofia's house and another two on the ferry as they neared land, but now he took two more. They felt comfortingly scratchy going down his throat.

He had found a red women's bicycle the woodshed with crooked handlebars that he had managed to extract. He had nearly crashed into the waterlily pond in front of the house, but he had managed to get the bike going the right way and had ridden the two miles to the harbor without encountering Sofia or anyone else. It had started to rain when he was about halfway there, a steady, angry rain.

He looked at his reflection. His face was dim and blurry around the edges. The result of the pills and the beers he had drunk with Marianne and Tord.

He definitely should not drive a car today.

Tuesday, June 25

30.

She was already awake when Tord put his key into the door. She had been awake for long stretches of the night, sitting in the rocking chair out on the deck. The rain had let up and left the air clear and easy to breathe. Even so, every breath caught in her throat.

He was gone.

His clothes were gone and his cell phone was turned off. She had called about ten times and then given up. Fredrik obviously wasn't planning to answer. She felt so incredibly humiliated, and yet she didn't have the energy to be angry.

Fredrik's disappearance couldn't mean anything other than that he was guilty. Why else would he leave? What was she going to say to Vera? The word *misconduct* darted through her head and her dream of one day taking over Vera's job fell apart in her heart. Would she even still have a job once all this got out?

"Are you sitting out here in the cold?" Tord tromped over and sat down on the sofa facing her.

"I can't sleep."

"Where's Mr. Zero Eight?"

"He's gone." The tears burned inside her eyelids and she turned her face away in annoyance. Tord leaned forward in dismay and hugged her.

"Oh, little girl, what happened?"

His hug was warm and smelled of coffee and fabric softener, the wonderfully safe way he had always smelled. Her father, Sten, and Tord had known each other since they were kids.

They had been like brothers only better, Tord liked to say. For as long as Sofia could remember, they had wrapped up each workday together down by the dock with a thermos of coffee, regardless of the weather. On Saturdays they used to take a six-pack of beer and submerged it in the icy seawater to cool while they left their fishing rods unattended on the rests. Sofia had joined them occasionally. Those were some of her best memories from her childhood.

"Let's hear it."

The tears exploded out of her in hard bursts, impossible to hold in. Tord patted her back and said there there, rocking her gently in his arms until her tears petered out.

"Don't cry. He'll be back. You'll see."

Sofia didn't know why she was crying. She was furious! A liar, possibly a murderer, had smiled his way into her home and now he was going to rob her of the career she had fought so hard for. She had been invaded, intimately—although she had been the one who initiated all of that. She had invited him to stay, offered herself to him.

"He's not coming back."

"You don't know that."

Tord leaned back on the sofa, but still kept his hand comfortingly on her leg.

"He's not a good person."

Tord chuckled.

"I said that about Yvonne, too. But I've never loved anyone the way I loved her. And she me. We drove each other crazy, but even so, we couldn't tear ourselves away from each other. If she hadn't gotten that job in Eskilstuna, we would probably still be standing there in the same kitchen screaming at each other. And loving each other."

"This is a little more complicated than that." Sofia looked at Tord dejectedly.

"Believe me," Tord insisted. "He's coming back."

Fredrik parked his car in the Lindén family's driveway and walked up the front steps. The door was locked. Their unit was at the end of the line of townhouses, so he walked around the back and, uncharacteristically, found Philip out there. He was sitting in a white Adirondack chair with the morning sun on his face. Big, mint-green earphones on his head and his cell phone propped on his knee, which he had pulled up. Fredrik sat down across from him and moved the chair so he was under the shade of the awning.

"You look like shit."

Fredrik nodded, well aware that the fatigue must be obvious. It was a miracle that he had survived the drive home. Somewhere near Gävle he had nodded off behind the wheel and almost clipped the center divider.

Philip leaned forward and lit a cigarette. He held the pack out to Fredrik, who shook his head.

"I haven't had time to check into Ceder, if that's what you're wondering. But I read about him in the papers. What the hell happened, Freddy?"

Fredrik looked down at his hands.

"It's so stupid. I followed him. I wanted to talk to him, you know? And now he's dead."

"But how?" The next question came before Fredrik had time to answer the first one. "Followed him where?"

"To Örnsköldsvik, up north on the High Coast."

Philip stared at him bug-eyed.

"Örnsköldsvik? That's gotta be, what, 200 miles?"

"Three hundred."

Philip snorted cigarette smoke out of his nose.

"So you followed Ceder for 300 miles and now he's dead? What do the police say?"

The air went out of Fredrik. He tiredly rubbed the bridge of his nose. His hands continued over his forehead and unwashed hair.

"I don't know."

"Fredrik, what the hell…"

"I know, I know." He held up his hands and leaned back in the lawn furniture. "At any rate, I have his computer."

"Uh, how did you get that, if I might ask?"

"I don't know…"

Philip leaned forward to put out his cigarette in the cola can sitting on the table between them. He looked at Fredrik, appalled.

"Oh, come on!" Fredrik said exasperated. "You get that I didn't kill him, right? I probably found it somewhere. In the worst-case scenario, I broke into his hotel room. I was totally out of it that night, but I didn't kill him. I swear!"

He looked out at the minimal backyard. Two boys who were about twelve were running around with a soccer ball. That could have been them twenty years ago.

"What do you think? Can you help me search it? Since I might be a suspect." Fredrik pulled the laptop out of his bag and held it out beseechingly to Philip.

Philip hesitated, his eyes locked on Fredrik's.

"Do you understand how this is going to look if people find out?"

"I'm sorry," Fredrik said with a nod. "I…"

Philip softened.

"Ugh, give me that. I'll take a look."

He reached out his hand, grabbed the computer, and gestured with a jerk of his head that they should go inside.

"And what am I looking for?"

"A motive for murder."

31

Sofia hurried down the well-worn path to the red boathouse. She stepped out onto the dock and set her backpack down while she undid the mooring line holding the boat in place. The swim ladder, which she had forgotten to bring inside last fall, had been snapped off by the ice and dangled from the side of the dock, sad and unusable. She had to sit down on her butt to hop down into the boat. She started the motor and headed north through the channel between Runön Island and Ulvön, past the lighthouse just off the northern tip of Runön Island. Thinking about Fredrik made her want to throw up. What had she done?

As she came out of the channel, she sped up, allowing the boat to run at full throttle. Out on the open water, the wind was still cold despite the warm weather they'd had for Midsummer. The Horse chugged along beneath her, full of life. With the back of her hand she stroked the varnished wood. She wished her dad were here now. He would have known what to do.

As Sofia entered the police station, there was already a long line at the front desk.

"Good morning!" Eva said, waving through her opening, which made everyone in the line turn around and look at her. Sofia smiled halfheartedly at them and hurried in the door to the investigative unit's offices. She was a couple of minutes late and didn't have time to grab a cup of coffee. She went straight into the library where everyone was already waiting for her.

"Your highness." Mattias bowed elaborately to her.

"Let's get started then." Vera glared in her direction. "The autopsy is finished. They did us a hell of a favor by granting us priority, so don't forget to thank Fridell the next time you see her. The report will come in after lunch. The sister formally IDed our victim as Adam Ceder. He was married one time, no children. He got divorced in the mid 90s. His ex-wife's name is Mari-Liis Ceder, born in Pärnu, Estonia, in 1957. We'll question her as well, but I doubt she knows anything about Adam's current activities. She remarried a long time ago and emigrated."

"Let's go around the table," Vera said, opening things up. "What have we got?"

"The rumors that the Ulvö Hotel is for sale are true," Karim began. "Several staff members confirm that Karst wants to sell. The interesting part isn't that she wanted to sell, but that people say Mona Höglund wants to buy it."

"Mona?" Sofia stared at Karim, taken aback. "Where's she going to get the money from?"

He shrugged.

"Maybe there's a motive here?" Marie turned to Vera, who stood up and started writing something next to Adam Ceder's picture on the whiteboard.

Vera slapped the pen against her hand a couple of times.

"Maybe someone wanted to stop Ceder from buying the Ulvö Hotel? We need to find out all we can about the sale. Were there multiple prospective buyers? Financial problems? Karim, can you keep digging into this?"

Karim nodded.

"We need to talk to the family and find out more about Ceder's background and what he was doing on Ulvön Island. Was he meeting someone there or not? Ask his employees, too, and see if the hotel chain had plans to expand to the north. Sofia, you can look into that when you get to Stockholm," Vera said.

Sofia nodded reluctantly.

"I've looked in this Fröding guy," Mattias said. He pulled a couple of printed pages out of a plastic folder and spread them out across the table.

"Fredrik Fröding, born March 5, 1981. Parents Göran and Gunnel Fröding, both deceased. Living on Brahegatan in Stockholm's Östermalm neighborhood since 1995. The apartment originally belonged to his maternal grandmother, but she has also passed away since then. No criminal record. Marital status, single. No children."

"Is that all?" Vera asked. "No ties to the Ceder hotels or the Karst family?"

"Not that I could find. He seems to have lived a fairly anonymous life. He started working for the passport office in Solna in 2006. Then he was registered with the Social Insurance Agency a couple of times, out of work on disability at various points. In 2015, he went back to work, but at the passport office in Sollentuna this time. No debt, but also no real assets aside from the apartment and a car that's practically an antique now."

"Do we think he did it?" Marie asked.

"Obviously he did it," Mattias scoffed. "Disabled, single, and mentally unstable. I wouldn't be surprised if he was working as a hit man for someone. Maybe someone who didn't want the sale to go through sent him up here to bump off Ceder."

"Bump off?" Sure, maybe Sofia didn't know Fredrik that well, but he wasn't a hitman.

"Why not? Do you have a better theory?" Vera interjected. "Mattias, you keep looking into Fröding. Find out more about him. Old girlfriends, classmates, bosses, case managers from the Social Insurance Agency, teachers. And fucking haul him in here for questioning! Sofia, you do the same thing, but for Christine Karst. The woman should understand that she needs to get in touch when one of her hotel guests is found dead. Talk to everyone on the Ulvö Hotel staff again today. You know the people out there. Maybe you can pry something more out of them. Bring Marie. And make sure you talk to Mona again. We need to access the server room and look at that surveillance footage. Ask if there's anything to the rumors that she was interested in buying the hotel, too."

Vera took a deep breath before she continued.

"Marie, you keep working on Ceder. Plot out a timeline of his final days. I'll get in touch with the prosecutor and give her an update. The investigation has been assigned Karin Åhlén."

A collective sigh could be heard throughout the room. Karin Åhlén was the most diligent prosecutor ever employed by the Swedish Prosecution Authority. She was always available by phone, even when she wasn't on duty, and it rarely took long to obtain arrest or search warrants. On the other hand, she demanded that the investigating officers for her cases constantly appear in district court, in case questions should arise, which made the whole station shun her like the plague. No one had time for that kind of additional work.

Everyone started to leave the table. Sofia struggled to get her backpack free from where it was stuck on her chair leg.

"Sofia, I want you on a plane to Stockholm no later than tomorrow. And get in touch with Marklund!"

Vera pointed her whiteboard pen impatiently at Sofia before replacing the cap with a click and setting it on the shelf below the whiteboard.

Marie had stopped just outside the door to wait for Sofia.

"Kaj Marklund? Isn't he the guy who's married to Mette Severin?"

Sofia nodded without making eye contact with Marie.

"She is so amazing! I loved her in that last production of Strindberg's 'Miss Julie.' Do you know her?"

Sofia shrugged in response. She could hardly claim to know Mette. Kaj, on the other hand, she knew.

–

Fredrik stood on the sidewalk gazing up at Torsten's office. He had swung by his apartment first to shower, change his clothes, and carefully brush his teeth. Nervousness crackled through his bloodstream. He hesitated before reaching for the intercom button by the door. He reviewed the speech he had prepared in his head and then pressed the button. The door buzzed and he stepped into the soft silence.

Torsten stood in his open doorway waving to him.

"You look good, fresh. Did you get some sun over Midsummer?"

Fredrik wondered at first if Torsten was making fun of him, but he quickly realized that he wasn't. He sat down in the visitor's chair and Torsten immediately started to fuss about, moving his chair around from behind the desk. He leaned forward and patted him amicably on the knee.

"Really fresh. How are you doing?"

"Good." Fredrik leaned back in his seat to avoid his psychiatrist's penetrating look.

Even though Torsten had made demands of him over the years, he was the closest thing Fredrik had to a parent and he didn't want to disappoint him.

"I was away for the holiday. I met a girl." To his astonishment, he blushed.

Torsten whistled, impressed.

"Well, well, well. What's her name?"

"Sofia."

"So, how does the future look for Fredrik and Sofia?" Torsten smiled knowingly.

"Bright, I hope."

A lie more based on hope than likelihood.

"So, I wanted to talk about the business with the clinic in Sundsvall. I know what you said about the pills and…" Fredrik sought out eye contact with Torsten and then held it. "But I'm feeling so good now. I really want to give it a try with this girl, and if I'm doing inpatient therapy, the whole thing might fall apart. Do you think you could prescribe the pills anyway? If everything falls apart with the relationship, then I promise I'll go."

Torsten contemplated him.

"And Niklas?"

Fredrik picked at the button on the cuff of his sleeve. He had trouble saying it. "Niklas is dead. I suppose I've held onto him so that I had something... someone. Now that I actually have someone, it's like my thoughts about Niklas are starting to fade away."

Torsten reached for his laptop, a sign that he was going to write out the prescription. Fredrik held his breath.

"You've made good progress, Fredrik. More than the whole time I've known you. Whoever this Sofia is, make sure you hold onto her. She seems good for you."

Fredrik smiled and nodded in agreement.

"So you won't be searching for your little brother anymore?"

Fredrik did his best to keep his eyes steady.

"No." He didn't know if he believed it himself, but he sounded sincere.

Torsten patted him encouragingly on the thigh as if Fredrik were a horse that had run a good race.

Fredrik looked out the window while Torsten typed on his laptop. His thoughts turned to that freezing cold night. The waves coming in so hard that the staff had to take the glasses and bottles down from the shelves in the bar. Drunk passengers reeling across the thick wall to wall carpeting with brightly colored drinks in their hands. One or two families with children who were still awake. Parents holding on tightly to their little ones to keep them from falling as the boat swayed back and forth. No one was afraid, not yet. No one realized that something that couldn't happen was actually going to happen.

Fredrik was roused from his thoughts by Torsten's phone ringing.

"I'm sorry, Fredrik. I forgot to turn it off."

He waved his hand to indicate that he didn't mind and Torsten answered the call.

"Do you mind holding for a moment?" Torsten didn't wait for a response, just held the phone to his chest while he whispered to Fredrik, who had gotten up and now had his hand on the doorknob. "Your prescription is in the system. You can just go pick them up."

Fredrik nodded in thanks and quietly closed the door behind him.

32.

"Let's start with the autopsy report." Vera pushed a stack of papers across the table. Everyone grabbed a copy and Sofia noted with satisfaction that Mattias was late for their afternoon meeting.

"The toxicology report isn't available yet. We have priority on that one, too, but it's still going to take a couple of days, next week at the latest. In terms of the autopsy itself, Fridell confirms that the blow to the head was the cause of death. That's not a big surprise. She thinks the murder weapon might have been a hammer." Vera flipped through the pages to a sketch that Fridell had made to describe the various parts of the murder weapon. "There are marks from a blunt hexagonal object, e.g., the head of the hammer. And from the claw on the back, which cracked the skull and penetrated the brain just above the right eye."

Marie pursed her lips in disgust.

"The location of the injury indicates that the killer was tall. It would also clearly take a hell of a lot of strength to kill someone in as few blows as Ceder received. Incidentally, where's Mattias?"

"He's on the phone with Fröding's psychiatrist," Karim said.

"And Christine Karst, have you gotten ahold of her, Sofia?"

"No."

"How about Mona Höglund?"

"No, not yet. But I did receive the passenger lists I requested for the flights to Alicante on Midsummer's Day. Christine Karst had a reservation on Norwegian Airlines flight DY4203, which departed Stockholm around lunchtime, but she was not on that flight or on any of the other flights to Alicante that day."

"Where the hell is that woman?" Vera flung up her hands in irritation.

"One of the housekeepers at the Ulvö Hotel mentioned that Christine has a private boat. It's apparently one of those big, expensive deals. I checked and it's not moored by the hotel and no one saw it dock at Köpmanholmen either."

"If she took her own boat, shouldn't we check Örnsköldsvik Marina instead of Köpmanholmen?" Marie asked. "That would be the closest if you were trying to catch a flight, wouldn't it?"

"Have you checked on that?" Vera asked, staring at Sofia, who shook her head.

"Go check it out," Vera nodded toward the door with her head. The marina was only a few blocks from the police station, and she could walk down there in under ten minutes. Sofia stood up, eying Vera uncertainly.

"Not right now," Vera hissed when she realized that Sofia had started to head for the door. Sofia stood there for a few seconds before taking a seat again, this time in the chair that was closest. Marie gave her a pitying look.

"If Christine isn't in Alicante, wasn't on any of the flights, and her boat isn't in the marina, maybe it's time we start considering whether she might be involved in the murder. Maybe she's deliberately staying away. We should go public with a description of her and say that she's wanted for questioning," Karim said. "Apparently she keeps a room at the hotel, too. We should see if we can gain access to it."

Vera nodded in agreement.

"Sofia, will you ask the staff about her boat as well? Find out if anyone has seen it around Ulvön since midsummer. I'll talk to Åhlén about a warrant so you and Marie can search Christine's room while you're there. Marie, how is it going with the timeline on Ceder?"

"I'm waiting for a list of his calls and bank withdrawals. I should receive them sometime today."

The door flew open and Mattias pushed his way past Sofia without apologizing. He walked right up to Vera and handed her a stack of papers. His whole attitude made it obvious that he had found something, and it didn't take long for Vera to react. She nodded, impressed, as she read, and then handed the stack of paperwork back to Mattias.

"The MS *Estonia*!" He shook the pieces of paper.

Images of empty life rafts from TV news broadcasts popped into Sofia's head. The bow visor being slowly hoisted above the surface of the Baltic Sea, grainy black and white photos of the text on the side of the ferry, deep underwater.

"What does the *Estonia* have to do with this investigation?" Marie asked.

Mattias cleared his throat. He like a proud rooster preparing for a cockfight standing there beside Vera.

"Guess who was onboard the *Estonia* when she sank that night?"

I suffer from PTSD... My parents died in an accident. In the fall of '94.

Sofia put her head in her hands.

Mattias took a few strutting steps over to the whiteboard and taped up the picture of Fredrik.

"Fredrik Fröding."

Marie's hand reached for the cross she wore around her neck.

"And...?" Karim asked, scratching his chin. "What does that have to do with this?"

Mattias made a big show of pulling out a chair, sitting down, and arranging his papers in front of him before he continued, fully aware that everyone's eyes were on him.

"According to Fröding's psychiatrist," he allowed his eyes to roam over the documents, even though he must have just spoken to the psychiatrist only moments before, "a Torsten Bredh, Fröding was onboard the *Estonia* with his parents and his younger brother the night it sank." Mattias made yet another ham-fisted attempt at a dramatic pause, which made Vera clear her throat, so he hurriedly continued. "Fröding and his brother made it out onto the deck. Against fucking slim odds, they made it into the same life raft and survived until well into the night. But just as they were being rescued, the brother, Niklas, was apparently washed off the life raft by a wave and disappeared into the Baltic."

Sofia stared down at the table.

Oh my God, no wonder Fredrik is a mess.

"According to Bredh, over the last twenty-five years, Fröding has never lost faith that his brother survived. He suffers from 'obvious symptoms of a panic disorder with clear signs of PTSD.'" Mattias made air quotes around the diagnosis as he read.

"Um, but what does that have to do with Ceder?" Karim persisted.

"I'm getting to that." Mattias placed his hands on the tabletop. "Bredh also said that Fröding suffers from hallucinations, and that these frequently occur when he takes a prescription medication that Bredh himself has prescribed for Fröding over the years... benzda... benzdio..."

"Benzodiazepines," Vera supplied the word with her back to them. She wrote something on the board and then turned to the group. "What Mattias is trying to say is that Fröding suffers from hallucinations and takes a strong, prescription medication. At his second to last appointment with his psychiatrist, Fröding reportedly said that he had seen his brother Niklas in Stockholm's Östermalm neighborhood, but that he disappeared again before Fröding could reach him."

"Disappeared where?" Sofia asked, staring at her.

Vera's eyes gleamed as she answered and Mattias grinned broadly.

"Into Adam Ceder's hotel."

33.

Sofia slowed down and stretched out over the helm so she could scan the wide dock below the Ulvö Hotel. Usually there was a jumble of wooden boats, motorboats, and German yachts here, but there weren't so many visitors today. She deftly maneuvered the Horse up to the dock.

There was no sign of the hubbub of a few days ago. The blue and white police tape was gone, although the few tourists who were strolling along the waterfront did appear somewhat subdued.

She squinted up at the white and gray painted wooden hotel. There had been a lot of debate about the construction of the new hotel. Change and development always brought up strong feelings, especially on a rural island where many people had lived the same way generation after generation. Some residents claimed the new hotel was a necessary investment to keep Ulvön Island thriving, whereas reactionaries felt like the modern hotel was going to irreparably alter the island way of life. Now that the new hotel had been finished for many years, the people who had embraced change had turned out to be right. The new hotel had brought with it a feeling of confidence in the future. It had created jobs and at the same time reinvigorated the island's other businesses.

"What should I do with this?" Marie held up the life jacket she had just taken off.

Sofia had almost forgotten that her colleague was in the boat with her. Whenever she was out at sea, the wind seemed to blow every thought out of her head. Now, as her feet touched land again, everything came back to her—Fredrik, the investigation, the *Estonia*, Ceder...

"Just toss it in the cockpit."

Marie stuffed the life jacket in and clambered out onto the dock. Sofia followed her up to the front entrance of the hotel. Mona Höglund stood just inside the glass doors. She picked up a couple of brochures that had been lying on the front desk and looked them resolutely in the eye.

"Good that you came. I've been trying to reach you."

Sofia gave Mona a questioning look.

"I was just in the server room, and it appears that the surveillance footage from the night that Ceder... Well, the footage simply isn't there anymore."

"Someone erased it?"

"I don't know."

"Who besides you has access to the server room?" Marie leaned in over the front desk and Mona immediately straightened up the brochures, which just slid into disarray again.

"No one, but I think maybe it happened because of the upgrade?"

Sofia nodded, and her eyes met Marie's.

"We'll look into it. Could you write down the name of the company that handled the upgrade?"

Mona reached for a pen and a pad of sticky notes.

"We'd like to take a look in Christine's room," Marie said.

"Why?" Mona stopped writing and looked up at them.

"We have a search warrant. Would you show us the room please?"

Mona reluctantly turned around and reached for a key from behind the counter before passing Sofia the yellow sticky note.

"There's one other thing, too," Sofia said. "We've heard that the hotel is for sale and that you're interested in buying it."

Mona laughed sarcastically.

"Me? Well, that would certainly be a dream come true, but there isn't a chance in the world that I could afford it. Who's saying that I'm interested?"

"That's not important. The question is whether it's true?"

"People gossip about so many things, but, no, I'm not going to buy the hotel." She nodded toward the stairs. "Shall we go up?"

The room was small but pleasantly furnished in the same white and gray nautical theme as the rest of the hotel. Sofia began in the bathroom. It wasn't big either. Light shades of gray that faded into each other, white porcelain bathroom fixtures, and a frosted glass enclosure for the shower. A couple of contact lens cases sat next to the sink. Most of the drawers underneath were empty, but she found a hairbrush and a toothbrush. There were bottles of shampoo and conditioner on the shelf in the shower, one of the more expensive brands, as well as a razor.

"Did you find anything?" Sofia closed the door to the bathroom behind her and looked at the items Marie had taken out of the nightstands and the desk. A notepad, some pens, a pair of headphones, and some other impersonal little things clearly showed that Christine didn't stay here very often.

"No," Marie replied from the floor under the bed. "How about you?"

"Nothing that suggests that she's deliberately staying away." Sofia looked around the room. Why would you keep a hotel room waiting for you year-round if you hardly ever used it? Surely that's a needless expense? Although if you owned the place, you owned it.

"A phone." Marie popped up next to the bed with a cell phone that was still connected to a charger plugged into the wall. "No passcode." She unplugged the charger and passed the phone to Sofia, who put it into a plastic bag.

"A cell phone isn't usually something you leave behind when you go abroad, is it?"

Marie shook her head in response.

"All right, I think we've done it." Sofia looked around the room one last time to make sure they hadn't missed anything.

Marie nodded and carefully replaced the items she had taken out.

"I can take that back to town with me," Marie said, pointing to the bag containing the phone. "There's a ferry leaving in 15 minutes."

"I'm staying here," Sofia said.

Marie gave her the thumbs up, took the bag, and disappeared out the door. Just then Sofia's cell phone rang. Vera's number.

"Did you find anything?"

"A cell phone. Marie is bringing it in now."

"And you?"

"I'm going to stay here and talk to the staff. We ran into Mona Höglund. She was adamant that she is not a prospective buyer for the hotel. But, listen to this. She claims that the surveillance footage from the night of the murder was erased due to an upgrade in the IT system."

"Oh paint me a fucking picture." Vera coughed on the other end of the call. "You'll have to ask the staff if it's really true, that she's not about to buy the hotel. At any rate, Mattias has been looking into Fröding. Åhlén approved us to run a full check on him. Our colleagues in Stockholm were going to go by his apartment tonight and see if they can get ahold of him. What do you think?"

Say it now.

No matter how Sofia looked at it, her actions were going to be interpreted as her deliberately withholding information. It wouldn't merely cost her her job. There would also be legal repercussions. She made sure the door to the hotel room was locked and then walked downstairs to the front desk before she responded.

"We don't have any motive to suggest it could be him."

"No, but we do have a bunch of fucking clues," Vera said.

"I have to return a key now. We'll talk when I get back from Stockholm."

Then she hung up.

–

When Fredrik stepped in the front door of his building on Brahegatan again, he ran into the manager, who was also the owner of the building. He was on his way out to the courtyard in the back, a half flight of stairs up from the front door. Fredrik nodded in greeting but didn't slow down so as to avoid being pulled into conversation. The manager's job seemed to focus more on roaming around gossiping with the residents than anything more practical. He could easily spend half an hour talking—without even pausing to take a breath—about how few residents had attended the last co-op board meeting, and Fredrik had no desire to listen to the whole rigamarole now.

All he wanted was to tumble into bed. He had picked up the pills Torsten had prescribed, and two of them were already spreading a chemical calm through his bloodstream. He took the stairs two wobbly steps at a time and after numerous attempts he succeeded in inserting his key into the keyhole. There were a few pieces of junk mail and a bill left on the hall carpet. He scooted them aside with his foot and went to open his bedroom window. A warm summer breeze blew into the room. Since his sheets were anything but clean, he just lay down on top of the blanket without even taking off his shoes or his clothes.

Sleep was slow in coming even though he was more tired than he had ever been in his whole life. His thoughts came like molasses and rapidly, both at the same time. Fragments of memories from the last few days blended with the familiar smell of his grandmother's apartment and his hometown. The look in Sofia's eyes when she hugged him on her deck, Tord with his lip full of snus, Adam Ceder's angry face, Niklas, the bag, that hanged teenager… His thoughts were like a thick porridge and soon he was there again. On the ferry, yelling for his parents and his brother.

A signal suddenly caught his attention, someone talking, echoey voices, then the signal again.

Fredrik sat up in bed, wide awake. He had only been asleep for a few minutes, all his senses were on high alert. The window had blown all the way open. He leaned over the deep windowsill and looked down. Down below, he discovered what he had already suspected. A police car with its door open. A uniformed policeman climbed out of the passenger door and the sound of the police radio followed him like a tail onto the sidewalk.

Fredrik looked around his apartment in a panic. Ceder's bag was sitting just inside his front door. Without the computer, but still, full of his clothes. He pulled it open and started dumping his own clothes into it from his closet. Cell phone charger, passport, his own laptop, a spare pair of shoes, a hoodie, and a hat from the hat shelf. Before he left the apartment, he ran to the freezer and grabbed the bag of 500 kroner bills that he had been saving for emergency situations. It was thinner than he remembered, but it was better than nothing. One last glance out the window. The police were still standing on the sidewalk down below. One of them was talking on the phone.

He walked back to his front door and cautiously opened it. No one on the landing. As quietly as he could, he ran down the stairs to the exit that led to the courtyard. Just as he felt the fresh air hit him and smelled the scent of the plants, he heard the police yanking on the front door of the building.

He adjusted Ceder's bag on his back, aimed for the door directly across the courtyard, and ran.

34

By the time Sofia returned to the front desk, Mona had disappeared. She handed in the key to the young woman behind the counter and asked to take a look in the server room, which was now unlocked. Sofia was quickly able to confirm that the door had not been jimmied or forced in any way. Maybe Mona's theory was right, and the surveillance footage really had been erased by mistake during the upgrade. She took out the sticky note with the name of the company that had done the work and dialed the number. Five minutes later she was talking to a technician. He confirmed that the footage could very well have been deleted since the storage was connected to the rest of the system.

She realized that she hadn't eaten anything since breakfast and decided to eat out on the patio before she started talking to the staff members. She ordered a cup of black coffee and a sandwich.

"I heard things got a little out of hand on Midsummer?" An older man in a red Helly Hansen fleece and rain boots leaned over to her familiarly from a neighboring table: Birger Hedlund, who had been the Ulvö Hotel's head cook since time immemorial. Next to Tord, Birger was probably the one who kept the closest tabs on what went on on the island.

Sofia smiled disarmingly at him. With fewer than 35 year-round residents on the island, she couldn't set foot here without running into someone who knew who she was, what she did for a living, and whose kid she was. She nodded gratefully to the waitress as she placed her coffee and sandwich down on the table.

"How's the investigation going? You must be busting your chops at the station now. But I suppose you're used to this kind of thing from your time in the big city?" Birger didn't wait for her to respond before he continued. "Personally, I've never understood the appeal of city life. A bunch of crazies getting in gang wars, people working twenty hours a day and paying millions of kroner for apartments that are no bigger than some Jukkasjärvi outhouse."

"Oh, it's not that bad." Sofia smiled and took a bite of her sandwich. Salami and brie, her favorite, but it didn't taste good today. She set it down on the plate and folded up her napkin.

"Poor guy, beaten to death and dumped in the ocean. What a fate," Birger continued, surely fishing for her to divulge some tidbit about the investigation.

"Hey, have you seen the Karsts' boat around here lately?" Sofia asked.

He thought about it for a bit before he replied.

"No. It's usually down at the end of the guest marina, but now that you mention it, I haven't seen it since before Midsummer. Why?"

Sofia pushed away her plate, the sandwich almost untouched.

"Do you know them well?" she asked, nodding back toward the hotel.

"The Karsts? No better than anyone else. I mean, they're never here." He scratched the underside of his chin, thinking. "Do you think Christine has something to do with this whole thing?"

"We don't think anything. We just want to get in touch with her. How about Mona Höglund then?"

"You mean Little Boss?" Birger laughed. "She's probably around here somewhere..."

"But what do you know about her?"

"Not so much. I mean, she's been running around here since she was a child, but I can't exactly say that I know her. Her father was the supervisor at the old hotel. You remember Yngve, don't you?"

Sofia nodded. She remembered him well. He had been Gisela Karst's right hand, running the hotel when she was out traipsing around the world performing as a concert pianist. She hadn't seemed interested in her daughter or the hotel. She had left them both in the hands of other people to look after. Yngve had been fond of booze, Sofia seemed to recall. She didn't know when Mona officially took over as manager, but it wasn't so far-fetched to think that she had already been doing the work for years before that. It must have happened back when Sofia was living in Stockholm. Still, she thought, funny that both Christine and Mona had taken over their parents' jobs.

"Mona has a husband, two kids, and a house on the mainland," Birger continued, trying to pick something out from between his teeth with the corner of his napkin. "I think she moonlights as a nurse in town over the winter."

One of the servers came out onto the patio and Sofia finished her coffee, nodded a quick goodbye to Birger and headed after her.

"Excuse me?" Sofia began.

The young woman turned around with a smile. Sofia recognized her from the swimming lessons that used to be offered out at Sandviken. She was the daughter of one of the residents and usually took shifts at the hotel in the summer.

"I'm Sofia Hjortén. I'm with the local police. Do you have a couple of minutes to talk?" She held out her hand and the server shook it after slipping her cell phone into the pocket on her server's apron.

"Linda Pihlgren. You're Sten's daughter, aren't you?"

Sofia nodded.

"Is this about the murder?"

"I'd actually like to talk to you about Christine Karst," Sofia said. "Did you know that she was planning to sell the place?"

"I've only heard the rumors. People in the kitchen have been saying that Ceder was here to buy the hotel. Is that true?"

"We don't know, but it's one possibility that we're looking into."

"I also heard that Mona was going to buy the place, but I don't actually know," Linda said, smoothing her carefully combed bun. "Although, you know, how could she afford it?"

"When did you see her last?"

"You mean Christine? On Midsummer's Eve."

"Do you know when she left the hotel?"

"She was going to leave the next morning, to go stay with her mother in Spain, I think. She was planning to take the first boat on Midsummer's Day."

"Did you talk to her on Midsummer's Eve?"

"Yeah, I did actually. She came up to me and asked me how things were going at school and if I wanted to pick up any hours this year working at the Christmas buffet again."

"How did she seem?"

Linda thought that over.

"Stressed? But she always seems kind of stressed." Linda leaned closer to Sofia. "They say she's got a problem with her nerves."

Sofia was taken aback to hear someone as young as Linda use an expression like "problem with her nerves." Hadn't we made more progress than that when it came to mental illnesses?

"What happened after that?"

"Nothing. She moved on to talk to some of the other staff members and I kept working."

"Do you know where she went after that?"

Linda shook her head and then said, "she had a meeting. It sounded like maybe with some kind of bigshot. Maybe it was with that Ceder guy?"

Smart girl, Sofia thought.

"On Midsummer's Eve?"

"She's only here once or twice a year and when she is, she always holds an all-hands meeting."

"How about Mona then? Did you see her on Midsummer's Eve?"

"No, I was serving the tables out on the patio all night. The crowd was really rowdy. One girl fell over the railing and had to be bandaged up. And one really drunk guy had to be escorted back to his room."

Sofia's cheeks felt hot.

"Fredrik Fröding?"

Linda narrowed her eyes, thinking back.

"I think that was his name. He was staying on the second floor. Just for one night, I think."

Two men in matching t-shirts advertising jet skis walked by and unabashedly checked Linda out. She smiled and gestured courteously toward the stairs, encouraging them to just walk on by.

"Was he here the whole evening?"

"I think so. He sat in the bar to begin with and then over there." Linda pointed to a table in the corner of the patio. "I served him, but I had to stop taking his orders right before closing because he was so drunk he could hardly stand up. I went to go get security to escort him, but when I came back he was gone. I saw him standing down by the pool talking to someone, but it didn't really seem to be a very pleasant conversation. He was practically yelling and then he left."

"Was Fröding the one doing the yelling?"

"No, the other guy."

Hadn't Mona said that Fredrik had been yelling at Ceder? Yes, Sofia was positive that that's what Mona had said. She would have to discuss this with Mona again.

"And then Fröding came back and then you helped him up to his room?"

Linda nodded.

"The security people were busy, so Mona took him up to his room."

"Did you see him again after that?"

"No."

Sofia handed her one of her business cards with her phone number on it.

"Could you ask Mona to contact me when you see her? And if you think of anything else that might be good for us to know, I want you to give me a call."

Linda nodded, took the business card, and was starting to head toward the stairs when Sofia stopped her.

"One last question. Can you think of anyone who wouldn't want Adam Ceder to buy the hotel?"

Linda contemplated that for a moment before responding with a shrug.

"That would probably be Mona."

35·

Christine stopped below the front stoop and looked wide-eyed at the group standing there. Adam, Mats, and Thomas were crowded around Marianne. The girls from the Soviet Union were also there. Loud pop music was blasting from the radio on the kitchen windowsill. Thomas applauded so that his fat belly jiggled. Adam was leaning against the outside wall of the house and petting that cat he was always lugging around. He seemed more interested in it than he was in her.

Marianne stood at the center of the circle. She was swaying back and forth and singing along to the radio. Shaking her hips and pouting with her full lips. She was dancing as if she was in a trance, as if she didn't see them, but she saw. Christine noticed how she opened her eyes every now and then to check and see if the boys were paying attention to her. They were.

They all followed every move her body made. Then she stopped abruptly and pointed to Christine.

"Come here!"

"Birger sent me over with some pickled herring from the hotel," she ventured. "He told me to give it to Bodil or Ester."

Marianne stopped and adjusted her t-shirt. Her shirt said "Hooked on a Feeling" on the front, written in ornate lettering. It was so short that when she raised her arms, the bottoms of her breasts showed.

"God's chosen monstrosity can wait." Marianne scoffed, enjoying the laughter she elicited from the boys. "Come dance with me instead!"

Marianne came over to her and took the baking dish of fish out of her hands and set it on the steps. Adam immediately set the cat down and let it eat from the dish. Marianne pulled her into the circle and Christine started awkwardly moving to the music. Even though she felt embarrassed, she started imitating Marianne's movements. She fixed her eyes provocatively on Adam. He looked into her eyes and she felt tingly inside. He was so good-looking. Marianne, who seemed to see everything, looked at Adam with burning eyes.

"Do you think Christine is pretty?" The music was still pouring out of the window, but no one was moving anymore. Adam shrugged and Christine blushed.

"If you think she's so pretty, maybe you want to kiss her? Come on, Adam, kiss her!"

The cheering section immediately joined in and started chanting loudly.

"I dare you!"

Christine looked at Adam. He looked hesitant, but took a step forward. She so desperately wanted him to kiss her. The others' chanting grew louder. Just as he leaned forward, the music stopped, and a head poked out the window.

"What are you doing? Don't you guys know Ester is resting? You can't be making noise down there!"

Bodil pulled her head back in, disappearing back into the house. She promptly came storming out the front door. She aimed a hard kick at the cat that was still eating out of the oven dish. It slid off the steps yowling and disappeared into the woods.

"Don't just stand around out here. Go set the table for breakfast!"

Marianne exchanged looks with the others and rolled her eyes. Without a word she sashayed past Bodil into the house, her parade of subjects following her. Adam walked with his head down, without looking Christine in the eye.

"What are you doing?" Bodil held her hand up to stop Christine. She stared reproachfully at her with her sharp bird's eyes. "Don't you know how nasty they are to Ester?"

"It's not that bad, is it?" she lied.

"Don't play dumb, Christine! You know how it is. Do you really want to be one of them? After all my dad has done for you?"

That was what she wanted. Christine wanted so desperately to be liked, to be one of the gang. She was going to die soon in her mother's shadow. She was her own person, but no one seemed to want to see that. Aron had been nice, though. He really had. He had let her spend the night so many times over the summers. As if she were one of his own daughters. She should stick up for Ester. She knew she should.

"Is this because of Adam? Are you turning your back on Ester because of him? Are you willing to just whore out your loyalty... for him?"

Christine didn't respond.

"God holds his hand over Ester. You know that, right? Anyone who harms her will be punished. Don't you understand that?" Bodil gasped for breath. Her eyes were wide and her voice was trembling with rage. "God will send an angel and to destroy those who harm Ester. They will burn in hell!"

36.

Fredrik parked the car on the steep hill near the entrance to Ersta Church and sat for a while to reflect on the absurdity of his situation. Right now, at this very moment, the police were in his apartment digging through everything. That's how he pictured it anyway.

He looked around a few times to make sure the police hadn't followed him here and then got out of the car, walked through the arched gate, and followed the paved walkway to the bell tower. Some kids were sitting on their jackets on a patch of grass and eating sushi, each from their own plastic container. He turned off the gravel walkway and went over to the fence. He had a well-rehearsed routine. Before he could even look at the monument, he had to stop and take in the amazing view. With your eyes raised, you could pretend you didn't see the ferries lined up at the port's ferry terminals down below. He focused instead on Djurgården Island across Saltsjön Bay, the rides spinning at Gröna Lund amusement park, the sun setting over all the little islets. It was heartbreaking and beautiful at the same time.

Then Fredrik finally looked at the monument. The beautiful, dark brown wood with its two simple plaques. An unassuming cross, but with the water and the sky as a backdrop, it was as striking as anything could be. He sat down on the bench directly facing it and looked at the cross for a long time.

He came here when he was missing them. It was the only grave he had to visit. For the first time now it hit him that this was Niklas's place as well. But to have a grave, you had to be dead. He felt around within himself. Was Niklas dead? Had he been chasing a ghost for all these years?

It occurred to him that this might be the last time he would sit here. The police might show up at any point, but he just couldn't be bothered to care right now. He just wanted to be for a while, to allow his thoughts to rest in the cotton wool created by the pills, to feel his breathing.

Soon he couldn't sit up any longer. He bunched up his hoodie into a pillow and lay down on the bench.

It didn't take very many minutes before he was asleep.

37.

The sounds of applause and cheering could be heard from Zinkensdamm Field. Yet again Mats Dahlman wished he had bought an apartment a few blocks farther from the sports facility so he wouldn't have to listen to this noise every single summer night. He closed his window and pulled the black-out curtains. He settled unsteadily into his armchair and reached for the remote control. His glass sloshed over a little as he leaned back, but that didn't matter. His suit pants still needed to be dry-cleaned. He put his feet up on the leather footstool and tried to focus on the show. The Alaska Gold Rush, perfect to doze off to.

He looked for his phone on the armrest to switch off the ringer, but couldn't find it. He couldn't handle any more calls from her. She had called so many times he had lost count. He had answered the first time, conversing politely about the wind and the weather and the old days, but he had quickly realized that something wasn't right. He had tried to explain that someone was pulling her leg. That the threat wasn't real, but she had raved about guilt and revenge. It was so absurd that he wondered if she'd somehow lost her mind. He had absolutely no desire to start digging into the past. What had happened was long forgotten now. They had been kids after all, scarcely dry behind the ears. He wasn't going to sit here four decades later and accept responsibility for a little schoolboy prank, was he?

Then it had arrived, just like she had said it would, an anonymous envelope, no return address. Just that threatening text, circled, and then the color copy of the photo from camp with them standing in a row in front of the chapel. His eyeballs had been poked through with a needle. That had been enough to scare him.

Mats looked at his glass, a little less than half full. He shouldn't drink any more now, his head was really spinning. He took a mouthful of whiskey and felt the pleasant burn in his throat. *Oh, one little glass won't matter.* There were only empty bottles on his drink cart, so he had to get up from his chair again and go to the kitchen.

On his way down the hall he heard a scraping sound by the front door. Through the peephole he saw that the stairwell was empty. The sensor for the overhead light was still broken in the stairwell, but he could see the faint glow from the elevator indicating that it had recently stopped on his floor. He couldn't understand why. The neighbors across the hall had been away for the last month. Then he heard the scraping sound again, followed by a metallic clicking. Mats pressed his ear to the keyhole. He had heard that sound before.

Cautiously, he undid the deadbolt and opened the door. In the light that seeped out from his apartment behind him, he could just make out something white moving a little way in front of him, movements that were jerky and rhythmic. He soon saw what it was.

At the far edge of the landing there was a white toy angel with transparent wings. She was spinning around on a platform and the clicking sound was coming from the wind-up spring in her back. Each time she spun around, a bell dinged.

At first he was scared, but then it hit him. Ah, yes, that must be it! Those darned kids, running around bothering people! Oh, he would definitely give that mother on the ground floor a piece of his mind when he spoke to her next.

He stepped out into the stairwell. The elevator light had turned off and he could barely see the floor in front of him. He swept his hand across the floor, feeling for the angel. The instant his hand closed around it, he discovered a pair of eyes staring at him. A woman sat huddled a couple of steps down, her legs pulled up under her chin.

"Hi," he whispered softly.

Mats backed away toward his apartment, the angel in his hand. He stumbled and lost his balance. She struggled to her feet and walked slowly toward him, her head bowed. Her long hair hung over her face and the grit under her bare feet made a scratching sound.

Mats stared at her, unable to understand what was happening. He did have time to notice something between her raised hands.

A hammer.

Panic-stricken, he lunged backward into his apartment and tried to close his door, but she was faster. The hammer hit him on the forehead. He lost his balance and fell into the apartment. His shoulder hit the tile floor hard and he rolled over onto his back and lay there.

Blood was pulsing out of the wound over his eyebrow in bursts. Through a red fog he saw her raise the hammer again. He screamed but couldn't move.

The second blow came down on his temple. He heard something inside break.

Wednesday, June 26

38.

By the time the taxi driver dropped her off outside the glossy, brownish-red police building on Kungsholmen Island in Stockholm, Sofia was so nervous she was feeling sick to her stomach. After meeting Kaj, she would go to the headquarters of the Ceder hotel chain in Östermalm. They were going to hold a memorial service for Adam Ceder there tomorrow and Vera had asked her to stay in Stockholm until that was over. After that she intended to return home as soon as she could.

She rubbed her belly. She always had problems when she was stressed. And stressed was hardly adequate to describe the situation she found herself in now. Her whole life was a joke. She was single and childless and there was a good chance she would be unemployed soon. And to top it all off, she was currently involved with two men, one of whom was married and the other a murder suspect.

She walked through the main entrance and told the receptionist who she was. With a phone receiver in one hand, the receptionist waved to the sofas, where Sofia should have a seat and wait.

Fifteen minutes went by without any sign of life from Kaj. Some plainclothes officers passed her in the lobby. An older woman with sunglasses on top of her head nodded at her in recognition and Sofia nodded back even though she couldn't place who the woman was. What was taking Kaj so long? She knew that it only took a minute to take the stairs down to the lobby from his office.

"Detective Hjortén. It's been ages!" Sofia jumped when she heard Kaj's formal, professional voice behind her. Apparently, he had decided not to acknowledge their relationship at work, and he politely shook her hand before they took the elevator up to the offices that housed the criminal profiling team.

His office looked the way she remembered it. Nothing seemed to have been moved. The crystal ball sat neatly on the windowsill from the time when Kaj and his colleagues had pretended to be fortune tellers at the employees' talent show. They had called themselves the "Saida Group," after the cookie manufacturer. A comic relic, and a symbol of how intractable and traditional some lines of work could be sometimes. The only change in the office was that the bookshelf was now full of books instead of three-ring binders. Kaj sat down behind his desk and crossed his long legs.

"Mette's not a fan of books, so I've given them a home here in the office instead."

Sofia noted that the first edition of Bo Bergman's The Heart Grows from Dreams, which she had bought him for his birthday, occupied a place of honor at the top left. Kaj smiled at her.

"I'm glad to see you here in Stockholm again. Have a seat."

Sofia felt a pang in her stomach and decided to get straight down to it.

"As I said on the phone, Vera wants your help profiling the killer. I'm going to talk to the staff at Ceder Hotels headquarters today and try to figure out if any threats had been made against him. There is a rumor that the Ulvön Hotel is for sale, and we need to find out if Ceder was planning on buying it."

Kaj furrowed his brow.

"Just off the cuff, I think this feels more like there's probably a personal motive. Maybe jealousy? Unrequited love? The murder weapon was a hammer, right?"

Sofia nodded.

"Where should we have lunch?" Kaj quickly changed the topic. As usual, he was completely unaffected by the grisly acts of violence he was investigating, a prerequisite for maintaining focus in this line of work, an ability that Sofia had never fully mastered.

"I promised the hotel manager that I would be at Ceder City East in half an hour, so I probably won't be back in time for lunch." She walked toward the door. "But maybe we can talk this afternoon about how we'll proceed and when you can come up? I'll be in town until tomorrow."

Kaj had stood up and stopped her with a hand on her arm.

"We can discuss it over dinner. At our place? Mette wants to meet you. Shall we say eight o'clock?"

His fingers burned through her shirt. Sofia carefully freed herself and nodded in response. Dinner with Kaj and his wife.

Hell must have frozen over again.

Fredrik looked at his watch. Eight thirty. At some point overnight he had woken up freezing on the bench outside Ersta Church and returned to his car to sleep in the back seat. He had slept fitfully and his back ached from the uncomfortable sleeping position. Every time he heard a car go by, he had huddled under his hoodie and hoped he wouldn't see flashing blue lights lighting up the ceiling of his car. But the police hadn't come.

To be on the safe side, he had turned off his cell phone and removed its battery. He didn't know what sort of resources they would put into finding him. He knew that he couldn't stay away forever, but he wasn't ready to turn himself in to the police yet.

He tentatively unfolded his sore body and, stooped over, emerged from the back seat. He was still freezing. Yesterday's sun was gone, and Stockholm was covered in a thick dome of heavy gray clouds.

There was a Seven Eleven farther down the street and he needed coffee and something to eat. He had been so tired that he hadn't even needed any pills to fall asleep last night. If he was lucky a little food would keep his anxiety sufficiently at bay and he could make it through the day without needing to take any of his precious and rapidly shrinking supply of pills.

Fredrik walked a few blocks away from his car before sticking the battery back into his phone and turning it on. Philip had called five times. The police had called and left a message urging him to get in touch with them for further questioning. Sofia, on the other hand, hadn't called again. He was just about to dial Philip's number when another one appeared on the screen. Marianne Nordin.

"Is this Fredrik?" The voice sounded tentative.

"Yes."

"Are you busy?"

He glanced around discreetly at the street before stepping into the Seven Eleven.

"No, why?"

"This feels a little uncomfortable, but..." Her voice faded away and Fredrik moved his phone to his other ear as he pointed to the sandwich he wanted. The store clerk nodded in response and started entering the amount into the cash register. She pointed to the tower of coffee cups behind the counter and Fredrik nodded and gave her the thumbs up when she got to the largest one.

"What happened?"

"I'm missing a photo. A framed photo that used to be on the chest in the parlor."

He paid for his items, with Marianne still on the line, and waved goodbye to the clerk.

"You didn't just move it and forgot where you put it?" He drank a tentative sip of coffee through the opening in the plastic lid.

Marianne laughed joylessly.

"I'm not actually old enough to be senile. No, I'm quite sure it's missing."

Fredrik stopped on the sidewalk, attempting to open the plastic wrapper around the sandwich while balancing the coffee and the phone. Hunger tore at him now and he didn't really understand what this had to do with him.

"I'm sorry, but how can I help you with this, Marianne?"

"I don't know... but I happened to think of you."

"Why?"

"It was the same picture you had with you when we saw each other, the one with the Dirk sisters in it."

39.

Ulvön Island, 1979

Adam leaned out the window and called quietly. He thought he saw something light moving in the bushes outside.

"Cookie," he whispered enticingly. The last few nights he had left the window to their room open. She had snuck in on the first night. The package of herring he had hidden under the bed had lured her in and after she ate, she had fallen asleep in his bed. Her gentle purring had lulled him to sleep and, for the first time since he had arrived at camp, he had slept the whole night through.

Adam peered out into the darkness again, but realized in disappointment that it wasn't Cookie he had seen. The other boys were asleep so he tiptoed out of bed to go outside and try to entice the cat to come in. By the main staircase that led upstairs he ran into Bodil on her way back from the bathroom. Her hair was a mess and she was wearing her nightgown, but her eyes were alert. She jumped when she saw him "Where are you going?"

Adam shrugged and kept moving toward the front door without answering. He waited until she had disappeared up the stairs before he opened the door. He called for Cookie, but there was no sign of her. She'd probably come when she got hungry, he thought, and was about to shut the door when he heard a sound from outside. When he realized it was Cookie yowling, he was happy at first but quickly realized that something was wrong. The scream was shrill, piercing. He put on a pair of boots, ran out onto the front step, and listened. The noise was coming from over by the swings. It was cold and dark out. He was only wearing his underwear and the boots, but even so he started searching through the dewy grass. It didn't take long to locate the cat. She was hanging from the swing set by a thin cord. Her legs were flailing frantically, which was causing her body to spin in the air as it hung there. Adam tried to make sense of what he was seeing. Then he ran over there and lifted her up. She wailed and scratched his face and hands. Panicking. Adam screamed, too, yelling for help. Thomas peered sleepily out the window.

"Come outside!" Adam yelled. "Now, right away! Bring a pair of scissors!"

A moment later, Thomas came running out the front door with scissors in his hand.

Just like Adam, he was wearing only his underwear. They quickly cut the cat down from the swing set. They tugged and pulled on what was now effectively a leash. Thomas held her with one hand while Adam tried to pull the cord off her neck. The cat kept twisting and he kept losing his grip. The cat's eyes were wide with fear and she kept hissing uncomfortably from her throat. No matter how they struggled they couldn't get the noose off.

"Get it off!" Adam yelled to Thomas, but the harder they tried to remove it, the tighter the noose became. The cat's movements were beginning to slow now, and it gazed helplessly up at Adam. When nothing else seemed to help, Thomas pushed the scissors in under the cord and cut. He got both the cat's skin and fur, but the cat didn't react. Even though the noose was now off, the furry body dangled limply in Adam's arms.

Thomas stood holding the cord in one hand and the bloody scissors in the other. Adam picked up the limp animal and hugged it. He cried and buried his face in its fur. Thomas stood beside him without saying anything.

Not a sound could be heard around them. The silence was palpable.

"Who the hell would do something like that?" Thomas whispered.

Still in shock, Adam just shook his head and then wiped away the blood from a scratch under his eye.

They stood there in silence for a bit looking at each other and the dead cat.

Somewhere over them they heard the sound of a window being closed.

40.

"Ah, I presume you're with the police?"

Sofia nodded and they shook hands.

"Sofia Hjortén."

"Theodor Hake, nice to meet you." The young man smoothed his hair, which had been slicked back with water. "We've prepared a room for you back here. If you would please follow me."

The contrasts between them were painfully obvious. Sofia's shabby civilian clothes and rural Norrland dialect compared to the dazzling hotel manager's dark-blue blazer, his nasal "i" vowel in his pretentious Lidingö accent, and the register of his speech which seemed to have come right out of Downton Abbey. And to top it all off, he refused to use the informal "du" with her!

Theodor showed her to a conference room behind the front desk. As soon as they sat down, a woman came in to offer them coffee from a cart just inside the door.

"Would you like anything else?" Theodor raised his eyebrows expectantly.

"No thank you," Sofia replied and took a mouthful of coffee. It tasted far more expensive than her percolator coffee, although not better.

"So," Theodor began, as if he had been the one to request the meeting. "Obviously we're all appalled at the news of the death of our boss and friend. We're like one big family here at Ceder Hotels and it pains us so immensely to have lost one of our own." He drank a sip of coffee and looked at her over the rim of his cup, as if granting her permission to speak.

"I'm glad to hear that you're one big family," Sofia began cautiously and set down her cup. "Then perhaps you can shed some light on who Adam was. We've been having a hard time getting a fuller sense of him. Do you happen to know if he had a girlfriend?"

"No, unfortunately, I don't know."

"A boyfriend perhaps?"

Theodor shook his head and allowed his eyes to strafe the wall clock mounted next to the conference table.

"Unfortunately I don't know anything about Mr. Ceder's private dealings. As hotel manager here, I'm responsible for Ceder City East and I worked very closely with him in its daily operations, but we did not socialize outside of work."

Sofia nodded.

"We'll leave no stone unturned as we look into Ceder Hotels, Theodor. If you're worried about your future, I would advise you to tell me what you know. You'll gain nothing by shielding Adam now. If it turns out that he was involved in anything illegal and you've failed to inform us, that could have legal repercussions."

This seemed to deflate Theodor a little.

"OK…" He sighed and set his cup down with a little bang. His pretentious Stockholm accent was suddenly blended with a more rural dialect from the valleys of Dalarna. "All right, well… Everyone knows that what happens here stays here. That's the rule. This is a great place to work. A gateway to the crème de la crème of Swedish business life, but in exchange your lips must remain sealed."

With a look, Sofia encouraged him to continue. Theodor flung up his hands.

"What should I say? He was a businessman, a cunning bastard. He wouldn't hesitate to step on anyone's toes to get what he wanted." The obvious admiration in Theodor's voice was unmistakable. "Maybe he wasn't always entirely on the up and up, but he could fool anyone into anything and then call it 'healthy hospitality sector M&A' to the press." Theodor made exaggerated air quotes.

Sofia cleared her throat and asked, "And what's M&A?"

He looked at her as if she were from another planet.

"Mergers and acquisitions," he replied with poorly concealed contempt.

"So someone might have had something against him? Had it in for him?"

"As I just said, Adam was involved with a great many mergers and acquisitions."

Theodor articulated the words with exaggerated clarity and then gave Sofia a little nod as if to make sure she understood. "He had an uncanny ability to sniff out people with problems. If it wasn't financial difficulties, it was personal ones—gambling addicts, sex addicts, drug addicts, people with mental health problems, or people who were dying of some ghastly disease. Then he would swoop in and go for the attack. He was also very well connected in the industry. He knew people in public health, too. They were amply remunerated for looking the other way when it came to his hotels and taking an extra hard look at his competitors. If he couldn't buy a hotel, he would do whatever it took to interrupt its business or dismantle it. So, yes," Theodor summarized. "I'd be surprised if he didn't have some enemies."

Was that what had happened to the Karsts' hotel? Had Christine and Gisela been pressured into selling?

"Do you know if Ceder Hotels was planning to expand in northern Sweden?"

"Yes, but I don't know any of the details."

"Have there been any… incidents here at the hotel lately? Has anyone threatened Ceder?"

"No, we have top notch security. A lot of diplomats and foreign bigwigs stay here."

"Are you positive that there haven't been any incidents here?" Sofia repeated.

"Actually, wait. There was one bozo in here making a big fuss the day before Midsummer's Eve." There was no trace of posh Stockholm left in Theodor's accent now.

"He was mouthing off and yelling. He was quite threatening. Adam had him thrown out, but according to the security guards, he hung out in front of the hotel for the whole day. I thought we should call the police, but Adam didn't want to involve... well, you."

Sofia reached for her phone, scrolled through to a picture of Fredrik, and held it up for Theodor.

"Was this him?"

Theodor looked at the picture and sniggered.

"Yeah, that's him."

She stuffed her phone back in her pocket.

"OK. If you happen to think of anything else, could you let us know?"

"Of course," Theodor replied, and Sofia noted that his supercilious attitude had returned. He smoothed his slicked-back hair, buttoned up his blazer, and stood up to signal that their meeting was over.

–

Fredrik parked his car a few blocks from his destination and walked in between the buildings instead of along the street to reach the end of the row where the Lindéns lived. It was impossible to tell whether it was drizzling or if the air was just humid.

Neither Hans nor Inga's cars were there, so Fredrik went straight to the basement entrance. He let himself in and encountered Philip's back. He was sitting at his desk. Fredrik looked around at the floor in surprise. Every inch of the room's herringbone patterned oak parquet was covered with paper. It looked like it had snowed. The printer, which sat on the wide window ledge, was spitting out page after page. Philip raised a hand in greeting without turning around, familiar with the sounds of Fredrik's footsteps. After a moment, he waved for Fredrik to come closer. Fredrik stepped carefully over the stacks of paper and stopped next to his friend's desk. Philip bored into him with his eyes.

"I have called you a thousand times."

"Five times."

"I have called you five times," Philip said. "Where the hell have you been?"

"Ersta."

The questions ended there. Philip knew what was there, on the hill over the hospital. He lit a cigarette and tried unsuccessfully to blow the smoke toward the half-open basement window.

"The hardware in the computer was clean, but I found a lot of shady discussions in Ceder's work email. He seems like an unscrupulous son of a bitch. Some of the acquisitions Ceder Hotels has made in recent years look like they were made with brute force… or blackmail."

Fredrik nodded. That explained the papers and the mortgage deed in Ceder's bag, but nothing else.

"But…" Philip spun around in his desk chair theatrically. His eyes gleamed with barely restrained hunting instinct. "I found other things. An encrypted cloud storage account." He pointed to a stack of papers in one corner of the room. "Newspaper articles, at least fifty of them. And this." Philip pointed to another stack. "A police investigation."

"What kind of police investigation?"

"It's not exactly recent. Scanned-in paper copies."

"What about?"

"You can read it for yourself."

Fredrik picked up some of the printouts lying closest to him. There were pictures of a group of young people playing soccer on a grassy lawn in front of a big, orange-colored house. There was a magnificent maypole in the middle of the lawn. The pictures had yellowed and had been copied with a scanner, but the quality was good enough that Fredrik was able to make out several familiar faces. He recognized Thomas Nilsson, the boy who had hung himself. Ester Dirk was there in her wheelchair, a cute girl with a gentle smile, flanked by a tall, skinny figure with a dour expression on her face. She looked several years older than the others, even though Fredrik knew the sisters were born only a couple years apart.

He took a couple of steps farther into the room and picked up some of the pages from the pile containing the police investigation. The transcript of an interrogation record from a cross-examination containing a few thin depositions from the kids who had attended the summer camp in 1979. None of the kids who had been staying in the house at the time had seen or heard anything when Thomas Nilsson killed himself on Midsummer's Eve. None of them seemed to believe that it had been anything other than suicide, despite Marianne's assertion. Either opinions were divided on that issue or the kids had lied, Fredrik thought.

The police report also contained some grainy, black and white photos of the dead boy. Fredrik turned the page and let his eyes slowly adjust to the sight. An overweight boy with blond hair, wearing only his underpants, was hanging on the outside of the front of the parsonage. The noose was secured to center post of a window frame and was less than two feet long. His feet were dangling freely in the air and his crooked toes hung like a curtain over the window on the first floor. The boy's mouth was open and his tongue hung from one corner of his mouth, limp and dark.

"Fuck," Philip whispered, looking over his shoulder.

Fredrik put the picture back face down and picked up another stack of pages.

One person was found dead in Sörbyn, north of Ulvö Harbor. An investigation is underway to determine the cause of death. Based on statements and forensic evidence at the scene, the investigation has ruled out any criminal activity.

Fredrik flipped further through the police report.

Thomas Nilsson's body was recovered with abrasions on the hands and knees, broken fingers, flakes of paint under his fingernails, and ligature marks on his neck. The doctor at the scene described these as normal, self-inflicted injuries, consistent with hanging.

He skimmed through a few paragraphs until he came to the last one. He read there that the family claimed the boy would never have voluntarily taken his own life, but the author of the police report had accepted the doctor's opinion anyway and determined that there was no evidence to support the theory of murder. In addition to the police report there must have been about fifty other documents and articles about the Ulvön Island death and the fire in the St. Paulsgatan apartment building in Stockholm's Södermalm neighborhood in which Ester Dirk had died, as well as a long list of Bible schools in Sweden and the other Nordic countries in the late seventies and early eighties.

"Why did he have all of that on his computer?"

That question hung there in the air between them. The printer stopped feeding out paper and a gentle silence filled the room. Fredrik looked around for somewhere to sit down. The sofa was covered with printouts. Not finding anywhere else to sit, he carefully sat down on the floor after scooping several pieces of paper out of his way. He picked up another stack of papers and started flipping through them. Philip regarded him from his throne at his desk without saying anything.

"Blackmail? Could Ceder have dug all this up to put someone away or frame someone?"

Philip let him go on talking. His work was completed now. He had broken through the protective plastic shell and revealed the contents. His part was done, and he leaned contentedly back in his chair with an unlit cigarette between his fingers.

"You don't think this is starting to look like a job for the police?" Philip asked and reached for a lighter and lit his cigarette.

Fredrik ignored him. It couldn't be a coincidence that Ceder had died on Midsummer Eve, just like Thomas Nilsson forty years earlier. The summer camp had something to do with Ceder's murder. Fredrik was sure of that. That had to be the case. The picture and the text he had found in Ceder's bag was a threat. But what did it mean? Fredrik pulled out the printout of the photo of the kids playing soccer again. What did you do, Adam, that you deserved to die for? He needed to find out.

Which meant another trip to Örnsköldsvik.

Fuck.

41

Sofia arrived at the address Kaj had specified at seven forty-five. She glanced up at the sky. It was clearly going to rain soon. She regretted having worn only a thin cardigan over her tank top.

Her gladiator sandals slapped against the pavement as she cut across the street toward Kaj's door. *Mette wants to meet you.*

The actress, Mette Severin. According to the gossip rags, she and Kaj had gone to elementary school together and had then run into each other again when they were older. They had fallen in love and within a few months they were married. It didn't make any sense. Sofia couldn't understand how Kaj could choose a wife who lived her life in the limelight. Mette was anything but shy when it came to the press. She was a highly publicized prima donna with an incredible range and a youthful face. The first time she saw her on TV, Sofia had thought she looked like one of those voluptuous nudes in an Anders Zorn painting.

Kaj lived on the fourth floor of an apartment building only a few blocks from police headquarters on Kungsholmen. Sofia had scarcely rung the doorbell before the door opened and a neatly made-up face appeared.

"How lovely to finally meet you! Kaj has told me so much about you," the plump woman chirped and kissed her on both cheeks in greeting. She introduced herself as Mette and then amiably ushered Sofia into the apartment.

"Would you like a drink, my dear?" She darted off into the kitchen without awaiting a response. Sofia stood there in the doorway to the living room. There was no trace of Kaj's fastidious style to be seen in the home he and Mette had bought together. The living room was overflowing with knick-knacks and plastic flowers. Each cushion on the sofa was upholstered in a different color and the curtains and the rugs had mismatched patterns. There was a purple hand-cranked phonograph next to a doll in a hula skirt in the middle of the coffee table. Kaj was sitting on the jarringly garish sofa, leaning back with his legs crossed in front of him. From a distance he looked a bare patch the artist had forgotten to paint, pale and uncomfortable. He was holding a green plastic wineglass in his hand. He unobtrusively sipped the contents and gestured with his hand for her to have a seat.

"Sit down and appreciate the peace and harmony."

The cacophony of colors and shapes was enough to trigger an epileptic seizure. Kaj burst out laughing when he saw her appalled expression.

"What's so funny?" Mette asked, standing in the doorway holding another plastic glass. This one was yellow and filled with something resembling fruit punch.

"Nothing, dear."

"You can enjoy your inside jokes later." Mette sat her capacious backside down on a round, green ottoman. "Right now I want to hear all about you."

Sofia sipped the contents of the yellow glass. It was strong. The first sip burned in her belly. She could count on one hand the number of times she had drunk alcohol in the last twenty years, and yet if ever she had needed something fortifying, it was now.

"There's not so much to say about me," Sofia said noncommittally and set her glass on the coffee table. "I'm a police detective in Örnsköldsvik now, but I lived and worked in Stockholm for almost ten years."

Mette nodded for her to continue.

"I met Kaj for the first time when I was a cadet."

"Is that how he became your lover?" Mette asked, perfectly at ease.

Sofia was stunned and didn't dare look Mette in the eye. Kaj cleared his throat, feeling uncomfortable.

"Oh come on, stop fooling around!" Mette exclaimed, looking at Kaj. "We don't keep secrets from each other, do we? Keep going, my dear. Why did you leave Stockholm? Was there some kind of trouble in paradise between the two of you?"

Kaj, who had been sitting quietly, cut his wife off, and tried to shoo her into the kitchen to check on the food.

"Harumph," she snorted in response. "Come on, Sofia, let's go open a bottle of wine and gossip a little about that old sourpuss." She took Sofia by the arm and pulled her out of the room. Sofia looked back over her shoulder and her eyes met Kaj's. He downed what was left in his green plastic glass and got up off the sofa to follow them.

Mette turned out to be a charming hostess. There wasn't a soul she hadn't met or worked with as she had traveled around the world for various theater productions and filming locations for movies.

Sofia even said yes to wine for once. The aperitif had settled like cotton around her raw nerves. She felt tipsy after just the first glass, but she still drank the second as well. The turbulence of the last few days had left her feeling both sleep-deprived and without any appetite. A night of pleasant company was exactly what she needed. Even if it was with Kaj and his wife.

Once they had cleared the table and finished off two bottles of wine, Mette excused herself and disappeared into the front hall. Kaj sat down on the sofa in the living room and opened a third bottle, but Sofia had the presence of mind to say no. The two glasses she had already consumed were zooming around her bloodstream along with the aperitif and she was having trouble concentrating. Kaj poured himself a glass and was feeling relaxed. He leaned back into the fluffy pillows and closed his eyes. Sofia sat down on the very edge of the sofa with her hands awkwardly resting on her lap. Mette soon appeared in the doorway again and solemnly announced that she intended to leave the party and would be gone for the rest of the night.

"It was lovely to meet you, young Sofia from the North. I have a feeling that we'll meet again!" Mette bowed theatrically and vanished back into the hall again. Kaj waved without opening his eyes. The front door closed behind her and the atmosphere in the room changed immediately.

"Where is she going?" Sofia asked.

"To her boyfriend's," Kaj replied, unconcerned. He sat up and put his hand on her leg as his lips found their way to her neck.

Sofia moved so that Kaj's hand fell onto the sofa's floral plush upholstery.

"Like I said," Sofia reiterated. "Vera wants you to come back north with me. We're facing a large investigation, and a profile of the culprit would be a big help."

Kaj didn't seem to be listening. His hand found Sofia's leg again and when she pulled away again he furrowed his brow.

"Did we have some falling out that I'm not aware of? I thought we had a pleasant evening?"

Sofia nodded in agreement.

"I'm tired and I want to go back to my hotel and go to sleep. Ceder's memorial starts at ten tomorrow." She really was tired. And tipsy, which she hadn't been in years.

She had questioned at least ten employees at Ceder City East that afternoon after her conversation with Theodor Hake. It had very quickly become clear that Adam Ceder had truly been interested in buying the Ulvö Hotel. A welcome piece of information that could help move the investigation forward. Now they just needed to find out if his death had anything to do with the intended real estate transaction. Had he threatened Christine Karst to get a better price, and if so had that devolved into an argument that got out of control? Or were there other interested parties who wanted to stop him from buying the hotel? Mona came to mind, but she had told Sofia herself that she wasn't a potential buyer. Plus she had said that she could afford it. Ceder's staff weren't aware of any competing offers for the hotel from other bidders.

Sofia was looking forward to sharing that information with the investigative team. If the motive for the murder was financial, that significantly reduced the risk that Fredrik was involved.

Kaj reached for her and put his arm around her waist.

"Kaj, I'm really tired." All she wanted to do was crawl under a fluffy hotel comforter and shut out the world. The last thing she wanted was to spend the night in Kaj and Mette's rainbow-colored sheets.

He shrugged and relented.

"As you wish. Mette has a premiere on Friday. But I can come up the next day."

Sofia was content with that. She hurried out into the front hall, thanking him for dinner as she put her sandals back on.

Kaj was still on the sofa, sulking, when she let herself out and closed the door behind her.

Thursday, June 27

42.

The oppressive heat was making the ground steam. Short rain showers alternated with baking sunshine. Occasionally thunder could be heard over the part of Lake Mälaren called Riddarfjärden, or the Knight's Firth. Sofia pulled her cardigan tighter as she ran down Swedenborgsgatan. Her tank top was wrinkled and she hadn't showered.

She had tumbled straight into bed the moment she had gotten back to her hotel room. She had slept on top of the comforter without taking off her clothes or her shoes. When she woke up, she only had twenty minutes until Ceder's memorial service began. She hadn't had time to shower or change her clothes.

The burial couldn't take place until the body was released and that would take a while, but the family had decided to hold a memorial service in the meantime. According to Nina Ceder there were many people who wanted to show their support for the family. She had humbly explained that she was something of a central figure in their congregation. It was going to be a large gathering and Sofia would be very welcome.

She had a pain in her abdomen and her upset stomach had now been joined by a hint of a hangover. When Sofia reached Mariatorget Park, she was forced to stop and lean on one of the park benches to catch her breath. She was so thirsty her fingers were tingling so she drank some of the orange juice she had grabbed from her hotel room minibar. No matter how hard she tried, she couldn't swallow. Her stomach protested wildly against the acidic liquid and she lurched forward and vomited next to the bench. Two teenage girls who were walking by tactfully jumped out of the way. They turned around to look at her. Sofia raised a hand to show that she was OK or maybe to show that they didn't need to be afraid of her, she wasn't sure which. Her pulse was pounding in her ears and her mouth was tinder dry.

She collapsed onto the bench and wiped under her nose with the sleeve of her cardigan. This is exactly what Sten had been through, her beloved father, Sten. She remembered how she had teased him. Even Claire had told him to go see a doctor, but he had refused. It's just a stomach bug, he had said. When he finally realized that something wasn't right, it had been over a year and it was too late to do anything. Tears welled up in her eyes. She inhaled and looked up at the sky.

She needed to be professional, look professional. Her mouth smelled sour and the snake in her belly wouldn't stop wriggling around.

When Sofia finally arrived, the church green outside Maria Magdalena Church was full of people dressed in black. A man was smoking a pipe over by the grave of the singer Evert Taube, and groups of people stood chatting in subdued voices outside the front door of the church. A few laughed nervously. Others adjusted their hats or their ties. They were all preparing themselves to face the discomfort of death, together. Some were hugging and crying.

Adam Ceder's sister stood with the priest at the base of the steps. Her coloring was the same as her brother's, but she was in significantly better physical shape than he had been. Her tight dress revealed a woman who spent so many hours at the gym that her body had begun to resemble a man's.

"I want to begin by expressing my condolences," Sofia said after she had introduced herself. Nina Ceder was in her fifties. She looked vaguely familiar, but Sofia couldn't place her. She smiled uncertainly and shook Sofia's hand.

"Where's your mother?"

"At home. She wasn't up to coming today."

"I understand that you live together?"

Nina nodded.

"I take care of her at home. She has fibromyalgia. We live in separate apartments," she hurried to add as if to stop Sofia from judging their housing situation.

"I see. That must take up a lot of your time?"

Nina nodded.

"This is the role God gave me."

For some reason, she had expected Nina to be a more rough-and-tumble sort of person, maybe because she knew Nina had done time in Ystad Women's Prison. But the woman before Sofia was both calm and composed, despite her muscular body. Maybe her time in prison had caused Nina to turn to God? If so, she wouldn't be the first person that had happened to.

"How's the investigation going?" Nina asked her, looking up at the ominously dark clouds.

"Slowly, I'm afraid. We're trying to figure out a potential motive. Can you think of anyone who might have wanted to harm your brother?"

Several people pushed past them on their way into the church. The priest suddenly appeared in the doorway and waved to let them know it was time to get started.

"Maybe someone he had a score to settle with?" Sofia continued. "A business rival? Or was he having any difficulties in his personal life?"

Nina's face remained blank. She rubbed her mouth and scanned the church green.

"He was a difficult child." The statement was abrupt and delivered without any emotion.

"Why?"

The priest was now waving his hand urgently for Nina to join them inside the church.

"He was quiet and withdrawn. At the same time, quite a prankster. Today you'd probably call him one of those...

'letter children,' you know, kids with some kind of letter soup diagnosis."

"What kinds of pranks?"

"He set off the fire alarm during graduation, dropped an anchor into the school swimming pool, and poured dish soap all over the hallways. He was too much for Mom to handle and she eventually had to send him away."

Sofia pulled out her phone and showed Nina a picture of Fredrik.

"Do you recognize this man?"

Say "no".

Nina studied the photo.

"Yes, maybe."

Sofia again felt her stomach begin to ache. She wanted to ask more, but something acidic had begun to work its way up her throat and her armpits felt sticky. She was going to throw up again. She quickly thrust a business card into Nina's hand.

"If you think of anything, anything at all, please give me a call."

Nina took the card and tucked it into the clutch bag she had under her arm.

Sofia looked around in a panic. She had to get out of here and lie down. The church grounds were empty aside from a couple of journalists who were packing up their camera tripods and microphones. Ceder was a well-known name and reporters had been covering his murder with a feverish intensity for several days now, just as Vera had predicted.

Sofia had to go rest for a while at the hotel before she headed to the airport. She couldn't be shut inside a church full of dead people and sniffling family members. She needed to sleep and shower, eat something to alleviate the nausea. She started walking down the hill toward Hornsgatan, leaning forward slightly and pressing her hand to her stomach. Far too preoccupied with herself to notice that Nina was still standing there, following her with her eyes.

43.

In an Upstairs Bedroom

You see, that wasn't hard. The sinners' knees soften when they see the true face of God. Let them scream and bleed all they want. Your heart will still never yield. Because you bear the burning sword in your belt, and when you swing it at them, they will be cleft asunder. Limbs will fall from bodies and you, my child, will wash yourself in their blood, wash clean your conscience and your soul.

With God's hand behind you, no one can stop you.

44.

By the time the plane took off, it was raining again and there was considerable turbulence due to the strong winds. Sofia clutched her armrest convulsively and looked out the window. She tried to recall the statistics about flying being ten times safer than driving. Or was it a hundred times?

The knot in her stomach wouldn't go away and her hangover had now exploded. She had thrown up twice at the hotel and yet again at the airport. All her thoughts about Fredrik and Kaj and this entire investigation made her head throb. Kaj had sent her a text that morning to wish her a pleasant trip. He had written that he very much looked forward to seeing her in Örnsköldsvik. All the things she so desperately wanted to hear, but not from him.

Sofia took a deep breath and strained to focus on the gray clouds passing below her window. Kaj was a kind, honest, honorable man, who loved her. Fredrik was a liar and an addict, a suspected murderer, who didn't love her.

She wanted him anyway. She longed to be with him again.

A quiet whimper escaped her, so miserably pathetic. Was it just the loneliness of Örnsköldsvik that had got her into this situation? No, it was something else, a burning sensation deep in her chest. Something inside her had changed. She had taken risks she would never have dreamt of before, put her job and her own reputation on the line, lied to Vera. Had the burning knot inside her made her do all that? That couldn't be it, could it? Whatever it was, she realized that there was no chance that this would end well. Even so, it was too late to change course.

At best, Fredrik would be innocent, and she would get to keep her job. At worst… she didn't even want to think about that.

In the library, Eva had laid out a small smorgasbord with soda, light beer, coffee, and sandwiches from Lundberg's bakery. Sofia suspected that this unusual extravagance had been intended to impress Kaj, who wouldn't arrive now until the day after tomorrow.

"How did it go with the sister?" Vera asked, turning to Sofia.

The pit of her stomach was still churning and the fluttering in her chest wouldn't go away. Her body was rebelling.

"It went well."

Vera raised her eyebrows.

"Apparently Adam Ceder was a handful as a kid. His family situation doesn't seem like it was all that stable, but I don't think that has anything to do with why he died. I asked around among his colleagues and several of them thought it wasn't out of the question that someone might have threatened him. They described him as completely unscrupulous when it came to business deals and said he could definitely have picked up some enemies over the years."

"And what about buying the Ulvö Hotel?" Marie asked.

"Both the company controller and several other staff members confirmed that Ceder was interested in buying the hotel. And given that the hotel manager said that Ceder's tactics for acquiring new hotels often involved both bribery and intimidation, it seems quite possible that Christine and Gisela Karst might have been pressured to sell at a much lower price than was reasonable. Maybe he had already dug up some unfavorable information about them that he threatened to publish if they didn't sell to him?"

"That would be a clear motive for the Karsts to want to get rid of Ceder," Karim noted.

Vera looked satisfied.

"Anything else?"

Yes, Fredrik went to Ceder City East and behaved in a threatening manner. And Nina Ceder thought she recognized him.

"No, nothing else."

"We should still take a closer look at Ceder's history, his schooling, friends, girlfriends. Marie, you keep focusing on Ceder."

"What else do we have?" Vera looked around the table.

Marie waved a stack of papers.

"I went through the call log his carrier provided. It supports our theory that the murder is related to the hotel purchase. The bartender at Ulvö Hotel confirmed that the last number Ceder called was one of Christine Karst's cell numbers."

Vera nodded and said, "Another thing to add to the stack of evidence."

"Christine apparently uses an unregistered, prepaid SIM card when she's in Norrland county because her usual carrier doesn't have very good coverage up here. The prepaid card is in the phone that Sofia and I found in her room at the hotel."

"Could there have been someone else who didn't want to see the Ulvö Hotel become part of Ceder Hotels?" Karim asked, reaching for the call log that was sitting in front of Marie.

"According to the staff at Ceder Hotels, there weren't any other bidders," Sofia said. "But we know that Mona Höglund wasn't thrilled with the idea of the hotel being sold." Her voice sounded high pitched and wobbly. She cleared her throat and sat up straighter in her chair. The breadbasket made another round and she helped herself to a roll with liverwurst, although the odds that she could get that down were minimal.

"She could have hired Fröding," Mattias suggested.

"He hardly seems like a professional hitman, does he?" Marie said, eyeing him skeptically. "Why would a professional allow himself to be seen out in the open arguing with his victim, not to mention getting so drunk before doing the deed?"

"He's still in serious trouble," Mattias said sulkily. "His apartment on Brahegatan was empty. We put out an APB on him and I ran the full package on him: call log, financial transactions, the whole thing! We'll get him…"

"The problem with Fröding is that he doesn't have any motive," Karim interrupted.

"No known motive," Mattias continued. "But he was seen arguing with the victim just hours before he was found dead. Just because we can't see the motive doesn't mean it isn't there."

Vera held her hand up tiredly to Mattias.

"He's one of our suspects, yes, but at the moment it's just as important that we reach Christine Karst as it is that we talk to him."

She was about to say something else, when Sofia interrupted.

"Mona Höglund is the only person who actually has a motive to make Ceder disappear, aside from possibly Christine Karst," Sofia heard herself say.

Was she trying to steer the investigation away from Fredrik?

Mattias leaned back in his chair and defiantly crossed his muscular arms over his chest.

"Look," Sofia continued, "it's true that Mona said she couldn't afford to buy the hotel, but according to the hotel staff she was interested. Given that she has been running the place for many years in a practical sense, it's not hard to imagine her disappointment if it were suddenly sold to a big corporate group. Right?"

"Well, there's a big difference between being disappointed and murdering someone." Vera sounded dubious.

"Mona found the victim. She's the only one besides Karst who has a key to the server room where the surveillance footage suddenly went missing, and she lied about what had happened between Ceder and Fre... Fröding."

"What do you mean lied?" Mattias leaned in over the table.

"Linda Pihlgren, the server who summoned the security guards to escort Fröding up to his room on Midsummer's Eve, said that Ceder had been yelling at Fröding, not the other way around."

"That doesn't mean anything." Mattias shrugged. "That argument could have led to anything. Maybe he decided to pay him back later that night?"

"Even though he was so drunk he could barely stand up?" Sofia argued. "So he supposedly went and found Ceder, killed him with a hammer, dragged him to the water, and threw him in without anyone noticing it?"

"Yeah, why not?"

Vera intervened.

"We have three suspects: Christine Karst, Fredrik Fröding, and Mona Höglund. We'll keep the investigation as broad as we can. We don't need any of your own personal opinions, thank you very much. We work with evidence here, in case you've forgotten that?" She looked back and forth between Mattias and Sofia. When neither of them said anything else, she pulled out her chair and got up.

"Well then. Let's get to it."

45.

Their Midsummer party was already in full swing. Mats had obtained beer. He was coaxing all the girls into tasting it.

"Hey, it makes your body feel so relaxed and nice. Come on, Christine!" he bellowed as he staggered out onto the lawn. Adam had had some and so had Marianne. Mats was slurring his speech and laughing at how drunk he was. Everyone was saying they felt drunk. Christine was the only one who hesitated, too chicken as usual. Finally Thomas got tired of her dithering and came up behind her and grabbed her arms from behind. Marianne tipped Christine's mouth up and poured the beer into it. It sprayed out her nose and mouth, down over the tips of her long 70s collar. It tasted awful at first, but after a couple of gulps things did start to feel better inside. Nice, just like Mats had said.

The music was blaring from the record player. Donna Summer was singing about girls on the street, walkin', sad girls. A group was dancing. The boys were sitting in the kitchen playing dice and making noise. They were being much louder than they needed to be, boisterous laughter that confirmed their intoxicated states.

There was no sign of Bodil. Maybe she had gone to midnight mass with Aron. Christine didn't care. For once she got to hang out with the cool kids, to be one of them. She swayed along with the music with yet another beer in her hand. Mats, who was sitting in the chair closest to her, fondled her butt and then gave it a smack.

"There, you see? You can trust me. I know what chicks want. If we can't go to the party, then the party will have to come to us."

Marianne squeezed between them and sat down on Mats's lap. Christine moved willingly, happy to get away from Mats's far-too-long arms.

"At least you know what I want, don't you?" Marianne flirted.

She puckered up her lips and pushed her heavy breasts into Mats. Christine had seen Marianne do that many times before. And Mats took the bait, every time. Marianne crooked her index finger, got up and walked toward the stairs, her hips swaying. Mats was right behind her, following her as if in a trance.

"I have a job for you!" Marianne commanded.

Thomas finished his beer and burped loudly. Adam joined them as well. On the way out of the kitchen, Thomas grabbed Christine's arm. He tugged her hard and she teetered after him. As they reached the stairs she was walking at an angle. Marianne turned around and laughed. Not derisively, intimately, as if Christine was one of them now. When they got upstairs, Marianne stopped outside Ester's door.

"Didn't somebody say that Ester should be taught a lesson? A little smack on the butt, wasn't that what you said, Mats?"

A shadow of doubt came over Mats's face.

Thomas laughed.

"Oh come on, Mats! Why don't you go in there and give her a little spanking right on her bare butt? I've heard some girls like that kind of thing. Although maybe you're not brave enough?"

Mats stretched cockily and lifted his chin.

"Sure, I'm brave enough!"

"You don't even know how to take off a girl's panties." Thomas laughed so that his belly jiggled.

"Are you dumb, or what?" Mats protested. "I've been with a ton of girls."

"Want to bet on it?" Thomas reached around and pulled his wallet out of his back pocket and then took out a wad of lumpy ten kroner notes. "A hundred kroner says you can't get Ester into bed."

"Why don't you do it yourself?" Mats stared angrily at Thomas. The mood had turned from jovial to aggressive. The steady throb of the music could still be heard from downstairs. Marianne's eyes gleamed in the darkness. Christine tugged nervously on her soiled silk blouse. The beer was starting to burn in the pit of her stomach, and it didn't feel pleasant or nice anymore. She was a good girl after all. This all felt wrong.

"Maybe you should both go in?" Marianne smiled mischievously and Thomas shrugged.

"Well, at least I'm not a coward," Thomas said.

But Mats still looked skeptical.

Then Marianne leaned forward and whispered hoarsely into Mats's ear, "If you do it, maybe I'll let you take my underwear off next."

That did it. In one assertive yank, Mats pulled the door to Ester's room open. Thomas wasn't far behind. Ester looked up as they came in, dropping the book she was holding so she could turn her wheelchair to face them. The look on her face would forever be etched in Christine's memory. Ester looked hopeful, believing that she was finally going to get to be part of the gang. A second later she realized what was going on and the look on her face immediately stiffened in fear. She opened her mouth to scream for Bodil, but Thomas's thick hand silenced her. Christine was still standing in the doorway with her arms hanging limply at her sides. She watched in fear as they dragged Ester out of her wheelchair. Clothes were pulled off bodies and hands restrained. She wished that someone braver than her would come and put a stop to the whole thing. She wanted to run and get Bodil or Aron or someone, but she just stood there.

A coward as usual.

Friday, June 28

46.

"Hello? You can't sleep here!" The woman's voice sounded distant through the windshield. Fredrik blinked drowsily. At first he thought he was dreaming, but he could plainly and clearly see the woman wagging her indignant index finger through the fogged up glass. The clock on the dashboard said quarter past ten.

"This isn't a campground, you know! There's hotels in town," she yelled and pointed at the Stadshotel which was right across from the harbor parking lot overlooking Örnsköldsvik Bay. When Fredrik didn't respond, she turned on her heel and clip-clopped away across the parking lot.

Fredrik rolled down his window and raised his seat back. A strong gust of wind off the water blew the receipts and trash off the dashboard onto the floor. He had spent one night at Philip's place. Then he had gathered up all the printouts, tried to pull himself together, and driven up to Örnsköldsvik. That was yesterday. He had driven almost a thousand miles in just a few days now. It must be some sort of record. He was dripping with sweat and the seat beneath him felt wet when he moved. He really needed a shower pronto.

Fredrik drank a swig from the bottle of warm soda that was sitting in his cup holder and felt the blister pack of pills in his jeans pocket. Did he need a pill? No, better to save them for a bit longer, to be on the safe side.

He was in trouble, he realized that. Continuing on this path was going to result in disaster sooner or later. But if he was being honest with himself, how much worse could things really get?

He thought about Ceder. If only he could remember what they had said to each other. He had no idea what he had done for large swaths of that night. His eyes were drawn to the bag sitting in his passenger's seat, staring brazenly back at him. What if he was the one who had...? No, that was totally ridiculous. Sure, he had some gaps in his memory from Midsummer's Eve, but surely he couldn't have killed a person and then forgotten about it? He scratched the back of his hand.

All the paperwork Philip had printed out was in the back seat, in stacks with rubber bands around them. He reached back between the seats and picked up one of the stacks, propping it against the steering wheel as he flipped through it. He couldn't find the copy of the summer camp photo from Ceder's plastic folder anywhere. Had he left it at Gösta's place? No, he'd had it with him the afternoon he spent with Marianne and Tord. Ah, it didn't matter.

There were several similar pictures in the material that Philip had found. He flipped through to a picture of Thomas Nilsson. He looked happy, not at all like someone who was planning to commit suicide. Had he been murdered as Marianne had claimed? But if so, by whom?

Christine Karst, who owned the Ulvö Hotel, turned up several times in the police report and in some of the various newspaper articles. Apparently she was the daughter of a famous pianist, which seemed to have brought extra notoriety to the case. "Pianist's Daughter in Death Drama," one newspaper headline proclaimed. "Summer Camp Death Mystery—World-Renowned Pianist's Daughter Caught up in the Drama", read another. The other young people Gösta had mentioned were also included in the materials, Siw-Inger and Annika Hörnberg and two Russian-sounding names that Fredrik assumed were the girls from the exchange program. And then the boys, Adam Ceder himself, Mats Dahlman, and Jan Dagegård. They had all been questioned by the police, but none of them had reported any information that could prove that Thomas's death was anything other than a suicide, Fredrik found Marianne's name in an appendix to one of the reports. She had been there on Midsummer's Eve, but not at the time of Thomas's death, and the police had questioned her by phone. Jan Dagegård had also been questioned by phone since he was no longer on Ulvön Island when Thomas was found.

Fredrik ran his finger along the row of kids in one of the pictures and stopped on Bodil, the missing daughter. He hadn't read anywhere in the material where she had gone. It was as if she had gone up in smoke, just like Gösta had said. Could Ceder have been looking for information about her? Was that why he had so eagerly gathered documents and newspaper articles about the family and looked into Bible schools? But Gösta didn't seem to believe the rumor that she had been sent to some school in Uppsala. Fredrik picked up his phone and typed "Bodil Dirk" into the Swedish search engine hitta.se. No hits found in Sweden. He googled the name and found two grainy, black and white photos showing the parsonage and Ulvö Church, but nothing else. He gave up on her and tried the other names: Christine Karst, Siw-Inger Hörnberg, and Annika Hörnberg. They had all been there when Thomas Nilsson had been found dead, and they had all been staying with the Dirk family. One of them must know more about what had happened.

After a quick search, he found that there were seven people named Annika Hörnberg in Sweden, so he tried Siw-Inger Hörnberg instead. There was one Siw-Inger Dagegård-Hörnberg, living in Bonässund a little way outside downtown Örnsköldsvik with a Jan Dagegård. That must be the same Jan who had attended the camp.

"Hörnberg-Dagegård," Siw-Inger said, answering on the second ring.

"Hi, my name is Fredrik Fröding."

"OK," the woman on the other end replied, sounding distrustful.

"I have a few questions for you about Aron Dirk's 1979 summer camp on Ulvön Island."

"OK?" Siw-Inger still sounded wary.

"Do you think I could stop by and ask you a couple of questions?"

"I guess that would be fine." She still didn't sound completely sure. "But you have to come when my husband is home. How about four o'clock?"

"Great, I'll see you at four then."

—

Vera squeezed past Marie to get to her desk. The library was being used for a training session, so the investigative team had had to pack into Vera's office for their morning meeting. She had reluctantly let them in, but not without first muttering a few choice curse words that had made Marie blush. Sofia still felt sick, and the stuffy air in Vera's office and the combination of everyone's deodorants and perfumes was not helping. No one dared open the window out of fear that the strong winds outside would create a vortex out of all the loose papers on Vera's desk.

In addition to the five people in the group, they also needed space for the whiteboard. Karim was leaning against the book-shelf behind the desk and Marie was also standing, pressed against the windowsill, while Mattias had afforded himself the honor of sitting in the guest chair. Sofia, who had been the last to come in, had to make do with the edge of the desk.

She had cautiously pushed aside a couple of binders before sitting down, careful not to disturb the orderly chaos that prevailed.

"This is like being in a tin of fucking sardines!" Vera bumped her bookshelf with her shoulder and several folders tumbled out. She swept them out of the way in annoyance with her foot and sat down in her chair.

Mattias cleared his throat.

"I can start," Mattias began, "by announcing that we're down to only two suspects now. One if you ask me, but at any rate we can take Mona Höglund off the list. I spent last night piecing together every single witness statement from Midsummer's Eve about her. She has alibis for her whereabouts for the whole night. Obviously it was a really busy day of work at the hotel, holiday weekend, peak season, and Mona worked until the bar closed at two. When she wasn't at the front desk, she was helping the kitchen staff or relieving someone at the bar. Then after that she helped clean the kitchen. She was around people until she went to throw the trash into the dumpster out beyond the guest pier and discovered Adam Ceder's body. And as we know, he had already been dead for several hours by then."

"Damn fine work, Mattias! Then we're one step closer," Vera crowed contentedly and Mattias looked as if he might burst with pride.

Sofia opened her mouth to say something but realized that she didn't have any sensible objections. The fact that she wished Mona would turn out to be the guilty one was hardly sufficient.

Vera pointed to Marie who reached for the whiteboard and moved Mona's picture down to the bottom corner.

"So, what does the timeline look like for Ceder?" Vera asked.

Maria flipped through her printouts.

"We know that he had a board meeting Thursday afternoon and that he received some Hungarian diplomats at Ceder City East on Friday morning. So the earliest he could have arrived in Örnsköldsvik was Friday afternoon, in other words on Midsummer's Eve. His car, a black SUV, was found at the Köpmanholmen Ferry Terminal. It's registered to Ceder Hotels, but according to a Theodor…"

"Hake," Sofia offered.

"Exactly, Hake. He confirmed that that was the car that Adam Ceder used personally. Neither the staff at Restaurant Kajen at the ferry terminal nor the personnel on the ferry recognized Ceder, but given how many visitors came through there around Midsummer, he certainly could have been on the ferry without anyone noticing him. There are surveillance cameras on the boat. And he could have caught on film when he disembarked in Ulvö Harbor. We've requested the footage. If we're lucky we can find out when he arrived on the island and whether he was with anyone."

Vera nodded and Marie continued.

"We know that Ceder checked into the Ulvö Hotel late in the day on Midsummer's Eve, and that he called Christine Karst's cell phone at precisely 7:15 p.m."

She drew a red line to a bubble with Christine Karst's name on the board and noted the time of the conversation.

"He was seen arguing down by the pool that night, but we don't know yet what happened after that or exactly when or where Ceder was murdered. The call logs are supposed to take another few days, but when they're ready, we should be able to get a clearer picture of which towers Ceder's cell phone connected to, which should tell us something about his movements."

"When does Kaj get here?" Vera looked at Sofia.

"Tomorrow morning."

"How's it going with Karst?"

"No one seems to have seen her after her conversation with Linda Pihlgren on Midsummer's Eve. All the airports and border crossings have been alerted, but she could have left the country by car or boat just as easily."

Vera pulled her reading glasses up and propped them on top of her plum-colored hair like a diadem. She leaned back in her chair.

"This is pretty damn scary. Karst must have been up to some kind of shit since she's staying away. We can put out an APB. And what about her boat?"

"It's still missing. I've been in touch with every single yacht club and marina from here to Nynäshamn. No one has seen it. And according to her ex-husband, Christine is very familiar with boats. She could stay away for a long time in the boat. I'll check and see if it has Meta Trak."

Everyone in the room turned to look at Sofia.

"Meta what?"

"Meta Trak. It's a kind of GPS transmitter that people use on boats." When no one said anything, she added, "I'm a competition pike fisher."

Mattias gaped in surprise at her admission while Karim nodded, impressed. It struck her how little she shared about herself at work.

"What, like you're competing in the Pike Challenge or what?" Mattias sneered. It was common knowledge that he considered himself to be a bit of a big-shot fisherman. He liked to go fly fishing and enjoyed talking about his exploits.

"Yeah," Sofia said. "I trolled up a 117.5 cm beauty this spring. How about you?"

Mattias clouded over.

"Fredrik Fröding fits the profile a lot better than Karst," he said peevishly when the group refused to take their eyes off him as they waited to hear what his comeback would be in this impromptu office game of fishing one-upmanship.

Sofia caught a glimmer of amusement in Vera's eye.

"He was probably the last person to see Ceder alive," Mattias continued. "He has mental health problems, was drunk at the time, and is keeping his distance from us. If that doesn't scream suspect, then I don't know what would. We're waiting on the tower dumps to determine where he was in the days surrounding Ceder's death, and ideally where he is now."

"I agree." Karim pulled his hand over his chin and then yawned discreetly into his cupped hand. It was almost noon and they were all starting to feel hungry.

Vera started putting on her jacket, which had been hanging over the back of her chair.

"We're not going to get any farther on this right now. Let's break for lunch. Sofia, do you want to join me?"

47.

Several of their colleagues were sitting in the small outdoor seating area at Port Nio having lunch. They waved in bewilderment to Sofia and Vera as they walked by down the cobblestone street that led to Örnsköldsvik's marina. As far as Sofia knew, Vera had never socialized with anyone from the office before. The unexpected lunch invitation had surprised everyone. Especially Sofia, although she couldn't help feeling flattered. No one had missed Mattias's obvious disgruntlement and even though Sofia didn't want it to, that had made her happy.

They strolled quietly down Nygatan side by side. The wind had died down, but the outdoor furniture at the cafes and restaurants was still wet from last night's rain. A thin ray of sunshine had broken through the clouds and Sofia greedily raised her face to the sky as she walked. Given how the weather had been so far this summer, you never knew how long the sun would stick around.

When they reached Allstar by the marina, Vera sat down at a table in the glassed-in sidewalk seating area and ordered a beer for each of them.

"It's Friday," she said before Sofia could object.

She sat down across from Vera and looked out at the crowd in the marina. Sweden's summer vacation was just getting started and the temporary pause in people's business lives had lured folks out into the light. Couples in love strolled among the tourists and families with kids with folding strollers. Sofia noted that very few of the boats moored in the marina seemed to belong to locals. From the open aft decks of the flashy high-end boats there was nothing to hear but southern Swedish dialects and she sighed wearily when the very caricature of an urban Stockholmite appeared in red shorts with a long-sleeved shirt tied casually around his neck over his piqué-weave shirt.

Her quick trip to Stockholm had made her appreciate Örnsköldsvik even more. No traffic, no hectic people pushing to the front of lines that never seemed to end. She couldn't understand why people would choose concrete and asphalt over the scent of moss and pine needles, although she did realize that maybe not everyone got the opportunity to choose.

"Well, what do you think?" Vera's voice roused Sofia from her thoughts.

"Uh, about what?"

"The pork tenderloin?" Vera pointed to the menu. "They make their own béarnaise sauce."

Sofia wasn't hungry, but she accepted the suggestion. She took a sip of the cold beer that the restaurant owner had brought out to them in person. Then she remembered the taste of yesterday's hangover and set her glass back down.

The owner stood at their table for a bit and chatted with Vera after he had taken their order. Sofia could tell from the conversation that they knew each other from before. Vera had worked with financial and narcotics crimes before she switched to the major crimes unit, two areas that unfortunately often led specifically to the restaurant industry. Despite her gruff image, Vera was popular and respected, and not just by her colleagues. Sofia was convinced that Vera could have had a distinguished career with the police if she had been willing to relocate, but she seemed to enjoy small-town life. No case was too small for her. Eva had said that Vera hadn't left a single unresolved case behind during her time at the station. True, one murder investigation had ended with the verdict being overturned on appeal and the perp had been acquitted, but Vera probably slept well at night knowing that she had gotten the right person even if the evidence had fallen somewhat short.

And one day, soon, someone would take over her position. Although the odds were minimal now that it would be her. It was dubious that she would even get to keep her job.

"Do you enjoy your work?" Vera asked, as if she had read Sofia's mind.

"Yes."

"What's your next move?"

"Move?"

"Life is like a game of chess, you know. You've got to think ahead and plan your moves accordingly. I know you're hoping for my job. I think it would be a good fit for you, but, well… I'm not the one who decides."

Sofia blushed.

"Oh, it's nothing to be embarrassed about!" Vera drank a swig of beer. "Just as long as you're prepared for what the job entails. You'll spend eighty percent of your time writing and reading reports. It wouldn't be a good fit for someone with a Gunvald Larsson complex; this isn't TV crime drama, you know? No so much running around in dark alleyways and chasing bogeymen, if you know what I mean?"

"I don't even own a trench coat," Sofia laughed. "And considering your figure, I'm guessing you don't do a lot of running around in alleyways during work hours."

Vera blinked, stunned, and then burst out laughing. The nervousness and the beer had loosened Sofia's tongue and Vera seemed to appreciate her candor. She chuckled happily as she prepared to dig into the piece of meat that had just been placed in front of her.

"So what's there to say about this damn investigation then?" Vera asked with her mouth full of tenderloin. She swallowed her bite before answering her own question. "There's something that doesn't add up about Christine Karst, I can say that much anyway. She's got something to hide. Why else would she be staying away? Maybe Ceder really did try to blackmail her and she had enough, just like we mentioned."

Sofia cut off a tiny piece of meat but didn't stuff it into her mouth.

"Very unusual M.O., though, for a woman if it was Christine," Vera said, wiping her mouth on her napkin before continuing. "Murder is rarely this complicated, you know. Humans are simple creatures with base, animal urges. The killer is almost always someone from the victim's inner circle. But that Fröding guy. I don't know. He doesn't seem squeaky clean either."

Say it now. Say now that you had sex with one of main suspects and then let him get away.

Sofia took a hesitant sip of beer and looked out at the marina without knowing where to begin. What was up with her? Was Fredrik really worth losing her job over?

"So, are you seeing anyone?" Vera raised her fork and pointed at her.

Sofia looked down at the table self-consciously.

"No, why do you ask?"

"It's important to have someone to share your feelings with when you work with the things we work with. It's not good for the soul to wallow in a ton of fucking misery day in and day out and then go home and sit alone in the evenings."

"But I don't usually wallow in misery, you do. I don't suffer from not having anyone to discuss stolen boat motors and pub brawls with in the evenings."

"Think about it anyway," Vera said with a smirk. "Loneliness is a disease of the soul. And it will be even more important for you to have someone in the future. If you want to do my job, I mean."

"What about you? Who do you share your feelings with?" The question just slipped out of her mouth and she regretted it the instant she saw Vera's face. Her lower lip was trembling. Sofia went completely cold inside. She searched desperately for something to say.

"I'm so sorry. I didn't mean to pry."

Vera wiped her nose with the back of her hand.

"My wife and I are getting a divorce," she stated briefly.

Sofia had always assumed that Vera was married to her job, but she was married to a real person, a woman. Sofia put her hand on Vera's arm.

Now she understood why Vera was so tight-lipped about her private life. Örnsköldsvik had been included on lists of Sweden's most homophobic cities several times, a shameful title that still lingered. And Vera was a prominent figure in the local police force, who appeared in the papers a lot. It would be hard to avoid unnecessary flak as the lesbian chief police inspector in a small town in Norrland. After a bit, Vera pulled her arm back and finished her beer in a few quick gulps. She set her glass down on the table with a bang.

"Now, that'll have to be that. We need to sort out this damn case."

–

Fredrik pulled up in front of the white house in Bonässund at four twenty. He had changed his shirt, put on a little deodorant, and combed back his dark hair. A shower would have been preferable, but it was still a significant improvement from this morning.

He parked his car next to a fastidiously pruned arborvitae and got out to check the name on the mailbox. Yup, this was the right place. The carved wooden mailbox had "The Hörnberg-Dagegård Family" painted on the side of it. A freshly waxed, older model Jaguar sat in front of the garage, and beside it a shiny, gleaming motorboat on a boat trailer. The house itself was made of sand-lime bricks and you could see the water down at the bottom of the grassy yard.

When Fredrik stepped inside the hedge, he discovered that Jan and Siw-Inger were already standing there waiting. They looked nice and neat, formally dressed like two tin soldiers under their front porch roof.

"Welcome, Fredrik!" Jan took his hand in both of his and shook it vigorously. "I must admit that Siw-Inger and I think this will be a little exciting. She said you're writing an article on the Dirk family?"

He couldn't remember having mentioned that, but since it seemed to appeal to the couple, he nodded.

"Siw-Inger and I went to summer camp with Bodil and Ester Dirk."

The man's enthusiastic tone and thick Norrland dialect made his wife's hyphenated first name melt together into a single word: Swinger.

"Come on in. Siw-Inger made coffee."

Fredrik obediently followed Jan and Swinger into the house.

The Dagegårds had prepared quite a spread. There were three matching cake plates and china cups. A strawberry and whipped cream cake towered like a centerpiece in the middle of the table. Jan and Siw-Inger giggled nervously.

"I'd like to start by showing you some pictures," Fredrik began.

The couple looked at each other excitedly as Fredrik pulled some of the pictures out of the stack of papers he had gotten from Philip and wedged them between the plates. Siw-Inger snatched them up immediately.

"That's you, isn't it?" Fredrik said, pointing over the table to the young girl on the far left.

"Oh, man!" Siw-Inger put her hand to her mouth. "Look at how cute I was, Jan!" She nudged her husband in the side and he nodded in approval.

"Hey, what about this doofus?" Jan said. He pointed to a pimply boy with shoulder length, curly hair. Siw-Inger laughed.

"That's Jan, you see?"

Fredrik nodded.

"We've been together since we were fourteen." Jan looked proudly at his wife.

"I understand that the Dirk family was a little... odd?" Fredrik said in the hope that the Dagegårds would stop focusing on themselves for a second.

"Oh yeah, you could definitely say that." Siw-Inger tossed her curly hair over her shoulder with an easy twitch of her head. "Real fanatics."

"You can say that again," Jan said, sounding uncomfortable.

"But hey, come on. No one believed all that. 'Spared by the holy angel,' what bullshit! Where was God when their apartment caught fire? That's what I want to know. Where was he then, hmm?"

The coffee machine grew quiet and Siw-Inger got up to transfer the coffee into the formal coffee pot. She started serving them without asking. She made a big deal of pouring it, so that Fredrik could see that the coffee pot matched the expensive china set on the table. He commented on the quality of the porcelain and Siw-Inger grinned as she sat back down.

"Yes, well, we don't want to seem stuck up or anything, but I think if you can afford it, you should treat yourself."

Fredrik took a sip and nodded in support.

"Did you know the Dirk sisters?"

"To a point," Siw-Inger said. "Bodil wasn't really someone you got to know. She lived like a shadow behind Ester. The rolling saint's eternal protector."

"Well, she didn't really have much choice but to shoulder that role," Jan continued carefully. "But she did it with such fervor that it felt uncomfortable sometimes."

"I understand that Ester was bullied?"

Jan looked down into his cup.

"Yeah, you know, we teased her quite a bit. About all that stuff about being spared by an angel and all that."

"But I wasn't the worst," Siw-Inger hurried to interject.

"I understood that Thomas was the instigator. Is that true?"

Siw-Inger nodded so her curler-curls fell forward again.

"And the suicide?" Fredrik asked. "That happened on Midsummer's Eve, right?"

"Yes, that night," Jan replied. "I had gone back to the mainland, but Siw-Inger and her sister were still there."

"If it was suicide," Siw-Inger said with a note of self-importance.

Fredrik leaned forward, interested.

"I understand that there were several people who suspected the death wasn't self-inflicted?"

She smiled conspiratorially.

"You don't touch 'God's chosen one' with impunity, if I can be so bold." Siw-Inger took a sip of her coffee and held eye contact with Fredrik.

"What do you mean?"

"I don't mean anything," Siw-Inger said with a knowing smile. "But you're probably smart enough to put two and two together." She nodded again.

Fredrik looked over at Jan questioningly. He was still peering into his coffee cup.

"Actually, the weird thing is that even the next day, rumors were flying that it hadn't been a suicide at all," Siw-Inger said. "And then it only took a week before Bodil disappeared."

"Disappeared in what sense? You mean to Bible school?"

Siw-Inger snorted.

"She didn't go to any Bible school."

Jan finally looked up and over at Fredrik.

"Aron sent her away. To a foster home."

"Why?"

Siw-Inger eyed Fredrik over her coffee cup.

"Maybe you should ask him."

48.

Gabriella was alone in the office. The other assistants who worked at Dahlman, Björc & Bergström had been let go when the company had lost several big clients. She had enough time to assist all three of the partners now. Both Johan Björc and August Bergström had started talking about selling the nice space in the stylish old building where their office was now and buying a smaller office somewhere outside of the city. If the company moved out to the suburbs, Gabriella planned to switch jobs. For her, working in the city was what mattered.

There were restaurants, shops, and all the status she had struggled to achieve since she left the little village outside of Jönköping where she had grown up. She had scrubbed away her dialect as soon as she set foot in the city limits, and as her salary had increased she had been able to clean the H&M clothes out of her closet and replace them with stylish suits from Karen Millen and handbags from Louis Vuitton. No, Gabriella really hoped the law firm didn't decide to move. This was a good job in every way. And if only Mats Dahlman could stay sober, it would be a dream job.

She had found him sleeping in the leather armchair in his office several times. She had lied for him even from the beginning, to avoid embarrassing him in front of waiting clients. "Unfortunately Mr. Dahlman has been held up in another meeting," or "Mr. Dahlman was summoned to court on an urgent matter." But she was starting to run out of excuses.

At any rate, he had promised to come in tonight. One half of a very famous TV duo had filed for divorce. The husband worked as program presenter on channel TV4 and he wasn't available for daytime meetings. His wife also worked at TV4, where she did the weather reports. They had been the media's darlings for many years and Gabriella had already read page after page about the divorce in the tabloids, but she would never have dreamed that they would turn to Dahlman, Björc & Bergström to handle the legal side of it.

She turned on the computer and switched on the overhead light. She had forgotten to buy fresh flowers for the vase across from the elevator, but after clearing away a few withered petals from the fragrant pink lily she determined that the current bouquet would last for another day. She dimmed the lights and set out a crystal pitcher of water and three clean glasses.

Everything was ready, but Mats still hadn't arrived. She knocked on the double doors that led into his office even though she knew he wasn't there, then she stepped in. His office was in good shape aide from a whiskey bottle and a glass sitting on his leather desk pad. She cleared them away, noting in irritation that the glass had left a ring.

A second later the bell dinged announcing that the elevator was on its way up. Gabriella sighed in relief. Mats had kept his promise. Now she just had to cross her fingers that he was sober.

She hurried out into the hallway to meet him, but when the elevator doors opened, she was dismayed to discover that it was the client, who was early. He had a young woman with him who definitely wasn't his wife. Based on the woman's stylish outfit, Gabriella guessed that this was probably only their first stop for the night. Who brought his mistress along to prepare for his divorce negotiations?

She nervously shook his hand and invited them to have a seat in the waiting room. There was still no sign of Mats. This was the last straw. She wasn't going to cover for him any more after tonight.

Gabriella snuck back into Mats's office and pulled the door closed behind her. After calling his home number several times without any answer, she dialed his cell phone. At the first ring tone, something started vibrating underneath his desk. She leaned down and discovered Mats's work cell phone, crestfallen. It must have slipped off the edge of the thick mahogany slab and was now dangling from its charging cord. She unplugged it and looked around his office. Had he really not noticed that he had forgotten his phone? Oh God, if so he must be in pretty bad shape. So much for the meeting with the waiting client. She unlocked his phone with the pin code that all of the partners used and started scrolling through his contacts. Maybe she could reach Mats's mother. She seemed to recall that she lived in Hökarängen and that he went out there sometimes when he wasn't working. When his mother didn't answer her phone either, Gabriella started looking through his phone. Twelve texts and nineteen missed calls. Three of the calls had come from the same number and had come in over the course of ten minutes on Midsummer's Eve. Only one minute later, a text had arrived from the same number: "Call me." Gabriella stood there looking at the phone in her hand, wondering what she should do. In the end, she made up her mind and dialed the number the missed calls had come from.

–

Karim waved and smiled as he pulled out of the police station garage in his green Saab. The evening sun gleamed off the car's finish and Mattias couldn't help noticing several rust stains around the wheel well. Karim could be so careless sometimes when it came to taking care of his cars.

Mattias waved listlessly back. He was tired, both of Karim's eternal optimistic way of looking at life and of his own naiveté. Didn't Karim see what was happening at the station? How he was being outmaneuvered in favor of Sofia. The whole thing just made him want to throw up.

His own car was parked on the next street over. Just as he hit the unlock button on his fob he realized that he had left his sunglasses on his desk. He slapped the roof of his car and swore to himself before relocking the car. Nothing was going right today. Now not only had he been forced to work late into the evening, but the whole investigation was also a big mess.

And to top it all off, in front of everyone, Vera had asked Sofia out on a private lunch date. He did not understand what Vera saw in Sofia. He had done everything she had asked, worked late, worked weekends, taken extra shifts, attended training courses, and Vera still didn't seem to see his potential. He could just imagine Sofia sitting there at lunch, smiling at Vera, lapping up every word she said, and sucking up to her for brownie points. Did she think one lunch was going to win her the coveted spot as Vera's successor? Then she thought wrong. He had been here longer and had better qualifications. He was not only stronger and smarter, he was also better liked by their coworkers. Sofia barely bothered to say hello to people and always remained aloof, so ridiculously snooty just because she had lived in Stockholm for several years. No, let her sit out there on Ulvön Island in her shockingly expensive house and look down on everyone and everything. At least he worked hard and made the effort to get to know his coworkers. His house in Husum may not be the classiest place and his finances were maybe not what they should be, but he was still careful to dress nicely and expensively and always have a car and a boat of the latest model. Viewed from the outside, he was very successful, much more so than Sofia, and surely that was something the higher-ups were looking for in choosing a replacement, that the person had social skills and cared about their relationships?

Mattias swiped his ID to open the door and sighed his way back up the stairs to his office. The offices along the corridor were empty except for one of the women from financial crimes. She sat bent over her reports without noticing him as he walked by. His own office was all the way at the end, next to Vera's.

As Mattias walked by, he heard a sound from her office. He stopped and listened. He could hear a muffled hum from her desk. At first he thought it was the fan in Vera's computer, but this sounded more rhythmic. It sounded like a cell phone. He walked in and quickly glanced around at the clutter on Vera's desk to try to find her old, dark–blue Motorola.

Mattias could still hear the sound and he realized in surprise that it was coming from the cardboard box underneath her desk, the one that contained the evidence material, which the forensics team had not had time to come pick up yet. He threw himself down there and started tossing the things out onto the floor. The plastic bag containing Christine Karst's cell phone was flashing and vibrating like crazy. Mattias held the bag and looked at the display.

Unknown number. What should he do? It had already rung several times and he had to decide if he was going to answer it or not.

With a decisive jerk, he ripped the plastic bag open and pushed on the green phone icon.

"Hello?"

Mattias listened intently to the person on the other end of the line.

"Yes, whom am I speaking with if I might ask?"

49

"Would you like the room for two nights then?"

"Yes, please." Fredrik took off Ceder's bag and set it on the front desk in Örnsköldsvik's Stadshotel. Then he realized what he had done and went to move it, but then he decided that he was the only one who knew who the bag belonged to. Here he stood with a murdered man's bag, checking into a hotel less than a mile away from the police station that housed the very police officers who were pursuing him.

"Good. Then all I need is a credit card."

"I'd prefer to pay cash if that's that all right?"

The clerk blinked in surprise, but immediately recovered her composure and smiled.

"Sure, but then unfortunately I need to ask you to pay for your room in advance."

Fredrik pulled two five-hundred-kroner notes from his plastic bag, which was hidden in Ceder's bag, and handed them over. He explained that he had lost his credit card and was still waiting for the new one to arrive. The clerk, who didn't ask for any further explanation, good-naturedly accepted the bills. Apparently the police hadn't asked them to be on the lookout for him at the hotel. And why should they? Surely no one expected him to be so idiotically stupid that he would return to the lion's den, with the whole flock of them standing outside, waiting?

Fredrik looked out the glass doors while the front desk clerk handled the transaction. The sun had set outside and there was a nice view of the water.

She passed him a key card and briefly explained which room was his and pointed up to the second floor. Unfortunately she only had one room left and it was a smoking room.

As he came up the wide stone staircase, his cell phone rang. He realized that he had forgotten to pull the battery out of it after his visit to Bonässund.

"Hi, this is Marit Sandgren, the director of Vedbacksgården. You had tried to reach me?"

"That's right," Fredrik replied, struggling to get his keycard to open the hotel room door. A strong cigarette smell hit him. He set the black bag down on the wall to wall carpeting, but kept his shoes on.

His visit to Siw-Inger had not resulted in a clearer picture of what had actually happened at that summer camp. But it was obvious that there was more to Thomas Nilsson's suicide than the old police report let on. It was clear that Siw-Inger considered Bodil to have been involved somehow, just as Adam Ceder seemed to have, if Fredrik was interpreting Adam's research inquiries correctly. But even if Fredrik hadn't learned that much more about the camp, he had come away with the name of a private nursing home. Aron Dirk's nursing home. The former Ulvön Island pastor was over ninety and lived in Vedbacksgården Nursing Home in the village of Kornsjö outside Örnsköldsvik. He had been living there for the last thirty years. It hadn't taken Fredrik very long to find the place online.

"I'd like to come visit Aron Dirk, and I was wondering if that would be all right? Maybe during the day tomorrow?"

"You're most welcome. What is this regarding?"

Fredrik thought it over. He couldn't really lie. What if Aron were with it enough, despite his age, to expose the lies?

"I have a couple of questions about the summer camps he used to run on Ulvön Island back in the late seventies."

The director breathed heavily into the phone. The clap of wooden clogs echoed in what must have been a stairwell.

"I'll let the staff know you're coming. I suggest you visit him in the morning. He's clearest then."

"I'll be in tomorrow then. Thank you."

Fredrik set the phone on the nightstand and lay down heavily on the bed.

He needed to sleep.

Saturday, June 29

50.

The town was empty and quiet when Sofia stepped out the door of her building. The sky looked as if it would open up soon, and the wind was blowing pretty strongly as she walked toward the station. She had not slept well. A thick porridge of nightmares had churned in her head and the deep sleep that she so needed had remained elusive. At around 4:30 a.m. she had given up and started getting ready for the short walk to work.

The brown brick building that housed both the police station and the Enforcement Authority, which was responsible for debt collection and evictions, was just across Highway E4 from the condo she had bought a few years earlier. She could see the window of Vera's office and the park below town hall from her kitchen table. As she had tried to force down a cup of coffee, she had seen the Persian blinds being raised down there. Vera was almost always at work by seven. Lately she had started staying later in the afternoons, and her occasionally grumpy image had been replaced with a look of constant anger. Now Sofia knew why. Going through a divorce took its toll on people. That much she understood, even though the only divorce she had observed at close range was Tord's. When he and Yvonne separated, Tord had seemed blasé and had claimed that the decision had been mutual, but Sofia knew that Yvonne had left him for a plum position as Eskilstuna's municipal administrator. And Tord had never met another woman after that.

Sofia pulled out her access card and entered the police building. Marie had gone home to Sundsvall the previous evening and would come in after lunch. Mattias didn't usually get in until eight. She and Vera were the only ones here at this hour.

She swallowed some acid reflux. She had to tell Vera today. The longer she waited, the worse it would be, guaranteed suspension and in a worst-case scenario, fired. This wasn't going to be a cheerful conversation.

Possibly her last one as a police officer.

As she approached Vera's office, she could hear her whispering, or rather hissing, at someone over the phone. Sofia stood outside her door, not knowing what to do.

"Lillemor, I can't do anything about that. Things are the way they are now. I'm not ready to retire yet. You're the one who made the ultimatum. Now this is how it's going to be."

The person on the other end of the call seemed to talk for a long time, or maybe they were both sitting there in silence. Sofia didn't know if she should go do something else or stick around and wait until Vera was done with her call. She shifted her weight from one leg to the other and a loud squeak from the linoleum flooring made Vera hang up abruptly without saying goodbye.

"Sofia!" Vera called her in without looking up. Her face looked strained and Sofia lingered in the doorway indecisively. Highway E4 curved around outside Vera's dusty office window. Traffic was light at this hour, but later in the morning it would pick up and the exhaust would be so thick that people with windows facing the highway couldn't open them. On the other side of the highway and the town's angular silhouette, you could just make out the water.

"Come in," Vera finally said, getting up to push the door closed behind Sofia.

Two empty coffee cups sat atop a pile of folders on her desk. A half-eaten cheese sandwich lay in the trashcan. Sofia sat down on the well-worn visitor's chair. The padding in the cushion had long ago disintegrated into dust.

Vera looked up, her eyes locked on Sofia.

"It would be ridiculous for us to pretend you didn't just overhear that." She nodded her head toward her phone.

Sofia stared at the jumble of documents posted on the wall behind Vera as she desperately tried to think of something to say. Every spare inch of wall space was covered with pictures and newspaper articles from Vera's career. Sofia's eye came to rest on a photograph that showed a scarcely twenty-year-old Vera shaking hands with Olof Palme himself. She looked young and serious, whereas the prime minister had a huge smile on his face.

"My wife has issued an ultimatum: retire or divorce," Vera continued when Sofia didn't say anything.

"Maybe that could be nice?" Sofia began. "I mean, you have been working here for…"

"But shouldn't I damn well be allowed to make that choice on my own?" Vera slapped her hand on the desktop, making Sofia jump. "It doesn't matter. It's already been decided. I apologize for dragging you into my private shit. Forget about it."

"But…"

Vera held up her hand to silence Sofia and pointed urgently to the investigation materials which were covering her desk in drifts. Sofia reached for a stack of papers, but left it sitting on her lap without starting to read. Sofia wanted to say something more, but Vera's focus had already returned to her screen.

51

It was just after nine when Fredrik arrived in Kornsjö. He was nervous about meeting Aron, but he managed to keep his anxiety in check. It was as if having a purpose had a calming effect on him.

From the nursing home's website, Fredrik had learned that Vedbacksgården was for patients who required round the clock care. Idyllic images showed smiling young men and women in purple polo shirts leading life drawing and pottery activities with the residents. Fredrik wondered if the reality was as harmonious as the pictures portrayed it.

He parked on the unpaved driveway and got out of his car. Vedbacksgården was housed in what looked like an old yellow school building. Tall Norway spruce trees swayed in the wind over the roof of the nursing home. Fredrik got out of his car and pulled his hood up over his head to shield himself from the rain. The wind was so strong that he was barely able to pull the building's front door open.

"Oh my God, can you believe the rain and the wind out there?!" the man behind the reception desk asked, handing him a paper towel.

"Yeah, that's some storm," Fredrik replied even though that was obvious.

"No worries. You can hold onto me if you're afraid you'll blow away," the man flirted with a wink.

Fredrik laughed shyly and dried his face with the paper towel.

"So, what can I help you with?"

"I'm looking for Aron Dirk."

An extremely heavy woman appeared out of nowhere and squeezed behind the front desk.

"John you're needed in the shower room."

The man, apparently named John, gave the older woman a defiant look, but then reluctantly did as instructed.

"John's a little… chatty," the woman said as John disappeared out of earshot. She sat down behind the computer, the springs in the desk chair protesting ominously under her considerable weight.

"I'm Marit. We spoke on the phone yesterday."

Fredrik shook her sweaty hand.

She eyed him compassionately over the edge of her glasses.

"I'm terribly sorry to have to tell you this, but Aron passed away during the night. Obviously we should have called, but we didn't have your number and…"

Oddly enough, Fredrik was seized by a feeling of sadness, even though he had never met Aron.

"I don't understand?"

The director laboriously stood up and walked around the counter.

"We're just as surprised as you are. He was feeling fine at bedtime, but when we went up this morning, he had passed away. I'm truly sorry. Would you like to come and say goodbye?"

Fredrik nodded, without knowing why. He wasn't family. The whole thing felt highly unethical, even though he was curious. After all, the director hadn't even asked him what his connection to Aron was.

She led him up a flight of stairs at an incredibly slow pace and then down a long corridor.

"Have you been here before?" she panted between steps.

"No."

They reached a room that had an adhesive label on the door with Aron Dirk's name on it. The director pushed open the door, which had been ajar, with a fleshy index finger and stepped into the room.

"Here he is."

The room looked freshly painted and sterile. There was a bouquet of summer flowers on a dresser and someone had hung up a pair of outdated, frilly floral curtains in the window in an unsuccessful attempt to give the room a personal touch. On a shelf over the head end of the bed there was a well-thumbed Bible sitting open beside a notebook and a pair of reading glasses. Aron Dirk lay on top of the made bed, his face turned out toward them. Someone had placed a rose on his chest and a candle was burning on the nightstand next to him as they waited for the funeral home to pick him up and transport him to the morgue.

Fredrik could not suppress the shiver that traveled down his spine as he saw Aron's terribly disfigured face. His injuries must have been caused by the fire in the apartment in Stockholm. His skin was pink and scarred, one ear was missing, and his hair grew only in tufts scattered here and there over his head.

"Did he ever have visitors?"

"No," the director replied. "Or, yes. Of course his daughter was here. Most recently yesterday, actually."

She turned around and looked at him as if she had said too much.

"We're not actually supposed to discuss the residents' visitors."

Bodil was here just a day ago? Fredrik didn't know what to think.

"His daughter? She was here?"

The director nodded, but with an expression that clearly showed that that subject was now closed. She walked over to Aron and tenderly adjusted the white sheet over his chest. Fredrik looked around the room. It was strange to think that a living person had lived here only a few hours ago, eaten, slept, and watched TV here. A half-filled glass of water and a pitcher stood on the nightstand. There was a plastic bin with rubber gloves and diapers in it.

"Would you like to stay for a bit?"

"No, that's not necessary," Fredrik replied quickly. He absolutely did not want to be left alone with the dead man.

She held out her hand to indicate that he should walk out the door before her.

"I have to see to a resident in the next room, but just follow the hallway back. You'll find your own way out, won't you?"

Fredrik nodded.

John was back manning the front desk downstairs. He was typing away briskly on Vedbacksgården's desktop computer and humming along contentedly to the music from the radio that sat behind the counter. When he heard Fredrik's footsteps, he spun around in his chair and grinned broadly.

"I knew you wouldn't be able to stay away!"

Fredrik came over to stand on the other side of the counter from him.

"I've just been up to see Aron."

John's eyes were filled with compassion.

"I heard he had passed away. He was so perky last night, but unfortunately age catches up with everyone eventually."

He watched Fredrik expectantly.

"Is there anything else I can do for you, my friend?"

"Yes, there is one thing you could help me with."

"Fire away." The sad look on his face was gone and he was once again smiling broadly. Fredrik assumed that he must be pretty used to having residents pass away.

"As I understand it, this is a private nursing home?"

"That's right."

"So who pays for the residents to stay here?"

"Some of the funding comes through various government programs, but generally relatives pay for the majority of it."

Fredrik took a step closer and leaned in over the counter.

"Could you tell me who was paying for Aron?"

"Unfortunately I'm not allowed to share that information. Although obviously we could discuss it over dinner sometime. Say at my place, maybe?"

Fredrik blushed.

"I'm sorry, but I'm not…" He shrugged apologetically.

John smiled again.

"Oh, the best ones never are, but maybe you could make an exception?"

Fredrik shook his head.

"I'm afraid not. But… maybe you could?"

John laughed as he rolled his chair over to a filing cabinet behind him.

"You know what, sweetie? For you I will."

–

A sharp tone signaled a call waiting on the speakerphone. They sat down around the conference table and Vera pushed the button with the green phone icon. The library was finally available again and Sofia was grateful not to have to meet in Vera's hot, cramped office.

"I've just come through Sundsvall," Kaj's deep voice filled the room from the speakerphone, "so I should be up with you in about two hours."

Mattias was leaning back in his chair, waiting for his turn to talk. After yesterday's shakeup in the case, the spotlight was on him and he knew it.

"Wikström?" Kaj said.

Mattias leaned closer to the phone. Kaj continued.

"Gabriella Johansson, the woman who called you yesterday, or to be more precise, who called Christine Karst, works as you know as an assistant in the law firm of Dahlman, Björc & Bergström and… fuck!"

They heard him messing around in his car.

"Um, hello?" Vera drummed her fingers on the table impatiently.

"I spilled coffee on my pants." Kaj muttered another several swear words before he cleared his throat and continued. "Where was I? Right, Christine had called one of the law firm's partners, Mats Dahlman, several times on Midsummer's Eve and when Gabriella couldn't reach Mats, she tried calling some of the people from his call log. It was very lucky that you happened to be there to take the call, Wikström."

Mattias crossed his arms over his muscular chest and shrugged casually.

"Some people diligently burn the midnight oil instead of going home and sleeping away their lives," Mattias said with a laugh and then stole a peek at Sofia.

"But that's not the most remarkable aspect of the story," Kaj continued. "The most noteworthy thing is that Mats Dahlman was found in his apartment this morning, murdered."

Vera who had just started hunting for her reading glasses froze in mid-motion, staring at the speaker. Mattias opened his mouth to say something, but Kaj beat him to it.

"I gave the medical examiner, who examined the body at the discovery site, a quick call. His informal guess was that Dahlman was murdered with a hammer."

Karim whistled. Mattias made another attempt to interrupt, obviously disappointed at how short his time in the spotlight had been, but Kaj kept talking.

"So there are a number of signs that we're looking for one and the same killer, a person who knew both victims. If we find out what the connection is between the victims, we'll be one step closer to finding who did this."

"What a fucking mess!" Vera blurted out, finally locating her reading glasses on top of her head. "So, two men have been murdered with the same or a similar murder weapon and both were in contact with Christine Karst. We have an APB out for her now. We can only hope that that will lead to something."

"If our earlier theory holds," Marie suggested, "that Ceder was pressuring Christine to sell the hotel, maybe Dahlman was somehow involved. Maybe if Dahlman agreed to fudge some legal aspect then he would get a piece of the pie? He did work in a law firm."

Marie and Vera exchanged glances and nodded.

"That is entirely possible," Vera agreed.

"But how does Fröding fit into that picture?" Mattias spluttered before anyone else had time to wedge themselves into the conversation.

"We don't know if he does," Kaj's voice sounded scratchy through the speaker. "But we're looking for someone with strong feelings about the victims. That's what the M.O. suggests. These were not random killings."

"Two victims... Does that mean we could be dealing with a possible serial killer?" Marie asked, her voice scarcely more than a whisper.

"So it seems," Kaj said and they could hear the highway noises in the background coming through the speakerphone.

52.

Ulvön Island, 1979

Thomas rolled over in bed and tugged on the duvet cover. It was pouring outside. His blanket had fallen on the floor and there was a cold draft from the window. He opened his eyes again and stared into the darkness. Mats was lying in the bed next to his, snoring with his mouth open. It smelled faintly of the green soap they used to clean the wood floors and the beer from his clothes, which were lying in a heap by the foot of his bed. The Midsummer party had just ended. They had left the kitchen and the patio in a shambles with beer bottles and cigarette butts all over.

Thomas got out of bed and tiptoed down the hallway to the stairs. He needed to smoke but in this weather he didn't even want to go out onto the front step. Bodil and Ester were the only ones with a bedroom upstairs, so he snuck up there. That was the only thing Aron had been careful about. The camp kids had to sleep downstairs. For his part, Aron slept in the little bakers' cottage on the property because he was such a light sleeper. Thomas had to admit that the pastor was pretty great. Everyone was welcome and they actually came up with fun stuff. Like the baseball tournament. He felt a bit guilty about the party, but he shook that off just as quickly. What had happened with Ester was not good, not at all, but what was done was done. Even if she blabbed, no one would believe her. Christine, Mats, Adam, and Marianne would all back him up. They would say that they were out in the yard when it happened. No one could prove otherwise.

Upstairs there was an unused room with a deep window ledge you could sit on. He had sat up there many times at night, secretly smoking and looking out over the fields that stretched down to the road. Bodil had caught him doing it several times. No one was allowed upstairs and there was no smoking in the house, but he didn't care. She might tattle to Aron, but he didn't care. What was the worst that could happen?

He lumbered across the room, heading for the window and the pack of John Silvers that he kept hidden under the window ledge. He carefully undid the latch as quietly as he could and reached for the pack of cigarettes. Cold, rain-laden air blew in over the floor.

He had just sat down when the floorboards behind him creaked. A gentle puff of air on the back of his neck made him stand back up. He turned around but there wasn't anyone there. He waited a moment and then sat back down and lit a cigarette.

It was beautiful outside. Dark and yet there was still a hint of twilight. Not at all like the rainy summer nights back home. He wondered what his friends were doing tonight. He couldn't wait until he could go home to the city.

Thomas dropped his finished cigarette out onto the lawn and leaned out to grab the window and pull it closed. A reflection flickered by in the pane of glass. A pale face just behind his shoulder. He tried to stand up, but someone prevented him, and he thumped back down onto the window ledge.

"What are you doing?"

A strong hand grabbed him around the neck, and something was placed over his head and tightened. He was yanked up onto his feet and then punched hard on the chest. It all happened so fast that he had no chance to defend himself. He fell helplessly out of the window, but he managed to grab hold of the sill. The noose around his neck was tied to the center post and must have already been hanging there when he sat down. How had he missed that? Thomas tore at it with his free hand, but he couldn't get it off. The fall he could handle, but not the noose.

Soon a little doll face appeared above him, a toy angel with white wings. It smiled at him ever so slightly. Thomas yanked hard at the noose, which was begging to cut into his skin at the base of his throat. His fingers ached. He wasn't going to be able to hold himself up any longer.

A shiny object was held up over the edge of the windowsill. Thomas had time to see the hammer as it approached his fingers in slow motion. One blow was enough. He didn't feel the pain, only a terrible fear. The crushed fingers lost their hold and he fell backwards. With a jerk, the noose tightened around his neck. The more he flailed, the harder it got to breathe. His tongue was forced up out of his throat. The blood in his head felt like it had stopped moving altogether.

He saw the doll lean out the window above him.

It felt like his eyes were being forced out of their sockets. He closed them and thought of God.

Hadn't Aron said that He welcomes everyone to His heaven?

53.

"Mats Dahlman and Adam Ceder." Kaj had scarcely made it into the library before he started discussing the investigation. He was still struggling to extricate himself from his sports jacket as he reached for the whiteboard pen.

"One of the neighbors said she saw a blond woman standing outside the building and looking up at Dahlman's apartment just a few days ago." Kaj tapped meaningfully on Christine Karst's long, blond hair in the picture on the whiteboard. "I know that you've been speculating that Ceder may have been murdered to prevent him from buying the hotel, but in my opinion there were strong emotions behind both murders. So we should be open to the possibility that it may not have had anything to do with the business deal. Perhaps Christine had a different motive for hating both Ceder and Dahlman."

Vera sighed.

"So you think that Christine might have stopped in Stockholm to murder Mats Dahlman before continuing on to wherever she is?" Mattias asked skeptically.

"It's possible," Kaj replied without turning around.

Eva knocked on the door and as usual came in without waiting for a response. Her eyes froze when they hit Kaj's wiry figure up by the whiteboard.

"Yes?" Kaj said.

"Um, the toxicology report came back," she said and handed it to Vera.

"Thank you. Was there anything else?" Her assistant shook her head and flashed a big smile at Kaj before making herself scarce.

Vera flipped back and forth through the papers and then handed them to Karim who was sitting next to her. He nodded, surprised, and stretched across the table to hand them to Sofia.

"The blood samples collected from Ceder showed a significant quantity of benzodiazepines," Vera reported, looking at Kaj.

"How large a quantity? Was it a lethal dose?"

"No," she shook her head, "but it was enough that he would have been pretty fucking impaired."

Sofia went completely cold. That was the same medication that Fredrik's doctor had prescribed.

"Well, we all know who's been munching on that type of pill, don't we?" Mattias said, immediately putting her thoughts into words.

"Although they're really common these days, aren't they?" Marie said, looking thoughtful. "As far as I know they're also used for epilepsy and sleep disorders. Maybe that's all it is. Maybe Ceder had trouble sleeping? If the pills weren't what killed him, then it doesn't really mean anything in terms of our investigation."

"What have you had time to find out about Dahlman, Karim?" Vera asked.

Karim reached for his computer and opened up Dahlman's murder investigation.

"We didn't get anything actionable from the forensics investigation of his apartment," Karim began. "He was probably attacked right outside his front door and then made his way back into his front hall where he later died. The murderer then closed Dahlman's apartment door. There were traces of blood in the stairwell, but nothing noticeable enough that, for example, the mailman would react." He looked up at Vera. "Apparently Dahlman's worked focused mostly on divorce law and dividing couples' property during a divorce. So it's not clear that he would have been able to help Ceder buy a hotel. But I'll contact his coworkers today and find out if maybe he had some professional involvement in some way with Ceder Hotels."

"Then I'll take another look at Ceder's call history and see if Dahlman's phone number shows up," Marie said and patted the stack of papers sitting in front of her on the table.

"Sofia, do you have anything new on Karst?"

"None of her credit cards have been used since the night before Midsummer's Eve. Her boat on the other hand has been found. It turned out that one of the chefs had borrowed it. He's been on vacation since Midsummer. Christine had personally given him permission to borrow it. And the boat wasn't equipped with Meta Trak, not that that matters now…"

"OK, then we know that she didn't use her boat to leave the island either," Vera said, looking around at the group in frustration. "How the hell did she leave then?"

"But how do we proceed with Fröding?" Mattias was like a badger when he got his teeth into something. Sofia knew that he wouldn't let go until he heard bones breaking.

"See if there's any way to speed up the tower dumps. We need to get in touch with him and find out what the hell he has to do with all of this. In the meantime, I want everyone to keep looking for any commonalities that might tie Mats Dahlman, Christine Karst, and Adam Ceder together."

After the meeting, Sofia had made sure to leave the station before Kaj managed to catch her alone. Linda Pihlgren had called and left a message on her phone. She wondered if Sofia was coming out to the island, but she hadn't said what it was about. Sofia had tried calling back but hadn't gotten any answer. Kaj had sent her several texts asking if they were going to see each other and if he could take the ferry over. He sounded eager, but she couldn't answer him. She just couldn't deal with any more sappy emotions. Things were complicated enough as they were. Although she was grateful that they got to benefit from his professional expertise. They didn't have the experience to conduct an investigation like this on their own, not even with Marie's help, but he would have to stay at the hotel and under no circumstances did she intend to share either a bed or meals with him.

Nausea churned in her stomach. She felt like she was going to throw up several times before she finally climbed aboard the Horse and made it out onto Örnsköldsvik Bay. A half hour on the water helped for a while, but as soon as she stepped ashore at Ulvö Hotel that gnawing sensation was back again. It felt like her stomach was full of rats, trapped panicking rats. She needed to make an appointment to see her doctor. Her father's oncologist in Umeå had said she could call anytime.

Linda Pihlgren was standing up on the hotel's patio with a tray full of glasses, pouring some rosé.

"Would you like a glass?" Linda asked. "Or maybe you're on duty?"

The thought of acidic wine made Sofia turn up her nose.

"I got your message. What did you want to talk about?"

"Do you have time?" Linda said quietly and set her tray down.

Sofia nodded and they sat down at an empty table.

"This might sound stupid, but I've been wondering about that Fredrik guy who was staying here."

Sofia tried to appear impassive.

"I heard that he might be a suspect," Linda said. "Is that true?"

"Unfortunately I'm not at liberty to say."

"No, of course not." Linda looked down at the table. "I didn't mean to pry, but… Um, there've been some rumors and I was wondering about how he looked when he checked out. You know, the way you think about things. Like, did he look like a murderer?"

It was touchingly naïve. Sofia didn't know if she felt sorry for Linda or envious of her.

"Well, you see, I saw him when he checked in and he only had this little fabric sack with him. I noticed it because I thought that was odd."

"And?"

"When he checked out he had two bags, the fabric sack and a black back with a Henry Lloyd logo on it, the same kind of bag that Adam Ceder had with him when he checked in. My brother has one like it. So, I don't know if that's of interest or not, but I thought I would mention it."

Sofia stared blankly into space. Her mind was racing, the thoughts spinning faster and faster until they came to an abrupt halt on the memory of her and Fredrik down by the pier the evening of Midsummer's Eve. That light hug, the painful silence. What had he looked like? Jeans and a light-colored shirt, black leather jacket. And a fabric sack. Nothing else.

When she found him on her front porch, he had had a bag.

With a Henry Lloyd logo.

54.

As she skidded in with her red Golf and came to an abrupt stop, she made four new parallel gouges in her gravel driveway, which had been so neatly raked. She took the three front steps to the front door in one leap and jogged down the hall without taking off her shoes. The bag. Fredrik had been sitting on her front step with that damned bag in his lap when she came home on Midsummer's Day. His pale face as they walked inside, his anxious body language. And yet she hadn't reacted. How blind could a person be? Her skin stung with shame. She didn't know what part of her was most embarrassed, the policewoman or the daughter of an alcoholic. She was usually so good at being able to sniff out a lie and yet she had allowed herself to be blinded. She had invited him into her home. Offered herself to him.

She remembered how she had walked around at night after he had fallen asleep, turning things off in the house, bewildered by the situation, but those butterflies in her stomach had clouded her police instinct, which had never failed her before. Now it was screaming inside her. That was Adam Ceder's bag he had been carrying. She had protected him from her colleagues, refusing to believe that he was anything other than innocent.

She yanked open the door to her guest room and recoiled from the unmade bed, where they had made love, one of the locations. Her whole house was sullied. Her father's pine bed, the rug in the living room. Had they done anything else in the few days he was here?

Sofia stripped the covers off the bed, flipped the mattress up. The bedside lamp followed in her rage, but she kept going, throwing things onto the floor. She kicked the rag rug that her grandmother had woven into the corner, yanked out all the drawers from the nightstand. Allowed this physical outlet for her anger.

That's when she noticed it. Under the chair next to the bed, one sleeve of a leather jacket stuck out, now half hidden by the rag rug. Fredrik's jacket.

Winded, she sat down on the now mattress-less bed frame and picked the jacket up onto her lap. She checked her impulse to inhale his scent from the collar. She sat like that for a long time with the jacket on her lap, allowing her breathing to calm down. Then she began slowly and methodically going through all the pockets. She didn't know what she was looking for until she found it, a folded piece of paper in the inside pocket. She carefully pulled it out and unfolded it, fully aware that she was breaking all the rules for how to properly handle evidence. She turned on the light and looked at the piece of paper. It was a color printout of an old photograph. The date stamp showed that it was from June 22, 1979, and it showed a group of young people, in their early teens, standing neatly lined up in front of Ulvö Chapel. A beautifully greenery-covered maypole had been set up on the lawn. Sofia pulled her finger over the line of well-groomed, well made-up faces. A man in a black cassock and white collar stood behind the young people: Aron Dirk. The picture must have been taken at one of the summer camps he had run. Those camps had been held for several years in the late 70s, but as far as she knew, they hadn't continued after that. She had heard terrible stories about Aron Dirk growing up, the almost fanatical pastor who lost both his daughters and his wife. Or was it only the one daughter? It was unpleasant at any rate. Those must be the daughters standing in the front, since one of them was in a wheelchair and the other had her hand on the wheelchair's handle. Bodil and Ester Dirk. Yes, now it came back to her. The family had left the island before Sofia had been born, but talk in the village had lingered on.

The pastor whom God forgot. And there was something more. Wasn't Bodil the one people whispered about? Sofia looked out over the water, thinking back to her recollections of her father and Tord mumbling to each other at the kitchen table, but their words slipped away, like freshly caught perch from a dip net.

Several of the faces in the picture were familiar. Her gaze stopped on a girl with long, blond hair on the far right, Christine Karst. Now missing, suspected of being involved in one murder, possibly two. At that time, the forgotten daughter of a world-renowned pianist who put her career before everything. Was it a coincidence that she found herself looking into the missing hotel owner's eyes now?

A clicking sound out on the deck made Sofia stand up. She kicked the covers that were lying on the floor aside and walked out there. The door was ajar. Had she forgotten to close it yesterday morning? Her thoughts expanded and the churning in her stomach once again asserted itself. The rocking chair had tipped over in the wind and was lying there with its runners up in the air. It seemed like it was crying out for help. She stood it back up and sat down, still with the printout of the photo in her hand.

Why did Fredrik have a picture from an old summer camp held on Ulvön Island, a picture that included Christine Karst? She ran her thumb over the paper as she contemplated that. There was a redheaded boy with curls at the back of his neck also on the far right-hand side. He looked familiar. It wasn't until her thumb grazed the boy's face that she felt a change in the texture of the paper. She held it closer to her face and saw that the eyes had been perforated with a pin.

A shiver ran down her spine.

She had seen him before.

Once the trains of thought finally came together, the terrible realization knocked the wind out of her. Sofia raised the picture again up to the light.

Even without his eyes, she recognized him.

She was looking at Adam Ceder.

55.

In an Upstairs Bedroom

It's time now. The work that God has charged us with must be finished.

"The righteous shall rejoice when he seeth the vengeance: he shall wash his feet in the blood of the wicked."

Feel how true those words are. For you and for me, my child.

You must strike back against those who have done wrong and come forward in your true garb.

They will bow before us and beg for forgiveness.

But you will not grant them any.

Sunday, June 30

56.

Tord lifted the coffee kettle off the wood stove and removed his snus, his phone, and his wallet from of his pockets before he sat down at the table with the moisture-damaged cardboard box on the floor below him. The top was dusty, but he was astonished that it had held up so well even out in the shed for all these years. It contained papers and photos that he and Gösta had found after the Dirk family had left the island in a hurry. They had probably planned to come back and get them, but that had never happened. Tord cautiously lifted the lid. There was an envelope with color photos and negatives on top; birth certificates for the daughters, one for Bodil and one for Ester; a few photos of the girls when they were little; a baptism certificate and a death certificate and a cause of death certificate for Elisabeth Dirk. Tord shivered and quickly set that aside. In the bottom there were loose sheets of paper and envelopes. There was something that looked like journal pages at the bottom of the stack. They seemed to be photocopies of handwritten notes.

> *The patient exhibits strong auditory hallucinations. The patient should be admitted for further testing. The patient may have violent and suicidal tendencies.*

Who had written this? And why did Aron have these? A sudden bang on the wall that abutted the shed made Tord jump. He stood halfway, about to go out and see what it was, but then he realized he probably forgot to close the hasp on the shed door when he got the box out. The wind must have blown the door out against the wall. Even so, an uneasy feeling crept over him that he couldn't explain. Although maybe it wasn't so strange after that miserable reading, he thought. He put away the unintelligible documents and opened another few envelopes of photos. Tord smiled when he saw photos of the kids dancing around the maypole, running with eggs balanced on spoons, and rowing out on the strait. He didn't know what Fredrik was actually planning to write, but if he was interested in the camps this would surely make him happy. He flipped through several stacks of pictures and eventually came to 1979, the year when the last camp was held. Tord studied each picture for a long time, trying to remember the children who had attended. His memory wasn't anywhere near as sharp as Gösta's and the only person he could actually remember was Aron. Obviously he could pick out Ester because of the wheelchair, but he had only met the girls a handful of times. Bodil was close to her sister in all the pictures. A pale copy of the bubbly girl with the long, blond hair and clear blue eyes. They were nearly identical, but it was as if Bodil had lost all her color compared to her sister. Tord set the pictures down and looked out at the rain, which was beating on the windows again. This summer would go down in history for its fickle weather. He scratched his scalp and reached for his snus tin. His eyes stopped on one of the pictures on the table. He leaned forward to study it. He held it up closer to his face while he felt around for his reading glasses in his chest pocket. When he didn't find them, he got up, still with the picture in his hand, and went to look in the storage bench in the kitchen to try to find a magnifying glass. A feeling of urgency came over him. He rummaged around in the junk drawer, among the pens, pads of paper, and card games until he found what he was looking for. He quickly sat back down at the kitchen table again, pushed aside the other pictures, and set the one he had in his hand on the tablecloth. With his back bent, he studied it through the magnifying glass.

That couldn't be possible. He looked over at Marianne's house. It was almost six o'clock in the morning, and it was still dark over there. Marianne was usually as much of an early riser as he was. A streak of worry came over him. It felt urgent that he get ahold of her. Tord reached for his cap, pushed everything into the box and tucked it under his arm. Then he called Sofia. Her voicemail picked up and he left her a brief message. Before he walked over to Marianne's place, he turned around and did something he hadn't done for many years. He locked his door.

—

After all the rain last night and this morning, her bedroom felt humid. This weather took a lot of the sting out of having to miss her vacation, Sofia thought. She pictured her coworkers—who were always going on about the delights of the outdoors—floating around in their tents.

The wind picked up so the rain was hitting the window panes almost sideways. They needed to be reputtied. Yet another thing on the list of tasks she hadn't had time to tackle yet. Sofia pulled the covers up around her ears. She didn't want to get up. She didn't want to do anything, didn't want to go to the station and see Kaj, and she absolutely didn't want to have to tell Vera about Fredrik. There was no getting out of that now. Fredrik had something to do with Adam Ceder's murder. The only question was what. Could he really have killed him?

And what did the picture mean? There was no way to look at those poked-out eyeballs as anything other than a threat against Ceder. But from whom? Fredrik? That didn't fit with their suspicions about Christine or with Mats Dahlman's murder. Was Kaj's suggestion right, that maybe the whole thing wasn't related at all to buying the hotel?

She wanted to pull the covers over her head and scream. Everything was going to hell. She thought about her fishing reel, which was still unopened, and wished fervently that she had never gone out to the island house before Midsummer. Then she would have avoided all of this and gotten to go on her trip to Northern Norway along with her fishing friends.

Instead, now she was lying here alone with DNA traces from a suspected murderer in her bed.

She had to tell Vera. Today. Not only had Fredrik gone to see and argued with Ceder before he died, he had also been seen with Ceder's bag and had been walking around with a picture of him with his eyes poked out. Even so, there was something that didn't add up, something she wasn't seeing.

Ceder and Karst had clearly known each other since they were young, and according to the hotel manager at Ceder City East, Ceder had a way of sniffing out people's personal problems. Both the guard at the property in Alicante and Linda Pihlgren had said that Christine was mentally ill. Had Ceder gone after the wrong person, someone who was willing to fight fire with fire? Maybe the picture was a warning from Christine, a threat about what would happen if Ceder didn't stop blackmailing her. That was a theory that fit well with their working hypothesis, but what did Fredrik have to do with that? And the camp? Her mind was racing with so many thoughts whirling around faster and faster and she couldn't seem to catch any of them. The knot in her stomach tightened and her mouth filled with saliva. Sofia swallowed with difficulty.

This was an opening in the investigation. They were on the verge of a breakthrough, she sensed that. If only she could put all the pieces together before she dropped the bomb, maybe she would have a better chance of protecting herself from the shit storm that would arise once Vera found out how big a mess she had made of things.

Her phone buzzed on the nightstand. The message on the screen said that the pike fishing team was going to meet tonight to plan for this weekend's prize ceremony. The team had ended up landing a spot on the podium in the Norwegian competition and several of the Swedish fishing teams were going to attend the awards ceremony. Sofia had really been looking forward to seeing some of the people she socialized with online through the fishing forum, but it would have to be another time. She was just about to set her phone back down when she saw that she had a voice message. She clicked on her voicemail.

"Hi, Sofia." Tord sounded serious and she was filled with apprehension. "I have a little information for you, and I need to talk to you. But not over the phone. Could you call me as soon as you get this?"

Sofia looked at the call log. Tord had called her before six a.m. that morning. What in the world could be so important that he would call that early? She dialed Tord's number and heard his phone ringing. After seven rings, she hung up.

She might as well go over there.

57.

Sofia closed the door to her house in Norrbysbodarna and hurried to her car. She drove aggressively, changing gears assertively. One early-bird tourist with a dog quickly jumped out of the way to avoid being splashed by the vast quantities of water that had accumulated on the roadway. She raised a hand in an apologetic wave to them.

She left her car by the fire station, jogged past the chapel, and then turned up toward Tord's house. The rain-soaked grass was like a skating rink under her sneakers and she had to put her arms out to keep from slipping. His windows were dark. She knocked several times, but no one came to open the door. Sofia pressed down on the door handle. Locked. She cupped her hand over her eyes and tried to look through the windowpane. There was no one in the kitchen. Tord's cell phone, wallet, and snus tin were all lined up on the table. The rain was lashing the window in irregular sheets depending on how the wind changed. He wouldn't have taken the boat out in this weather, would he? She looked around his yard. Tord's cargo moped wasn't where he usually kept it down next to his deck. She saw the light on in Marianne Nordin's place. She squeezed past the lilac in the opening in the wall that separated the properties while clutching her unbuttoned jacket closed over her chest. The rain picked up.

She knocked hard on the door and then stepped inside.

"Sorry to just barge in, but it's pouring out there!"

There was no sign of Marianne, but Sofia could tell that there was a window open somewhere. The wind was blowing right through the house. There were two coffee cups sitting on the kitchen table. A carton of milk had tipped over and the embroidered tablecloth hung over the edge of the table like a downspout above a puddle of milk on the floor.

"Marianne?"

Her hand went to the holster at her hip, her muscles reacting reflexively to the surge of adrenaline, but there was no weapon there.

"Is anyone here?"

There was a newspaper on the floor next to the milk. Sofia jumped when a gust of wind suddenly made the top few pages move.

"Marianne, it's Sofia Hjortén!" she called into the house.

She turned the corner into the living room and saw the lavender tulle curtains hitting the ceiling in the strong gusts of wind.

"Oh my God, oh my God," Marianne moaned. She was kneeling on the parquet floor, feeling around on a body. There was broken glass on the floor inside the door to the glassed-in veranda. And blood.

"What happened?" Sofia screamed.

Marianne didn't respond. Her hands moved back and forth over the lifeless body as she slipped around on her knees in the pool of blood. She put her cheek to the man's chest to listen for heartbeats and a bloody tuft of gray hair stuck out into Sofia's field of vision.

Something inside her turned off.

As if from outside her own body, she saw herself run over and push Marianne away. She dropped down to her knees and mechanically and purposefully begin doing compressions. She stopped to try to breathe air into the blood-covered mouth, but the heart still wasn't beating.

"Call 911!" she yelled, trying to establish eye contact with Marianne who sat hunched over beside her, crying quietly. Sofia managed to get her cell phone out of her back pocket and tossed it onto Marianne's lap.

"Marianne, call now! He's dying!" Marianne slowly looked up and looked into Sofia's eyes in despair. After what felt like an eternity, she nodded weakly and reached for the phone. "Speaker. Put it on speaker phone!" Marianne's bloody fingers were slipping on the smooth screen, but she succeeded in activating the speaker and the operator's voice could be heard, authoritative and inspiring confidence.

"Emergency Call Center, what is the nature of your emergency?"

Marianne held the phone up to Sofia who was furiously struggling to do chest compressions and count, her hands clasped together over the man's chest.

"This is Sofia Hjortén with the Örnsköldsvik Police. We have an injured man, head trauma. He's bleeding out of one ear."

"Does he have a pulse?"

"No!" Sofia practically screamed. She was on the verge of succumbing to the fear, but she cleared her throat and tried to pull herself together.

"We're doing chest compressions."

"Good. Where are you?"

"Northern Ulvö Island, in Ulvö Harbor. You need to send a helicopter!"

The dispatcher typed on a computer and simultaneously began a second call. Sofia could hear her start arranging the emergency response.

"Are there other people there with you?"

Sofia looked at Marianne, who was sitting as if turned to stone, holding the phone out in her bloody, trembling hand.

"No, well yes, but no one who can relieve me."

"If possible, ask someone to go call for help. It's going to take us a while before we can get there. You need to keep the heart going until we arrive."

Sofia knew it would take them at least an hour, maybe more.

The dispatcher's voice slipped over to her other conversation. Marianne was alternately weeping and sobbing. Sofia had to yell to get her to react.

"Marianne, look at me! Look at me! You have to go outside. We need help. It's going to take them a long time to get out here. Go out and yell for help!"

"I don't dare," Marianne said, shaking her head in jerky motions.

"Do you know who the injured person is?" The dispatcher was back on the line.

Sofia looked up and saw the curtains whipping against the ceiling. Again she felt as if she were looking at her own body from the outside. She looked at those long pieces of fabric that had picked up blood from the floor and were now splashing it on the walls in the driving wind.

"Tord. His name is Tord Grändberg. Please, hurry."

"Marianne!" Sofia yelled again. "You have to go get help. Can you do that?"

A tremor ran through Marianne's body and the phone fell out of her hand. It splashed as it landed screen-down in Tord's blood, making Sofia's stomach lurch. Marianne stared at her in terror.

"Now, Marianne! Run and get help!"

58.

Fredrik stopped his car in the turnaround that separated the virgin forest from last remnants of civilization and looked around. The woods became dense only a few meters in, and the dirt road up to the house was practically overgrown. It wasn't possible to drive all the way there. He sat there in the car with his hands on the steering wheel. On the passenger's seat beside him sat a photocopy of the invoice with the address he had received from John at Vedbacksgården. After visiting Aron, Fredrik had returned to the hotel mulling over how to proceed. Eventually he had fallen asleep and hadn't woken up until late in the afternoon. It was starting to get dark now and he regretted not having made it out here earlier.

He did not want to be here. All his senses screamed to him that he should turn around and drive the other way, back to something that at least from a distance could be mistaken for a normal life. Right now he didn't care if it involved a lifetime in some treatment program in Sundsvall or dying alone in his grandmother's apartment. The shadows crept closer and closer to him. The only reason someone would choose to live out here is that they didn't want to be found.

Images of Aron's badly burned face flitted through his head and he shivered. How had he ended up in this situation? Adam Ceder, the bag, the police... Sofia. This couldn't end well. He understood that, but there was no going back now.

Fredrik opened the driver's side door. The green mailbox at the end of the road lacked both the house number and the owner's name, but he didn't need those.

This was Bodil Dirk's house.

Aron's missing daughter, who had paid for her father to live in the private hospital for 38 years. The girl who had been accused of murder by her own father and then sent away to a foster family. The girl that Adam Ceder had researched.

Fredrik did his best to shut his car door quietly and was careful not to lock it. He turned around and looked back down the dirt road... no neighbors. The rain had eased up and a milky mist had settled over the grasses along the sides of the road. The gravel crunched loudly under his shoes. In the distance he could hear the birds' persistent blend of alarm calls and song.

The forest had closed in so much on the dilapidated two-story house that only the front steps were visible through brushy undergrowth. Heavy cotton curtains were drawn, covering the windows along with a thick layer of dirt and pollen on the windowsills. His hand trembled as he raised it to knock on the textured glass panel in the front door. Not a sound was heard from within. He knocked again, a little harder. No signs of movement.

Fredrik stepped back, walked back down the front steps, and looked up at the upstairs. The paint was peeling off in several places and the gutters were overflowing with rotten leaves. The house looked abandoned. Had he come to the wrong address after all?

He decided at least to walk around back and look. It was hard to move around because of all the vegetation. The tall birch saplings tore at his arms. The ground squelched as the soles of his shoes sank into the mud. When he finally made it around to the back, he found himself standing in front of a wooden basement door, painted blue. It was secured by a bolt with a hefty, newer model padlock, but there was no sign of anyone. Fredrik looked around before going down the steps that led to the basement door. He tried the door handle even though he knew it was futile. He knocked hard a few times and put his ear to the door. Not a sound.

He was about to walk back around to the front when his foot knocked something on the top step over, a metal bowl. He looked at the contents that slid out. It looked like dirt, but when he leaned in closer, he smelled something bad. He turned the bowl back over with his foot to discover rotten cat food teaming with maggots.

So someone was living here.

He looked around indecisively at the overgrown property, but couldn't detect any other signs of life. He jogged back to his car, turning now and then to make sure no one was coming after him. He rummaged around for a pen and a scrap of paper from the glove compartment and wrote "Call me." Then he scribbled his name and phone number and left the note in the mailbox.

Back in the car, he made sure to lock his doors properly and inserted his key into the ignition. He drove quickly around the turnaround and cast one last glance into the rearview mirror.

It wasn't until he had left that the curtains upstairs began to move.

59.

In an Upstairs Bedroom

"And shall not God avenge his own elect, which cry day and night unto him, though he bear long with them?"

His own elect.

She was one of God's own elect.

She who had been sullied and ridiculed.

Revenge has not yet fallen on everyone who deserves it. We still have work to do.

They desecrated God's own elect, let their eyes and hands touch her sacred body.

And for that they must die.

60.

"Go home!" Vera said. "It's late and there's nothing you can do now."

"I can't sit around doing nothing," Sofia insisted. "I need to work."

She pulled her hands through her wet hair and then pulled the hair band off her wrist. Kaj came in with two cups of coffee and handed one to Vera and one to Sofia. His hand reached out and touched Sofia's shoulder, but he backed away when he saw her face and sat down on the chair across from her instead.

"You haven't heard from them?"

She shook her head and blew on the coffee.

"They won't know anything until tomorrow at the earliest."

"And Marianne?"

"She had some lacerations on her hands from the broken glass on the floor but was mostly in shock. She didn't want to stay at the hospital. They sent her home with a dose of sedatives. Two nurses live on the island, and they promised to keep an eye on her for the next few days and make sure she's recovering."

"We sent a forensic team out to the house, but they couldn't say very much," Vera said, pushing her glasses up on top of her head. "The window glass in the door to the veranda broke when the door was flung open, no fingerprints. Were you able to get any sense of what had happened?"

Sofia shook he head. Marianne had been so out of it that she hadn't been able to get anything out of her, and by the time the ambulance helicopter finally arrived, Sofia had been so mentally and physically exhausted that she could barely climb into it.

She swallowed a gulp of coffee. Even though she had showered several times and changed her clothes, the smell of Tord's blood lingered. She felt empty and sick to her stomach.

"No, just that someone had come in. We'll have a proper questioning session with Marianne tomorrow."

Vera nodded matter-of-factly.

"Although, there is something else I need to tell you," Sofia said.

Both Kaj and Vera watched her attentively. Sofia wished Kaj hadn't been there, but she couldn't put it off any longer now.

"Fredrik Fröding," she began. Vera crossed her arms in front of her chest as if she knew she wasn't going to like whatever she was about to hear. "He was at my house on Midsummer's Day. We are... were in a relationship. Or, not a relationship, more of a..." Sofia's voice faded away when she saw the look in Vera's eyes. "I did not know at the time that he was a suspect," she tried to defend herself.

Vera stared at her, her forehead deeply furrowed. Kaj, who had been leaning forward toward her in his seat now leaned back. There was no missing the hurt look on his face.

None of them said anything.

"I think that Fredrik may have had Adam Ceder's bag when he came to my house. One of the waitresses at the Ulvö Hotel had seen him checking out with the same sort of bag that Ceder had had when he checked in, and I'm quite sure that that was the one, a black bag with a Henry Lloyd logo."

Vera got up and paced back and forth across the library's worn linoleum, agitated. The damage was already done, so Sofia continued.

"And then there's this. I found it yesterday in Fredrik's jacket, which he had forgotten and left behind at my place." She handed Kaj the printout of the picture, which she had placed in a plastic bag. He looked at it for a long time.

"Is this...?"

Sofia nodded.

"And this one? With the eyes…?"

Kaj handed the picture to Vera who exhaled loudly when she noticed the same thing he just had, that both Christine Karst and Adam Ceder were in the photo.

"That one must be Mats Dahlman." Vera looked like she was about to explode.

"It's possible," Kaj said, taking the picture back and nodding. "We'll find out."

"I know how this looks," Sofia said, squirming in her seat, "but I'm still not sure that Fredrik… I don't believe that he… I'm not trying to defend him. I just…"

One look from Kaj silenced her.

Vera walked over to the window and looked at the pink Elim Church building across the street. Her voice was scarcely more than a whisper at first.

"Look, I cannot tell you how to conduct your private life, but I fucking can tell you how to do your job. This is outrageous." Her eyes flashed as she spun around. "I'm trying to give you greater responsibility and a chance to show everyone what you can do, and what are you doing? Hopping into bed with a suspected murderer and then lying about it after the fact."

"I didn't lie. I…"

"What the fuck?!" Vera slammed her hand down on the tabletop causing the little archipelago of Ramlösa mineral water bottles to rattle.

"Vera…" Kaj had gotten up and was now standing protectively between Sofia and her boss. Without responding, Vera held up one hand and then vanished out the door.

61.

Anders Bohman stepped into his boathouse and walked around his suspended boat to make sure everything was in order. A musty smell made him wrinkle up his nose and he left the door open so the cross breeze could air the place out.

The vacation had been amazing, two weeks in Mallorca with Agneta and the kids. They had scrimped for the whole year so they could splurge on the most luxurious hotel they could find. The kids had their own room and he and Agneta had sat up late on the balcony, drinking beer and talking about old times. He couldn't remember ever having been so relaxed since the kids had been born. They had made love every night and hadn't said one nasty word to each other the whole trip. Even the kids had gotten along.

Marianne Nordin had picked up their mail and watered their flowers while they were away, but he hadn't spoken with her yet to hear how things had gone. He had walked straight off the ferry, right to his boathouse to check on his Anytec A21, which was waiting to be relaunched following repairs. He had been working on her all spring and the first part of the summer, and now that his vacation was behind him, it was time.

There was a discreet knock on the open door and Alvin's fluffy blond hair appeared in the doorway.

"Mom told me to come get you. It's time for dinner."

"I'll be right there. I just want to check on Josefina. Want to come?" He held his arms out to his son who immediately darted to him and climbed up into his arms. He hugged him and inhaled the scent of his summery-warm little body. Anders never ceased to be surprised by the little burst of joy he felt when he hugged his kids. They were the best thing that had ever happened to him, and he loved them so much it almost hurt. Alvin held onto his neck and laughed.

"Oh, you and your Josefina, Dad!"

Anders walked another circuit around the boat and then activated the switch for the winch. They could squeeze in a quick jaunt around the strait. Sure, it was late, the weather wasn't at all right for a trip in an open boat, and Agneta would be mad, but it would be worth it. The winch creaked, slowly lowering the boat toward the surface of the water. He enjoyed the sound and he was euphoric at the thought of taking his son out on the water.

Suddenly Alvin stiffened and grabbed his neck tightly in a panic. Alvin's little fingernails pressed into his skin and he could feel them breaking the skin.

"What are you doing, Alvin?" Anders shut off the winch with a bang. The boat stopped, hanging there in front of them swaying gently. He took a firm hold of his son's arm and urged, "Let go of me!"

"Dad, look," Alvin stammered, pointing down beneath the surface. The wake from a passing boat came in, splashing water between the planks. Through sheer strength he succeeded in pulling free and set the boy down on the walkway.

"I don't see anything."

"Down there," Alvin said. His son's voice was barely more than a whisper.

Anders lay down on his belly and leaned out over the edge of the walkway, out over the water.

The waves from the passing boat's wake ceased and the water grew still. He turned his head up to look at his terrified son.

"I still don't see anything, Alvin."

That very instant, the boy's piercing shriek cut through the boathouse.

Anders looked down again as the bloated gray face broke the surface of the water.

62.

"How are you feeling?"

Sofia turned her head away and looked out the window. The only noise in the library was the steady ticking from the wall clock. A reminder that the hour was late and that conversations like these were best put off until the next day.

"Why didn't you say anything to me when he became a suspect? I could have helped you."

When she didn't respond, Kaj pulled out a chair and sat down beside her.

"I didn't know you were seeing anyone else. I thought you weren't dating." That word sounded out of place in his mouth and the insecurity in his voice irritated her.

"I'm not dating. And even if I were, what business is that of yours?"

He looked embarrassed.

"I guess we never really discussed any ground rules. When you left me, I wanted nothing more than for you to come back, and then when you did…"

"…you had gotten married. I don't understand why we're talking about this now."

"We can get through all of this, together."

Kaj tried to put his arm around her, but she shook it off.

"What makes you think I want your help?" Her voice sounded more caustic than was necessary.

"I don't want to lose you," Kaj insisted. "I want to be there for you."

Sofia shook her head.

"So you can just pull away again without any explanation at all?" Her voice, which was usually so calm, definitely had a sharp edge to it now. "Do you really think you can just come and go in my life as you please?"

"I don't owe you anything!" he said, getting up out of his chair. "Meanwhile, you owe me an explanation."

"You have no idea what I've been through, Kaj," she hissed.

"No, I don't," he said, flinging his arms up in frustration. "How would I know that? You didn't say anything. You just left."

"I was pregnant."

The silence that followed made it hard for Sofia to breathe. The hands on the wall clock sounded like they were punching holes in the wall.

"Was the baby mine?"

"Yes." A sob escaped from her and she cleared her throat in annoyance. "I had a miscarriage, five months in."

Kaj looked at her in horror.

"I'd only been working in my new position here for a couple of weeks. We had gone out to question someone, but when we got there the man was drunk and strung out. He had cut up the family dog and assaulted the son. I had no choice but to intervene. As I went to cuff him, things got out of hand. When my colleagues saw that I was bleeding, they thought I'd been stabbed."

The clock kept ticking.

"Something happened, a complication. They had to remove one of my ovaries. I won't have any more chances."

Kaj didn't even seem to hear what she was saying anymore. He was just staring blankly into space.

"I could have had a child?"

"A daughter."

"But why didn't you say anything? I would have supported you. I would have taken care of you and… her."

"I was afraid that you'd force me to have an abortion."

Every time they had discussed children, he had made it explicitly clear that men his age shouldn't have any, that it was cruel to bring children into the world if you weren't going to be around to get to see them grow up.

"I would never have forced you to…" His voice faded away only halfway through the sentence.

"It doesn't matter. It doesn't change anything between us. I don't want to discuss this anymore now. Our relationship is over and what's done is done."

He nodded absentmindedly and rubbed his mouth with his palm. A firm knock on the door interrupted their conversation. Without waiting for a response, Vera walked into the conference room.

"The county communications center in Umeå just called. A dead body has been found on Ulvön Island. We're leaving now. I'm assuming you'll want to come along?"

Kaj nodded, more to Sofia than to Vera. Then he pushed his way unsteadily past Vera in the doorway and disappeared down the hallway.

"I'll be waiting in the lobby," Vera said, shutting the door behind her.

Sofia sat there, her hands clenched tightly over the little scar next to her belly button from the operation and a lump of tears in her throat.

Monday, July 1

63.

Sofia stood frozen stiff, watching as two members of Ulvön Island's emergency response team struggled to pull the bloated body out of the water. They had just woken up, their hair tousled with pillow marks still on their faces. They stood in water up to their waists, maneuvering the tarp into place that would hoist up the limp body in the boathouse.

A work light on a tripod lit up the subarctic predawn. The light cast long shadows over the plastic sheeting that had been hung over the open end of the boathouse to shield the site from view from the strait, as if they were performing a macabre shadow play. Midnight had come and gone as they had mobilized crews to come and salvage the body. The sun would be rising soon, before 3 a.m. at this latitude. A couple of people from the Sea Rescue Society were also on the scene. They were used to handling accidental drownings and didn't seem particularly affected by the body as it was slowly hauled up. After a couple of attempts, working together, they succeeded in bringing the bundle up over the edge and onto the boathouse floor. The body was tangled in a net and the nylon lines had cut into the loosened skin in several places. Sofia felt her morning coffee pushing its way up her throat and she excused herself to step out and get some air.

From the shore side there was no indication of the grisly spectacle underway in the boathouse, aside from the blue and white police tape stretched between the Bohmans' property and the neighbor's up by the unpaved pedestrian street. She leaned

307

heavily on the fence and took a few deep breaths. The cadaver smell lingered in her nose.

Death was so strange. When her father had been dying, she had sat with him all night, holding his rough, heavy hand in hers. Spasms of pain had cut through his gaunt body. When death finally came, he had fallen asleep with a gentle smile on his lips, without fear and without struggle. It hadn't been at all the same thing as the dead people she encountered at work. They had rarely departed their lives from natural causes and often their despairing and shocked relatives were nearby needing support and comfort. The body in the boathouse was one of the worst she had been forced to see. Even so, her years on the beat had done their part to increase her tolerance. Traffic fatalities were generally the most awful. She remembered one summer when she and two colleagues had had to spend a whole night walking along the shoulder, searching for an arm that had been ripped off in a multiple-vehicle collision. That was the day she had turned twenty-eight.

Sofia shivered, trying to shake off the memories. As she turned around to return to the boathouse, someone called her name. A reporter from the Örnsköldsvik *Allehanda* newspaper snapped a string of pictures including the police tape in the background and shouted loudly, "What happened? Did someone die?"

Sofia had encountered the reporter many times before. As far as she could remember he had been on the crime beat since she was a kid.

"You know I can't answer that."

He rolled his eyes.

"Oh, come on. Give me something, otherwise I'll print the gossip I've heard."

"What have you heard then?" Sofia asked, feeling annoyed.

"That you found a dead body in the water and it's another murder victim."

The reporter already seemed to know quite a bit and there would be no quashing the rumor once the Coast Guard arrived to pick up the body.

"I can confirm that one person has died," Sofia finally responded. "As to whether or not it was murder, that I can neither confirm nor deny. The details will have to wait for the press conference." He was content with that but made no effort to move away from the barrier. Sofia shook her head at the reporter and returned to the boathouse.

Medical examiner Caroline Fridell and one of the techs were kneeling over the tarp and calmly debating how the transport to handle the transport to the mainland. Vera was standing over in the corner with Kaj. Sofia seemed to be the only one struggling to keep her breakfast down.

"Whose boathouse is this?" Kaj asked.

"Anders Bohman's. He's been away recently. Marianne Nordin usually keeps an eye on things for him when he's away. I can walk over to her place and ask if she saw anything unusual." Sofia was hoping for a chance to get away from the smell and the nauseating sight of the body.

"Will you come take a peek first?" Caroline interjected, tugging on the sleeve of her protective suit.

"Drowning?" Vera walked over to Caroline, wrinkling up her nose at the stench.

"Nope," Caroline said, shaking her head. "Look at the temple. Reminds me quite a bit of the guy we found on Midsummer. Obviously I can't say anything definitive until the autopsy, but I wouldn't be surprised if a similar murder weapon were used for this."

Sofia and Kaj looked at each other. The third victim in less than two weeks. What was going on?

"We haven't found any ID, but I also don't want to move the body around too much before we've wrapped everything in plastic for transport. It looks like the victim was tied up and weighted down with something. So you probably ought to send divers down to try to find whatever the weights were. It seems like they came loose, which allowed the body to float to the surface. The mistake made here was that they didn't perforate the body."

"Perforate?" Vera asked with her hand over her mouth and nose.

"If you perforate the body the right way, the gases leak out and the body stays on the bottom."

Vera scrunched up her face in horror and said, "Thanks, you can stop there."

The medical examiner shrugged slightly and turned back to the body.

"Could you try and turn the head so we can see the face?" Sofia asked. "It could be someone from the island."

Caroline snorted cheerlessly.

"If you can succeed in identifying this poor thing, that would be impressive."

With her glove-covered hands, Caroline grasped the damaged head and tried to turn it toward the work light. Her fingers slipped, and she kept having to get a new hold. Wisps of thick hair were tangled in the fishnet. She struggled to pull them aside so that they could see the whole face. When she felt satisfied with the hairdo, she leaned back and let the gleam of the work light fall on the body.

64.

Fredrik sat down at the table by the window in the Stadshotel's dining room and let his gaze rest on Örnsköldsvik Bay outside while he waited for his tea to cool down enough to drink. It was almost nine, but the dining room was empty aside from himself and two women in their mid-sixties who had sat down at the next table. One was carefully buttering a piece of crispbread while the other was scrolling on an older model tablet.

He hadn't slept more than a couple of hours overnight. He had woken up several times because of noise drifting in from the hallway and he had had trouble falling asleep again. He had just been waiting for the police to storm in and arrest him. But they hadn't come.

The thought of visiting Bodil had settled like a cold blanket around his shoulders. Did he really dare go back out there again? But he had to. Bodil must have been involved in what had happened to Thomas Nilsson that night. Was she the one who had threatened Adam Ceder and then murdered him? But if so, why? What had Ceder discovered? A thought struck him.

Bodil had visited Aron the same day he had died. Had she had something to do with his death? No, that couldn't be possible. Or...?

"It happened again." The woman at the next table pointed to her screen and her friend sitting across from her put her hand over her mouth.

"Another one? On that same little island? Wow, you really have to wonder what's happening to the world."

"What happened?" Fredrik asked, stiffening.

"Another body. See for yourself!" She held up the tablet so that Fredrik could see.

The news photo showed police tape around a red boathouse. The blue and white crime scene tape was in focus, but farther back you could make out a blond woman in street clothes, who without a doubt was Sofia. The thick black headline read: "Second Ulvön Death in Two Weeks." The woman passed the tablet over so that Fredrik could read the story, which described the discovery of a body in a boathouse in Ulvö Harbor. The owner had returned home from a trip to Mallorca and discovered the body.

"This one appears to be a woman." The woman shook her head to her friend across the table. "An island resident."

Fredrik gasped.

I usually borrow the Bohmans' dock. They're in Mallorca.

Oh my God, Marianne! She had called and told him about the missing photo. Had that been a threat, like the one Ceder had received? And he had brushed her off. Fredrik muttered a farewell to the women at the next table and left the breakfast room. He stopped in the lobby, put the battery back into his cell phone, and dialed Marianne's number. No answer. He hung up and instead searched her name and location to bring up the number for her land line instead. The phone was finally answered after the sixth ring, but the voice on the other end wasn't Marianne's.

"Hi, this is Fredrik Fröding."

"So I hear."

"Who is this?" he asked, even though he could clearly hear who it was.

"This is Sofia Hjortén with the Örnsköldsvik Police."

Fredrik had no idea what was going on. He heard male voices in the background.

"Why are you answering Marianne's phone? Could I please speak to her?"

Sofia was quiet for a long moment and Fredrik began to feel uncomfortable.

"If you have any questions regarding the investigation," Sofia said, "please contact the head of the preliminary investigation."

"Did something happen to Marianne?"

The silence on the other end of the line was deafening. He could hear Sofia moving away from the other people in the room.

"I can't discuss this with you, Fredrik. We're in the middle of a murder investigation. You're wanted by the police, are you aware of that? We've been looking for you for days. I would strongly recommend that you go to the police station and talk to Karim Jansson if you don't want to make things worse for yourself."

"Where's Marianne?"

When Sofia answered, her voice was ice cold.

"Come in now, Fredrik, for everyone's sake."

Then she hung up.

—

Sofia sat between Caroline Fridell and Kaj in the prow. It had taken all night to get the right people out to the site where the body was found, salvage the body, and get it onboard the boat. For the second time in just a couple of weeks, Fridell had had to drive down from Umeå and then get out to Ulvön Island.

The cold hull seemed to absorb the cold from each wave and press it into her back. The smell of the saltwater and the corpse lying on the floor between them in the cramped space made Sofia's gorge rise. Caroline had handed out barf bags to everyone and they left the door to the cabin open. Kaj had protested half-heartedly but had still accepted a bag and stuffed it into his pocket. Sofia sat holding hers on her lap. Both Kaj and Vera were holding their jacket sleeves over their noses and breathing through their mouths. No one spoke. The crewmen from the maritime search and rescue team, who had had to be called in yet again due to a lack of Coast Guard and police boats in the area, discussed the bearings every now and then, but otherwise it was quiet. She doubted anyone would have spoken to her anyway. Neither Kaj nor Vera had said anything to her since they left the station late last night, only exchanged a few isolated words to move along the work of identifying and transporting the body. Other than that, things had remained chilly between them.

Sofia leaned her head against the hull and closed her eyes. This would probably be her last day of work as a police officer. Tomorrow she would be suspended pending the internal investigation. In just a few months, she would be a civilian again. Anything else was unthinkable. She had withheld information and in a worst-case scenario, she would be prosecuted for intentionally obstructing the investigation. She also hadn't told anyone that Fredrik had called when they were at Marianne's house, but she had asked him to come in. The knot in her stomach was pulled so tight now that it was hard to breathe. Every time she swallowed, she imagined she could taste death and the cloying sweetness of decay.

Worrying about Tord made everything worse, but even so she could no longer ignore the fact that there was something physically wrong with her. Not going to see a doctor now would be downright irresponsible. Sten's colon cancer had spread at record speed. The doctor had informed her that it was hereditary and had recommended that she come in if she experienced any abdominal pain or digestive tract changes. If this didn't count as a change, nothing would.

Less than half an hour later they tied up at the Järved Boat Club dock, a couple of miles east of downtown. They had agreed that this was a better option since the visitors' marina in town would be full of tourists looking for lunch at this hour. A hearse and two unmarked police cars were already waiting for them. Without a word, Vera and Kaj walked over to one of the cars and got in. Karim, who was sitting in the driver's seat, waved through the windshield for her to come. Sofia hesitated.

After a while the back door on the passenger's side opened and Vera stuck her head out so the sea breeze caught her red bangs.

"We don't have all day. You coming or what?"

65.

The library was full of journalists. Most were Swedish, but there were also a few Norwegians and one Dane. The noise level was far louder than was comfortable, and Sofia's head was throbbing after the sleepless night and the trip over from Ulvön in the stifling, cadaverous air. TV cameras, microphones, and cords were being moved around by eager men and women who were all trying to move their equipment into the most advantageous location.

They had called an immediate press conference to discuss the discovery of another body. There was a lot of interest and Sofia was grateful that Mats Dahlman's murder and the suspended link to Adam Ceder hadn't come out yet. The media hadn't learned of Tord's assault yet, either. The surgeons at Örnsköldsvik Hospital were in touch with the forensic medicine department in Umeå but hadn't been able to narrow down the type of weapon he had been attacked with. Sofia realized that in a worst-case scenario, it could be a hammer.

The conference table had been moved, and Mattias and Vera were sitting at a folding table at the front of the room. A man in a green hoodie attached body mikes to their clothes. Sofia could see the drops of sweat glistening along Vera's hairline. The detective superintendent let the reporters chat for a few more minutes before she cleared her throat. The buzz of voices in the room abruptly stopped. Twenty-five pairs of eyes were focused on the pair at the front and Mattias began to speak in broken English.

"As was previously reported, the body of a deceased individual was found in Ulvö Harbor yesterday."

A plump woman from the *Jyllands-Posten* newspaper immediately broke in, speaking a throaty Danish, ignoring their previous request for questions to be asked in a language everyone understood.

"Was this a crime?"

"Probably."

"Is there any connection to the murdered man you found on Midsummer's Day?" she continued still in Danish.

"We cannot rule that out," Vera stated.

The reporter smiled in satisfaction and jotted down a couple of lines on a notepad. A serial murderer sold newspapers.

"Have you identified the body?"

"Yes."

"Will you be sharing that information with us?"

Vera glanced briefly over at Marie who sat at the far end of the first row and then nodded to the journalist. There was a rustle of pens and paper and every neck in the room stretched a tad closer to the table where Vera and Mattias were sitting.

"We informed the next of kin overnight, and since the information has already leaked out online, unfortunately we must confirm that the deceased is Christine Karst, the owner of the Ulvö Hotel."

A murmur ran through the room.

It was only half-true that the next of kin had been informed. They had been in touch with Christine's ex-husband. He had caught the first flight up to Umeå, had met Fridell in the forensic medicine department, and had confirmed her identity. The body they had found was his ex-wife's. But they still had not been able to reach Gisela Karst. Sofia couldn't help thinking that the news of her daughter's death wouldn't affect her all that much. It had been several days since Christine was supposed to arrive in Alicante and Gisela hadn't tried to contact them or the Spanish police. Far too busy with her career, same as always.

"How was she killed?" asked a male journalist with short hair and glasses.

"Unfortunately I can't comment on that," Vera said.

"Do you have any suspects?"

"Unfortunately I can't comment on that either."

"Given what happened on the island just a couple of weeks ago, you've probably concluded that there is some connection?"

"We cannot comment further on that, but as we said, that is a possibility," Mattias said, trying to take charge of the press conference.

But the reporters continued peppering Vera with questions. The reporter from *Expressen* broke in, "Where was she found?"

"In a boathouse."

"You already said that, but I was wondering where. In the water?"

"I can't answer that."

"Was she in her own boathouse?"

"No." Vera shook her head, her lips pressed together.

"Did you find any evidence in the boathouse?"

"Unfortunately I can' t answer that either."

"Why haven't you identified any suspects?"

Sofia could tell that Vera was starting to lose her patience with the journalists.

"Hasn't it occurred to you that both people owned hotels? That's a possible motive."

"Yes, we are aware of that and if you're insinuating that we haven't…"

"We're in the thick of a complex, fast-moving phase of the investigation," Mattias interrupted. "So we're going to wrap up our press conference now and get back to you once we have more answers for you."

Fredrik sat on his hotel bed with the purple blackout curtains drawn. The sun had broken through the rainclouds for a little while outside, but he didn't want to see or be seen.

TV4 Västernorrland had just concluded a live broadcast from the Örnsköldsvik police station. Vera Nordlund and Mattias Wikström, who had questioned him on Ulvön Island, had just given a brief, vacuous press conference. The journalists who had been permitted to speak had been persistent in trying to obtain more information about the two murders, but without success. The most important detail, however, had come to light—Marianne was not the one who had died. The body belonged to Christine Karst, who had owned the Ulvö Hotel and was the daughter of world-renowned pianist Gisela Karst. The fact that it was somehow connected to Adam Ceder's murder was evident from the evasive responses the police had given.

He stood up and walked a lap around his temporary jail. The yellow walls seemed to sway.

After a few local ads, there was a brief interview with just the blond police officer with the model looks. The same questions that had just been asked at the press conference were now revisited in the hope of coaxing out some new piece of information.

"Do you have any suspects?"

Mattias Wikström pulled back his hair and eyed the reporter somberly.

"The police are very interested in getting in touch with a man who was seen with Adam Ceder the night he was murdered, on Midsummer's Eve."

"Do you think he could be the killer?"

"As I said, we are very anxious to get in touch with this man. He was a guest at the Ulvö Hotel on Midsummer's Eve."

"Can you provide any more information? A description?"

Mattias Wikström cleared his throat and nodded. The reporter's delight was practically palpable. The microphone was thrust forward, so close that it nearly touched Wikström's mouth.

"He's 38 years old, six foot one, and has dark hair and brown eyes. The man we're seeking should be considered extremely dangerous. There is probable cause to suspect him of at least two murders and he has a previous history of mental health problems. He lives in Stockholm but may still be in the Örnsköldsvik area."

He concluded by turning toward the camera and looking directly at the viewers.

"If you see him, we ask that you contact the police immediately."

66.

The investigative group was already in the library following the press conference when Sofia snuck in and took a spot at the very back of the semicircle that had formed around the whiteboard. The chairs were still in disarray and no one had managed to put them back in place.

Vera ignored Sofia's late arrival. She was focused on Kaj, who stood at the front, rearranging the photos on the board. Sofia was only there out of charity. She knew that, but at least she was there. Vera had taken the risk of not passing on what she had been told. Yet.

Four pictures were lined up on the board side by side: Adam Ceder, Mats Dahlman, Christine Karst, and Fredrik Fröding. All of the pictures aside from Fredrik's were perfectly lit studio photos, taken from homepages. His was blurry, taken from his rarely updated Facebook page.

"So," Vera began, "Christine Karst was found dead in the water in a boathouse in Ulvö Harbor last night. Her body was wrapped in a fishing net and probably sunk with two anchors. Even at first glance, Fridell was able to say that her head injuries resembled Ceder's. The forensic team in Solna confirmed that Mats Dahlman's injuries are also consistent with this. There is every indication that we're talking about one or two good blows to the head with a hammer. We won't know for sure until the autopsy report comes back, but according to Fridell, Karst's body could have been in the water for up to two weeks. That could mean that she might have already been dead when Dahlman and Ceder were murdered."

Vera glanced briefly at Sofia before continuing.

"As we know, an Ulvön Island resident, Tord Grändberg, was also attacked. We need to consider that this might be related to the murders."

Kaj took over from her.

"The techs found traces of blood from two different people in the boathouse. We can assume that one of them is Karst and it's not unreasonable to think that Ceder might be the other one. That may be where he was thrown in, and then maybe carried from there to the beach below the Ulvö Hotel by the currents and the wind. Maybe the murderer was in a hurry or was interrupted. Or maybe sinking his body just wasn't part of the plan."

"On the other hand, if it turns out that the second set of blood doesn't belong to Ceder... well, then there's a risk that we have a fourth victim waiting to float to the surface," Vera interjected. "If we're really fucking lucky, then it's the murderer's blood, but that's not especially likely."

Before any of the others had time to ask questions, Kaj continued in a steady voice.

"As I said before, every indication is that we're dealing with a very purposeful killer who selects victims carefully. At first the murders seemed to have been well planned, but Dahlman was attacked in his stairwell. Anyone could have come along, but the killer took the risk anyway. If we include the assault on Tord Grändberg, which happened while Marianne Nordin was in the house, that suggests that the killer is no longer worried about the risk of being caught. We should therefore be open to the possibility that the culprit could be a mentally unstable person who is not fully able to predict the consequences of his or her actions."

Mattias straightened up in his chair as if he were about to say something, but Marie beat him to it.

"Have we completely ruled out the possibility that this is related to buying the hotel now? Could there still be some

322

competing prospective buyer for the hotel that we've missed, someone who was ready to do whatever it took to get their way?" She looked at Vera, but Kaj shook his head.

"Our focus has been on finding commonalities between the victims that might be related to a potential sale. What we've overlooked, however, are connections that go farther back in time."

Kaj looked at Sofia before he almost apologetically pulled out the plastic envelope with the picture she had found in Fredrik's leather jacket and he attached it to the whiteboard.

"Our colleagues in Stockholm discovered this when they searched Fredrik Fröding's apartment."

He seemed to have made a conscious decision to spare Sofia from embarrassment by not telling the truth. She had no idea how he had convinced Vera to go along with that, but she felt immensely grateful.

Vera pointed to the image.

"As you can see, this was taken on Midsummer's Eve in 1979 during one of the summer camps the Church held on Ulvön Island. I received the list of campers today from the Nätra parish pastor's office archives."

The names of all the campers were now neatly noted at the bottom of the printout of the photograph. Mattias was the first one to walk up to the whiteboard for a closer look.

"Damn!" he exclaimed. "That's Christine Karst!"

Karim, who followed him up, nodded and pointed farther down. Mattias leaned in closer and stated the obvious out loud.

"And Mats Dahlman and Adam Ceder. Hey, it looks like his eyes have been poked out."

He flung up his hands. "So you're telling me that Fröding had a picture of all three victims in his apartment and he's mentally unstable. It's got to be him. That's just what I've been saying all along."

"You mean that he's our 'suspect with probable cause' person?" Marie's voice was unexpectedly gruff. "I don't know what you think your role is here, but I am the preliminary investigation leader."

Sofia saw Vera open her mouth to say something but then close it again. Marie clearly wasn't kidding around. She may have been happy to take a step back when it came to the operational details, but when her reputation was on the line, she took the reins.

"It's my call what information we share with the media. From now on, I want you to talk to me before you go off on any public digressions about whom we're looking for. Or maybe you wanted to alert him that we're on his heels?"

"But…" Mattias began, but one look from Vera silenced him.

Kaj cleared his throat.

"We obviously need to interpret this picture and the poked-out eyes as a threat against Adam Ceder. Anything else is really unthinkable. But the question is whether we can be equally sure that Fröding is behind it?"

"I'm with Mattias," Karim said cautiously. "Who else would it be?"

"So you think that he murdered Adam Ceder, Christine Karst, and Mats Dahlman because he thought he saw his brother outside a hotel with Ceder?" Sofia couldn't keep quiet any longer. Fredrik wasn't a triple murderer and he hadn't attacked Tord. There was just no way.

Vera immediately turned her eyes to Sofia, who promptly averted her gaze.

"It's definitely not impossible that it could be Fröding." Karim flipped through a few plastic folders and pulled out a couple of map images that he handed to Sofia. "According to the mapping info from his cell phone based on the mast dumps we received, he was in Södermalm in Stockholm at around the time when the Stockholm police believe Mats Dahlman was murdered."

She eyed the maps skeptically.

"There," Karim said, pointing to the top, "by Ersta Hospital. That's not all that far from Krukmakargatan where Mats Dahlman lived."

Sofia handed the printouts back to Karim. They didn't prove anything.

"Fröding drove back and forth to Stockholm over the course of a few days," Karim continued and showed her another map with dots marking the locations of the cell towers nearest to his route.

"Why else would he do that if not to murder Mats Dahlman?" Mattias scoffed.

Karim nodded in agreement.

"And he's back in Örnsköldsvik now. His most recent tower connection occurred in Bonässund three days ago. We're waiting for the next set of location tracking records to confirm that he's still in the area, although none of his credit cards have been used around here."

Karim passed the maps on to Marie.

"I agree that he's clearly a suspect, but what would his motive be?" Marie asked, looking at Vera and Kaj.

"We don't have an alternative suspect," Mattias said, sounding upset.

"So what do we do now?" Marie asked.

Vera was looking at Sofia. She thought she detected a glimmer of compassion in her eyes but wasn't sure.

"We find Fredrik Fröding."

67.

Ulvön Island, 1979

Mats was sitting in the grass, ripping out blade after blade without looking down at his hands. His eyes were on the policemen who were coming out of the parsonage. They carried a stretcher with a white blanket over it between them. A nurse from the village was there, too.

She wiped her nose and shook her head. Adam stood next to her along with some of the neighbors. He was crying so that his shoulders shook. They had been friends. Or, as much as anyone could be friends with Thomas.

Mats just couldn't understand it, that Thomas was dead.

When he had woken up that morning, the house was already full of police, clomping around and taking pictures and jotting down notes. Everyone was taken one by one into a room where Aron and a policeman were waiting. They briefly explained that Thomas had tied a noose around his neck and jumped out the window. They asked if Mats wanted to call his parents, but he said no. His mother wouldn't care anyway. He had learned that a long time ago. A horrible thought darted through his head. Was it feeling guilty that had made Thomas take his own life the same night that... He didn't want to think about that. He was so terribly embarrassed about what they had done, but he had done it for Marianne. To get her to finally notice him. He had thought she would be happy when he tried to please her and that she would want him, let him get close. He had so wanted his first time to be with her. Instead it had been with Ester, dirty and unwilling. Mats sighed. And now Marianne had gone to her new home in Ireland, without even saying goodbye.

He looked out at the courtyard. The girls were sitting there wrapped in blankets, watching the car that was going to take Thomas's body to the mainland. Siw-Inger was holding her sister and they were crying. Several of the others were crying, too. Ester was sitting in front of them on the grass. Someone had lifted her out of her wheelchair and she was sitting childlike with her legs stretched out in front of her. She was staring intently down at her dress. Bodil was kneeling next to her and patting her hand. The saint at the center, as usual. Christine sat on the other side of Ester. Sanctimonious, fucking Christine. As if she were the lamb of God with a spotless, white conscience.

The stretcher passed in front of the group of kids and was lifted into the long hearse.

The girls held each other tighter and their faces crumpled into tears and commiseration.

Everyone's except Bodil's.

She looked coldly right back at him.

68.

It was already late at night. Fredrik lay in his hotel bed, trying to fall asleep. His anxiety grated at him, and he longed for the chemical warmth of a pill. But he resisted. He needed a clear head if he was going to investigate this. Even if the story was still full of loose ends, at least he knew that he wasn't a murderer. Although that was really the only thing he was sure about. He would never take someone else's life in cold blood. He was not the one they should be looking for.

Every three hours he put the battery into his phone and turned it on to see if he had received a message from Bodil. Philip had called a few times and sent two text messages. Both asking questions about how things were going and how he was doing.

Fredrik's body was on autopilot. He had almost started wishing that someone would come storming in and slap some handcuffs on him. That would break this impasse and release him from the tension.

Sofia's words echoed in his ears. Come in now, Fredrik, for everyone's sake. She had spoken to him as if he were a complete stranger. He had not been able to discern even a trace of compassion in her voice. He was just an obstacle on her path forward, a problem that needed to be solved for everyone's sake.

Fredrik rubbed his face hard. He had to find out what had happened. Bodil had pushed Thomas out a window with a noose around his neck, made it look like suicide. That was what Marianne had insinuated. Then Aron had sent Bodil away and she had never been seen again.

Several people had substantiated that. Forty years later for some reason Adam Ceder started looking into the old suicide, which had led to his being threatened and finally murdered. Was it Bodil? Had she wanted to stop Ceder from saying what he knew? But then why would she have attacked Christine Karst and threatened Marianne?

He turned over restlessly in his bed, trying to find a cool area on the pillow. Thoughts of Bodil and the kids at the camp swirled around in his head. He was missing something. Both Marianne and Siw-Inger had said that Ester was bullied. Could it be that Bodil was actually trying to get revenge on the people who had attacked her disabled younger sister? That Ceder had received the threatening photo first, and then started digging. That would fit better with the murder of Christine Karst and the threat against Marianne. However unbelievable it sounded, that was the most reasonable explanation he had right now.

He reached for his phone and put the battery into it even though it hadn't been three hours yet. It took forever for the white apple logo to appear. He could already sense it before he had even navigated to the text app.

He had a new message.

–

Sofia was the only one left in the investigative team's offices. Her colleagues had left for the day and there wasn't anyone in the financial and drug crime sections either. The sun was setting, and thick clouds had crept in so that half the sky was now covered. It was going to rain again. You could feel it in the air.

She poured herself some water from the glass pitcher she kept on her desk and drank some. Karim and Mattias had driven out to Bonässund where Fredrik's last cell phone signal had been located and then they were going to go home after that. Marie had taken the ferry out to Ulvön to talk to the techs who were still working in the boathouse, and Kaj was on his way to Umeå to meet Caroline Fridell who was examining what remained of Christine Karst. All of the beat cops had been instructed to be on the lookout for Fredrik. She, however, had been assigned to desk duty until Vera had time to figure out how they should proceed.

Sofia rubbed her stomach. The nausea wouldn't go away. She forced herself to take another gulp of water and caught herself running her fingers over the scar next to her belly button. She had learned to suppress this involuntary motion a long time ago, but everything had been dredged up to the surface again now. Fuck Fredrik and Kaj and this whole investigation.

For the fourth time today, she dialed the direct number for the intensive care unit at Örnsköldsvik Hospital but was informed yet again that Tord was asleep. He was in a critical but stable condition. They were going to ease up on his anesthesia tonight and see if he was stable enough to transfer to the regional hospital in Umeå. They had asked Sofia to come back tomorrow.

She dialed Marianne Nordin's number, but there was no answer. They had only been able to question her briefly earlier in the day. She had been far too worn out and distraught after what had happened. Physically she had fared better than Tord. She had only needed a few stitches in her hand. Sofia inserted her ID card into the reader and started up her computer. She clicked on the case. The technicians had been to the crime scene, but they hadn't found any sign of forced entry. Marianne hadn't been able to answer the question of who had attacked Tord. She and Tord had drunk coffee together in the kitchen and then he had gone to go close the window on the glassed-in veranda and had been attacked by an unknown assailant who had gotten into the living room.

Was the attack somehow related to the murders? It seemed as if Kaj thought it was, and now that Christine Karst was dead, Fredrik was their only remaining suspect. But it couldn't be him. It had to not be him. The investigation was expanding every day, but it also felt as if it was slipping away through their fingers. They had requested the surveillance footage from the ferry and the door-to-door canvassing which they had just wrapped up had been started again. Three parallel incidents were being investigated at the same time on an island with 35 year-round residents. Nothing like this had ever happened in the history of Ulvön Island before.

The sound of someone's rubber Crocs walking down the linoleum hallway interrupted Sofia's thoughts. Eva poked her head in and held up a stack of paper.

"Where is everyone?" Eva asked.

"Out," Sofia confirmed. "Can I help you?"

Eva came over to her and set the stack of paper on her desk.

"New cell phone tower hits from the operator for the Ulvön case. Will you make sure Vera gets them?"

Sofia nodded.

"Oh, and Mona Höglund is here to see you. She called from the intercom at the front door. I wasn't sure what to do, but she seems really sensitive, and she refused to leave…"

Sofia looked at Eva and then at the clock on the wall behind her.

"At seven thirty at night?"

Eva nodded.

As the squeaking of Eva's Crocs faded away down the stairs, Sofia picked up the stack of papers, but before she had a chance to read them, Mona appeared in the doorway to her office. She had been crying and looked ashen and washed out.

"Have a seat," Sofia said.

Mona sat down with her purse in her lap. She focused her attention on playing with the zipper and did not look up. When she finally opened her mouth, her voice was scarcely a whisper.

"It's about the surveillance footage. I was the one who…" Her sentence faded away into silence.

"You erased the footage?"

"Yes." Mona nodded and then looked Sofia in the eye.

"Why?"

Mona gave a piercing sob. Her voice was suddenly loud and strident.

"That's just what happened. Christine had warned me that he was coming, Adam Ceder. They were supposed to meet on Midsummer's Eve to sign the papers. She had promised me. I was going to buy the hotel, but suddenly she was going to sell it to that... that idiot instead!" Despite her tears, something sharp gleamed in Mona's eyes.

"What happened, Mona?"

She wiped her eyes with her sweater sleeve.

"I didn't plan it, I promise!" She looked up at Sofia as if she was looking for support, but when she didn't receive any, she continued.

"On Midsummer's Eve I was in the bar for a while after dinner when he came by. He ordered whiskey. I knew who he was right away." Mona scoffed loudly. "That arrogant pig! But do you think he recognized me? Nope, of course he was too posh for that."

Sofia nodded for Mona to continue.

"Sorry, I just get so upset when I think about it. I mean, the hotel should go to someone who at least cares about the island, right?"

Sofia nodded.

"Anyway. I have some trouble sleeping, you know? So I take these pills to help me relax, really strong pills, actually."

It grew quiet and Sofia asked Mona to continue.

"Well, I put a couple of pills in his glass."

"Um, why?"

"I don't know. I was just so pissed. Christine had promised me that I would get first crack at buying the hotel. She even said that I could have it for a lower price so that I could afford it. And when I saw him it just popped into my head. He was a rotten person. I wanted him to miss the meeting so Christine would realize what an irresponsible guy he was and change her mind. But then... then he was just lying there. Dead!"

"You have to help me understand, Mona. What does this have to do with the surveillance footage?"

She paused for a moment before answering.

"When I realized he was dead, I panicked. I saw him there by the water when I went to take the trash out to the dumpster. He was so bloody and the head wound…"

"Did you think it was an accident?"

Mona looked at her pleadingly.

"Yes. And, I mean, if he fell, it was my fault, but then I remembered that argument and the guy who was yelling. He was drunk. I mean, it was Midsummer. Everyone was drunk, and…"

"What happened after that?"

Mona looked up.

"After I found Ceder, I fetched his bag from his hotel room. Then I stuck it in that Fröding guy's room, the man I had helped up to his room. I thought you would be sure to find it there. When you didn't get in touch about that then I called and reported the fight instead. So that you would think he was the one who… Oh my God." She moaned. "What's going to happen to me now? Am I going to jail?"

Mona was crying uncontrollably now, and Sofia put a comforting hand on her arm while she reached for her phone with the other hand. This information did not cast Mona Höglund in a good light, but it was pretty clear that she hadn't murdered Adam Ceder. Sofia felt a sense of distaste creeping over her. Had she been wrong about Fredrik after all? Although, if Mona had planted the bag in his room, he couldn't have taken it from Ceder, could he?

"Here's what we'll do." Sofia got up and carefully helped Mona to her feet. "You and I are going to walk down to lock-up together and then I'll call a colleague and we'll work through what happened in detail. How does that sound?"

Mona nodded indifferently and allowed herself to be led down the corridor and down the stairs. Sofia delivered Mona to the officer on duty by the holding cells and then returned to her office to call Vera and tell her what she had learned. As she picked up the receive to her landline, her eyes fell on the list of cell tower hits that Eva had delivered. She hung her phone back up, reached for the stack of papers, and flipped through them to today's date. Fredrik was still in Örnsköldsvik. He hadn't made any calls, but his phone had connected automatically just a few hours ago.

To a cell tower less than 100 meters from Stadshotel.

"Do you recognize this man? His name is Fredrik Fröding and he may be staying here." Sofia held her phone closer so the front desk staffer could see Fredrik's face better.

"Unfortunately we're not at liberty to disclose information about our guests," the woman responded without even looking at the picture.

Sofia pulled out her police ID and showed that to the young woman. The clerk cast an anxious glance at that and started typing on her keyboard.

"First floor, two doors down to the left. Would you like me to come up there with you?"

"No thank you."

Sofia looked at her watch. It was eight thirty at night. She shouldn't go up there alone, but Kaj wouldn't be back from Umeå yet. Marie was still on Ulvön. Mattias was surely already home, but she couldn't bear to see his smug smile one more time. She picked up her phone and dialed Karim's number. He had had to return to work to deal with Mona.

"How did it go?"

"She's been crying since we booked her in," Karim replied. "In the end, one of the guards had to drive her up to the psychiatric emergency room. Her only motive appears to have been stopping the sale of the hotel."

"What are you doing right now?"

"I'm on my way home, back to the beer I had just opened when Eva called me."

Sofia half-heartedly apologized and told Karim to have a nice night before she hung up. She could call Vera of course, but she realized that call wouldn't end well. She had been ordered to stay at her desk and that wasn't where she was right now.

It bothered her that she was looking forward to seeing him. Here she was, standing outside the door of a suspected murderer's hotel room, tucking back wisps of hair that had come loose from her ponytail. As if this were part of some fucking beauty contest. What had happened to her professionalism? The image of Fredrik between her legs as she leaned back against her refrigerator flitted through her mind. That was pretty much where everything had faded away—professionalism, career, brains.

Sofia adjusted the holster under her jacket and got ready.

Then the door opened.

The housekeeper screamed and grabbed her chest.

"You scared me. Is this your room? I'm almost done."

"I'm with the police." Sofia got out her badge again and showed it to the dark-haired woman, who immediately backed away, taking a few steps back into the room. She dropped the trash bag onto her housekeeping cart and quickly started retrieving the various spray bottles and rags she had set on the desk.

"Just leave everything," Sofia instructed.

The housekeeper nodded, pushed her way past Sofia, and vanished down the hallway.

Sofia closed the door with her foot and looked around. The room smelled stuffy and also like cigarette smoke. She opened the curtains and let the rain-laden night air pour in the window. The stacks of paper on the desk trembled in the wind. A cell phone charger sat in the wall outlet and the bed was unmade. She had to quash her impulse to run her hand over the dip in the pillow, which revealed that Fredrik had lain there.

There was no doubt that he had been staying in this hotel room. Nor that he planned to return. Sofia leaned over and peeked under the bed, but there wasn't anything there. She picked up the clothes that had been thrown over the armchair and then walked over to the closet and opened it.

There it was, Adam Ceder's bag. Why hadn't Fredrik turned it in to the police?

She pulled a latex glove from her pocket and opened the bag. Clothes, a toiletries bag, and an electric razor.

Why the hell did you hold onto this bag, Fredrik?

The lump in her stomach was back. Nausea flooded through her body and Sofia quickly backed away from the closet, looking around for a trash can. She just had time to reach for it before she threw up. On all fours, she heaved out what little there was in her stomach and then wiped her mouth on the back of her hand. Her heart was racing, but she managed to get up into the desk chair.

That was when she saw it.

In the closest stack of papers, underneath a Pepsi can, there was a well-thumbed invoice with the recipient's name and address circled, a name that she recognized.

What was Fredrik doing?

69.

For the second time, Fredrik parked in the deserted turnaround and looked up the overgrown dirt road that led to Bodil Dirk's house. He pulled out his phone and read the message again:

Come alone.
Bodil.

Her tone was menacing and he was struck again by how absurd this whole situation was. Was he just going to traipse in there and ask Bodil if she murdered Thomas Nilsson that night in the parsonage almost forty years ago? And then Adam Ceder and Christine Karst. *Hey, are you a serial killer?* He laughed. What did he really expect her to say? And what would he do if the answer was yes?

He dialed Philip's number. After a couple of rings his voicemail picked up.

"Hi, Philip. I'm calling to… I just want you to know where I am in case something happens. I found Bodil Dirk. I think she might be behind all of this. At any rate, if you can't reach me, call Sofia Hjortén with the Örnsköldsvik police." He gave Philip Bodil's address, then hung up. He took a few deep breaths to steady himself.

When he put his hand on the handle to open his car door, he suffered an abrupt and intense panic attack. His back broke out in a cold sweat and his breath came in jagged jolts. He sat there until his breathing had calmed down a bit and then got out of the car.

After he walked up a bit closer to the house, he could make out a dim light in one of the downstairs windows. A shadow passed behind the ribbed glass in the front door, revealing that his arrival was expected. A shiver ran though his body. He turned around, but he could hardly see his car anymore through all the undergrowth and scrub brush. He really hoped he would have cell coverage in case something happened.

He knocked cautiously on the front door. After a few seconds, he thought he heard a shuffling noise inside. A silhouette appeared behind the glass. They stood like that for a few seconds, each on their own side.

He held his breath.

The door opened. A thin figure came into view in the open doorway. She quickly waved him in and shut the door behind him with a bang. The front hall was dark, but the light from the kitchen allowed him a glimpse of the skinny woman in front of him. Fear flooded into him and he had to fight his impulse not to shove her away and run back outside. He opened his mouth, but she tersely shushed him.

"Did you come alone like I asked?"

He nodded.

His eyes began to adjust to the dark and now he saw that she had her ear pressed to the front door. They stood like that for a few minutes before she limped past him, mumbling, into the kitchen. Fredrik followed.

There was a walker waiting by the stove.

"I have arthritis," she noted briefly. "Would you like some coffee?"

The inside of her house was the complete opposite of the outside. Every window was covered with thick curtains and blinds, but the windowsills were crowded with plastic flowers and knick-knacks and there were embroidered pictures on the wall with Bible quotes. Fredrik quickly tallied up at least eight porcelain cat figurines on the windowsills in the kitchen alone.

Without a doubt this was the most cluttered home he had ever seen, but unexpectedly enough, both welcoming and

338

clean. Bodil pointed to the six-foot-long cross-stitched table-cloth depicting a bouquet of flowers in yellow. She smiled proudly.

"It took me a year to finish. Looks great, doesn't it?"

She sat down at the kitchen table with difficulty and pointed encouragingly to a plate heaped with homemade cookies. Fredrik sat down on the bench and, feeling bewildered, helped himself to a sugar cookie, which he set on a floral cake plate.

"So, Fredrik Fröding. I understand that you want to talk about my family."

"What makes you think that?"

"Why else would you be here? No one knows where I am or even that I exist. If you managed to ferret that out, it means that someone at Vedbacksgården let the cat out of the bag. They're the only ones who have my address."

"I'm trying to find out what happened to a man named Adam Ceder. Also a boy named Thomas Nilsson. He died in 1979."

She nodded resignedly.

"You forgot Christine." She carefully smoothed the table-cloth.

Fredrik nodded and tried to hide the shiver that traveled down his spine. Bodil's voice was so chilly that it cut into him.

"They were terrible to her, you should know that. Ester told me everything, the night after it happened. What they did. How they forced themselves on her. He deserved what he got, even though…"

"Thomas?"

Fredrik's eyes locked onto Bodil's hands. They were running over the stitches in the cloth as if she were redoing each stitch again with an invisible needle. A sob shook her body and she pulled a cloth handkerchief out of the sleeve of her sweater and dried her eyes with it.

"Yes."

Outside they could hear the birds singing in the dense forest around the house, but in the kitchen it was quiet. Fredrik felt at a loss. Was this a confession? What should he do now?

"So, you did it?" he whispered finally, moving his hand to his phone, which was in his jeans pocket.

Bodil looked up at him.

"Me? I can barely walk." She pointed awkwardly to her walker.

"But then how did you know that Christine was dead?"

Bodil pointed to the stack of magazines and newspapers on the bench next to Fredrik.

"The world forgot about me. I didn't forget about it."

Fredrik stared at the stack for a long time and then picked up the one on the top. He read the address printed on the back.

"Asta Norén?"

"One of father's churchgoers here on the mainland. She became my foster mother and then formally adopted me. I've been Bodil Norén for almost forty years. After my father moved into Vedbacksgården, I stayed here so I could visit him. I took care of Asta, too, when she got old. She died years ago now, but the paper keeps coming."

"I don't understand, Bodil. People on Ulvön Island think that you killed Thomas. Why are you hiding here in this house if you don't have anything to do with what's happened?"

"I didn't kill anyone." Bodil shook her head.

Fredrik was struck by an uncomfortable realization: he believed her.

"But then who's behind all of this?"

Bodil looked over at the drawn curtains and then ceremoniously folded her cloth handkerchief back up into a square. When she looked back up at him, her eyes were unwavering.

"Ester."

"Ester?"

Bodil nodded.

"I don't know how it happened," she explained. "I was down in the kitchen, trying to clean up after the party. When I came back upstairs, Thomas was already dead. Everyone thought I had done it, even my dad."

"Ester killed him?"

She nodded.

"Your sister Ester killed Thomas Nilsson? But how? And why didn't you go to the police?"

Bodil looked at him, shamefaced.

"I didn't have the heart to let her spend the rest of her life in jail. She was sick, you see, very sick. When our mom passed away, Ester started hearing voices. She thought she had healing powers, that she could heal injuries and cure diseases. She used to cut herself and then try to make the wounds close with the power of God. Dad took her to a doctor, but they didn't understand what it was. Neither did Dad. His only explanation was that Ester must have been chosen by God and the voice she heard was God's own voice. Plus, Thomas sealed his own fate with what he did. So I looked the other way."

Bodil sobbed and eyed him pleadingly.

"I just went to bed, as if nothing had happened. While he hung there outside the house, dead. Everything that happened after that was my fault."

"You mean the fire in Stockholm?"

She nodded. Fredrik pushed his coffee cup away and leaned on the table on his elbows. He rubbed his face and tried to process the information he had just received. Bodil watched him as her tears dripped down onto her folded handkerchief.

"So Ester put a noose around Thomas's neck and pushed him out the window? Even though she was in a wheelchair?" Fredrik asked, confused.

"Yes."

"But then who killed Adam and Christine? And why?"

Bodil's face twisted in a tormented grimace and her hands flew up to cover her face. She was sobbing.

"Bodil?"

She shook her head. Fredrik reached across the table and put his hand on her arm, but she jerked away.

"Help me understand, Bodil. You can tell me."

She lowered her hands from her face and looked him in the eye.

"Ester isn't dead."

The silence that followed was so thick, it was palpable. Bodil's body trembled. Somewhere outside, Fredrik though he heard a twig snap. At first he thought it was his imagination, but then he heard the sound again.

"She's out there. I've been afraid of her my whole life. She'll never let what she's done come out." Bodil sounded preoccupied now, almost unresponsive.

"We have to get out of here," Fredrik said.

He stood up and walked around the table. He put his hand on Bodil's shoulder, but as soon as he touched her, she screamed and lashed out at him. He realized that she wasn't going to leave the house voluntarily.

"Listen, Bodil. We're not safe here. I have to warn Marianne. She might be next. We might be next. We have to get out of here."

Before she had time to protest, he grabbed her hand, pulled her toward the front door and flung it wide open. He saw the blond woman waiting for them outside with her gun raised too late.

70.

Södermalm, 1980

The doorbell rang. Dad wasn't home, but he had left the front door unlocked so I wouldn't have to go out into the hall if anyone came. I quickly threw myself back into my wheelchair and straightened the blanket over my legs. Mom could stay on the floor inside the bedroom door.

"Come in!" I called.

I sat up straight in the wheelchair and smiled. I only just barely made it. Only a moment before I had been practicing my balance on the floor. I'd gotten really good. With Mom's help, I'd started to be able to use my legs again. They were never broken, she said, just asleep. Every day I grew stronger and stronger. Soon I would stand up before Dad and show him how God brought my legs back to life. He would be so happy.

Don't forget, my child. You are God's chosen one. You have God's approval in everything you do. Don't let anyone tell you otherwise.

Mother's whisperings strengthened me.

The door opened, pushing Mom, who slid under the bed. I gasped but was so surprised at who had come that for a second I forgot Mom. Bodil was standing in the doorway.

"Ester." She leaned forward and tried to hug me, but I pulled away. I didn't want her here mucking things up. We were a family now, me, Mom, and Dad. She couldn't come here and blab. Right, Mom?

Bodil sighed and sat down on the bed.

"Ester, you have to tell them now."

343

I shook my head.

"Don't you understand? We have to tell Dad, and the police. You have to tell them what you did. I can't take this any longer."

Bodil looked at me beseechingly, as if that was going to help. I couldn't hold back my giggles. They escaped between my teeth and Mom joined in. She was rolling with laughter under the bed, but Bodil didn't notice anything.

"What's so funny?"

"I haven't done anything."

"You killed Thomas," Bodil said, staring at me dumbfounded.

"I didn't kill anyone. We helped."

"Who helped you?"

"Mom."

Bodil looked around the room in despair, her eyes filled with tears.

"My sweet, sweet sister, Mom is dead."

"She isn't dead! I am her child, God's chosen one. You know that, right, Bodil?"

She put her hand over her mouth and shook her head.

"She's here. Come out, Mom, and show yourself to Bodil." I tried to coax Mom out, but she was shy and didn't want to come out.

Bodil burst into tears. She turned on her heels and left the room. I followed in the wheelchair. I sped up to make it over the threshold Dad hadn't had time to remove yet.

"Where are you going?"

Bodil undid the lock and opened the front door with her back to me. Before she closed it behind herself, she turned around without looking me in the eyes.

"I'm going to the police now, Ester."

"No, Bodil! Wait. Don't say anything to the police. They'll separate us, take Mom away from me!" I heard how my high voice echoed in the stairwell. "Please, Bodil. I'd rather die than leave Mom again!"

But Bodil didn't respond. The door closed before I could get to her. I quickly rolled back to my room and slid out of the chair. My legs weren't steady enough yet that I could run, even though we trained every night. I crawled under the bed and blew the dust off Mom.

"Mom! You have to help me. Bodil says she's going to go to the police. What are we going to do?"

She eyed me reproachfully.

My child! But it was supposed to be our secret.

"I'm sorry, Mom. Please, forgive me. What are we going to do? We have to get away and find somewhere to hide."

Mom didn't have a chance to respond before the phone in the kitchen rang. I hobbled out there as quickly as I could. I had to pick it up before it stopped ringing.

"Bodil?"

But it wasn't Bodil. The voice on the other end was the same, even though I hadn't heard it in over a year. Not since Midsummer's Eve.

"I thought you were in Ireland?"

"My parents moved to Ghana," Marianne replied guardedly. "I've been staying with my grandmother in Dalarna for the summer."

"Really?"

Marianne continued in a haughty voice.

"Then I'm going on to England, where I'm starting at boarding school. My bags are already packed at the hotel. I'm leaving tomorrow. How about you, Saint? What are you up to? Going to wheel down to the park and feed the birds every day for the rest of your life?"

She laughed.

Mom said something from the bedroom, but I wasn't able to catch it.

"What hotel are you staying at?"

Marianne seemed put out at first but recovered quickly.

"The Kung Carl Hotel, why?"

345

Mom yelled again.

"Can I stop by?" Marianne asked.

"Why?"

"I need to drop off some English Bibles for Aron, from the congregation. Mom said I had to. Why, did you think I wanted to see you or something?"

Same old Marianne. She hadn't learned a thing, had not felt God's scourge. But Bodil would be back soon with the police. I didn't have time for Marianne and her Bibles, I had to get Mom and escape. I looked into the bedroom. Mom looked into my eyes from the bed. At first she was looking at me sternly, but then she smiled and nodded.

And I understood what Mom wanted me to do.

"Yes, Marianne. That would be fine. You can stop by."

71.

Bodil stopped by the fountain at Maria Square and sat down. She contemplated the bare-chested sculpture of the Viking god Thor with his hammer raised over Jörmungandr the serpent. The water in the fountain was turned off today, but the dramatic sculpture still felt just as alive.

She was at a loss. She loved Ester. And she wanted to help her, but she couldn't keep quiet any longer. Her bad conscience was eating her up from the inside.

Dad was going to be disappointed. After all, she had promised to protect Ester. And she really had done everything she could to accomplish that. She had let her life revolve around her sister, forsaking all her own needs to be the mother they had both lost. She had even played along with her father's sermons about how chosen Ester was. How she was beloved by God, and how their mother had died to become an angel to watch over them. She had hidden Ester's illness and the voices she heard. She had accepted the blame, had let her father banish her. She had done everything to protect her sister from their friends' taunts. And still it had turned out like this.

Bodil started crying again. She couldn't lie anymore. Her conscience shouldn't be tarnished by what Ester had done.

She got up, decisively wiped the tears from her face, and smoothed her blouse and skirt. When she looked up, there were two men standing in front of her.

"It's on fire!" They were pointing behind her.

Bodil turned around. It was really burning. Black smoke filled the sky. Without thinking, she began moving toward the apartment. At first she made her way out of the park slowly, out into the street, following the smoke with her eyes. Then she started running. Her heart was racing. When she was almost in front of the terracotta-colored apartment building, she saw angry yellow and orange flames pouring out of the roof of the building.

Ester, oh my God! Ester was in there and couldn't get out.

Although she didn't want to think the thought, it grabbed hold of her anyway.

This is my fault.

A crowd had gathered outside the front door. A woman came running out with a baby in her arms, crashing into a man who was on his way in.

"Stop! You can't go in there!" the woman yelled, but the man disappeared up the stairs anyway, protecting his nose and mouth with his sleeve. It was her father. Bodil saw that it was him. He was going in to save Ester.

Everything happened so incredibly quickly and at the same time slowly. People ran past, but they seemed to be moving in slow motion. A firetruck wailed somewhere far away. Bodil stood there, as if turned to stone. Several people were helping receive those who escaped from the building. The firemen and emergency response personnel toiled away with ladder trucks and firehoses. The fire had now spread to multiple units and black smoke was billowing out of the windows. She didn't see her father or Ester anywhere.

As she stood there, she saw the building's side door open. A long-haired figure slowly pulled itself up the handrail from the basement level. She was limping, and seemed to be injured. Her legs were unsteady. The silhouette was so familiar. Bodil squinted through the smoke and all the people running.

The girl suddenly stopped and looked into her eyes. They looked at each other for a long time.

Ester held her index finger up over her lips and then smiled. Then she vanished down the street.

72.

"Freeze!" Sofia stood, legs apart, both hands on her drawn weapon. Her voice was commanding. Fredrik let go of the crying Bodil and they stood there on the front step. Sofia holstered her gun.

"Back up!" She pointed to the door and he did as she instructed. Sofia quickly climbed the stairs and went over to Bodil. She placed her arm protectively around Bodil's narrow shoulders and leaned forward so that their faces practically touched.

"Bodil, I'm Sofia Hjortén. I'm a police officer. What's happened here?"

Bodil looked up, looking at Sofia for the first time.

"Ester," she whispered, "you have to find Ester."

A couple of minutes later all three of them were sitting in Sofia's Volvo. Sofia drove, her lips pursed. The car zipped along, way above the speed limit, and Fredrik had to hold onto the door handle to avoid being tossed around like a ragdoll. Fredrik had left his grandmother's Skoda in Bodil's turnaround, but he was glad not to have to drive. It had started raining and the wet roadway gleamed eerily in the light from the headlights.

In the rearview mirror he could see Bodil vacantly staring at the road ahead of them.

"Do you realize how crazy that sounds?" Sofia asked.

He nodded without saying anything to Sofia. It was crazy, even though it was the most likely explanation.

"I swear, if this is something you made up to save yourself…"

He opened his mouth to start to say something, but Sofia wasn't done yet.

"So Ester Dirk supposedly murdered Thomas Nilsson, survived the apartment fire, came back, and murdered three more people? How is that even possible?"

"I don't understand it either," Fredrik said. "Wait, what do you mean three more?"

For the first time, Sofia looked over at him in the passenger's seat.

"There's one dead in Stockholm, too. Mats…"

"Mats Dahlman." The voice from the back seat made both Sofia and Fredrik jump.

Sofia looked in the rearview mirror and found herself looking into Bodil's eyes.

"She's going to take them out one by one, everyone who wronged her."

The more Fredrik thought about it, the more convinced he became that Marianne was going to be next. That was why her picture from the camp had been stolen. It was a warning from Ester.

"I need to see Marianne," he said. "She might be in danger."

Sofia shook her head, but he could tell that she believed him. The realization left him on the verge of tears with relief.

"You're not going anywhere," Sofia said. "You're going to the police station, do you understand? We'll deal with Marianne and the others who attended the camp later."

"But what if…"

"Fredrik." The sharpness in Sofia's voice silenced him. "Let the police deal with this now. We'll send someone out to Marianne, but first we need to get to the bottom of this."

Sofia picked up her phone and dialed a number. She quickly updated the person on the other end about the situation.

"We're looking for an Ester Dirk, born in 1965. Description unknown. She was presumed to have died in a fire in Stockholm's Södermalm neighborhood in 1980, but she is suspected of still being alive and being at large. I have reason to believe that Ester Dirk is responsible for the three murders we are investigating and a fourth, a 14-year-old boy, who was killed in 1979. She should be considered extremely dangerous. I'm on my way in with two witnesses in my car. We'll be there in twenty minutes."

She had scarcely hung up her phone before it rang. She exchanged a few sentences with the person on the other end, but Fredrik wasn't able to get an impression of what the call was about. When she hung up, her face was white.

"I have to go to the hospital."

73.

Fredrik looked at the keys sitting in the tray between the front seats of Sofia's car as they drove through the gates into the police station's garage. Her keys were attached to a ball of brown cork and he wasn't such a fool as to not realize that they were for her boat. Contemplating even just the fleeting hint of that idea for a second, he realized that it was sheer lunacy. Even so, he readied himself. He leaned toward the passenger's side door and snuck a peek back at the metal gates behind them in the sideview mirror. They hadn't begun to close yet. He couldn't sit tight at the police station through endless questioning sessions while Marianne was in danger. Three people were already dead and she could be next in line. He felt a responsibility, as if he himself were the catalyst of everything that had happened.

Sofia steered her car into a parking spot and reached for the key in the ignition. He saw his chance. In one move, he grabbed the boat key and threw himself out the passenger door. The gates had just begun closing, but he managed to throw himself out before they slammed shut. When he rounded the corner of the brownish red brick building that housed the police station, he heard someone calling after him, but he already had too much of a head start. They would obviously catch up with him at some point. He understood that, but no matter what happened he wouldn't end up in prison. He was no murderer.

–

Sofia jogged down the white hallway toward the nurses' station.

She tried not to think about Fredrik. That fool! What was he doing?

Karim, who met them in the garage to see to Bodil and Fredrik, had sent a patrol out to look for him. He wouldn't get very far on foot. Karim had assured her that she wasn't needed at the station and she should focus on Tord. Even so, it bothered her terribly. Who did Fredrik think he was?

When she reached the nurses' station, the charge nurse was talking on the phone. The stout woman mimed that she would be done in a second. Sofia forced herself to smile, but immediately began pacing back and forth in front of the counter waiting for the woman to finish her call. After five minutes, she couldn't take it any longer and pulled out her police badge and held it up right under the chatty nurse's nose. With her eyes locked on Sofia, she wrapped up her conversation and hung up.

"Oh dear. What happened?" The nurse seemed completely beside herself at having made the policewoman wait.

"I'm looking for Tord Grändberg. He had surgery this morning. I need to speak to him right away."

"I'm afraid you can't," the nurse said, shaking her head firmly. "We're easing up on Tord's anesthesia, but he's sleeping now. He needs his rest."

"Maybe I wasn't clear just now, but I need to see him right away! His doctor called me less than an hour ago and told me Tord was asking for me, that it was important!" Sofia's loud voice echoed down the hallway and a couple of nurses farther down the hall turned around in concern to see what the commotion was about.

"I don't care if you're the National Police Commissioner. He is not receiving visitors right now. He is still hovering between life and death at the moment. Do you understand?"

A jolt of worry shot through Sofia. Tord couldn't die. That just could not happen. He was the closest thing to a relative she had left in the world. She just had to see him.

"I apologize for my strident tone, but I'm a bit distraught. I'm not actually here as a police officer. Tord is my family."

The nurse eyed her skeptically.

"Please," Sofia urged. "I don't have anyone else left. Tord has been like a father to me. I just want to see him one more time in case he... in case he..."

Panic welled up inside her and she suddenly had a hard time breathing. Her eyes filled with tears and she had to double over because of the pain in her abdomen. The nurse quickly leapt to her feet and came around from behind the counter. Before the nurse reached her, Sofia threw up right on the floor.

"Oh, there there, sweetie." The nurse patted her comfortingly on the back. "You can't go in and see him if you have a stomach bug. He's not strong enough for that."

Sofia wiped her mouth with the back of her hand. Her stomach was tensing and churning.

"I don't have a stomach bug. I have cancer."

A half hour later, Sofia was sitting on a gurney in the hallway with a plastic cup of water and a couple of painkillers in her system. The nurse had insisted that she be examined, but she had refused. In the end they promised her she could go in and see Tord for a brief visit.

A nurse stuck her head out of a room a few doors down the hall and waved her over. When Sofia saw Tord lying there in the bed with his eyes swollen shut, the tears caught in her throat. There was an enormous bandage behind his left ear, held in place by gauze that had been wrapped around the top of his head several times.

It was still unclear exactly how he had incurred the head injury, but the nurse had explained that because his skull was broken, that had allowed his brain to swell, which in turn had saved him from a massive cerebral hemorrhage. Unfortunately there was still a risk of hemorrhaging and clots. They couldn't say for sure whether he would survive, and even if he did, he might not ever be himself again.

Sofia tiptoed into the room, pulled a chair over next to the bed, and sat down. She put her hand over Tord's big fist and leaned her forehead down onto the yellow hospital blanket that covered his body. His breath came in little puffs and he had a tube in his nose. She stroked his cheek reassuringly. Every now and then she glanced at the door, afraid the nurse would come in and shoo her out. But no one came. She had almost fallen asleep in her chair when a wheeze from Tord roused her.

"Hi, little girl."

His voice was cracking and hoarse.

"Thank goodness you're alive!" Sofia felt the tears welling up in her eyes again. "You have no idea how worried I've been."

Tord moved his head, but the pain made him grimace. She very cautiously ran her finger over his gray hair.

"It's going to work out, you'll see. You'll be back on your fishing boat in no time. Rest now. We can talk later." She got up and put on her jacket, patting his hand farewell. "I have to get back to the station. We have a breakthrough in the investigation."

She took a step toward the door, but Tord grabbed her hand with surprising strength. The look in his eyes, behind those half-closed, swollen, bruised eyelids, told her that he had something to say that was worth staying for. She sat back down again.

"What is it, Tord?"

"Marianne Nordin. You have to find… She… The scars on…" He took a deep breath and his lungs made a nasty rattling sound. His eyes rolled back in his head and he started having a seizure. A loud alarm went off and one of the machines next to his bed started blaring.

In a second the room was full of doctors and nurses. The door slammed shut right in front of Sofia's nose, and she was left alone in the hallway.

74

His lungs burning, Fredrik ran the ten or so blocks down to the marina with his phone glued to his ear. It had rung ten times, but Marianne still hadn't answered. He gave up and stuffed his phone into his pocket and looked around at all the boats moored there. He immediately recognized the unusual mahogany boat that he had seen at Sofia's dock over in Norrbysbodarna. He got the motor started after a couple of tries and pulled away from the dock.

He had driven motorboats before, before the *Estonia*. Philip's family had had a boat and Hans had let him drive it out to Sandhamn several times, but that was more than twenty years ago. He had trouble controlling the speed, going too fast sometimes and too slow other times, and the boat bounced alarmingly in the waves. The wind tore at him and he was grateful for the green raingear he found in the storage compartment under the seats.

A nautical chart in a protective plastic cover was secured to the control panel. He had to empty his mind of all other thoughts in order to decipher it. If he strayed into the rocks in this weather, he would be done for.

Fredrik struggled for over an hour, parrying the waves and trying to maintain a steady course before Ulvön Island finally came into view. He slowed down as he approached the strait between North and South Ulvön, maneuvering the boat carefully. The wind eased up a little once he made it into the strait, but it was still pouring. Once he reached Ulvö Harbor, Fredrik realized he didn't know where to tie up. The guest marina by all the businesses, where the ferry had dropped him off, was full. The only other place he knew about was the Bohmans' boathouse, and he turned in toward the narrow dock there at far too high a speed. He couldn't remember how to tie any real knots, so he just wrapped the boat's bowline around a wooden pole a few times and hoped that would be adequate.

The boathouse still had blue and white police tape around it. This was where she had been found, Christine Karst, right under the dock where he and Marianne had sat and had coffee and chatted, completely unaware. It was so awful it turned Fredrik's stomach.

It was only a few hundred meters up to Marianne's house from the boathouse. Fredrik crouched down in the rain and sprinted up to the white house. To his relief he saw that there was a light on in one of the windows upstairs. Just as he put his hand on the handle of the front door, his phone rang. He took it out, hoping it was Marianne finally calling him back, but he didn't recognize the number. That probably meant it was the police, and he declined the call.

If Marianne was asleep, he didn't want to ring the bell and bother her, but if Ester was already here… he didn't even dare think about that. Fredrik tried the door and discovered that it was unlocked. He stepped quietly into the front hall, the water pouring off his raingear. He kept going farther into the house without taking off his shoes.

There was no sign of Marianne, but her cell phone was sitting on the kitchen table with the ringer off. Fredrik swore to himself at how no one around here seemed to care about being reachable. Why even have a cell phone if you couldn't hear it ring? He tried a door in the front hall that led to the basement and found it unlocked as well. He tried to convince himself that surely everything was fine. Marianne was probably just asleep.

"Marianne?" He turned on the light by the stairs. "Marianne? Hello!" he called a little louder but received no response.

After a second's hesitation, he decided to go upstairs. One wooden step creaked loudly as he went up. A dim light seeped out from one of the rooms. Fredrik knocked on the thick pine door. When he didn't hear any response, he cautiously pushed it open.

The room was decorated in a romantic style with lace curtains and dried roses in a vase. There were several framed photos on the wall. The bed was tightly made with a crocheted bedspread. A summer dress hung on a hanger on the front of the closet door. Fredrik stopped to look at a picture on the dresser just inside the door. Marianne's grandchildren, the same picture that she had shown him on her cell phone. Several similar pictures were hanging on the wall over the dresser. He noticed that the children were wearing the same clothes in all the pictures. As he leaned in closer, he realized that it was the same picture in the frames. He counted at least ten pictures all around the room, all the same photo.

On the nightstand next to Marianne's bed there was an old toy angel. Fredrik carefully picked it up. It was dressed in white and had blond hair. The doll's face smiled serenely, and its hands were clasped in prayer. The fabric the wings were made out of was almost see-through and was stained with something that looked like rust.

He was just about to set the angel back down when he heard one of the floorboards creak behind him. Fredrik turned around and saw Marianne standing in her nightgown in the doorway. He was so startled that he dropped the angel on the floor.

"Oh my God, you scared the hell out of me!"

"Don't touch anything!" Marianne's voice was shrill. "You can't touch anything! You mustn't grope at anything and ruin it."

"I just wanted to…"

She held up her hand to silence him and Fredrik immediately realized that something was wrong. Her glazed eyes were looking right through him.

"We have to get out of here," Fredrik urged her. "You're not safe here. I've been trying to call you. I've called you so many times. This is going to sound completely unbelievable, but Ester Dirk is alive. She killed Thomas at that summer camp. And now she's back and she's killed several other people. You need police protection."

Marianne laughed.

"You think Ester is alive?"

"Yes. We have to get out of here."

Marianne nodded thoughtfully, her eyes fixated on the angel lying on the floor.

He was starting to feel uncomfortable. Something must have happened. She looked like she had aged several years since he had last seen her. Her hair was unbrushed and lank and she had dark circles under her eyes. There was something about her eyes, too. Hadn't Marianne had brown eyes?

"It may be true, what you're saying Fredrik, that Ester Dirk is alive."

"I'll call Sofia and ask her to come pick us up."

"Good, good. You do that. But pick Mother up first, please. She doesn't want to lie on the floor." Marianne pointed to the angel.

Fredrik gave her a questioning look, but decided to do as she said. She seemed confused. He bent down and reached for the angel.

She was on him in only two quick steps. Fredrik just had time to catch a glimpse of the shiny hammer out of the corner of his eye. The crunching sound when it hit his jawbone was the last thing he perceived.

Tuesday, July 2

75.

When Fredrik opened his eyes, it was starting to get light out. Gray fog was visible outside the rectangular window up near the ceiling. It smelled musty and dank and he quickly realized that he was in a basement.

The pain in his jaw hit him like a tidal wave. For a second he thought he was going to throw up. Large amounts of blood had dried into his shirt. He tried to lift his hand to feel how bad it was, but he couldn't. His wrists were duct taped to the armrests of a wheelchair.

He tried to get free, but the movement made his head roar with pain and his field of vision blurred. What the hell had happened? Where was Marianne?

When his eyes cleared, a face appeared right in front of him. He jumped and tried to back away. A floral perfume scent mingled with the nauseating smell of iron. He looked up to meet Marianne's gaze. She was wearing a long, blond wig and shaking her head pityingly. There was a gas can sitting on the floor beside her.

"It's such a shame, Fredrik, that it had to end like this." She sat down on the basement stairs a little way from him. The slanted, green exterior cellar door was behind her.

Fredrik opened his mouth, but his jaw throbbed so much he could scarcely get any words out.

"Who… you?"

He sounded like his grandfather had after his stroke. Marianne adjusted her wig and smiled serenely at him.

"Who am I? I'm God's chosen one. I'm Ester."

A strong sense of unreality came over Fredrik. He struggled to try to comprehend what Marianne had just said. How could she be Ester?

"You… killed…?"

She looked at him in surprise.

"Not me. We, Mother and I. They'll never be mean to me again, will they, Mother? No one can touch God's chosen one. And no one is going to give away my secret. Absolutely no one. Not Bodil, not Tord, not my father, and not you, Fredrik."

The pain made it hard for him to focus. His tongue still wouldn't obey. His words came out as a thick porridgey mess.

"Elisabeth… dead."

"Mother isn't dead. She's right here," Ester hissed, tenderly caressing the white toy angel that was sitting on the steps next to her. "You see, Mother promised me there in the car that she would never leave me, and she never has either. She has held her wings over me." Her voice was childish and high-pitched. "No one should touch God's chosen one. Right, Mother? He who touches God's beloved must burn in hell."

She's crazy. I'm going to die in this cellar.

"They didn't understand that the one God loves can never die. Not even when I warned them with the picture. They didn't understand until their very last moment, but by then it was too late. Right, Mother?"

"Why now?"

Ester looked up as if she had forgotten that Fredrik was there.

"When I returned to Ulvön, I knew it was time. It was time for me to exact the revenge I had been waiting for my whole life."

She got up off the step and walked around the wheelchair once with the angel in her hand.

"Christine was the first, impressionable, fragile Christine. She hardly resisted. Adam didn't either. So preoccupied and arrogant, and so eager to get his hands on Christine's hotel. They allowed themselves to be herded right into death like a flock of sheep. Only Mats tried to fight back, but what good did it do him?" A look of disgust came over her face at the mention of his name. "He floated ashore just below the hotel, Adam did. It doesn't get any more poetic than that. A sure sign of God's approval, that He was satisfied with the way we had carried out His work. Don't you think?"

Fredrik tried to shake his head but wasn't able to. Pain shot through his jaw, right up to his temples.

"Where's Marianne?"

"Ashes and soot in a grave that's not hers. Gone. Just like Christine and Mats. They had to pay for what they did. God's work will be done soon."

Ester disappeared from his field of vision. He heard her mumbling behind his back, but quickly realized that she wasn't talking to him. He carefully put his feet down between the wheelchair's footrests and managed to scoot the chair enough so that he could see her over his shoulder.

"You will leave this earthly life in flames, Fredrik, just like Marianne did. Everything must be purified by fire. And as for me, I will once again rise from the ashes."

"No, wait!"

Ester crouched down in front of him. She put her hand on his knee.

"Are you afraid?"

Fredrik nodded feebly.

"Don't be. It only hurts for a little while. Then you're free."

She stroked the toy angel's head and then left him to push open the cellar door. A tremendous panic seized Fredrik. He kicked desperately at the cold floor to get away, but he didn't get anywhere.

The faint sound of the lid being unscrewed from the gas can seemed to echo off the hard walls. She carefully poured gasoline around the wheelchair, over his legs and arms. She dropped the can, which rattled away across the cellar floor, and looked into his eyes one last time.

"Goodbye, Fredrik." She smiled.

In slow motion he watched her raise a match and pull it over the striking surface.

A spark flared up but then went out.

Ester laughed and shrugged at him. She tossed the match aside and took out another.

Fredrik closed his eyes.

He saw his mother's gentle eyes before him and heard his father's ringing laugh. Saw the ocean, Niklas, the life raft. And Sofia. Her blond hair backlit by the bright light of the open cellar door. Her beautiful face in deep centration. The tall, wolf-like Vera beside her. But why were they holding guns? That didn't fit at all.

A shot was fired. He felt a burning pain in his stomach.

And then everything went black.

Epilogue

Her cell phone sat quietly in the pocket of her hospital night-gown, worn to softness from being washed so many times. Sofia picked it up for the hundredth time to check if Vera had called, but the screen was blank. She stood there outside the nondescript, yellow hospital door, watching motes of dust float through the sunbeams. She had passed this door countless times in recent weeks without daring to go in. She knew she should. He needed all the support he could get. Even so, she couldn't make herself open the door and walk inside.

Some of her colleagues had been by to try to question him. She had read their report, but they said almost nothing about what had happened in that cellar. But Fredrik was alive. That was all that mattered.

Ester Dirk's grave would be opened today. Sofia would have liked to have been there, but her doctor had protested loudly the minute she mentioned traveling to Stockholm. He was skeptical enough that she was still working, albeit from her hospital bed. Travel was absolutely out of the question.

Since Ester Dirk was the only person who had been missing after the fire on Sankt Paulsgatan in 1980, no one had questioned the identity of the burned body. Aron Dirk himself had confirmed that that was his daughter's body they had found, and thus the matter was settled. But given this summer's events, they were now pretty convinced that they would find Marianne Nordin's remains in Ester Dirk's grave.

Marianne's parents had already moved to Ghana by the time Ester took Marianne's place at the boarding school in

Cambridge. This was long before the digital era. There were no cell phones, no passwords to know, no social media to update. A new haircut and color were enough. When Marianne's parents died a year later of dengue fever, that was yet another obstacle out of the way, and Ester had been able to fully become Marianne Nordin, now with a sizeable inheritance in her pocket.

Vera had flown to London to meet with Marianne Nordin's ex-husband, or Ester Dirk's, as now appeared to be the case. He was heartbroken when he heard what had happened, but he admitted that he had been afraid of where her mental problems might lead for a long time. Throughout their entire marriage, Marianne had struggled with auditory hallucinations and grandiose delusions that she had been chosen by God. She had been involuntarily committed several times over the course of their marriage. In the end, he couldn't take it any longer and had filed for divorce. When Vera had asked if she could speak with their son, the ex-husband had shaken his head in surprise. There was no son, no grandchildren.

The media coverage had been a zoo. Serial killers are incredibly rare, and the case had received a tremendous amount of attention. Sofia had missed all the fuss since she was stuck in the hospital, but Vera had complained about being harassed by journalists for days on end.

They still hadn't discussed Sofia's part in what had happened. The internal investigation was still underway. Vera had been responsible for the stray bullet in the cellar, and she was also under investigation.

Sofia had no idea how it had happened, but somehow Mattias had managed to get himself transferred to Umeå, to their communications department. More than once she had caught glimpses of his suntanned face on various news broadcasts, and she guessed that he was very happy in his new role. He had found something he desired even more than being in charge—media exposure. In another situation, Sofia would have seized her chance to claim the position as Vera's successor now that Mattias was busy elsewhere. But the position was no longer a good fit. Even if she did manage to hold onto her job, she wasn't going to be allowed to leave the hospital anytime soon.

Despite so many things falling into place with Ester Dirk's arrest, her nausea had not subsided. Even when Tord's condition was upgraded and he was transferred out of the intensive care unit and the doctors were able to say that he would likely recover, she didn't start feeling any better. In the end, she had no choice but to make a doctor's appointment. The doctor who examined her had quickly determined that she needed to be admitted, and five weeks later she was still there, cooped up inside the hospital walls with only her anxiety and her own thoughts for company. The incomprehensible news still hadn't sunk in.

She had been sitting with a bag under her chin and throwing up bile while a plump nurse comfortingly patted her head. Images of her father's emaciated body, ravaged by the spreading cancer, had darted through her mind as she awaited word. The doctor's compassionate eyes when she entered the room had convinced her right away. She knew what she was going to hear. Even before the doctor had opened her mouth, tears were already pouring from Sofia's eyes. She had cancer. She was going to die.

Even so, the shock was greater than she could have expected.

"Oh, I remember what it was like, honey. It's not easy. I threw up for five months straight with my first. It's unusual for it to start as early as it has for you, but don't despair. It'll pass."

The thing that could never happen had happened.

Sofia hadn't believed it until she had seen with her own eyes the tiny beating heart on the ultrasound. Against all odds, a small life had held on and started to grow inside her, with everything that entailed. The doctor had explained that she was suffering from a type of severe morning sickness that affects only a small percentage of pregnant women. It could begin almost immediately once the egg attached to the uterine wall and sometimes continued well into the pregnancy. Sofia's case, however, was the most extreme any of the staff had dealt with firsthand.

She looked down at the still invisible bulge, caressed the faded scar and the little life that was now growing underneath it. She tried to imagine what it would be like once the nausea subsided, but that was impossible. All joy was drowned out by the vomiting, the IV, and the worry.

"Oh, honey... don't cry. This is going to be so great. Having children is the most joyful experience you'll ever have. Believe me. I have three of my own and seven grandchildren." The doctor had wrapped her arms around Sofia and hugged her to her ample bosom until she could hardly breathe.

"Have you told the father?"

Which one?

"Not yet."

ⓒ **CANELO**CRIME

Do you love crime fiction and are always on the lookout for brilliant authors?

Canelo Crime is home to some of the most exciting novels around. Thousands of readers are already enjoying our compulsive stories. Are you ready to find your new favourite writer?

Find out more and sign up to our newsletter at canelocrime.com